Praise for the Novels of Karen Kendall

Fit to Be Tied

"Sexy-hot delicious and laugh-out-loud delightful! Karen Kendall is my new favorite author!"
—Nicole Jordan, *New York Times* bestselling author

"Kendall's lively tale about breaking up, making up, and shaking it up is funny and poignant. Fans of Lori Wilde, Susan Donovan, and Connie Lane will appreciate Kendall's humorous take on tying the knot." —*Booklist*

"Kendall again presents a story that mixes humor with a more serious plot. The journey of the two main characters toward an awareness of what really matters, and secondary characters who make their own discoveries, give this lighthearted romance substance." —*Romantic Times*

"This funny, sexy romance will keep you reading."
—Fresh Fiction

"Be prepared to laugh, cry, and feel some emotions for the characters and their plights . . . an unforgettable read."
—Romance Reviews Today

First Date

"Hilarious and downright sexy! Karen Kendall will delight you!" —Carly Phillips, *New York Times* bestselling author

"Lighthearted comedy . . . the snappy talk keeps the plot in constant motion. . . . Something fun . . . to read on the beach."
—*Publishers Weekly*

"A sharp, sexy, and fun read with engaging characters who steal into your heart right away. Karen Kendall's newest romance contains all the ingredients required to make it a supersassy ___ vibrant, snappy dialogue. ___ecommended!"
—The Best Reviews

continued . . .

"*First Date* is a magnificent, captivating read that will keep you totally entertained from the first page until the last."
— The Romance Reader's Connection

First Dance

"Kendall's sparkling third installment in [the] Bridesmaid Chronicles series offers both zany romance and serious probing of her protagonists' emotional depths. This witty, well-crafted entry bodes well for the final volume."   — *Publishers Weekly*

Someone Like Him

"Karen Kendall has a gift for the turn of phrase . . . [her] prose reads like poetry . . . yet the comedic elements of the story likewise sparkle with her original style, [which] readers will treasure."   — WordWeaving.com

"A lovely story, *Someone Like Him* has humor entwined around the characters' self-discoveries."   — *Romantic Times*

"A charming cast of characters. . . . Readers will take pleasure from this lighthearted romantic romp."   — The Best Reviews

I've Got You, Babe

"Exciting and fun, wonderful and beautiful, perfectly paced, sexy and sassy, emotional and very satisfying . . . excellent secondary characters . . . a perfect balance of tender, serious, and funny moments. . . . If you find a Karen Kendall book up on the shelves, don't hesitate to grab it. You'll enjoy it, guaranteed."
— A Romance Review

"The incomparable Karen Kendall is back with yet another rollicking comical romance, which will have the readers laughing their hearts out. . . . Karen Kendall is indeed a masterly writer. . . . The characterizations are divine; the dialogue, more specifically every character's internal assessments and thoughts, is supremely candid, realistic, and altogether delightful—all in all, this is a gem of a book, which is a must-read for all kinds of readers!"   — The Road to Romance

"[Karen Kendall's] copious metaphors will leave you howling with laughter, and her portrayal of a gorgeous hunk in a classroom of hormonally charged teenage girls is a hysterical delight. Emotion and serious issues are tackled as well. . . . Read and enjoy!"   —*Affaire de Coeur*

"A battle of wits and attraction. Join the fun and read this delightful book. . . . Well done, Ms. Kendall."   —*Rendezvous*

"*I've Got You, Babe* is a terrific love story . . . filled with laugh-out-loud humor."   —Reader to Reader Reviews

"Humor and sadness blend well in rising star Karen Kendall's new novel. The moral dilemmas that the characters face make for interesting drama, and the humor just charms."
                                                           —*Romantic Times*

"*I've Got You, Babe* has 'winner' written all over it. It's funny . . . it moves quickly, and it sizzles right when it should. . . . Smart, sassy, and sensational, this is the contemporary romantic comedy of the year."   —Romance Reviews Today

To Catch a Kiss

"Karen Kendall's second book, *To Catch a Kiss*, will have you laughing so hard you'll cry. A hot and hysterical read. The scenes with 'Pedro' are particularly memorable."
                                                           —*Romantic Times*

"*To Catch a Kiss* is a very amusing romantic romp . . . reads like a 1930s madcap comedic romance set in contemporary times. It never slows down. . . . The support cast adds depth and much humor."   —The Best Reviews

Also by Karen Kendall

Take Me If You Can

karen kendall

For Lou —
All Best,
K dall

A SIGNET ECLIPSE BOOK

SIGNET ECLIPSE
Published by New American Library, a division of
Penguin Group (USA) Inc., 375 Hudson Street,
New York, New York 10014, USA
Penguin Group (Canada), 90 Eglinton Avenue East, Suite 700, Toronto,
Ontario M4P 2Y3, Canada (a division of Pearson Penguin Canada Inc.)
Penguin Books Ltd., 80 Strand, London WC2R 0RL, England
Penguin Ireland, 25 St. Stephen's Green, Dublin 2,
Ireland (a division of Penguin Books Ltd.)
Penguin Group (Australia), 250 Camberwell Road, Camberwell, Victoria 3124,
Australia (a division of Pearson Australia Group Pty. Ltd.)
Penguin Books India Pvt. Ltd., 11 Community Centre, Panchsheel Park,
New Delhi - 110 017, India
Penguin Group (NZ), 67 Apollo Drive, Rosedale, North Shore 0632,
New Zealand (a division of Pearson New Zealand Ltd.)
Penguin Books (South Africa) (Pty.) Ltd., 24 Sturdee Avenue,
Rosebank, Johannesburg 2196, South Africa

Penguin Books Ltd., Registered Offices:
80 Strand, London WC2R 0RL, England

First published by Signet Eclipse, an imprint of New American Library,
a division of Penguin Group (USA) Inc.

First Printing, April 2008
10   9   8   7   6   5   4   3   2   1

This book is dedicated to my parents, all three of them. See, that art history degree was good for something after all, you guys!

Acknowledgments

Many thanks to the following people, without whom I couldn't have written this book. I hope you know how much I appreciate all the answers to those bizarre questions I threw at you.

George De Prado, the best SIU guy in Florida and probably the nation. (Next time, we'll make it Cuban food, and I'm still dying to know who called my husband to tell him I'd been out with Another Man!)

The Babes in Bookland Plotting Group. (You get credit for the original suggestion that the villain become the hero, but that means you also get blamed for me having to throw out two hundred pages . . . LOL.)

Carol Stephenson, font of knowledge on all things cockatiel. (Kong thanks you for not letting me give him a toucan beak or a parrot's vocabulary. And he sure does dig those Nutri Berries.)

James O. Born, author, police officer, and all-around good guy. (Knows his guns and which ones have safety catches. Of course, I may have read my notes wrong, but that's in no way his fault.)

Lisa Fugard, for invaluable advice.

Kimberly Whalen, my agent, who believed in this project from the very beginning.

All the people at Penguin, especially my editor, Kara Cesare, because I know how hard you guys work to get my mad scribbles edited, produced, packaged, and marketed. Thanks is an entirely inadequate word.

chapter 1

Some people steal for thrills. Others steal for simple profit or for dark psychological reasons. Art recovery agent Avy Hunt stole for justice—or so she liked to tell herself. The truth was a little more complicated.

Avy certainly wasn't a femme Robin Hood, since she worked on commission and eschewed green tights for the sheerest of thigh-highs. She preferred a 9mm SIG Sauer P230 to a crossbow, and usually avoided bands of merry men, since they tended not to keep their hands to themselves.

Only in the name of a job would she deliberately go home tonight (from the raucous Clevelander Hotel on South Beach) with this particular merry man. Dave Pomeroy, with his greasy, lurid grin and I'm-a-multimillionaire strut, gave her the creeps.

But here she sat in his giant black Hummer, dressed like the Cheap Trick he'd cranked up on the CD player.

South Beach on a late August Saturday night was a fast, sexy samba in a salt-tinged sauna. Spotlit against a moody night sky, royal palms waved in the humid breeze like passing acquaintances who wouldn't remember your name.

Sand and ocean stretched to the right beyond the palms, and art deco hotels rose along the left, past Dave's shoulder on the driver's side of the vehicle.

Collectively, the facades of the lighted, pastel buildings looked like a Hollywood backdrop for some steamy soap opera. People were out on the town, dressed up or dressed down, indulging in dinners, drinks, dancing, deals, and drugs. Laughter mingled with shouted insults and the bass of crawling car engines, their stereos playing everything from rap to rock to Brazilian dance music.

It was a short drive to Star Island, where Dave's status symbol of a house stood. They were waved through at the guarded gate to the causeway, and repulsive Dave decided to caress her knee as they traversed the water.

Avy forced herself to sit still until his fingers crept higher, at which point she dredged up a vacuous giggle and caught his hamlike hand in her own.

They turned into a long drive, where a pair of ornate wrought-iron gates opened as if by magic. The house that stretched before them looked more like a government building than a home. The architecture, with its harsh angles and sterile feel, was a bad rip-off of Le Corbusier.

Inside it was a mirrored white palace with all the warmth of a hospital. Their footsteps echoed like gunshots on the ceramic tile.

Pomeroy had the taste of a Vegas pimp. He'd decorated in Early Eighties Nightclub, except for the occasional big-game trophy, such as the twelve-foot alligator in the corner of his living room. That added a cozy touch.

Avy let out an appropriate squeak of excitement, though, and Dave puffed up with pride. "You live here *all by yourself*?" she asked.

"Well, I have staff, honey, but they have the night off.

Hey, you need to take a whiz? The john's right there. I'll make us some drinks."

As she stood in his bleak silver powder room, Avy's heart throbbed against her rib cage and her stomach slid around like a big glob of mercury. *Not fear,* she told herself. *Adrenaline. Nerves on edge before the job. Normal.*

She took a disgusted look into the mirror at her temporary persona, vaguely surprised that she could even see out from under her tarantulalike false eyelashes.

A tight, shiny black spandex microminiskirt rode her hips. A red push-up bra promoted her assets like a media blitz; the matching thong peeked out above the skirt like a paid endorsement. She'd done unspeakable things to her hair and applied her makeup with a trowel.

Bile rose in her throat—she looked a little too much like the type of woman her father occasionally took to seedy motels.

She fingered the deluxe Swiss Army knife that rested next to her lipstick in a satin cosmetics pouch. Normally she wore the Victorinox on a cord around her neck. Her dad had given the knife to her—his little tomboy—on her twelfth birthday, and in the seventeen years since, she'd worn off the brand name with use.

She'd cut her Barbie's hair into a punk style with it; she'd carved her initials into trees and benches; she'd employed the knife to open everything from beer bottles to car and apartment doors. And that was all before she'd *really* learned how to use it.

Though she felt more like opening the knife than the lipstick, the red schmear was, for now, the better weapon. So she used it without compunction, then blotted her lips on a tissue.

This guy Pomeroy didn't scare her. And besides, her trainee, Gwen, was right outside with her surveillance equipment. If Avy got into serious trouble, Gwen would have her back.

"Heads up," Gwen's voice said through the tiny electronic bud in Avy's ear.

Avy moved to the crack of the powder room door and watched, eyes narrowed, as her new friend Dave dropped something—definitely not a vitamin—into her drink.

A roofie? And here she was dressed like a sure thing, too. She'd known that Dave Pomeroy was a smug bastard and a thief, but she hadn't realized that he was also a rapist. How charming.

What are you up to, you bottom-feeder?

She backed silently away from the door and flushed the toilet, along with any vestige of guilt over what she was doing and how she was doing it. Dave Pomeroy had something that didn't belong to him, and as a full partner of ARTemis, Inc., stolen art recovery specialists, Avy intended to get it back.

She'd have preferred to do a clean break-and-enter, but security was tight here—no getting onto Star Island without the owner of the real estate. The likes of Shaquille O'Neal and Gloria Estefan wanted to enjoy their exclusive beach-front Pleasantville without security breaches.

So out of necessity she'd targeted Dave at the Clevelander, that famously rockin' South Beach institution that handed out complimentary drinks, earplugs, aspirin, and condoms upon check-in.

She'd rather have arrived on the island the way Gwen had, using a dive tank and fins, than let Dave practically hump her leg before inviting her home with him. But every job had its downside, didn't it?

Avy considered her next move as the cold metal of the 9mm strapped to her left thigh came into contact with the skin of her right one. Given the roofie, her first instinct was to pull the gun on Dave, demand the priceless bronze he'd had stolen, and walk out.

But she thought better of that idea, since if Dave turned ornery he could decide to press charges for armed robbery. Considering the hot art, it was doubtful . . . but it wasn't completely outside the realm of possibility.

Avy grimaced. Law enforcement didn't always take kindly to her methods of repossessing things for their owners. She figured it was mostly envy on their part—she had no red tape to deal with and a fat commission at the end, while they had that whole law-and-order thing going on, without much reward. She'd made more money in five years of art recovery work than her U.S. Marshal father had in his lifetime.

She'd taken her occasional slaps on the hand—plenty of agents on the art recovery team had. But she wasn't going to risk prison. So Avy settled on plan B: no cops, a little dramatic flair, happy ending.

She closed her eyes for a moment and channeled sexiness and stupidity and availability—which was the biggest illusion of all.

Okay, go.

She pulled open the door and sashayed out to Dave in the ridiculously high clear-plastic heels that were part of her costume. "Wow," she said breathily. "This is some place you've got here." She cast a look of awe out at the private beach, the infinity-edged pool and the forty-five-foot, state-of-the-art cigarette boat rolling on the waves.

Dave dragged his gaze up from her breasts and gave her the drugged daiquiri with an oily smirk, displaying too many yellow-brown teeth.

She was repulsed by the hair product in his sparse fringe, the diamond in his earlobe, and the sweet reek of his cologne. She wasn't sure she could bear him touching her again.

Just business, Ave. Not personal.

"Drink up, darlin'," he urged, swirling the ice in his snooty Scotch, an expensive, aged Laphroaig. Dave evidently had better taste in Scotch than he did in furnishings, but it gave him breath like moldy Band-Aids. She moved away.

"Drink up," he repeated. "I got a whole blender of those daiquiris with your name on it."

Do you, now? Well, I've got a toy surprise with your *name on it, buddy.* But Avy manufactured the most vacant smile in her repertoire and giggled before taking a "sip."

"How's that taste?"

Like anticipatory revenge. "Mmmmm. Perfect."

Dave eased his bulk over to her and slid an arm around her shoulders while Avy tried not to shudder.

"Steady," Gwen said into her ear. It was nice having company—usually Avy worked alone.

Dave didn't have a clue, but Gwen and her equipment were installed in his own sleek, phallic boat, completing Survey of Art Recovery 101. Her final exam would be her very own solo job.

Avy shifted uncomfortably and Dave grinned again, tightening his arm around her. He had sticky fingers on more than one level. Their moist heat seeped through the thin fabric of her belly-baring top, and she wanted to molt out of her own revolted skin and leave it behind with him. But that wasn't possible, so she stayed still. *Not personal . . .*

Her mind departed the scene as he copped a good feel. Art recovery *was* personal for her, and had been since a cold night in Boston when she'd been a clueless college student and museum intern. She'd been robbed at gunpoint, tied up, and locked with her two coworkers in the coat-check room while $3 million worth of art walked out the door.

She still remembered the shock of the easy ambush, the vulpine faces of the thugs, the fear, rage, and guilt . . . the smell of musty wool and stale sweat and urine in the dark. One of the night guards had pissed himself when a gun was held to his head.

All three of them had spent the rest of the night in the coat check, and when Avy got out she'd resolved never to be that helpless again.

She no longer felt fear.

Dave squeezed her ass—how she'd love to break his metacarpals for that—but she forced her body to stay passive. He would be expecting her to get woozy within minutes as she drank more of the drugged daiquiri.

They went through a few painful minutes of the smallest of small talk, during which she managed to distract him enough to pour some of the drink into a potted orchid.

Then she put a slightly trembling hand up to her temple. "Um, Dave?" she asked, laying her Southern accent on thick. "Do you have some saltine crackers or somethin'? I feel kind of . . . funny. Prob'ly just too many cocktails on an empty stomach."

He made an effort to appear sympathetic. "Sure, babe." Dave unstuck his fingers from her tailbone and lumbered off to the kitchen, where he rooted around, giving Avy the opportunity to pour more of the daiquiri into the potted fern near his terrace doors. When he came back with a plate of crackers she swayed a little, which he noted with apparent satisfaction.

"Do you want to lie down?" he asked with more false concern as he set the plate on the coffee table.

"No, no. I'll just sit here on the sofa for a minute."

Dave shrugged and looked at his watch. "Be my guest.

Listen, I'll be back in a few, babe—I've gotta make a phone call."

Avy nodded and sank down onto his inflexible black leather sectional, leaning back against a prickly calf-hair pillow. She closed her eyes until his footsteps retreated, his hard-soled shoes echoing on the white ceramic tile that lined the whole house. Unfortunately his cloying cologne hung like a fat cumulonimbus in the air and refused to blow away.

Avy opened her eyes, turned her head, and stared straight at the ancient Chinese bronze Dave had arranged to have stolen when the owner had refused to sell. Imprisoned in a Lucite box, the bronze looked utterly out of place in this house, as if it had been accidentally beamed here, an unfortunate victim of an evil time-travel machine.

A serene, dignified Tang-dynasty Buddha in the classic lotus position, the figure sat with hands clasped under its chin. It seemed to be praying for release—not only from the box, but from Pomeroy's ugly, stark, contemporary interior and its stink of polyurethane and too-fresh paint.

This particular Buddha was worth a cool million, but the little guy didn't seem to know or care. He just kept his eyes firmly closed against the spectacle of the only other statue in the room, a tasteless erotic nude on a lighted revolving pedestal.

Avy eyed the Buddha with sympathy. *Hang on for a few more minutes, okay? I'm about to get you out of here and back to your rightful owner.*

Maybe it was crazy, but she often felt a kinship with the stolen art objects she repossessed for their owners, as if they had a spirit and that spirit had been kidnapped, too— held hostage in the name of acquisition, greed, or money.

"Gwen," she said softly into her wrist unit, which was disguised as a chunky gold-plated bracelet. "Confirm that alarm is still off." Dave had disarmed it when they'd come in the front door, but she couldn't be sure that he hadn't turned it back on when she was in the powder room. You couldn't be too careful in this business.

"Alarm off. Avy, watch out. The sick twist isn't making any phone call. He's setting up a video camera in the bedroom."

Nice. Avy slid something that looked like a pink cell phone out of her big, shiny pleather bag. She stuffed the phone behind the calf-hair pillow.

"And he's got, um, outfits on the bed for you to wear."

Outfits? Dear God.

"Heads up. He's walking your way now."

Avy slumped a little lower on the uncomfortable couch and let her head roll back. She channeled linguine as Pomeroy's heels slapped back across the tile. Eyelids half-closed, she made a good show of struggling to a sitting position as he approached.

"Dan?" she murmured blearily, locks of teased hair falling into her face.

"That would be Dave," he said.

"Dave . . . I don' feel s'good. C'you take me . . . home?"

"Darlin', I'm not taking you anywhere," he said in a voice like WD-40. "Except to bed."

She nodded. " 'Kay. Wanna . . . go sleep."

"Yeah, that's it. You go to sleep."

Avy slid her hand under the calf-hair pillow and curled her fingers firmly around the pink plastic cell phone she'd hidden there. Then she let her eyes fall closed and her limbs go limp.

"Stupid bitch," Dave said pleasantly. Then he bent forward and yanked down her bra and top to check out the goods.

Avy shot into motion, whipping out the pink cell phone

and pressing it to his chest. Dave howled as nine hundred thousand volts of electricity knocked him backward to the floor. He lay there immobilized, eyes bulging, as Avy furiously righted her clothing.

"Self-defense, Dave," she said. "A girl's gotta do what a girl's gotta do."

Avy walked calmly over to Pomeroy and set the toe of her plastic shoe against his chin. "You're a real sad sack of shit, buddy. You know that?"

All he could do was drool like a baby, which was perfect, since she was about to take his ill-gotten candy away from him.

Avy resisted the urge to kick Pomeroy and removed her shoe from his chin. "They make Tasers in all shapes, colors, and sizes now. Cute little thang, isn't it?" Avy dropped the pink "phone" back into her pleather bag and made her way to the Lucite case. She lifted the cover off its stand and picked up the Buddha with care.

"Dave," she said, shaking her head. "Didn't your mama ever teach you that it's wrong to steal? This doesn't belong to you, honey, and the insurance company that wrote the policy on it . . ." She shrugged. "Well, they want it back. So does the owner."

Dave just lay on the floor like a large, diseased catfish that had floated, belly-up, to the surface of a dirty Miami canal. She smiled sweetly at him, as she'd been taught to do almost from birth in her hometown of Atlanta.

"I'm a high-class repo man, honey, and I show up just when people like you least expect me."

Avy held the Buddha in her left hand—it was much heavier than seemed possible—and traced its contours with her right index finger. "What are you doing with this, Dave? I don't think it speaks to you on any artistic or spiritual level. You sure don't have anything else like it."

She looked around the big white living room, at the television the size of Texas, the fully stocked bar, the retro pinball machine, and the fierce twelve-foot alligator in the corner, its tail curled into an unnatural swirl.

"Nope. This statue is not your style. So why'd you steal it? Just because you didn't like being told no? That's my theory."

"I'll bet he tried to buy it to impress a woman," Gwen said, entering from the terrace doors. She had a thin, almost fragile figure, big, sweet eyes the color of dark honey, and skin like café au lait. "It made him look bad when the guy said no. That's the only possible explanation." She recoiled when she saw the gator, and Avy grinned.

"Want to hire his decorator?" she asked as Gwen shivered and ran a hand through her short, spiked dark hair. The orange streaks in it were oddly tasteful. Only Gwen could make the touch of punk look elegant.

"I think I'll pass, thanks."

"We need to get out of here," Avy said. But, conscious of her manners, she leaned down to say good-bye. "Dave, you reptile, since you like to drop pills into women's drinks, I will be more than happy to drop a *dime* on you to the local cops. Don't take care of yourself, you hear?"

Pomeroy just lay there, gazing up at her with loathing.

The little bronze Buddha in her hands kept his eyes closed and his hands together in prayer, but Avy could have sworn he was secretly smiling. She kissed his generous belly before wrapping him up in a flannel cloth and dropping him into her handbag.

Gwen looked from the figure on the floor to the figure in Avy's hands and shot her a companionable smirk. She quickly changed into South Beach party-girl duds and stowed most of her gear in a messenger bag. Someone would pick up her air tanks later.

They shut Dave's frosted-glass doors behind them and stepped out into the humid Miami night, where his color-coordinated shrubs and flowers all stood at rigid attention, clearly terrorized on a regular basis by a landscaping service.

Avy's plastic sandals made hollow tapping noises on the brick pavers as they headed for Dave's golf cart, their getaway vehicle. Her damned skirt slid up to dangerous heights as she and Gwen got into it, and the backs of Avy's thighs stuck unpleasantly to the vinyl seat.

A symphony of night noises played for them as she turned the key in the cart and they drove quietly toward the island's guarded entrance gate and the causeway to the mainland. Palms whispered in the breeze, bullfrogs made their throaty mating calls, waves gently slapped the shore.

Moments later Avy pulled the golf cart up to the gate and she and Gwen flashed some helpful cleavage at the young, sandy-haired guard. "Hi . . . would you be a doll and call a cab for us? Our date kind of passed out and we want to get home."

He took a dazzled look at Avy's tanned, tautly muscled legs and dialed the phone without asking any further questions. When the taxi arrived they tipped the guard generously. Then they climbed into the car and—mission accomplished—blew a good-bye kiss to Star Island.

"Good job, Ave," Gwen said in a low voice.

Avy turned to her and winked as the cab sped away. She patted the little bronze guy in her handbag. "What can I say? I've never met a man I couldn't handle."

chapter 2

Disarming the alarm was child's play, which surprised the man. One would think that Ava Brigitte Hunt would have a better security system, given her occupation, but then, she counted on anonymity in her work, as did he.

He shut the door behind him and moved into the dimly lit foyer, where a hand-carved mirror made him look larger than life, shadowy and frightfully menacing in his guayabera shirt and dark trousers. He chuckled.

As he crunched down on a green apple, savoring the clean, tart flavor, he discovered that dear Ava also counted on an attack bird. An unholy screech caused him to start and drop the Granny Smith, which bounced once, rolled across the marble foyer, and then came to an abrupt stop due to a collision with a pair of high-heeled shoes.

"What the *devil*?" He peered around a white pillar that seemed to have no discernible purpose other than to knock one's elbow upon . . . and beheld Ms. Hunt's tiny but furious roommate, which was housed in a sort of airy faux château.

He pegged it as a cockatiel while the little bugger continued to verbally abuse him, sounding as if it were not only challenging his right to be there but also casting aspersions upon his character and his paternity.

Knowing full well that the owner of the condo was out for several hours, he made so bold as to turn on the lights, which seemed to displease his avian foe even more. He listened to it for a couple minutes, making soothing noises as he looked around the place. The condo wasn't large, about twelve hundred square feet, he guessed. It smelled faintly of cinnamon toast and butter, which was all right by him.

He rather liked Ava's quirky, modern decorating style. The walls were sand-colored with white crown moldings; the couch was ocean blue suede and formed a U around a plasma TV. Every pillow on the couch seemed to be different: a white sand dollar perched next to a peach starfish, a purple sea horse, a pale yellow angelfish, and a teal sailboat. The ones that amused him the most were the multihued plush octopus and the gray suede shark.

Miss Hunt, it seemed, had a sense of fun. Behind the seating area was a saltwater aquarium with dozens of colorful fish and small coral reefs. Lovely.

He scanned the paintings on the walls, which were abstract and of good quality. She had an eye—but then, he'd expected that, given her background at the famed Sotheby's auction house and her bachelor's degree in art history. He'd done his research quite thoroughly.

The bird's hostility mounted, as did its agitation. It now flew around the cage, hopping from a swing to grip the bars of its cage and poke its tiny beak out at him belligerently.

"Cheeeeeaaacchhh!" it said, or something along those lines.

"Now, stop that," he responded in severe tones. "You're absolutely right that I shouldn't be here, but there's not a damned thing you can do about it, so you may as well settle down, eh?"

The creature fell silent, amazingly enough, and simply glared at him. He raised an eyebrow at it and bent to get the wayward apple, which looked less appetizing now that it had gathered bits of dust and carpet fibers, not to mention hairs. Out of his pocket he pulled a small utility knife, which he used to cut a few tiny pieces of the fruit. Gingerly he extended one on his gloved index finger.

The bird hissed at him and flew back to its swing.

Unperturbed, he dropped a couple of apple bits into the cage, set the rest of the fruit on the edge of the kitchen bar, and continued his reconnaissance.

The kitchen was small and utilitarian, with granite countertops and white cabinetry. Next to the sink was a coffee cup, and in the basin was a clear glass plate scattered with crumbs and a crust of toast, the source of that welcoming scent.

She'd left a bottle of quite decent red wine on the counter, the only other item of interest being a live, healthy plant. A quick sniff told him that it was mint. Interesting. What did she do with fresh mint? Perhaps she put it in that horrifying American concoction, iced tea.

He pulled open a couple of cabinet doors. One held pottery dishes in a sort of blue and violet swirl pattern, while the one next to the ceramic cooktop held condiments, salt, pepper, and . . . cartridges for a 9mm handgun. Armed and dangerous, was she? A corner of his mouth turned up. He liked that she seemed to consider bullets a spice.

The body of the refrigerator yielded a couple of containers of Chinese takeout, an eggplant, three tomatoes, two oranges, and half a head of lettuce. In the door were two bottles of Dos Equis and a jar of balsamic vinaigrette. Evidently Ms. Hunt was a healthy eater with excellent taste in beer.

He moved out of the kitchen and picked up one of the high-heeled shoes near the small dining table. It was a silver Christian Louboutin, laced around the edges with a narrow black-satin ribbon that tied in a delicate bow on the toe. Size seven and a half. "Very nice."

"Pendejo!" said the cockatiel suddenly—and with feeling.

He swung around and stared it down. "Look, I didn't come here to be insulted, and I'll have you know that I'm in possession of a *delicious* recipe for Cornish game hen. I should think it would suit you very well."

The bird cocked its head at him.

"It's made with a brandy sauce, and I'd marinate you first, so I suggest that you shut your beak and mind your manners." He aimed a charming smile at it and set down the shoe exactly in the same spot that he'd found it, not a millimeter to the right or left.

He walked through the condo, stopping in the hallway that led to the bedrooms and baths. The walls of the corridor were lined with framed photographs of family and friends. Very few men, he noted. Except for the one who must be her father—or perhaps an uncle? At any rate, he looked quite a bit like Ms. Hunt, though he was easily twice as big as she. Handsome bloke.

They both had rich, light brown hair—his laced with more red, hers with gold. While the father's eyes were a dark brown, hers were hazel with a tinge of that same gold. Her nose was straight, neat, and narrow and she had a mouth made for long, slow, languid kisses. It was her mouth that gave him a hard-on. Christ Jesus, it was sexy.

He noticed her chin next, and it spelled trouble. Strong and angular, it promised that the woman was stubborn and competitive to a fault.

The rest of her was tall and firm and rounded in all the right places—fairly spectacular, in short. He shook his head and grinned. If she was half as good as they said she was, he was in for the roller-coaster ride of his life.

There were pictures of her and the older man (it had to

be her father) on a ski slope, with a beautiful older woman whose smile seemed rather worn and humorless. There were pictures of father and daughter on racing bicycles, in crash helmets; pictures of them about to hang glide; pictures of them BASE jumping.

His respect for Ms. Hunt went up another few notches. Not many women of his acquaintance did such things. His favorite sequence of photographs was of Ava Brigitte checking her harness in a small aircraft, waving at the camera before the jump, and then free-falling into the atmosphere at several thousand feet. She clearly had nerves of steel and a liking for adventure, didn't she?

He continued down the hallway until he got to a bedroom that seemed to double as both office and guest quarters. The bird screeched again, and he sighed, retracing his steps.

"Look here. I am fully aware of the fact that I'm a filthy snoop, but it's for my own protection. I've got to know what I'm up against, and if it's any comfort to you, she'd do the same damned thing to me. So have some apple and be a nice fellow, won't you?"

He peered at the floor of the cage and noticed that the two bits of fruit he'd pushed through the bars had disappeared. Pleased by this, he cut another couple of bits and extended one on his index finger, trying once again for friendship.

The bird stared at him without blinking.

"Come on, then. I may be wicked, but I'm not here to steal anything but information."

Still the bird hesitated.

Finally, at the speed of light, the cockatiel darted forward and snatched the morsel off of his finger, then flew back to a favored perch.

"So, we've reached an understanding, then? I'll be only another ten minutes or so, I promise."

"Coño," said the bird.

"Right, then." He moved back into Ms. Hunt's office, where he left her financial information strictly alone. He went straight for the file drawer that was labeled, CASES CLOSED, and flipped through it. "My, but we've been a busy little bee, haven't we, Ava?"

In the past six months she'd hunted down an heirloom necklace for Chubb Insurance, a rare and astonishingly valuable Mayan headdress for Hiscox, at least seven missing paintings for various other insurers—all syndicates of Lloyd's of London—and a Fabergé egg. "Well done, darling," he murmured.

Every file was neat and well organized, with detailed descriptions, photos, envelopes of xeroxed receipts, maps, and well-written reports.

After checking a stack of files on her desk, he finished in her office and went to the last room, her bedroom, where a lovely floral scent hung in the air—not the sharp essence of perfume, but the diffused one of shampoo.

A lemon yellow bath towel had been flung onto the bed, which was unmade. Queen-size with a modern maple headboard, it was a rumple of soft, pale blue sheets dotted with clouds, and a white cotton blanket. No sophisticated velvets or satins here—just pure, uncomplicated comfort.

On one of the matching nightstands was a silly stuffed sheep with googly eyes, which made him smile. On the other was a map of Star Island and the surrounding area and a water glass with a hot-red lip print on the rim. At the foot of the bed lay a book on Chinese art. The map and the book testified to what she was probably doing tonight—repossessing the Buddha whose photograph he'd seen in one of the files on her desk.

He took a cursory look into the bathroom before getting down to business. A red silk camisole and tap pants lay on the floor, as if they'd been tossed there on her way into the shower. He resisted the urge to pick them up and inhale her scent, which would, in his book, cross the line between reconnaissance and perversion. The fact that he was tempted bothered him.

A quick look into the drawers and linen cabinet yielded nothing of interest, so he returned to the bedroom and opened the lovely Ava's closet. *Hmmmm.*

On the left side hung strictly utilitarian clothing: several pairs of serviceable slacks and worn jeans; cotton tops she could move about in easily; rugged, lightweight jackets; rubber-soled boots and hiking gear—even a pair of waders.

The right side of the closet seemed to belong to an entirely different woman, a glamour-puss with expensive tastes. Here there were slinky cocktail dresses in every color imaginable, dressy designer suits, couture jeans, and sexy tops. The shoe collection alone represented a down payment on a nice piece of real estate.

On the top shelf of Ms. Hunt's closet were sweatshirts, sweaters, and a Winchester twelve-gauge shotgun with a box of ammunition. Very feminine, that—the perfect accessory for the Escada dinner suit hanging directly below it.

He closed the closet door and turned his attention to the highboy standing in the corner. Going through drawers of personal items wasn't his favorite activity—it, too, made him feel like a pervert—but he needed to gather every detail he could about her personality. So he delved in.

The highboy told the same story of a dual character, and one who traveled to different climates. The thick, woolly socks and athletic gear in two drawers seemed incongruous in comparison with the sheer silk thigh-highs, lacy thongs, and delicate bras in the other two. It was purely by accident, he told himself, that he happened to see the label of one bra, which was marked 34C.

In the very bottom drawer, under some filmy negligees and nighties, he hit pay dirt: a cache of surveillance equipment, listening devices, a handheld GPS, and a sweet little glass-cutting tool, along with a leather case of other useful tools that he easily recognized. Lock picks and a tiny ball-peen hammer. A wristwatch that doubled as a microphone. A lightweight climbing harness and thin cord that would hold her weight and then some.

All of these things told him about the way she worked and what she might have up her canny designer sleeve. Because he and Ava Brigitte Hunt were destined to cross paths and wills soon—and probably blades as well.

Before he left he removed all traces of his presence, even the last bit of apple in the bird's cage, which he speared with the tip of a kitchen knife through the bars of the cage while the cockatiel abused him some more. *"Chivo de mierda!"*

"I beg your pardon?" His university Spanish was beyond rusty. Had it called him a *shit-goat*? "I'm beginning to think that your mummy needs to wash out your tiny beak with soap."

When the creature fussed some more, he sighed. "Look, you bloody little raptor, I'll put my finger in and you can bite it. Will that relieve your feelings?" Doubting his own sanity, he put a still-gloved digit up to the cage.

The bird eyed him suspiciously.

"Well, go on then," he urged. "Attack!"

The creature opened and closed its beak a couple of times, no doubt anticipating its first taste of blue blood. Then it lifted its wings and settled them again. Finally it hopped to within a millimeter of his finger, clung to the cage with one claw, and gingerly put the other on the black leather over the finger—for all the world as if it were shaking hands.

"The pleasure has been all mine, I'm sure," he said dryly. He moved slightly and it disengaged. "*Au revoir*, then. I doubt we'll meet again."

And with those parting words he carefully reset the alarm, turned off the lights, and pulled closed the door behind him.

London, England

Monday morning Avy sat in a small meeting room inside the enormous, postmodern glass and steel Lloyd's of London building at 1 Lime Street.

They were high above the famous, bustling underwriting floor and the Lutine Bell, recovered from a sunken ship Lloyd's had once insured.

She demurely folded her hands into her lap and crossed her legs at the ankles while the Honorable J. Graves Sedgwick took his time inspecting the Buddha through a powerful magnifying glass.

He was a new client, one steered to her by the claims department at Lloyd's, the way most of her customers were. Though she often had meetings with them here, what many people didn't understand was that Lloyd's itself did not insure anything—their Names, or syndicates, did.

Lloyd's was a consortium of many insurers and reinsurers who underwrote risks. Sedgwick was a senior VP for fine-art claims at one of those syndicates.

The room itself was so quiet that she could hear his breathing, but the sounds of the ubiquitous London traffic—cars beeping, buses wheezing as their doors opened to disgorge passengers, engines idling—were still audible outside the window and several stories down.

Avy tried not to yawn, but the transatlantic flight yesterday had taken its toll. She'd exchanged her sleazy getup of Saturday night for a tailored black silk suit with a nipped waist and a pair of prohibitively expensive Giuseppe Zanotti sling-backs with four-inch heels.

She'd twisted her hair up into a smooth classic chignon. Minimal makeup and pearl studs in her ears completed the picture of professionalism. She looked every inch the Sotheby's associate she had once been.

"I must congratulate you, Ms. Hunt," Sedgwick said finally as he put down the magnifying glass and set the Buddha down on the table. He stripped off a pair of white cotton gloves. "You seem to have made a successful recovery. Pending further testing we will cut you the ten percent commission check immediately."

"Thank you, Mr. Sedgwick."

He leaned back in his chair and eyed her curiously. "Pardon me for saying so, but . . . you seem so young."

To all appearances he himself was at least a hundred years old. Mottled bags had settled under his intelligent, if watery, blue eyes, the tip of his nose was in danger of slipping into his withered mouth, and the poor man had wattles that grazed the knot of his necktie.

This was the first time Avy had met Sedgwick face-to-face, but she now understood why Sheila, the office manager and self-appointed mistress of disguise at ARTemis, unkindly called him "Old Chicken Neck."

"You were expecting someone older?" Avy asked with a smile.

"It's just that you have quite a track record, my dear. What's your background? How long have you been making art recoveries?"

"Five years. I graduated from Sweet Briar College with

honors in history of art and started with Sotheby's right away."

"And how long did you stay there?"

The cappuccino she'd downed in her hotel room roiled in her stomach. *I'd have been there a lot longer if not for a lecherous old client who couldn't take no for an answer.* He'd gotten her fired. But she kept her expression neutral. "Two years."

"And then?"

"I got some training and went to work for a private investigative firm, though I was never licensed."

"How did you end up at ARTemis? And by the way, what's the significance of the name?"

"The A-R-T stands for Art Recovery Team. Artemis was the Greek mythological goddess of the hunt. It seemed to fit." Avy took a sip of the chilled water with lemon that sat on the table in front of her.

"As for how I ended up there, I was . . . recruited . . . to help found the company. Fine-art crime is a serious, growing problem, and we have a silent partner who was looking to invest. He liked my skill set."

"Which is, specifically?"

"A background of extreme sports with my dad, a working knowledge of art, and research skills."

"Combined with great style and beauty, my dear." Sedgwick pulled at his nose reflectively and removed his spectacles, setting them on the polished table between them. "If you'll allow me to say so."

Avy smiled politely. "Thank you. I'm also known to be a tad stubborn."

"Yes. Just a tad," Sedgwick said gravely, tapping the Buddha on the head with one wrinkled index finger. But his eyes twinkled.

She liked him.

He polished the lenses of his glasses with one of the white cotton gloves and then set them back on his nose. "Well." He rose to his feet and extended his hand to her.

She got up and shook it. His palm was cool, dry, and a little papery.

"Thank you for traveling all this way to deliver the Buddha, Miss Hunt. I've enjoyed meeting you."

"You're welcome, and likewise." Avy moved toward the door with him and waited while he opened it.

"I'm happy to join the ranks of your professional admirers, my dear. I'll be in touch again soon—sooner than you might think." And with that cryptic statement the interview ended.

chapter 3

A day and a half later, Avy was back among the palm trees, steamy heat, and sexiness of Miami, driving down ritzy Brickell Avenue past some of the most expensive commercial office space in the city.

Most of the lush, tropical beauty of south Florida had long been paved over, and seeing those ubiquitous royal palms trapped in the scant dirt between concrete slabs always made her a little sad.

The trees that had once ruled the landscape looked like toothpicks in the shade of the massive glass and stone boxes that had taken over.

Unable to do anything about the development, she ruefully thanked God for her precious covered parking spot at her office (a rarity in downtown Miami). Avy left the air-conditioning of her Porsche Carrera and felt guilty as usual that it wasn't a Prius like the one Gwen drove. But Avy hadn't lived the high life long enough to be over it. She remembered all too well the days of her old battered Beetle and the boxy, utilitarian Nissan that followed it. She treasured the Porsche.

She had barely gotten through the minimalist modern reception area at her own office building when her BlackBerry chirped. She looked at the ID.

"Kelso," she groaned. "Give me a break." Kelso owned 51 percent of ARTemis, Inc. The real kicker was that she'd never met the man, and if he had it his way, she never would.

She opened the message. *We have a situation. Multimil sword missing from the Met. Stolen en route to Louvre. Best suspect: British thief Liam James. Details in 10 a.m. meeting. You're up.*

Got it, she typed back as she made her way to the wardrobe room to return her spandex duds. *Thanks.*

"So did old Chicken Neck slip you some tongue when you slapped that ugly statue onto his desk?" Sheila Kofsky asked as Avy came in the door.

Avy choked. Sheila was a certified pain in the ass, but she was very entertaining. She took care of reception and wardrobe, talked a lot of trash, and liked to war with anyone who'd take her on. Somewhere in her sixties, Sheila looked like a trendy white raisin with hair and always wore somewhat astonishing reading glasses.

Today's were purple and black zebra-striped, and as usual they had slipped so far down her nose that they seemed to defy gravity. It was Avy's theory that Sheila applied a dot of Gorilla Glue there each morning. That or rubber cement.

"Have some respect," Avy said, but her mouth quivered despite her attempt at gravity.

"I don't do respect, doll face. You know better than that."

Yes, I do. "Old Chicken Neck helps to keep the lights on. He paid for your fancy upgrades in here." She gestured around them and tried not to wince. "And no, he did not slip me any tongue. He's going to write us a fat check, though."

The two of them stood in the big storeroom that served as the costuming closet for the ten southeast recovery agents. Whereas they used to have rolling garment racks

and plastic drawers from Wal-Mart, Sheila had gotten up-
pity a few months ago and demanded California Closets.

She'd also installed a hideous fake Louis XIV dressing
table with a giant gilt mirror and a matching tufted stool
with enough decorative curlicues to strangle whoever sat
upon it. But the pièce de résistance was the polypropylene
rug shaped like a zebra skin, complete with nose and tail.

Avy said, "Dave Pomeroy sure did love your outfit. *He*
tried to slip me not only tongue, but a roofie."

"No." Sheila's head came up, her eyes narrowed. "What
a shitbag." She snapped the lid onto a clear plastic box that
housed the much-despised cheap pumps Avy had worn.
Only the "good" shoes got a place on the mahogany-veneer
shelves.

"Uh-huh. Too bad I'm not as stupid as I looked." She
gestured at the shoes. "Where did you *find* those things,
Sheila? They're beyond awful."

"Tag sale in Homestead," she said succinctly. "I think
the woman was a former stripper who got ripe and then got
married before the fruit spoiled, so to speak."

Avy's toes curled in protest. "They had *sweat stains* in
them."

Sheila grinned and shrugged. "Hazards of the job. You
should have seen 'em before I replaced the lining, honey."

"I'm going to soak my feet in Clorox."

"The purse came from the Salvation Army store in
Pompano Beach. It had a Church of Christ flier, an ancient
stick of Wrigley's, and a receipt for two bottles of el cheapo
gin in the back zipper pocket. How's that for a combination?" She cackled. "Now, the skirt I got from my friend
who used to be a madam in Little Havana—"

Avy wrinkled her nose.

"—so I'll bet that skirt's origins are *real* interesting.
Gwen e-mailed us one of the surveillance shots from the

other night, and let me tell you: If that skirt woulda got any shorter on you, doll face, you'da had two more cheeks to powder and a beard to shave."

Ugh! Avy was speechless for a moment.

"Thanks. Just tell me you washed it. About twenty times."

Sheila smirked at her, then relented. "Yeah. Wouldn't want that highfalutin Sweet Briar butt of yours contaminated by a Cuban ho, now, would we?"

"The nationality of the ho doesn't make any difference to me, Kofsky. And as for Sweet Briar, I was on scholarship there, and you know it. I scraped plates in the kitchen and worked in the library and tutored the brain-dead and bitchy, so don't give me any lip."

"'Don't give me any lip,' she says," Sheila muttered. "Miss La-Di-Da." She tossed her frizzy blond head and sniffed, bending over her inventory binder and making a check mark on a plastic-protected sheet. She shoved her zebra-print reading glasses up to the bridge of her nose— and pursed her stop-sign-red lips. "By the way, that green tea you gave me is nasty stuff. And it doesn't have any caffeine in it, far's I can tell."

"It's good for you. And it's full of antioxidants."

"Whatever the hell *those* are," Sheila growled. "In my day we lived on these mysterious oxidants—*and* cigarettes *and* martinis. We baked ourselves brown as nuts, and we didn't go around dithering about the ozone layer. We didn't know what ozone *was*, for chrissakes. And we were happier that way. . . ."

Avy rolled her eyes, grinned, and left wardrobe for the ten-o'clock staff meeting, where she and the other agents would be briefed on their new assignments.

The conference room was painted olive green, which complemented the light wood and the rust-olive and gold upholstery on the chair seats. Black-and-white photographs of architectural landmarks, framed in pale, textured gold, hung on the walls. A white screen had been pulled down at one end of the long, hexagonal oak table, and a laptop sat at the other end, ready for a PowerPoint presentation.

Gwen was already there, trying hard as usual to look dressed-down and average and failing miserably. She liked to wear gaudy, very feminine earrings and smoky eye makeup. She also stacked her slim wrists with "silver" bracelets that Avy was quite sure were platinum.

Darling, good-natured Gwen had been carried home from the hospital to a thirty-five-room house but had been trying to disguise the fact ever since. Her money and her sheltered background embarrassed her.

"Morning, Gwennie. Thanks ever so for e-mailing that picture to Sheila."

"Hi, Ave," Gwen said, fighting a smile. "Sorry, but she hounded me relentlessly."

"Uh-huh." Avy settled herself into a chair.

"Hey, while we're alone, can I ask you a serious question?"

"Shoot."

"Okay." Gwen sighed. "The boundaries of this job are feeling, um, blurry to me. How far would you go, exactly, to recover a piece? What if you had to take it further than you went the other night?"

Avy angled her head at her. "Further . . . how?"

"You know." Gwen hesitated. "Would you sleep with some creep?"

"I can't believe you're asking me that. We've known each other since college—what do *you* think?"

"No," Gwen said after a moment. "No, of course you wouldn't."

"But there are other team members who would. Valeria,

for example. Or McDougal. The boundaries you set are your own. ARTemis—Kelso—doesn't want to know how you get the job done, and neither does the client, just as long as you *do* get it done."

"Isn't that a little . . . I don't know . . . immoral?"

"I'd say it's more *a*moral. And yes, that suits Kelso to a T. But I'll counter your question with another one: Is it realistic, Gwen, to think you can always be aboveboard when you're dealing with thieves? Come on.

"The insurance companies or owners call us in when the police can't help. When the trail has gone cold, or the caseload is too high and the cops have better things to do than chase after some rich person's missing baubles. If we spent all our time dotting the I's and crossing the T's of the law, we'd never get anywhere."

"Does your dad agree with that philosophy?"

"My dad, despite his law enforcement background, views art crime as pretty much on a par with fashion crime. He doesn't take it seriously. And besides, he thinks I spend most of my time on my butt, doing investigations via computer. Don't even think about enlightening him."

"Wouldn't dream of it. You'd tell my mother what I'm getting into, and she'd have me knocked unconscious and married to some boring banker before I woke up."

Avy laughed.

"My mother asked about you, by the way. She wants *you* married and chained to a white picket fence, too."

"Not going to happen," Avy said lightly. "I like men. In fact, I adore them. But you know my philosophy: They have a biological imperative that's the opposite of ours."

"Not all men are like your father."

"True. They broke the mold when they made him," Avy said with affection. Her dad was one of a kind, a man larger than life and twice as good-looking as any mere mortal, a man's man who couldn't help enslaving women.

As his daughter she certainly wasn't immune. She'd jumped out of a perfectly functional airplane at age sixteen just to see him grin.

"Avy, not all men cheat. At some point you're going to have to acknowledge that."

"The ones *I'm* attracted to do." She'd been thirteen years old when she'd discovered that she and her mother weren't Everett Hunt's only girls. She'd been twenty-three by the time she realized that every one of her boyfriends had fit the same pattern: confident, good-looking men with outsize personalities who attracted other women like flies to peanut butter.

At this point Avy didn't blame the guys—she blamed herself for choosing them. *You can't change the spots on a leopard,* her mother had always said. Yeah, well, you couldn't blame the leopard for biting you if you snuggled up to it, either. It was, after all, a carnivore.

As they waited for the other agents to arrive, Avy sipped coffee and Googled Liam James on her laptop while Gwen finished the fruit smoothie she drank every morning. Out of the corner of her eye she saw Gwen, who pretended not to care about her appearance, surreptitiously use the sugar bowl on the conference table to check her teeth for berry seeds.

Google produced a Liam James property management company, a Liam James who was an actor, a Liam James male model. . . . Avy clicked on each of these, but none of them seemed right. Unfortunately there were dozens and dozens of Google references to slog through.

Other agents began to stream through the door. There was Valeria, her black hair streaming down over her tanned shoulders, white teeth flashing as she laughed into her cell phone.

She was followed closely by the quiet Zoe, whose rectangular-lensed black glasses screamed "creative type" from miles away and seemed at odds with her pale skin and short, white-blond hair.

McDougal strode in next in his signature baggy khakis, his narrow, intelligent face dotted with freckles and flushed as if he'd just run miles. He blew a kiss at Valeria, who responded with a disgusted look before scratching delicately at her temple with her red-tipped middle finger. McDougal grinned widely and sat across from her, his legs akimbo.

Dante came last, breathing heavily as he maneuvered his big muscular body on crutches. One leg of his black trousers had been cut off to accommodate the heavy cast he wore. He'd had a bad fall in Berlin on his last job.

"Everyone else is out on assignment or on vacation," Dante informed them. "Courtesy of my injury, I'll be today's game-show host, so who wants to buy a vowel?" He shot a pointed look at Valeria, and she ended her call abruptly, dropping the cell phone into her Louis Vuitton bag.

"All right, let's get started." Dante claimed the seat at the head of the long table, where his laptop sat. He brought up the first visual. "Gwen, would you hit the lights? Thank you."

The slide depicted a large, colorful rug that was clearly very old. Avy pegged it as French, probably seventeenth century, from the look of it.

"Valeria, this is yours. A Savonnerie carpet dating to roughly 1640, hand-woven at Chaillot, near Paris. It disappeared during a recent remodeling job in Lyons. Our brilliant and industrious Nerd Corps has tracked it to South America, where it was smuggled to a home in Rio de Janeiro belonging to this gentleman." He changed slides.

A paunchy man with a handlebar mustache and pomaded hair stared out at them, and Valeria made a face.

"Your best bet," Dante continued, "is to wait until he goes on vacation with his family in a week, but if you're in a hurry, he's known to have a weakness for beautiful women."

"What is the size of the rug?" Valeria asked in her heavily accented English.

"Roughly eight by twelve feet. You'll need help to get it out of there. Clear any customs issues ahead of time by getting money to the right people. Any questions?" She shook her head. and he slid a file down the table toward her.

"McDougal, you're chasing after a collection of watches, also French, also seventeenth century." The next slide was up.

"Not quite my style," said McDougal, giving them a cursory glance. "I prefer my Breitling." The delicate antique watches winked from a dark velvet background like brightly colored jewels. Some depicted myths and some displayed purely decorative motifs.

Dante ignored him. "Nine hand-painted, enameled pocket watches were lifted from a historical tableau at Baume and Mercier. They'd been loaned from the Louvre as part of a special promotion and were insured through Chubb.

"The thieves left thousands of dollars' worth of other jewelry untouched. They knew what they were doing and got in and out in seconds. This one looks like an inside job, but the police haven't gotten anywhere with it. Needless to say, the Louvre is most anxious to have them back, and Chubb doesn't wish to shell out for them."

McDougal accepted the file with a yawn but immediately began reading it.

"Zoe. For you we have a Chinese porcelain perfume brazier, essentially a potpourri dish, mounted in solid gold. Note the swan's head at one end, and the face of a bearded god at the other. They signify Zeus visiting Leda in the form of a swan.

"This piece disappeared from the home of the Chinese ambassador to France. There was no obvious break-in. The details are in the file, but it surfaced at an auction in Vienna. The current owner paid for it in good faith, so the situation is a delicate one. The auction house claims that the papers looked legitimate and it had no reason to doubt the brazier's provenance. You will need to proceed with the utmost caution."

Zoe nodded, and her file flew toward her, across the surface of the table.

"Gwen. Kelso has something special planned for you. He will text-message you privately and you'll receive your file later. After the assignment is complete, you'll stand by in case Avy needs help on her job."

Dante cleared his throat and flashed the next slide.

Avy caught her breath. A wicked steel blade dominated the screen. About three feet long, it glinted malevolently under the strong lighting that had been used to take the photograph.

The cutting edge of the sword, replete with dark smudges and stains that might have been ancient blood, was so chilling that its glorious gilded and jeweled handle at first escaped her attention.

"Avy. You've got a hell of a job, but Kelso thinks you can handle it. This is the Sword of Alexander, said to be worth eleven-point-three million dollars, and it's only been missing for a week. The insurer is Sedgwick's company, and he's beside himself."

Avy thought of the old man's odd parting statement and frowned. Meanwhile she felt the whole atmosphere of the room shift subtly; the envy of the other agents—even Dante's—was palpable. It instantly put her on edge.

"This is a historic sword, said to be the one given to Alexander the Great by his father, and used to rout the Persians in the Battle of Issus, 333 B.C. The blade itself is original; the pommel, tang and cross guard were modified several hundred years later, when the twenty-two-carat gold and the cabochon jewels were added."

McDougal said tightly, "The plum assignment goes to Ms. Hunt."

"Yes. Because she's a founding partner and because of her track record."

Ominous silence took over.

"Any other comments? Questions?" Dante asked in clipped, perfunctory tones.

Valeria stared at Avy with open hostility, Zoe gazed right through her, and McDougal, a muscle jumping along his jaw, refused to look at her at all. *Great.* There was nothing like having a fan club at work. If Avy didn't bring back the sword, the wolves would be on her. She kept her expression cool and indifferent, but the tension inside her ratcheted up another notch.

Dante continued with an overview of the situation. "The sword was en route to Paris as part of the Mobley costume exhibit, originating at the Metropolitan in New York and curated by world-renowned medieval art expert Saundra Heller. The theft took place outside of London, during transit from the Met to the Louvre. The police investigation has barely begun, and you won't want to get tangled in it."

Avy said, "Kelso thinks Liam James is the most likely suspect. I agree. Who else could pull that off? Security had to be damn near impermeable."

Dante drummed his fingers on the relevant file and nodded. "This one's going to be tough, because he's like smoke. We have too many visuals of the guy, and they're all varied. The name seems to have been chosen at random, and he has other aliases, too. He's a master at changing his voice and accent. The Nerd Corps has finally tracked down a London residence, though, which is in itself a little suspicious. Odd timing for that to surface, don't you think? The former owner is a holding company for an obscure corporation."

Avy had to agree. She was intrigued by the job, though—more intrigued than she'd been by one in a long time. Dante fired the file down the table at her with a level glance and got awkwardly to his feet. "Good luck, everyone."

chapter 4

As she did her research on Liam James over the next couple days, expertise and finely honed instincts told Avy that someone was following her. And he was good, too—not obvious. She had to give him points for that.

As she strolled down Brickell from the parking garage the Miami heat and humidity almost melted her to the pavement. The beginning of September might bring autumn in New England, but it was dead, sticky summer here in the Sunshine State. The sun didn't shine; it oozed and steamed and spit nasty yellow between thunderheads at this time of year.

Avy mopped at her brow and stayed calm, if not cool. She wasn't nervous, since she'd summed up the man's intent within moments. He wasn't tailing her in order to catch her by surprise and hurt her. He was simply gathering information. Watching her movements.

The moment she'd spotted him she'd run a few extra errands just to be sure. She'd taken him down Calle Ocho for a Cuban coffee. She'd stopped in at her favorite Columbian-run nail salon and left him cooling his heels while she had a manicure and gossiped in Spanish. And just for fun she'd run over to Coral Gables and taken her time looking at wickedly expensive shoes in Capriccio. Nothing drove a man crazier than a shoe-shopping woman.

The guy had garnered excellent training somewhere. He was taller than average, about six foot two, but he slouched to disguise it. He wore unremarkable clothes, nothing that would stand out.

And he'd switched out his car three times now in just a day and a half, going from a beige Maxima to a pale blue Windstar minivan to an older-model black Taurus. He'd worn a beard and mustache the first morning, lost the beard by evening, and today his face was clean-shaven.

During the few hours he was changing cars and appearance a stocky woman had filled in for him, but Avy had spotted her as well. She was a touch too studied, too by-the-book. The man was a natural, a real pleasure to watch—and not only for his skill. God certainly hadn't put him together on a Friday afternoon.

No, he'd taken his time with this guy's proportions: wide, tough shoulders and a trim midsection, narrow hips and long legs. He moved with a supremely masculine grace, had longish dark hair but wasn't too pretty.

She couldn't tell what color his eyes were. His casual slouch didn't completely disguise an intensity probably born of character, not just mission.

She wouldn't have noticed him if she hadn't been a recovery agent and a former investigator. That was just his bad luck. The question was: Why was he following her?

Avy watched him watch her as she walked casually across the street from the ARTemis building and down to the local Starbucks. She had two choices: lose him or bust him. Because she certainly couldn't go anywhere near Liam James in London with this guy on her tail.

And if she wanted to keep her reputation and get paid, she needed to go get that sword.

She made her decision: If she tried to lose her tail, he'd still eventually discover that she'd gone back to London. So bust him it was. She continued on her way to Starbucks, stood in line, and then ordered: a skinny no-whip mocha and a regular coffee, bold. She swiped two packets of Sugar in the Raw and a stir stick on her way out.

She smiled her thanks at a gentleman who opened the door for her and crossed Brickell Avenue again, headed for her building.

Mr. Mysterious had moved benches but still pored over the same page of the *Miami Herald*'s sports section. She wondered if they'd set up electronic surveillance equipment—maybe in an empty office across the street. They'd have had a hard time rigging anything near her condo without a big van, so they'd probably settled for watching ARTemis, Inc.

Avy walked right up to the man and sat down next to him. "I figured you might like some coffee after a tough morning of reading the same two pages of stats. Two sugars, right?" She handed him the coffee.

He lowered the paper, but she couldn't see his eyes behind the mirrored shades he wore. A muscle twitched in his jaw, the only sign of possible annoyance. "How thoughtful of you." He accepted it. She couldn't place his accent. It wasn't quite American. Scandinavian?

She held out her hand. "I'm Avy Hunt. But you knew that, right?"

He nodded. His strong, warm fingers engulfed hers, and of all things, he kissed them.

A shock fluoresced through her system, and Avy quickly repossessed her hand.

The stranger folded up his paper, unconcerned, as if he kissed women's hands every day. She still wasn't sure how he'd done it without seeming the least bit cheesy.

He stuck the stir stick between even white teeth, popped the plastic lid off the coffee, and tore the tops off both sugar packets at once. He dumped the contents into his cup, shoved the wrappers into his pocket, then removed the stick from his mouth and stirred the black liquid.

Finally he threw the stick, javelin style, into a nearby trash can, snapped the lid back onto the cup, and took a sip. "Mmmmm. Very good. I must say, it's been a sheer pleasure to watch you, lovely Avy Hunt, but it's an even greater pleasure to meet you up close. And you're cheeky. I do like that in a woman."

His voice was rich, saturated in luxury and garnished with elegance. It sounded like aged whiskey poured over rocks—not ice, but diamonds.

"And *your* name?" she asked.

He still didn't supply the information, just shrugged.

She sighed. "Okay, No-Name. What do you want with me?"

"Maybe I'm just some horrible man stalking you."

"Give me a break," she said. "You have a purpose other than that. Surveillance is part of my job, and my father is a U.S. Marshal who's passed along a few tips. But you knew that, too. You know the natural color of my hair, the kind of toothpaste I use, and probably the brand of my underwear."

He lowered his shades an inch. "Brown, darling. Colgate. And . . ." The right corner of his mouth turned up. "Various. You should know that I'm quite partial to the green silk pair trimmed in black lace." He shot her an utterly charming and thoroughly wicked grin.

Avy's mouth dropped open, and her first instinct was to smack him. Tightly she asked, "You've pawed through my lingerie drawer? Don't you think that's a little bit outside your job description?" *And how the hell did I not notice you'd been in my condo?*

He made a soothing noise. "You'd be amazed at how varied my job description is. But I don't paw, love. I'm much more subtle and practiced than that. Even you never knew I was there, did you?"

The idea of it made her furious—a lot angrier than having him go through her things. She glared at him, and he met her gaze unapologetically. His eyes were an amused gray-green with dark lashes. Intelligent. Provocative. Compelling. "Your bird likes me, by the way."

"Kong doesn't like anyone except for me and one other person."

"Make that two." He showed his teeth again.

"Great," Avy said. "That's just great. I'll bet you know my social security number—"

He recited it.

"—and yet you won't tell me your name or your affiliation. That ruffles my sweet Southern feathers."

He adjusted his shades once more so that all she saw was a double of her face reflected in them. "I daresay you'll recover," he said in cheerful tones.

"No doubt I will," she agreed. "And I'll also find out who you are. But you could make it easier by just coming clean."

"Oh, come now. That takes all the fun out of things, doesn't it?" Again he displayed his white teeth.

That was when she spotted the surveillance equipment, a tiny camera between an *arepa* and a *cachita* on a pastry cart across the street. "Okay, have it your way," Avy said. She waited for a couple of cars to pass by. Then she slung an arm around his shoulders, leaned in toward him, and waved merrily at the pastry cart.

"Bloody hell," he said, with grudging respect. "You aren't half-bad, are you?"

"Your partner's no match for you," she told him. "She's stiff and she doesn't play Hispanic well. Dark hair and eyes aren't sufficient—she's got to *move* like a Latina. Gracefully. Sexily. Not like a repressed WASP. That woman's also never handled an *arepa* in her life."

He reflected on this. "And an *arepa* is . . . ?"

"A South American corn-based pastry, often stuffed with meat or cheese."

"Ah."

Avy stood and kissed him on the cheek. He smelled great—of sandalwood, hard man, coffee, and some guava-cream confection. "Next time don't eat the camouflage, honey," she advised. "And try to behave. Stay out of my condo—and my panty drawer."

As she strolled away, Avy could feel the man's gaze right in the small of her back.

"It's not your panties I'm interested in, love," he called after her. "It's what's inside them."

Despite the flash of heat the words sent through her, Avy didn't stop walking.

He watched her hips swing as she made her exit, eyeing her rear with the expertise of a connoisseur. She was sexy, but in a no-nonsense, straightforward way. She had a natural grace that hadn't been learned in any charm school.

Even if he hadn't seen photographs of her high-risk adventures, he would have known that Avy was an athlete, with those broad, confident shoulders, narrow hips, and lean, muscled calves that would give a man a run for his money. She was nervy and intelligent to boot. Wary of men—he wondered if that came from experience or instinct.

Either way, the lady was impressive. He grinned. This was going to be good fun. He sipped at her sweetened up-yours coffee, rose, and spoke into his wrist unit. "I do believe we've been bested, Miss Bunker. I daresay your employer won't be at all happy. Seems that they should have sent you for some theater arts courses, my dear."

Kay Bunker's voice crackled back at him. "Yes, I heard. I'm not deaf."

"Now, now. There's no need for hostility. The hostility should be on my part, don't you think? After all, I'm here against my will."

"If you'd rather go to prison, we can arrange that. We can also arrange a very friendly cell mate with a raging hard-on for snooty Brits."

"I fear you are sadly lacking in subtlety, Miss Bunker," he said mournfully. "There is no need for threats, either." He removed his earpiece and sauntered away with his paper and coffee, leaving her to deal with the pastry cart.

He didn't care much for Bunker, and he'd far rather think about Ava Brigitte Hunt and her long, honey-brown hair. Of course, the long legs weren't bad, either. Nor was the quite exquisitely proportioned bosom.

Ava Brigitte could easily have modeled as an odalisque, reclining nude on a chaise longue for some nineteenth-century French painter.

And yet . . . he was most attracted to her very sharp mind. He hadn't been made by anyone *ever.* He was that good. Until she'd come traipsing up to him with that cursed cup of coffee.

"Very nicely done, Miss Hunt," he murmured. "But the next round belongs to me."

Instinct told him that she'd take the rest of the day to continue research on her next mark, Liam James, and then head for London. The insurer would spring for a first-class ticket. And then the games would truly begin—because Avy Hunt was not going to be easy to distract.

Back in his suite at the Mandarin Oriental, he poured himself a vodka and stared out at the water of Biscayne Bay, at the tall white buildings gleaming like shark's teeth under the hot Miami sun. Below him, at the bar, the fabric of the luxury umbrellas flapped in the breeze. Under them sat posh couples sipping mojitos and martinis. A small yacht backed out of a slip at the high-rise opposite him.

"Mmmmm." He raised an eyebrow and thought briefly about piracy. But it would be difficult to pull off a kidnapping of the crew as well—and who wanted to captain, clean, and cook on a seventy-five-foot yacht? It rather defeated the purpose of taking it. Then there were the facts that he didn't swim well and wasn't partial to sharks.

He pursed his lips and then frowned. Took another sip of the icy vodka. There'd been a day when he might have done it just for a lark . . . but those days were over.

He sat at the walnut desk in his suite and booted up his laptop. He pulled up the screen he wanted, one that displayed a clear view of Avy Hunt's front door, and settled back to wait.

Ah. There was the delivery girl with the gorgeous tropical arrangement he'd sent—of course, anonymously. There was Avy herself, opening the door, accepting the flowers, thanking the girl.

The door shut.

He pulled up another screen, which, thanks to the tiny camera he'd installed in the vase he'd asked the florist to use, displayed the interior of her condo. He grinned as he watched Avy run her fingers meticulously over every leaf and petal in the arrangement. *Clever girl.* She wouldn't think to look at the vase itself, though.

He took another sip of vodka as she proved him wrong.

He sputtered and choked as a feminine finger, not coincidentally the middle one, came toward the camera lens, magnified to fill the whole screen of his laptop. Then everything went black.

chapter 5

One of the oldest tricks in the book. He really must think I'm stupid. Avy scanned her condo unit, inch by inch, for bugs and other hidden cameras. She didn't really expect to find any, since if they'd already been in place Mr. Mysterious wouldn't have pulled the floral stunt.

Still, she checked the colorful, abstract glass piece on her curvy teak coffee table, and she felt around the edges of the plasma TV.

Just to be safe, she picked up every one of the pillows on the blue suede couch and checked underneath them thoroughly.

She scanned every wall and looked behind the art, even the huge mixed-media painting that was her single biggest retail sin.

An odd piece, it was a vortex of shapes and textures that escaped its rectangular frame, wrapped around it in a wave, and appeared to be pulling the right section of that frame into its center.

It reminded Avy of a tornado or a hurricane. She'd never seen anything like it, and when she'd walked into the gallery she'd been riveted. The painting seemed to suck her into it, and she'd felt compelled to take it home, regardless of the collapse of her savings account. She'd never been sorry—though she *had* investigated thoroughly to make sure it wasn't hot.

Avy checked the birdcage, the double bookcase, and even the powder room. She went over the whole interior of her condo, found nothing, and felt better. She wondered why the provocative spy hadn't taken care of surveillance while he was inside her condo—it didn't make sense to her. Had he been giving her a fair shot? Or had he simply been too busy in her underwear drawer?

It riled her that he'd broken in and gone through her things, but it wasn't as if she'd never done it while gathering info on a subject, and at least he'd been honest about his trespassing. It was the secretive, nebbishy, passive-aggressive types that gave her the creeps. She'd far rather deal with straight aggression, provoking or not.

Avy headed for her bedroom again and stopped as she caught the barest whiff of the stranger's scent near her dresser: the sandalwood and something male. Her skin prickled with awareness.

She looked around the room, trying to see it as he would have: the unmade bed, the silly stuffed sheep that stood on the nightstand, the discarded clothes draped over a yellow armchair. Why had he been following her? Why had he been in her condo, and when, and how had he gotten in? She resolved to find out the answers to those questions as soon as she got back from London.

She multitasked that evening, packing her carry-on while shamelessly bribing her nineteen-year-old cousin Shari via cell phone. "Free food, Shari! Free *booze*. All you can drink from the bar."

She threw a fake passport into the carry-on, along with a fake driver's license. She adjusted her fake boobs. They were the heavy, rubbery kind, and felt a lot like veal cutlets.

But they tucked easily into a massive bra, where they jiggled convincingly.

More annoying was the body padding surrounding her from waist to knee under her icky expando pants. She felt like a sausage stuffed into a casing.

"Will you leave me your car keys?" Shari asked.

Black cashmere cardigan, spike-heeled boots, Dior bag— "What? Are you smoking crack?"

"I think that's a deal breaker, then." Avy's cousin yawned. "I mean, I have to drive all the way from Tampa, and that bird of yours hates me. He's really nasty, and I should be well compensated for putting up with him."

Kong, Avy's cockatiel, currently stood on her shoulder, running his beak through her hair. He cocked his head inquisitively at the cell phone. *"Bruja,"* Kong said. He had a vocabulary of only sixty words, but many of them were Spanish insults.

"See what I mean?" Shari complained. "I definitely need you to throw in the car keys."

" 'Witch' is a term of endearment to Kong," Avy told her. "Really."

"I don't think so. Why don't you have that Jeffrey guy bird-sit? Kong loves him."

Jeffrey Kluber, a sous chef for a five-star restaurant in Miami, lived in Avy's building just down the hall, and what Kong primarily adored about him was his very prominent, active Adam's apple. The cockatiel could watch it for hours as it bobbed up and down, jutting out and vibrating madly as Jeffrey got excited by a topic like soufflés.

"Because Jeffrey doesn't look like me, Shari. I need to lose a tail—I want them to think I'm still here."

"Someone's following you and you want me to take your place? Are you *kidding* me?"

"He's just watching. He's harmless."

"Yeah, right. No, thanks."

"C'mon, what's not to like about a few days at the beach?"

"I'm already near a beach," Shari pointed out. "Without some weirdo looking at me through binoculars."

"I'll pay you a hundred dollars a day, plus expenses."

Silence followed. "One fifty," Shari countered after a moment. "Danger pay."

"I told you, it's only standard surveillance." Avy didn't mention the fact that Mr. Standard Surveillance had broken in. She didn't think he'd do it again—and definitely not while anyone was there.

"I don't care—it's creepy. One fifty a day and the car keys."

"Ladrona!" said Kong in the general direction of the phone.

"What did he just call me?"

Thief, in Spanish. "Nothing," Avy said hastily. Sometimes his timing was eerie. She tried to get Kong to leave her shoulder for her finger so she could put him back in his bird palace, but nothing doing. He curled one foot under the strap of her tank top and clung stubbornly.

"You have a car," she told Shari. "You don't need to drive my Porsche. And one fifty seems a little high."

"Well, but I have a research paper due on Tuesday, so this is really inconvenient."

"There's a computer here, DSL, everything you could possibly need."

Silence.

"Fine," Avy said, exasperated. "A hundred and fifty a day, but no car keys. You drive your own car. Do we have a deal?"

"Yesss," Shari crowed. "Be still, my new Prada handbag!"

Avy made a sound of disgust. "I'll leave the key with the concierge downstairs, okay? Can you be here by ten in the morning?"

Shari grumbled but agreed.

Avy finished tossing her toiletries into the carry-on, zipped it, and then again tried to dislodge Kong from her shoulder, uncurling one claw at a time. He fluttered his wings, squawked, and ascended to her head, where he danced around and tangled the hair of her wig.

"Kong, come down from there—I have to get to the airport!" She slipped her hand underneath his body and tried to pull him off as gently as possible. "Ow!"

Finally she got him settled onto a perch in his airy little kingdom, content with a Nutri Berry and some shredded carrot. She turned on some light jazz for him, grabbed her carry-on and her computer bag, and sprinted out the door. Sheila had left a packed suitcase for her at the reception desk, containing outfits and disguise possibilities for every occasion. Like Forrest Gump's box of chocolates, Avy never knew what she was going to get, and it was kind of fun that way.

In the basement parking garage she hopped on her building's courtesy shuttle to Miami International. A surveillance team looking for a tall, slender girl with long hair probably wouldn't take much note of a chunky, middle-aged woman in a bad pantsuit, with an auburn bob and heavy tortoiseshell glasses over too much makeup.

And if they were checking flight information, a Louise Houghton shouldn't raise any red flags.

As the van swung out of the parking garage and onto Alhambra, Avy buried her nose in a copy of the *Wall Street Journal* and tried to look myopic and bland. She paid little attention to her two fellow passengers, a dour older businessman who clutched a London Fog across his lap and a pert redhead who talked incessantly on her baby blue Razr phone.

They arrived at the construction zone known as Miami International Airport within minutes, but then waited in endless traffic, victims of poorly conceived rerouting and impatient, lunatic drivers. MIA was a disaster and never seemed to improve.

Miss Razr Phone ended her call and checked her makeup in the reflective screen of the device before climbing down from the shuttle at the Continental terminal. Avy and Mr. London Fog got out at the British Air terminal.

She and her padded thighs and veal cutlets made it through security with no incident, and she boarded her flight within the hour. As usual these days, the air-conditioning was insufficient, and in her middle-aged getup Avy began to have a very real hot flash. Over her head—in fact, directly into her left ear—hissed a lukewarm stream of recirculated air that provided no relief at all.

She fanned herself with the in-flight magazine, one whose cover taunted her with pictures of cool, mouthwatering cocktails.

Across the aisle from her, a woman Avy guessed to be in her fifties cast her a smile of sympathy. "It gets worse before it gets better," she murmured.

Avy returned the smile and then dug into the sturdy, battered Coach purse Sheila had checked out to her, producing a compact. She was positive that her carefully applied, heavy makeup was melting off her face.

"Ha!" said the woman across the aisle. "Try a whole container of talcum powder, dear. And a bag of ice across the back of your neck. And a bottle of Xanax so that you don't kill strangers who give you unsolicited advice on how to handle menopause." She winked.

Avy laughed. At least her disguise was convincing. Her

fellow passenger had no idea that she was in fact twenty-nine years old and roughly a size eight, not a fourteen.

"I'm Regina Davenport," the woman said. "My daughter and her husband live outside London. They just had a baby, so I'm going to visit my new grandson."

Avy wondered what it must be like to have a mother with a sense of humor, one who'd actually wink at someone she didn't know. "Louise Houghton," she said, regretting that she couldn't give her real name. "Headed to London on business."

"Oh? What do you do?" Regina probed as Mr. London Fog shuffled past, making his way to a seat behind Avy's. *Hmmmm. Surveillance?*

"I . . . Let's just say that I find things for people."

"Private investigator, are you?"

Avy smiled and nodded.

She felt a little guilty for not being straight with Regina, but telling people what she did for a living started an inevitable barrage of questions and always drew unwelcome attention.

Before the woman could ask further questions, Avy distracted her by asking if she had any pictures of her new grandchild. Regina produced an entire album and regaled her with tales of labor and delivery for two hours into the trip.

Liam marveled at the effectiveness of Avy's disguise. If he hadn't known for a fact that nobody had entered her condo, if he hadn't seen her walk out in this costume, he had to admit that he'd never have guessed it was her.

He settled back into his seat and admired her, comfortable in the fact that she hadn't seen through his own costume of baldpate, gray fringe, and tired-businessman aura. Her eyes had flickered over him as he got onto the plane, so she'd definitely noticed that he'd shared not only her cab but her flight. But for the moment he rather thought he was safe.

The weakly recirculating air brought her scent to his nostrils, and he savored it. Freesia. Jasmine. A touch of citrus. Mmmmm. Now he was even more certain that the heavy middle-aged woman in the seat ahead of him was Avy.

He enjoyed the sound of her voice, as well, as she chatted with the woman across the aisle from her. He analyzed her tones like a fine wine as she spoke: light, melodious, Southern-kissed—and, interesting enough, rather wholesome.

Now, that was unexpected. Spike-heeled, Dior-bagged, globe-trotting Ava Brigitte was wholesome? He found it charming, something to pursue further as he got to know her.

He rolled her name on his tongue without vocalizing it. Damned sexy. Had her mum been a fan of Ava Gardner and Brigitte Bardot? Avy managed to do them both justice— though not in her current garb.

As the flight attendants explained the use of seat belts and flotation devices and oxygen masks, he lazily imagined what Avy looked like without any clothes on. He intended to find out in the course of his mission, but in the meantime anticipation was sweet. Those high, proud breasts . . .

His BlackBerry buzzed in his pocket just as the flight attendants reminded all passengers to turn off such devices. He pulled it out and read a text message from Agent Bunker. *Confirm you are on board flight.*

With a slight shrug he hit the power button and turned it off without responding. *Just following rules and regs, love.* The bloody woman knew damned well he was on board— and all she had to do to confirm was to look at the flight manifest. Keystroke software had made an easy job of tracking Avy's movements, even traveling as Louise Houghton.

He ordered his vodka with tonic, since he considered the airline liquors inferior, and unfolded his *New York Times* to the crossword puzzle. The clue for number four down read, *Describes an individual with a penchant for theft.*

With a broad smile he set down his drink and found a pencil. Then, in bold letters, he spelled out the answer: L-A-R-C-E-N-O-U-S.

Under the imposing lighted portico of London's landmark Savoy Hotel on the Strand, Avy tipped her driver and made her way inside, happy to see Mr. London Fog nowhere in sight. She was probably just being paranoid.

She was thoroughly sick of her body padding after the long flight. Since she didn't want to check in as Louise Houghton, she headed straight to the nearest ladies room. She pulled her wheeled carry-on into a stall with her, laid it horizontally on the toilet seat, and began the metamorphosis back into herself. What a relief! And wasn't it every woman's fantasy to be able to shed forty pounds of excess body weight in approximately ninety seconds? It sure beat a starvation diet.

Padding, matron wear, and wig safely stowed away, she pulled on a black pencil skirt, high heels, and a formfitting gray cashmere sweater. She shrugged into a light jacket with a peplum waist, quickly switched out Louise's ugly square leather pocketbook for her own sleek Dior saddlebag, and Avy was reincarnated.

Moments later she checked in. Before going up to her room she took a few moments to wander and admire her luxe surroundings—even after five years of the high life, she never took five-star hotels for granted.

The Savoy's Thames Foyer was vast and gorgeous, with pastoral scenes painted on the walls, real and painted trompe l'oeil, marble columns, and a grand piano in the

center of it all. The American Bar there was an institution
and had been serving cocktails to the beau monde since the
1890s.

She'd have a drink there later, but for now she headed up
to her room. After a long, hot shower she fell soundly
asleep.

Hours had passed when she picked up a SIG Sauer iden-
tical to her own at a prearranged dead drop. Not even law
enforcement officers could pack heat and travel overseas,
so this was the simplest way to get around the issue. She'd
replace the gun at the same spot on her way out of town.

London at night was gray and chilly, much as it was during the day. An anemic sliver of moon did an ineffectual job
of lighting the somber sky as Avy walked to the confirmed
address of Liam James.

He lived in what she'd loosely term a gray stone garden
home on Palace Court, off Bayswater Road. A porch light
winked conspiratorially at her from across the street where
she stood in the shadows. Other than that the place was entirely dark—which was very convenient. According to her
sources, no lights had been on for two days.

She crossed the street casually and cased the back of the
place, which was sheltered by a small garden surrounded by
a five-foot wall of the same stone as the building. Two
doors down a couple was having a drinks party—not so
convenient. She hoped that they were all at the bottom of
their fourth cocktails and couldn't see straight.

She also hoped that Liam James still possessed the
Sword of Alexander. She was betting that he did—standard
operating procedure was to let the fuss over a heist die
down for a few weeks and then smuggle the items out of the
country. Better still was to smuggle them out before anyone

knew about the theft, but she didn't think he'd had a big enough window of opportunity.

She mentally reviewed the schematics of the home. Master bedroom at the rear left, converted from a study five years ago. Kitchen directly next to it, with the dining room at the rear right. In front of those was a spacious living room.

What made the most sense was to break in through the window of the master bedroom on the ground floor. She'd be hidden from sight by the stone wall, there was no climbing required, and as long as she succeeded in disarming the alarm system the cocktail partiers would never know she was there.

She flexed her fingers in their black calfskin gloves and felt the familiar surge of adrenaline begin to hum in her system. Checking to the right, left, and behind her first, Avy slipped through the garden gate unnoticed and latched it noiselessly behind her.

She took stock of the small yard. Liam James apparently liked a traditional English garden, with all sorts of flowers and shrubs she couldn't identify. A cherry tree in full blossom seemed to usher her graciously to the master bedroom window, and underneath the tree was a wrought-iron bench, painted white. *How picturesque.*

Avy took care of the alarm first. Then she walked through the grass, ducked under a large branch of the cherry tree, and inspected her target window, which had a somewhat complicated latch. No jiggling it loose. She reached into the zipper pocket of the black backpack she wore and removed a cutting tool that was standard-issue for ARTemis agents.

Carefully she attached it with adhesive to the window and began to cut a circular hole in the pane. When she finished she lifted the little glass circle out with the tiniest of scrapes. She detached it from the adhesive and placed it carefully under the window. Then she dropped the cutting tool back into her pack.

Her pulse had kicked up a bit during this process, and she listened indulgently to an earnest speech on friendship by one of the drunk guests two doors down.

"A man alone is nobody," he intoned.

And a woman alone is smart and free.

Avy put her hand through the hole she'd cut and groped for the latch. She unfastened it, raised the window as quietly as possible, and threw her leg over the sill. She slipped inside. It was pitch-black. As she stood there, trying to accustom her eyes to the darkness, she felt another presence in the room.

Her heart landed on her tonsils and she whirled, heading straight for the window and escape. But it was blocked by a large, powerful male figure. He flicked a switch and illuminated not only that corner of the room but himself.

Mr. Mysterious from Miami wore nothing but a pair of pajama bottoms and a very wolfish grin. In a lazy and highly amused voice he said, "Why, Avy, my darling. What took you so long?"

chapter 6

Gwen Davies still didn't like to fly, which was fine for an overprotected daughter but a problem for a recovery agent. In her orange leather carry-on there was a bottle of Xanax nestled with its travel companions: four minis of Smirnoff.

Along with the Xanax and the vodka, she'd packed an Eyewitness Travel guidebook to Rome and two romance novels by favorite authors. Since she hadn't had much luck meeting Mr. Right in Miami, she'd lose herself in someone else's love story for the flight—and anyone who scoffed just didn't know what he was missing.

So armed, Gwen fastened her seat belt, reassured herself that in the event of a crash her seat cushion was a flotation device, and clenched her hands around an airsickness bag until the plane reached a cruising altitude of twenty-two thousand feet. She was bound for Rome and one particular palazzo.

Sold in 2004 by Contessa Daniella di Benedetto, her notes read, *to Sid Thresher, lead guitarist and vocalist for the internationally known band Subversion.*

Gwen had a few Subversion CDs—who didn't? With the rest of the world she'd watched Sid's outrageous antics from afar.

He was best known for once having his Los Angeles

swimming pool filled with top-shelf tequila. He'd floated around in a blow-up raft during a well-publicized television interview, answering questions while bikini-clad babes lay around the edges of the pool, dipping in shot glasses and sucking on lime wedges. The object from which they licked the salt was too profane for television.

Sid, one of the world's most unattractive men, had gone through five wives, last time she'd checked. He had nine acknowledged children and probably countless others.

Gwen would have loved to meet the guy just for curiosity's sake, but that didn't mean she wanted to break into his home in the middle of the night. This whole caper was high-risk and stupid, yet she was committed now.

Joining the recovery agents at ARTemis meant living a life of adventure, not just reading about it in paperback novels.

While she'd traveled a bit with her parents, they were partial to cushy resorts and five-star hotels with room service, laundry service, every kind of service. Gwen wanted to see things off the beaten path, things more interesting than minibars and spas and boutiques. Real life, not American Express Black Card life.

She wanted to prove to herself that she was more than just a debutante with an art history degree. This crazy assignment of Kelso's scared her spitless, but it also made her feel alive. She was so tired of being insulated from everything.

Around her other passengers began to chat or peruse newspapers or sleep. The flight attendants muscled a big steel drinks cart down the aisle, and one of them reminded her a little of Avy, statuesque and calm but alert.

Ever since she'd met Avy at Sweet Briar in Art History 101, Gwen had been a little awed by her. She'd admired her drive most of all. Avy was a girl who was going places, even if she hadn't led as privileged a life as Gwen.

Avy had been fascinated with the art that Gwen had grown up with and took for granted, working hard to analyze pieces and remember every detail about them. She'd fallen in love with art and its history, while Gwen had chosen the major as an easy way to coast through school. She'd been attending museum classes in art appreciation since she was five.

She still remembered Avy that first morning of class. Same long hair, same body that managed to be voluptuous and athletic at the same time. Same intensity. She'd had a cheap spiral notebook and a plastic Bic pen. Gwen had brought her leather portfolio and Waterman pen.

They'd sat next to each other and introduced themselves, and when the lecture began Gwen started making notes. Avy sat there, pen poised, not writing anything. After ten minutes or so she leaned over. "How do you know what to write down, other than the name and the date of the piece? This class is so strange."

Gwen laughed and thought about it. "I guess it is strange sitting here in the dark and watching a slide show while some guy with a pointer calls everything 'compelling and monumental.'"

Avy nodded.

"You'll understand more when you start the text. But for now try to note the category he places the art in, where it comes from, what it looks like, and how it's similar to or different from the next thing he shows. If it seems to illustrate what's going on culturally or historically at the time it was made, then note that, too."

"Thanks," Avy whispered gratefully.

Gwen smiled at her. "You're welcome. If you want, we can get a coffee after class and I'll tell you more."

That was how she'd met Avy Hunt.

She and Avy had been friends ever since, even though Avy's idea of fun was to go to a shooting range with her dad and blow holes in paper targets, and Gwen's idea of fun was to go to Bliss or Dior and melt plastic with her mom.

Avy had come home with her for Thanksgiving one year, and Gwen would never forget the way she ran her hands reverently over the big bronze sculpture of a horse in the Davieses' foyer—the same sculpture that Gwen tossed her coat onto when she came in.

"You're sure it's okay if I touch this?" Avy had asked.

"Of course. We're not in a museum, and you can't hurt it. Get on and take a ride if you want."

"I can't believe you get to *live* with these pieces," Avy said. "It's so cool."

Gwen's parents had adored Avy, and when she and Gwen graduated from Sweet Briar they gave her a Dior saddlebag purse and a letter of recommendation to Sotheby's famed auction house.

Avy's mom made Gwen a quilt for the occasion, and Avy's dad gave her a wink and an antique ladies' derringer, in case the debutante balls got rough. Gwen still had the quilt and the Derringer and Avy still had the purse.

Gwen smiled just thinking about it, and then made the mistake of looking out the window. It reminded her that she was twenty-thousand feet in the air and had not an iota of control over the way she'd land.

She pulled the orange tote out from under the seat in front of her, unzipped it, and pulled out the Xanax, the vodka, and a romance novel. Then she anesthetized her fear with all three.

One Xanax was sufficient for the whole flight, if she drank a minivodka every two hours and fell utterly in love with the novel's hero. And so Gwen passed the time until the flight's descent, when she just gripped the armrests of her seat and prayed.

The Rome airport was a zoo, but she negotiated customs without any trouble and then made the mistake of catching a cab to her hotel. The driver had looked fairly normal when she got in, but turned into a raging psychotic with no regard for life or traffic rules as soon as the door closed behind him.

He floored the gas pedal and they shot forward so fast that she was positive they'd time-traveled into the future. He sped through intersections illegally, nearly sideswiping at least three other cars, stopping only to exchange invective and hand gestures with the drivers.

He violently wrenched the wheel to avoid unwise pedestrians who stepped in front of his taxi, while Gwen rolled around like a pinball in the backseat. He used his horn as a rude conversational tool and the brakes sparingly but effectively—almost ricocheting her out the front windshield.

By the time Gwen crawled, shaking, out of his taxi, she had no doubt that breaking into a famous rock star's residence wasn't going to affect her nerves at all—because after this and the flight they were already shot.

She checked in, let Sheila know she'd arrived, and then heartily cursed Kelso and his juvenile sense of humor. Surely stealing a rock star's dog, however temporarily, shouldn't be *anywhere* in her job description.

chapter 7

"What are *you* doing here?" Avy, at a total loss, said to her Miami stalker.

He bared his teeth at her. "I live here, love."

She stared at him. "You *live* here?"

He nodded and then added encouragingly, "Do the math, darling."

"But . . . *you're* Liam James?"

"Sir Liam," he said modestly.

"Of course. I should have known." Trying to get her head together, she looked around at the room. Brocade wallpaper in a pumpkin color. Chocolate brown satin sheets. An eiderdown quilt in a pattern of bottle green and pumpkin and burgundy. Museum-quality antique furniture, mostly in mahogany and walnut.

Heavy gilt frames on his walls burst with color—she recognized a genuine Reynolds, and what appeared to be a Gainsborough—very rare, since few of them existed. On the wall over the bed hung a gorgeous, lush Tintoretto nude. She looked sleepy, satiated, debauched.

As an art history major Avy had seen many nudes. But she'd never seen one that made her blush. This one, spread like a banquet over the head of Sir Liam James's rumpled, somehow wicked-looking bed, had her color rising. She averted her gaze.

"Inviting, isn't it?"

She said nothing.

"Cat burglar got your tongue, love?" His eyes roved over her. "If not, he'd surely like to." His lips curved.

"How did you . . ." Words failed her as her eyes fell to his chest again.

"How did I . . . ?"

She forced her gaze away from it and stared at the open window instead, uncharacteristically wanting to flee through it. "How did you know I was coming here? How could you possibly have tracked me? And why would you go to Miami to surveil me if you *did* know I was coming here?"

"Connections," he said enigmatically. "That's the answer to the first two questions. As for the third . . ." He shrugged. "Because it was amusing."

"Amusing?" The heat in her face began to seep into her veins and trigger a slow burn in her stomach.

He bared his teeth at her again. "Well, love, the more sinister answer is that I always track my prey and take careful note of any individual habits and quirks."

"Prey?" she repeated. The burn bubbled into a boil. "I don't think you quite understand the situation. You're *my* prey. Or something in your possession is."

"How delightful. It seems we have such a lot in common. Care to take off your knickers and stay awhile?"

"Take off my—!"

"Do you hear an echo? I believe the workmen must not have done a proper job of insulating." He scrutinized the corners of the room.

Avy was ready to simply take out her 9mm and shoot the man. "Look, *Sir* Liam, you're responsible for taking something of great value from the Metropolitan Museum of Art.

I'd appreciate it if you'd just turn it over to me and then we can be done with this farce."

"Oh, but this is no laughing matter, love," he said. "Besides, you'll hurt my feelings if you call it a farce."

I am *going to shoot him.* "Sir Liam—"

"Let's not stand on ceremony, shall we? You'll just call me Liam, and if I may I'll just call you Avy. Allow me to say that you look quite fetching in black."

"I specialize in fetching," Avy said.

"Oh, very good." He grinned appreciatively. "Drink?"

"No, thank you. If you'll hand over the sword I'll be on my way."

He threw back his head and laughed. "Come, now. Surely you don't expect it to be that easy?"

"Is the sword on the premises?"

"Let's not talk business just yet, love."

"I don't really feel like talking pleasure with you, under the circumstances," she said evenly.

"I don't talk it, my darling, I *take* pleasure." He came far too close and tilted up her chin. For a brief, wild moment she thought he'd kiss her. Then he flashed her a quick grin and walked out of the room.

She had no choice but to follow or leave by the window. She certainly wasn't going to make herself comfortable on his rumpled bed.

He turned quite suddenly in the hallway so that she came chin-to-chest with him. God help her, but she wanted to lick it—after she murdered him, of course. "I *give* great pleasure, too," he said softly. His breath ruffled her hair and tickled the lobes of her ears. A deep shiver spiraled down her spine.

Avy took a step back.

He lifted an eyebrow. "Disappointing." He turned back

around and kept walking. "But perhaps a world-class vodka will change your mind."

Her eyes riveted to his taut backside and the way his silk pajama bottoms rode his hips, she barely heard him.

"What's your choice? Belvedere, Grey Goose, or Chopin?"

The man had not an ounce of fat on his body and looked as if he could do pull-ups with a single index finger. In Miami he'd been clothed but still impressive. Here he was heart-attack material. He looked like blue-blooded, half-naked sin on the half shell.

"See something you like there, darling?"

Mortified, Avy realized he could see her fascinated reflection in the clear glass of his maple kitchen cabinets. She diverted her gaze from Sir Liam's spectacular buns to the rest of his furnishings.

The hardwood floors gleamed with polish under several very fine Oriental rugs—no polypropylene here. The ceilings were fifteen feet high, the elaborate trim painted white. His living room walls were a gorgeous deep crimson—Avy half expected to find the furniture trimmed in ermine.

But like the bedroom, it was a mix of fine antiques and comfortable, more modern pieces. Near an L-shaped white sofa sat an eighteenth-century carved French chair covered in what looked like the original tapestry of a hunting scene. Two sixteenth-century Spanish chairs framed an Elizabethan console.

A nineteenth-century English fainting couch stretched languorously in front of the fireplace, over which hung a fleshy young Bacchus that Avy hoped was not an original Caravaggio, but which probably was. Liam apparently had a long and colorful history of strolling through museums on shopping trips. According to his file, he would identify something that he liked, scope out security and convenient exit options, and return after dark.

The mantel boasted Sèvres and Limoges, not to mention the most elaborate sterling candelabra and what she thought might very well be a Revere teapot. Why he'd have an American Revolutionary piece she couldn't guess.

Had he stolen it all?

She felt his presence behind her and turned, though she hadn't heard a sound. Liam James gave new meaning to the term *light-footed*. A cat made more noise.

"Here you are. You didn't specify, so I chose for you." He handed her a Baccarat glass. "I'll challenge you to tell me which of the three vodkas it is."

She didn't want it, but then again, perhaps she needed to play his game in order to get what she did want. Avy accepted the heavy cut-crystal glass. "What were the choices again?"

"Belvedere, Grey Goose, or Chopin." His eyes glinted.

She could barely tell Diet Coke from real Coke, which meant she had a 33 percent chance of getting the answer right. Or did she? She'd seen a bottle of another vodka brand in his kitchen.

Avy took a sip and rolled it over her tongue, evaluating that particular glint in his eyes. It warned her not to trust him, not even on such a small matter as this. She took a gamble. "It's Skyy."

Those wicked eyebrows rose and his expression bore admiration. "Very, very good. You didn't let me get away with it."

She smiled as she took another sip and set the heavy glass down on his coffee table. "To catch a thief . . . ," she said, and sank into the white sofa. *Oh, heaven.* The pillows were stuffed with down.

Liam rubbed at his chin thoughtfully. "Well, now. You're

not really in the habit of catching us, are you? You're more dedicated to foiling us."

"If I wanted to catch you, I'd send my father after you." Avy crossed her legs. "Does that chair date to the Spanish Inquisition?"

He glanced at it. "Good eye."

"It wouldn't happen to be lifted from that contessa's home in Barcelona, would it? The same haul as the two missing Velázquez paintings I eventually recovered and the filched sapphire-and-diamond necklace?"

"Of course not, love," he said smoothly. "Just as the Daghestan rug under your feet didn't come from the palace of a sheikh in Dubai, and my delicious Tintoretto didn't come from the home of an exceedingly stupid magistrate in Venice."

"What would his stupidity have to do with anything?"

"It would have to do with the fact that he left the painting there during the summer months and refused to climate-control the room in which it hung. He was too cheap. And so his multimillion-dollar masterpiece was slowly rotting."

Liam took a sip of his own vodka. "Or so I hear. I wouldn't know anything about it personally." He shot her an angelic smile.

"Clearly you did the man a favor, then," Avy said in a voice heavy with sarcasm. She didn't like the fact that the statement was half-true.

He settled next to her on the couch, his hard, bronzed, nude shoulder nudging her own. She could smell a tinge of leather and sandalwood, as she had in Miami when she'd kissed his cheek. She could also smell his very male interest in her, as if he hadn't made it clear enough.

What can I do with that? Can I use it to manipulate him, or would it be unwise to try to beat him at what is obviously his own game?

"So tell me, Avy, what does Papa do? Under what circumstances would you send him after me?"

"You know what he does, remember? You have a dossier on me an inch thick. You know damned well he's a U.S. Marshal—and a very, very good one."

Liam studied her lazily. "Proud of him, are you?"

She folded her arms across her chest. "Why shouldn't I be?"

"Handsome man. Not home much, though."

"What are you driving at, Mr. James? Are you probing to see if I'm aware of my father's serial philandering? Yes. New topic, please."

"Touchy."

"What does *your* father do?" she asked pointedly. "I don't have quite such an extensive dossier on you."

Some of the glint went out of Liam's eyes. He laughed shortly. "I don't know. He certainly doesn't need to work, and he disinherited me years ago." An old pain flickered over his face and then was gone so fast that she almost imagined she'd seen it.

"Why?"

He turned his head away from her and pointed across the room, changing the subject. "That harp? Solid gold. Once in the household of Louis the Sixteenth. The little footstool in the corner used to caress the royal derriere of Marie Antoinette."

"Is that why you steal?" Avy asked. "Because your father disinherited you? Because you feel you deserve more?"

He looked skyward. "Amateur psychology. How old were you when you first stole something, love?"

"I don't steal. I'm a repo man."

He laughed. "You steal," he said. "You and I, we're just alike. The only difference is that you have a permit."

"That's not true," Avy said, but her heart began to pound and her palms began to sweat.

He leaned toward her, his eyes intent and very, very green. "You get a high from it. An adrenaline rush."

She shook her head.

"It makes you feel alive."

She looked away.

"It's like a great, fast fuck, isn't it, Avy?"

Shocked, she met his gaze again involuntarily. His face was inches from hers, his intensity rushed over her in a wave, and the truth in his words hit her right between the thighs.

"No," she said, because it was the only acceptable answer. "You're wrong."

Liam's eyes drilled into hers, his mouth quirked, and the tip of his tongue caught between his white teeth. For a moment he was the serpent of original sin. Then his expression changed.

"Disappointing," Liam said, as he had before in the hallway.

"You have no right to find me disappointing." Avy set her vodka down with a snap.

"You have no right to break into my house. Shall I call the police, or shall we sit here peaceably and share a vodka, get to know each other?"

"That would be lovely," she said tightly. Again, the only acceptable answer.

"Papa might not welcome the news of his daughter's arrest for burglary"—he eyed the bulge in her boot—"make that armed robbery—in another country. A smidgen professionally embarrassing, don't you think?"

She blanched at the idea of humiliating her father that way, at seeing disappointment in his eyes instead of pride. Though her dad had disappointed her, she'd never, ever let him know it. She'd just buried it deep. "You're *despicable*," she said.

"But at least I'm no liar." He grinned. "By the way, do you have a U.K. permit to carry that gun in your boot?"

She glared at him.

"Of course you don't. Add to that the fact that you traveled here on a false passport. If I called the police, you could be in a right shitstorm of trouble, love. Isn't that what you Americans call it? A shitstorm?"

Her eyes narrowed on a small bronze figurine that stood on a bookshelf across the room. It was Chinese and ancient—possibly Tang dynasty?—and looked very similar to the one she'd recovered in Miami. She saw herself in Pomeroy's living room, patting it smugly in the pleather purse. *Never met a man I couldn't handle . . .*

Avy picked up his damned vodka again and slammed the rest of it.

"But being a softhearted sort of fellow—a jolly good fellow, in fact—I shan't call the authorities. Isn't that generous of me?" His eyes danced.

Immediately she was suspicious. "Why not?"

"Because, my sexy Ava Brigitte, I should like something in return. A small thing, really. I do hope you won't begrudge it."

Her suspicions grew stronger. "A small thing," she repeated skeptically.

He nodded. "What I'd like in return . . . is a kiss."

chapter 8

Avy was allergic to sexual blackmail, especially given the way she'd lost her job at Sotheby's. The idea of it was anathema to her, and it kick-started an old rage.

The problem was that kissing Liam James didn't seem like such a terrible idea. She'd been fixated on his lips since he'd challenged her about liking to steal. Since he'd seen right through her to the darkness inside and lit a flame to illuminate it for her. *You're a thief with a permit.*

But every human being was capable of immorality or cruelty. It was all a question of how you were brought up, where you set your personal parameters, and how hard you fought against the temptation to stray over that moral line.

As she burned with angry resistance, Avy looked at Liam's mouth, at the way the almost sullen lower lip met the insouciant upper one. She noted the tiny scar that cut across the left corner and wondered if it had been made by a woman's fingernail. She imagined that mouth on hers and felt a mixture of desire and fear coil in her belly.

Stealing is like a great, fast fuck . . .

She got up and walked across the room, putting distance between them. Stepping away from the edge of her moral line.

If she turned him down and he did call the cops . . . if she went to jail . . . She saw her father's face as he whipped off the Maui Jims he always wore and gave her that hard stare he reserved for deadbeats and criminals.

Given his dogmatic views, there was no guarantee he'd even come bail her out. He was a tough man, under the charm. He had to be.

Her skin erupted in hot prickles as a tremor went down her spine. But she brought her chin up and looked Liam James right in the eye. "Call the cops."

Liam's brows shot up, and he evaluated her for a long moment before he grinned and said softly, "Brava." Then he got to his feet as well and walked toward the kitchen. "Do you fancy salmon or pasta primavera for your very late supper?"

She leaned weakly against the bookshelf where she'd braced herself. He wasn't going to call anyone? "You're crazy."

"Daft Liam, that's me," he said cheerfully. "Now, salmon or pasta? You can't tell me that the airline's revolting spongy substance quivering under a blanket of bad sauce assuaged your appetite. Nor the tiny teacup of salad."

"How do you know what they served on my flight?" But Avy had a sinking feeling.

Liam winked at her from the open kitchen and disappeared for a moment into his bedroom. She heard a drawer open and shut. He emerged with a bald rubber pate fringed in gray spinning on his index finger. He tossed it at her, Frisbee style.

"I really, really hate you," she said, catching it. "Mr. London Fog."

"Fine line between love and hate, Mrs. Louise Houghton," he called. He winked again. "Now, I'll ask you a third time: fish or pasta?"

Under the circumstances she felt the need for something fattening. "Pasta, thank you."

Was he honest-to-God going to cook for her, after she'd broken into his house and they'd exchanged countless barbs? After he'd threatened her? She didn't know what to make of this man. Liam James was confounding, annoying, offensive, far too perceptive—and yet somehow charming.

He uncorked a bottle of white wine and splashed some into two stemmed glasses. She was already a bit high from the vodka—and if she had any hope of finding the sword in this place, she'd be smart not to drink any more. Was the sword here? If not here, then where? Buried in the garden?

"So where's the sword, Liam?" she asked, casually strolling into his kitchen. He turned from the sink, a large ripe tomato in either hand, and flashed what she was coming to think of as his sin grin.

"What sword would you be referring to, love?" He bounced the tomatoes gently in his palms, and under her gaze began to slowly rub circles on the taut skin with his thumbs.

As she watched him, heat seeped into places she'd rather it didn't. "Don't play games," she said mildly.

"All of life's a game, darling. It just depends on how you choose to play it. What's your strategy? What's your attitude? What's your reaction when you lose a point or two? You make a decision to prevail or not in the end."

Liam squeezed the tomatoes and brought them up to his nose, never taking his eyes off her face. He kissed each one.

A hard, rhythmic pulse kicked up in Avy's most unmentionable body part.

Liam smiled, set down the tomatoes, and handed her one of the glasses of wine.

She took a sip. "Look, all I want is the sword, okay?"

"Point taken—I wish," he said, with a lascivious grin. "I'd be happy to drive it home."

Elements of her body that she didn't even recognize began to pulse at the idea of Liam driving home, stealing home, sliding home.

"Do you ever think about anything other than sex?"

He nodded. "Occasionally. But you provoke all sorts of forbidden fantasies, love. Visions having to do with my strong sword and your delectable scabbard."

First she snorted. Then she asked, "How can you possibly know it's delectable until you've tried it?"

He groaned. "Avy, darling, you're a wicked tease. And you won't even give a suffering cat burglar a kiss? A wee one, that's all I'd ask . . ."

Maybe it was the vodka. Maybe it was the challenge. Maybe it was the fact that he hadn't called the authorities and he was cooking for her. She took hold of the dish towel he was wiping his hands on and pulled him toward her.

Obviously she was just as crazy as he was. But Avy lifted her chin and closed her eyes.

The dish towel fell over her feet, and Liam's big hands caressed either side of her face. She shuddered at the contact of his warm, calloused fingers. And then, just as she almost thought he wouldn't kiss her after all, his lips whispered across hers.

Every nerve ending she possessed seemed to sigh, *Yes.* She opened to him as he deepened the kiss, threading his fingers through her hair and drawing her head firmly toward him. His mouth became hungry and demanding, but always stayed somehow tender under the urgency.

The heat of his chest burned through her light sweater, and she could feel the strong, steady rhythm of his heartbeat. She slid her arms around his waist and ran her hands over his naked skin, noting every ripple of muscle underneath.

She'd never been kissed like this—as if he wanted to consume her, make love to her mouth, possess her completely. Liam James kissed her almost illegally, as if he wanted to steal her. It frightened her and excited her simultaneously. Adrenaline surged through her body, chasing desire. Her blood seemed to hum with forbidden pleasure.

Avy, what are you doing? Avy, be careful.

But just as she'd stupidly gone skydiving the week after twisting her ankle, she let Liam kiss her again. He tasted of vodka and lemon, and he ignited her all over again. His arms folded around her, holding her close, and she felt, of all things, safe.

He stroked her back, traced a finger down each vertebra of her spine, snugged her against him so that they fit together like puzzle pieces. He was hard against her belly, her breasts pressed flat against his chest.

When he raised his head at last her lips felt bruised, and she could feel the razor burn on the lower half of her face.

"Ava Brigitte," he murmured, cupping her chin. "You're very disturbing to a man's peace of mind. Do that again, and the pasta can go right to hell."

"You asked me to, Liam."

"Yes, I did. I must have been mad." He ran a hand through his hair and lifted his wine to his lips, eyeing her over the rim. "Mmmmm. I want more."

"A nice Southern girl doesn't go all the way on a first date." She smiled sweetly.

"Does she not?"

Avy shook her head.

"May I point out, then, that this is really our third date? We first met in Miami. And then we shared a transatlantic flight."

"You were tailing me in Miami," she said, outraged. "And I didn't even realize you were on that flight. You were in disguise!"

He shrugged. "So were you."

She shook her head. "Those do not count as conventional dates," she said severely.

He grinned. "But breaking into my home does? Face it, Avy—if you were the conventional sort, you wouldn't be here. So don't give me any speeches about nice Southern girls. You're no magnolia blossom."

She flushed and swallowed a mouthful of her wine.

"Heard that before, have you? Mum doesn't approve of your occupation?"

"My mother doesn't approve of anything," Avy said. "Especially not my job."

"Nice girls with art history degrees from Sweet Briar don't break and enter and tangle with dangerous reprobates?" He aimed that mocking grin at her again.

"Not that she knows about any of that, but exactly."

"Well, love. Now that we've established the fact that you're not at all a nice girl, why don't we concentrate on being naughty?"

Avy hit her wine again and tried to come up with a suitably scathing reply.

Liam looked ruefully down at his impressive erection. "You want my sword, Avy? Then come and get it."

She swallowed and averted her gaze. "That's not the sword I want," she said, upending her wine.

"Liar."

She couldn't refute it.

"You're a risk taker, Avy. You cave dive, you hang glide—you love extreme sports. Why doesn't that apply to extreme *in*door sports?"

"It just doesn't," she said.

"Ah. We've found something that our Ava Brigitté is afraid of. Does it have something to do with that being your father's territory?"

"Leave my father out of this!" She was almost surprised at the ferocity of her response.

"Hate him, do you?"

"Not at all. I adore him. Now, this topic is closed for discussion."

Avy had never really recovered from the discovery that her father's high moral standards, his respect for the laws of God and the United States, didn't seem to apply to him when it came to his zipper.

Not only had he coveted his neighbor's wife, but a coworker's wife and one of her teachers and countless others. Even after the awful day when she'd seen him outside a motel door with Mrs. Kopek, Avy had pretended, like her mother, not to know.

"You adore him. It all begins to make sense," the bastard murmured. "The extreme sports with Papa. A way to . . . repossess your father's attention? His love? Is that what you've been doing all your life? Stealing him back from the other women by being more fun?"

She gasped with shock and the horrible truth of this before her temper ignited. *"You are so over the line."*

Avy stalked to the front door, almost tripping over a flat wooden crate leaning against the foyer wall. It was about forty-eight inches by thirty-six inches by eight inches. Attached to it was a familiar carrier label. Clearly he was shipping a painting.

"Overnighting a stolen canvas to a crooked dealer?"

Liam shrugged. "You forgot your backpack. It's still in my bedroom."

He was right, damn him. Avy turned on her heel and made her way back to the big, shadowy room. She picked up the pack from the floor near his armoire and headed for the window, which was now the easiest means of exit.

"My apologies," Liam said. "You're right. I was over the line."

She stopped, her back still to him.

"Please stay for dinner."

Her stunned, appalled, hurt ego warred with temptation. His insight had her legs trembling, and she felt cold inside. *"Why?"*

"Because I'd like to cook for you."

She turned to face him. "I don't understand you at all."

He winked. "But you like me."

Avy narrowed her eyes. "I wouldn't be too sure of that if I were you."

"You're hungry. I just heard your stomach growl."

"The Savoy has excellent room service."

"Please." He beckoned her. "Stay."

Not even knowing why, she hesitated. At last she asked, "You'll behave yourself?"

"You initiated that kiss, Avy. Not I. But yes. I'll behave myself—unless you ask me not to. Deal?"

She nodded. "Will you tell me where the sword is?"

He chuckled. "Of course not. But it's fair game if you spot it. How's that?"

She twisted her hair into a knot on top of her head and pushed up her sweater sleeves. "Deal."

chapter 9

Gwen had stayed at the Ritz in Rome with her parents on two other occasions, so she barely noticed the luxury of her surroundings—the beautifully wrapped, thoughtfully placed toiletries, the way her bare feet sank two inches into the carpet, the fresh flower arrangement, or the eiderdown quilt on the bed.

She wasn't going to experience gritty reality here, but it was a great place to try to repair her shredded nerves. She paced to the window and threw open the curtains. Rome sprawled before her in a maze of buildings and monuments and avenues to get lost in.

It was a marvelous city . . . and she was petrified of it. Gwen had no sense of direction, and without people to guide her or a taxi to drop her at her destination she was afraid she'd never get there.

She couldn't take a cab or ask directions to Sid Thresher's palazzo in the middle of the night, and she certainly couldn't ride public transportation back to the Ritz with his world-famous dog on a leash.

With despair she eyed the specially constructed, zippered nylon bag she'd brought with her—the dognapping sack with areas of mesh so that the creature could breathe while she sped away with it.

What on God's green earth was she doing? Why had she left her comfortable interior design job for this madness? Oh, right—because she'd felt as though she were sleep-walking through life, that all the action was on the other side of some window that she couldn't break through.

But at the moment Gwen would much rather deal with the horrors of various workrooms and fabric manufacturers and custom furniture orders than be here. She was losing her nerve.

Avy wouldn't hesitate in this situation. She'd get a map and go. Avy could deal with gritty reality. She kept lock picks and a glass-cutting tool in her Dior bag, along with the SIG Sauer handgun.

What had made Gwen think she could do this job? What had made her want to? She should have been careful what she'd wished for.

But things could be worse: For Avy's initiation, Kelso had made her steal an entire wine collection from some guy, replacing each bottle with one of Welch's grape juice. She'd returned the collection via UPS a couple days later.

This was only one dog, and Gwen could do it. Putting him back would be the tricky part. . . .

Gwen had learned from a boyfriend how to ride a Vespa, which was a popular choice for transportation in Rome. Like flies at a picnic, the city buzzed with them.

She reviewed the orange highlighter on her map one more time and then turned the key and started up the little bike. Left out of the hotel, north to the Viale dei Parioli. Right, or south, down that to the Viale Liegi . . .

In the end Gwen missed one turn and had to pull over to study the map and right herself, but other than that she had no trouble. She parked, swung her leg over the bike, and planted both feet firmly on the street. She wiped her hands on her pants, took a deep breath, and listened to the night noises.

It was a flat, still, warm night, and this was a quiet, very upscale neighborhood, so there weren't many. But a car door slammed one street over, a sprinkler hissed gently on the corner, and some insect crooned to another in the darkness.

Avy's right. I can do this. I can rise to this bizarre occasion.

But she was so scared she was sweating out half her body weight. Gwen walked around the block and approached the back of the monster Renaissance home. She scaled the garden wall of Sid Thresher's palazzo, swung herself daintily over the edge, and made a clean, silent drop to the damp, loamy ground.

Of all the stupid things I've done in my life, this has to rank number one.

She surveyed the dark garden and waited for a moment before zigzagging, in a crouched run, from the wall to a large clump of shrubbery, and then to yet another. In this fashion she made her way to the big bay window of the kitchen and flattened herself against the hedge as a security guard walked by on his routine nightly rounds.

As soon as his burly backside ambled past, she ran to a double-glass-paned French door and attached her cutting tool to one of the small rectangles. She made quick work of the outside pane, then had to detach and go to work on the inside one. Finally she stowed the tool and put her hand inside the perfect circle she'd made, unlocking the door.

Gwen's heart barreled around in her chest as she prayed that the next step went smoothly. She'd followed the schematics that the Nerd Corps at ARTemis had provided and cut the wire to the alarm. *Did I cut the right wire?*

She must have cut the correct one, or the silent signal

would have triggered and the *polizia* would be surrounding her.

She swallowed and turned the knob. She crept into the kitchen, closed the door behind her, and flattened herself against the side of a cavernous Sub-Zero refrigeration unit. Its steady hum comforted her as she steeled her nerves for what she had to do next.

Upstairs in this grandiose place lay Sid Thresher himself, his very young and beautiful blond wife and a fat, overbred, probably *in*bred shar-pei named Pigamuffin.

Pigamuffin went everywhere Sid Thresher did: strip clubs, leather bars, wild, drunken private parties. He took up his own seat in elegant restaurants and peed in the gutter in bowling alleys.

Pigamuffin took all of this in stride. What he might not take in stride was being temporarily dognapped. Gwen said a silent prayer that she wouldn't get shot or go to jail for this little stunt of Kelso's.

She flexed her glove-clad fingers and tried to steady her nerves by cursing him. Then she cleansed her mind and meditated on successfully completing her task.

Gwen moved into the hallway, carefully avoiding the motion detectors of Sid's security system. She waited, back pressed against a grandfather clock, while a guard and his flashlight crossed the front lawn.

She sprinted, hunched over, for the wide staircase and scuttled up soundlessly. At the top were the double doors of Sid's bedroom. She stood in a broad hallway and got her bearings, listening for any sound of movement. To the left was a children's wing and to the right guest quarters.

Only silence greeted her. Gwen crept to the doors and turned one of the knobs. Moments later she was inside Sid and Danni Thresher's bedroom, peering at three lumps in the vast king-size bed.

Logistics told her that the two heads on the pillows belonged to Sid and Danni, and the shape at the foot of the bed should be Pigamuffin. But as Gwen squinted into the darkness she got a surprise.

One of the heads on the pillows was indeed Sid's. The other was Pigamuffin's. It was Danni who was curled up near Sid's knees. *Nice.* Gwen began to feel a little less bad about stealing the dog—clearly this family needed a reality check.

She reached into the fanny pack she wore and pulled out a fat, juicy tidbit of filet mignon from an open Ziploc bag. Gwen approached Pigamuffin's side of the bed and extended the morsel to his mouth. His whole wrinkled face twitched at the scent, and he opened his mouth and eyes at the same time.

Don't growl. Please don't make a sound. Nice doggy.

Sid Thresher chose that precise moment to roll over and sleep-burp.

Gwen dropped and flattened herself on the carpet, where she remained, in a cold sweat, for a good five minutes. Any other dog would have gone looking for more filet mignon, but apparently Pigamuffin was so spoiled that he waited to be hand-fed. Unbelievable.

Finally, when nobody stirred, Gwen got to her feet, pulling out another piece of steak, a big one this time. She held it out to Pigamuffin, who, of course, accepted it as his due. As soon as his jaws closed over it, Gwen hefted him off the bed and ran, soundlessly, for the exit.

True to his name, he was heavy. She could barely support him in one arm as she closed the master bedroom door with the other. Pigamuffin grunted, still chewing, as she sprinted down the stairs with him and around the corner, through the kitchen and to the door. *Freedom!*

She'd put her hand on the knob and turned it when a small voice asked, "Mommy?"

Gwen froze.

She turned and forced herself to smile. The voice belonged to a little girl who closely resembled Cindy Lou Who. Gwen hoped her smile didn't look as smarmy and fake as the Grinch's.

"You're not my mommy," said the minuscule blond.

"No, sweetheart, I'm just the doggy nanny."

The child peered at her suspiciously. "We don't have a doggy nanny."

"You absolutely do," Gwen said, patting the heavy mass of furry wrinkles under her arm. Pigamuffin sneezed. "Your mommy and daddy hired me yesterday, while you were taking a nap. Why are you awake in the middle of the night?"

"I wanted a cookie. Mommy says not to talk to strangers."

Gwen nodded. "She's right. You shouldn't."

The child digested this, but apparently couldn't restrain her curiosity. "What are you doing with Piggy?"

"He needs to go outside and . . . er, tinkle."

"Oh. Okay. Will you get me a cookie first? I can't reach."

This is surreal. But Gwen nodded, and when the child pointed to a ceramic cookie jar shaped like a guitar, she lifted the lid in her gloved hand and gave the kid a cookie.

She immediately took a huge bite.

"What do you say? What's the magic word?"

Through the mouthful of cookie came a barely discernible, "Thank you."

"You're welcome," said Gwen. "Now, I'm going to take Pigamuffin outside, okay?"

"Can I come?"

"No, sweetheart. You don't have any shoes on, and you should go back to bed now."

"Oh. Okay."

"Sweet dreams." Gwen opened the door as the little girl turned around and shuffled in the direction of the staircase. Then, tightening her hold on Pigamuffin, Gwen ran.

chapter 10

Avy and Liam ate on Royal Doulton china with Francis I silver—solid, not plated. Liam had made a creamy white béchamel sauce as she watched, stirring in a little of his wine and adding nutmeg, of all things.

He'd steamed the vegetables to perfection: crisp broccoli florets, a lovely, mellow onion, chanterelle mushrooms, tender red peppers. He cooked the pasta al dente, heaped her plate, and grated fresh Parmesan over the top.

Avy dug in, famished. The golden chardonnay he'd chosen complemented the meal perfectly, and all the flavors sang in harmony on her palate.

Liam seemed to take pleasure in her appetite and clear enjoyment of his food. In between sips of his own wine he coiled the linguini around his fork with great finesse. How was it that she always either got too many strands wrapped to make a ladylike bite, or left stragglers hanging from the tines?

He did it without benefit of a spoon, too. A perfect, elegant forkful every time.

"How do you do that?" she asked.

"Do what?"

"Those perfect pasta coils."

Liam's eyes crinkled at the corners. He set down his

fork and reached across the table, wiping a trace of sauce off her chin.

The gesture was sweet, not meant to embarrass her or make her feel like a sloppy eater. But Avy's face heated.

"Lots of practice," Liam said. "Pasta is a great friend of the bachelor."

"I'm sure you have dozens of lady friends dropping by with casseroles."

Liam picked up his wineglass by the stem and rolled it back and forth between his long, lean fingers. He shook his head. "Not so."

She lifted an eyebrow. "You take *them* the casseroles?"

"I don't have many lady friends. In fact, at the moment I haven't any at all—except for you. And may I add that I hope we don't stay friends for long." He put the glass to his lips.

"That's not exactly music to a girl's ears, Liam."

"You're deliberately misconstruing my words. What I meant was that I want to be your lover."

Avy set down her fork and touched her linen napkin to her lips. She took a fortifying swallow of wine, draining her glass, and noticed absently that they'd finished the bottle over dinner.

The word *lover* echoed oddly in her ears.

"What I'd like to do to you at the moment is thoroughly ungentlemanly. Shall I tell you all about it?" His eyes looked seductive and drowsy in the candlelight, and his lips curved wickedly.

Sword. You have to find the sword. Focus on that, Avy. He is the devil.

"I should like to unbutton that sweater of yours, for starters, and touch my mouth to the soft skin at the top of your brassiere . . . slip my tongue under the edge of it to taste your breast . . . tug the lace down with my teeth."

She stood up abruptly. "Where is the powder room, please?"

Liam lounged back lazily in his chair, looking amused. "Just down the hall to the left, love. Or you can use the one in my bedroom if you like."

She headed that way, wondering how long she could take to search before he realized what she was up to. She made an auditory show of closing the door to the bathroom, flushing the toilet, and turning on the faucets while she looked quickly into the linen closet, the shower, and under the sink. Nothing.

Well, she hadn't really thought he'd keep it in there, anyway. She opened the bathroom door noiselessly, leaving the water running in the sink, and went to his armoire. She turned the key and opened it to find an array of very fine custom-made suits on polished cedar hangers.

Beautiful cashmere sweaters, precisely folded, lined the top shelf. She found no sword under or behind them, or on the floor of the armoire. She closed the doors and opened the drawer at the bottom, which held blue jeans and workout clothes.

Avy moved on to the highboy dresser in the other corner and discovered Liam's cashmere socks, his collection of driving gloves, and—she smirked—his boxers, which were mostly silk. He wasn't the only one who could go through an underwear drawer.

But she found no sword.

She eyed his unmade bed again, those rumpled, chocolate satin sheets. She dropped to her knees next to it to check underneath and couldn't help catching his distinctive male scent trapped in the silky material. She ran her fingers over the sheets and wondered what it felt like to sleep nude in them. And with him.

Get control of yourself. Avy bent down and checked

under his bed, only to jump back with a small cry as something with yellow eyes hissed and took a swipe at her with a hairy black paw.

Liam appeared in the doorway, hands on his hips. "Are you having a seizure? Is that why you're sprawled on my rug?"

"No, no! I, um, lost an earring. I was just looking for it, and your cat surprised me," Avy lied, covering the lobe of one ear.

"Of course. That explains it." Liam nodded and walked into his bathroom, shutting off the tap at the sink. He returned. "Though, come to think of it, you had both of them on at the dinner table. Come along and we'll have dessert."

"I couldn't possibly eat anything else. The food was delicious. Thank you."

"Tell you what—you sit and have a cognac by the fire while I prepare something sweet. It will take me a few minutes. You can just make yourself at home." He smiled and reached for her hand.

He'll be occupied in the kitchen? She couldn't have ordered a better opportunity to search the rest of the house. She smiled back and let him take her hand to lead her out of the room. "All right."

He squeezed her fingers. "I see you suddenly found your earring. How fortunate."

"Yes, isn't it?" She did her best to look innocent and, judging by his expression, failed miserably. "So, what's for dessert?"

"Brandied, spiced pears," Liam said. "And, quite possibly, you."

"Do you always sexually harass women?"

"It's not harassment if you enjoy it, love." Again the wicked glint appeared in his eye.

"I don't enjoy it."

"Then why do you allow that satisfied, feline expression of yours to indicate that you do?" They'd reached the living room again.

"Liam, pour me a cognac and tend your brandied pears."

He walked to the drinks cabinet and lifted a decanter. "I'd be happy to. I know you're itching to search the rest of my house for the sword while I'm otherwise occupied." He laughed at her expression and poured her drink. "What, do you think I'm a half-wit? You've my blessing to search. And if you find it, why, then, you may keep it."

Her heart dropped. "It's not here, is it?"

"Oh, I promise you it's here." He handed her the small glass. "Now run along, love, and pretend it's all a big Easter-egg hunt."

He laughed softly as she began to prowl the premises. She hadn't liked his Easter-egg comment one bit, but now that she knew the sword was here she was determined to find it. Avy Hunt didn't give up easily . . . but neither did he.

He hummed as he began to peel a ripe pear, slicing just under the skin to leave a maximum of tender, pale flesh. He held it easily in his palm, turning it as he went. Then he cut it in half and carefully hollowed out the centers of each piece.

Avy, by the sounds of things, had gone off to search his guest bedroom and was even tapping along the walls in the hallway.

Liam sprinkled cinnamon and ground cloves over the pears and then added a bit of honey. He finally drenched them in the brandy and placed the platter into the oven.

He went to find her, wiping his hands on a dish towel.

She was in the laundry room, gingerly lifting the lid on

a hamper, and started guiltily as he came in and leaned against the jamb, grinning.

"No, no, my dear Avy. I'd never find it again if I'd buried it in the laundry. You don't imagine that I do my own, do you?"

"Of course not. So who does do it?"

"Whidby takes care of all that." He looked around. "I'm not sure I've ever set foot in here, come to think of it."

"Of course not. As a thief, you only get your hands dirty, not clean. Where's Whidby now?"

"I gave him the night off, of course, since I knew you were coming."

She opened the cabinets near the washer and dryer, but all she found was bleach and detergent.

"Truly, the sword isn't in here."

"Liam, why should I trust you on that?" She closed the cabinets and peered behind the dryer. Then she bent over the washer to check behind it, too.

Liam examined *her* behind, thoroughly. In the end he couldn't help himself. He stretched out a hand . . . molded it to that utterly delicious curve . . . squeezed.

Avy whirled on him, her hand raised to slap him, but he caught it and held on. Her mouth hung open in outrage, her eyes glittered with anger, and he'd never wanted any woman so badly. Not ever.

"Don't you dare do that again," she said.

"Ungentlemanly, wasn't it?" Liam caught her other wrist and noticed that her breathing became fast and shallow. A pulse jumped in her throat. "What if I do this, instead?"

He captured her hot, sweet mouth with his, coaxing it open, and felt her body quiver against him. He pressed her against the cool metal of the washing machine and explored her lips with his tongue, biting gently at the lower one, tugging it into his own mouth and sucking on it.

She made a low, feminine sound that spoke to the most primal part of him, and in a single smooth motion he lifted her to sit on the washer and walked between her thighs. He still loosely held her wrists, but she made no attempt to get away.

He looked deep into her lovely hazel eyes and noted a reckless quality there. She looked the way he imagined she might before running off a cliff to hang glide.

Liam kissed her again and then dropped his mouth to the top button of her tight black sweater. He unfastened it with his teeth, pleased at her sharp intake of breath.

He made quick work of another three buttons until he bared a black lace brassiere and the high, plump curves of Avy's breasts. He placed a kiss between them, and then, just as he'd told her he would, he slipped his tongue under the top edge of the bra.

She let her head fall back, and he dipped lower, encountering a taut, pebbled nipple. He sucked it into his mouth, and her tiny whimper drove him mad. She trembled against him and stirred restlessly while he savored the small, pink, perfect bud, licking around and around it and then abrading it with his tongue.

Avy's breathing came in small pants now, and her legs wrapped involuntarily around him. He let go of her wrists and unhooked the brassiere, laying her bare to his gaze, a three-dimensional erotic painting in the frame of a cashmere sweater.

Her breasts were gorgeous, swollen with banked desire that he wanted to release in the worst way. Liam bent his head and smuggled her other nipple into his mouth, robbing her of the will to say no to him. Without stopping his provocative assault on her flesh he picked her up again, copping a very deliberate feel of her behind as he backed out of the laundry with her and strode toward his bedroom. No doubt about it—the pears were going to burn.

This time she didn't seem to have any objections. If she was wearing panties, he couldn't feel them under the fine wool trousers, and the thought of her bare and ready for him was almost too much to take.

The room was dark again except for a sliver of moonlight that shimmered across the dark chocolate satin sheets. He lay on his back, pulling her on top of him so that she straddled his waist.

Her breasts hung suspended above him, and her hair tumbled exotically over her shoulders. She looked like any man's wild fantasy of seduction—he felt almost humbled that she was, at least for the time being, his.

Liam pushed both of her breasts together and took the tips greedily into his mouth while Avy writhed against him, her fingers tugging at the waistband of his pajamas. Yes, it was decidedly time to be without clothing. He moved his hands to her zipper, made quick work of it, and tugged off her slacks. She peeled his pajamas off of him as he discovered, with seeking fingers in dark places, that she wore a tiny silk thong.

He left that in place for now. The rest of her clothing he stripped off her completely. In the meantime she'd wrapped her fingers tightly around his cock, and he couldn't breathe. Before he knew what she was up to she bent her head, and her hair spread over his abdomen in a river of chestnut softness.

Liam almost had a stroke as her lips touched him, enveloped him, welcomed him. His toes bloody well curled, and every nerve in his body coiled tight. *Sweet Jesus* . . . He had to stop her before he went out of his mind and lost control of himself. He'd been in the middle of seducing *her*, and now she'd stolen the act away from him.

Though he was clearly a madman, he pushed at her shoulders until she raised her head again. She looked down with a siren's smile, and he realized she'd reversed the power between them deliberately. She wasn't naive, even in passion.

But Liam was nothing if not competitive, and he wasn't going to take this lying down—or perhaps, come to think of it, he was. He'd been about to flip her onto her back, the consequences be damned, when he thought of a better idea.

Liam hooked his arms under her thighs and vaulted her forward so that she straddled not his waist, but his mouth. She was clearly horrified by her new position and tried to wriggle off, but he held her hips in place and stabbed upward with his tongue.

She gave a cry as he dipped under the scrap of material there and explored everything she had to offer while she trembled with shock and pleasure.

He caressed her smooth cheeks and held her to him as she took a much wilder ride than she'd planned, and he loved every moment of it as much as she did. Her breath was ragged and sobbing as she achieved what he thought of wryly as liftoff—and still he didn't let her go. Instead he made her come again.

Finally he released her hips, tore off her thong, and fumbled in his nightstand for a condom. She lay on her side panting next to him as he rolled it on.

"May I?" he asked politely.

She replied with a weak laugh. "Do you want me to beg?"

Liam kissed her breasts, opened her to him and finally, blissfully, unwisely . . . slid home.

It was clear long before he reached his own climax that

God had made Avy's body and her chemistry and her mind specifically for him, and him alone.

It was the devil who'd placed him in these particular circumstances.

chapter 11

Gwen ran like hell back to her rented Vespa with Pigamuffin bouncing in her arms, making groans and snuffles of protest at the rough treatment. "Sorry, boy."

She ran past dignified old villas and stone lions and sculpted fish spitting water into burbling fountains. She ran past Fiats and Mercedes and a rusty old push mower that someone had taken apart and not yet put back together.

At last she arrived back at the Vespa, where she zipped the dog into the specially constructed vented backpack, threw a leg over the motorbike, and peeled out of there. If Sid's little girl went and woke the couple up, she had no time to spare.

The Vespa seemed a less-than-stealthy choice of getaway vehicle, but they were so common on the streets of Rome that she'd actually attract less attention on it than she would on foot.

Gwen gunned it, paying little attention to her route. She just wanted to get as far away from the scene of the crime as possible. She careened down streets and around corners, past residential and commercial areas.

Pigamuffin squirmed against her back, and she prayed that nobody was paying attention. All she needed were more eyewitnesses.

After about twenty minutes she stopped and looked at her map, and she was nowhere near any of the streets with orange highlighter on them. It took her a bit of time to discern where on the map she actually was, but once she'd done that she easily worked out a route back to the friendly orange. Looked like a right, then a left and another left . . .

Gwen did it, in the dark, and though it was silly she felt a great sense of achievement—not to mention freedom. She was exultant as she rounded the last corner and found the Ritz, even though Pigamuffin was heavy enough that the straps of the pack cut into her shoulders through the thin black T-shirt she wore.

At three eleven a.m. she strolled into the Ritz-Carlton nonchalantly, key card in hand, and went straight to the elevators, keeping her back angled away from the front reception desk. Moments later she was in her room with the dog, who'd glared at her when she let him out of the carrier. "I know, boy. This has been a long, strange trip for both of us. I'm sorry. If it helps at all, I wouldn't normally even consider doing something like this."

He didn't seem mollified.

"And it wasn't my idea."

Pigamuffin sniffed around the bathroom and then waddled out into the bedroom. He checked out each corner and whuffled around the curtains. Finally he walked over to the bed and looked up longingly.

Gwen remembered that he slept in the bed with Sid and his wife. "Poor doggy. It's been a lot of excitement. You want to go night-night?" She picked him up and set him on the comforter.

He sank into the down almost up to the belly, but bravely soldiered on until he got to the pillows at the head of the bed. Gwen frowned, but then shrugged. He could have one of them as long as she got the other. It was only for a few hours.

Pigamuffin turned and looked at her.

"It's okay, boy," she said in encouraging tones. "Go ahead."

So the Pigster lifted his leg and peed.

Gwen attempted to wash the pillow in the bathtub with shampoo, which didn't work wonderfully well. Then she called Avy, wanting to share her success, but Avy didn't pick up. She must be in the middle of something or not have cell coverage.

Gwen thought about Avy delivering hundreds of bottles of vintage wine back to the owner via UPS, and stared at Pigamuffin, wishing that she could send *him* back by UPS. But no, tomorrow night she had to break into the palazzo yet again and put him back in Sid's bed, then escape without being caught. This part of the operation seemed grossly unfair and needlessly dangerous to her.

After all, if she were recovering a painting or a stamp collection, she'd be breaking in only once, unless the first attempt was unsuccessful. Ah—that was it. Kelso wanted to make sure that she could get in and out of a target building even under heightened security.

She wondered if Kelso had some odd connection to Sid Thresher. Avy's wine collection had belonged to a friend of his. Was Sid a friend, too? If so, Gwen wondered what Kelso did to his *enemies* for fun.

He was truly strange, whoever he was. While Gwen's job interview for ARTemis had been with Avy, Avy's had been conducted by talking to a camera, answering a typed list of questions provided to her by Sheila, who'd been hired by telephone.

It was all very mysterious, and much more intriguing

than ordering custom window treatments. Gwen made a last attempt to squeeze the water out of the soiled pillow and draped it over the edge of the bathtub. Who knew what the Ritz staff would think . . . ?

She left the bathroom, only to be greeted by snores from Pigamuffin, who'd made himself comfortable right in the center of the bed.

Gwen tugged at the eiderdown until she'd moved it, dog and all, down to the foot.

She slid under the sheet and blankets and shook a finger at him. "You shouldn't be allowed to sleep in bed at all, in my opinion. But if you must, that's where you belong—not with your head or your other end on a pillow."

Pigamuffin kept snoozing, but he proved that he was a multitasking sort of animal: He passed gas, too.

In the morning they ordered room service. If the Ritz staff thought it was odd that Gwen wanted a medium-rare steak for breakfast, they didn't mention it.They also didn't ask any questions about the three copies of the newspaper she requested.

Gwen had spent a restless night being worried and occasionally regassed. She poured cream straight into the coffeepot and added eight packets of sugar, stirring well. Then she swallowed two cups of the mixture in quick succession before blearily cutting up the steak into bite-size pieces for Pigamuffin, who took it as his due.

She set the plate down on the bathroom floor next to the bidet, which made a great drinking bowl for him, and imagined the look on the chef's face if he could see his carefully prepared, colorfully garnished meal now.

Pigamuffin was still disdainful of her but followed the aroma of the meat, waddling as fast as his wrinkly legs would carry him. He appeared very satisfied with the arrangement.

While he was eating, she spread two of the newspapers on the floor in the bathroom, hoping that they made an adequate landing pad for whatever the dog had to excrete. Then she shut the door on him and climbed back into bed with her coffee, a feeling of unreality enveloping her.

Was she really planning to spend the day babysitting an oversize, four-legged wrinkle? Had she really just "borrowed" the pet of the world's most famous rock star?

Gwen drank her coffee and felt sick when she thought about returning him to Sid Thresher's home tonight. Then she gingerly opened the door to the bathroom and felt even sicker at the mess that awaited her on the newspaper.

I deserve combat pay for this, damn it.

Avy awoke bathed in marigold light from the windows and a sense of bliss that unfortunately didn't last long. She stretched lazily under Liam's satin sheets and encountered his warm, strong, naked body next to hers. "Mmmmmmm." She opened her eyes, staring up at his fifteen-foot ceiling, and then closed them again before she sprang from the bed.

"You son of a bitch!"

The Sword of Alexander glinted in the sun. It hung suspended from a rafter in the ceiling with what she hoped was *very* strong fishing line, the deadly tip about six feet above them.

Liam lifted a tousled, sleepy head from his pillow, shielding his eyes. "I beg your pardon?"

"Has that been hanging up there the whole time?" she demanded, gesturing at the sword. "Is that your idea of a sick joke?"

He squinted up at it and chewed his lower lip. "You have to confess that it's rather amusing, love."

"Amusing? Are you smoking crack?! That's beyond dangerous. What *possessed* you?"

"The sword of Damocles and all that."

"Who?"

"You know, the Greek fellow who envied Dionysus's wealth. He changed places with him for a day, only to find a sword poised over his head, ready to drop at any moment."

She did vaguely remember some classical story along those lines, but it didn't make her any happier. "That thing could have fallen on us at any point during the night, you crazy bastard."

"No, no," he said soothingly. "I had Whidby buy very strong fishing line."

"Your buddy Whidby was in on this, too?" Avy was so angry that she was almost levitating. For the first time she understood the meaning of the phrase *hopping mad.* "Did you laugh with him about how you planned to seduce me under the very sword I was looking for?"

"No," Liam said without the trace of a smile. "That was not part of any plan. I swear to you."

"Right," Avy said bitterly. "God, I am such a fool." She stalked to where her slacks lay on the floor and pulled them on. She tried to disentangle her bra from her sweater, but her hands were shaking so badly that she made a hash out of it at first.

"Do you want help?" Liam asked.

"No," she said shortly. "I want you to make me some coffee while I figure out how to get that damned thing down. Because it's mine now. You said that if I found it, I could have it."

"So I did," Liam said carefully. "Ah . . . if you'd care to take a shower, there are towels in the linen closet of the loo."

"I'll shower at my hotel, thank you." She glared at him. "I don't suppose you have a twelve-foot extension ladder and a pair of scissors?"

His doorbell rang. "Excuse me. I'll be right back."

Avy furiously buttoned up her sweater and looked for her socks and boots. During the process she stepped on her torn panties, and, disgusted with herself, she marched them into the bathroom and flushed them down his toilet.

Liam had done something with her gun, damn it. She walked out into the foyer just as he closed the door behind someone. He held a folded shipping bill in his hand, and the crate she'd seen earlier was gone.

"My nine-millimeter, please." She eyed him coldly.

"Darling Avy, I really cannot allow you to shoot the sword down. I'll fetch a ladder and we'll take it down properly."

"Fine. I'd like my SIG Sauer back anyway."

"I cannot allow you to shoot me, either." He grinned cheerfully. "Would you care for a soft-boiled egg and some toast with your coffee?"

"Liam, I'm not going to fall for the whole charm and let-me-cook-for-you thing again."

"It's not a thing, love. I'm simply being a good host. I'd do the same for anyone who broke into my house like a thief. It's only professional courtesy."

"Do you screw everyone who breaks into your house, too?" Avy looked around for her backpack.

"No." His face grew sober for a moment, and she began to feel slightly mollified. Then he added, "Only you," with a wicked grin and ruined it.

She lunged at him but he sidestepped and dodged her. She went after him again, but this time he spun her and held her close against him, her arms trapped inside his. "How dare you?" she raged.

"How dare I? You broke into my house. Did you think I'd leave the sword waiting on the kitchen table for you with a glass of milk and a sandwich? For God's sake, woman!"

"You've done nothing but manipulate me since the first time we met, and I resent that."

"You resent it because you're used to doing the manipulating, darling."

Damn him, he was right.

"You didn't need to take it so far," she threw at him. "Seduction shouldn't have been part of it."

"Seduction *wasn't* part of it, believe it or not. That just happened."

"Sure it did."

He spun her to face him. "I didn't take anything against your will, Avy Hunt, and you know it, so don't play the wronged virgin now, or behave as if your feelings were engaged. You approached sleeping with me as if you were about to jump out of a plane. You got a charge out of it, an adrenaline high, because you took a risk. And you enjoyed it every bit as much as you enjoy what you call repossessing and I call stealing."

She wrenched out of the perceptive bastard's grasp. He was right. It wasn't as if she were in love with him, so there was no harm done. They were two consenting adults.

Liam put a pot of coffee on while she calmed down. Then he disappeared into the shower without getting her either a ladder or anything with which to cut the sword down. *Fine.*

She walked into his kitchen, found the knife block, and withdrew a long meat-carving knife. Then she took it into the bedroom, carefully gauged angles and distances, and threw it in an arc.

The cutting edge bit cleanly through the fishing line and

continued, embedding in Liam's wall. The sword plunged down, slicing right through his mattress and box springs until the tip of it hit the floor.

Oh, God, the cat! Avy panicked and dropped to a crouch, peering under the bed to make sure the creature was okay. A hiss and an angry yowl greeted her, and this time kitty came out fighting.

Avy jumped back and stood up, only to laugh when the cat, all black except for one white toe, stood on its hind-quarters like Godzilla and stalked her.

Just for fun, she made claws out of her fingers and roared at it. The cat ran back under the bed.

"Poseur," Avy said. Then she took the sword by the hilt and pulled it from the bed. It was broad daylight, and she'd look pretty odd walking down a fashionable street of London wielding a sword, so she wrapped it in a blanket before grabbing her backpack, throwing open the window, and exiting the way she'd arrived.

chapter 12

Avy was still angry with herself, but at least she now had what she'd come to London for. She sat on her bed at the Savoy and called ARTemis to let them know.

"Mission accomplished," Avy said to Sheila when she picked up. "How's everything in sunny Miami?"

"Peachy," growled Sheila. "Except that Marty got a prescription for that crap that gives even an old, fat bald guy a wonder-woody. He chased me around the damned dinner table last night. Spare me!"

Thank you for that very unwelcome mental image.

"Like I want him an' his two spare tires on toppa me? It was bad enough when he was somethin' to look at. These drug companies ask the *wives* before they develop this stuff?"

Avy fell into a coughing fit. "Yeah . . . um, has Gwen or Kelso checked in lately?"

"Yup. Gwen reports a successful dognapping last night—"

"Yay, Gwennie!"

"—but says security around Sid's palazzo today is unbelievable. She'll have to wait two or three days to put the pup back, so meanwhile she's stuck in the Ritz living on room service and watching Italian soaps. Poor, poor thing." Sheila's voice was heavy with sarcasm. "And Kelso left an envelope for you."

"What's in it?"

"How should I know—it's sealed."

"C'mon, Sheila. You and I both know that you steam Kelso's stuff open. I'm still in London. What's it say?"

"A real weird one. All he wrote is, 'Beware of what is too easy.'"

"Nothing else?"

"Nope. That's it."

"When did he leave it?"

"We locked up for lunch, and when I got back it was here."

"Did you turn on surveillance?"

"Yes, Avy. He just finds it and turns it off. Or if you remember that one time, he left it on but dressed up like Casper the friendly ghost."

"I'm going to figure out who he is one of these days."

"Right," Sheila said, her skepticism clear. "You back in the office tomorrow?"

"After I drop the sword at Lloyd's, yes. See you then."

Avy hung up the phone, feeling in her gut that something wasn't quite right. *Beware of what is too easy?* What was Kelso trying to say?

She hadn't had an easy time getting the sword back. She'd been caught by Liam, then cooked for by Liam and . . . She hastily turned her thoughts away from later events, specifically the ones that made her face burn to remember them.

Okay, so she'd made a mistake. A slutty mistake. What person of her acquaintance hadn't had at least a single one-night stand? She couldn't blame it entirely on the fact that she'd been drunk.

Liam, with his wicked gray-green eyes and dark stubble

and mouth made for sin, was just plain hot. He was close to irresistible, and worse, he knew that and played upon it. Had played upon her.

Avy brought her chin up and decided that she had no regrets. He was hung like a horse, he was a maestro in bed, and every girl should experience the likes of Liam James at least once. Plus, she'd gotten the damned sword in the end.

So why did she still feel . . . strange? Why did she still see his face and hear his laughter and smell his scent? He wasn't worth the time of day, and she'd never see him again.

She unwrapped the sword, which was so sharp that it had sliced through part of the blanket while she'd carried it. She didn't care about that, though she did regret the damage to those beautiful, decadent, Hershey-toned satin sheets.

The sword was made of tempered steel, as elegant as Liam and as wicked as his eyes. The hilt of the thing was gold, as was the cross guard, and encrusted with rubies, emeralds, and sapphires. She closed her hand around the hilt and tried to imagine hours of fighting in battle wielding a sword, slicing and dicing other men, oblivious of the gore.

She put it down on the bed next to her and got up to brush her teeth and take a shower. Avy was squeezing toothpaste onto the bristles of her brush when she noticed it: Gold flecks of paint adorned her right hand. She froze and set down the toothbrush.

She walked out of the bathroom and approached the sword with a sick feeling. Liam fenced, according to the information she'd been able to dig up on him. That meant he had blades of his own. He could have had one modified. Anyone—Whidby, perhaps?—could go buy a tube of superglue and a few rhinestones, a can of gold spray paint.

She picked up the "ancient" rapier and examined it

closely. She scratched at the paint with her fingernail and, sure enough, revealed base metal.

But how . . . ? She spied a faint seam between the cross guard and the blade and slipped her fingernail into it. She shouldn't be able to do that. Avy found, to her horror, that somehow another blade had been cleverly fitted onto a very narrow existing one.

She was an idiot. She should have known just from the weight and flexibility of the blade—something ancient wouldn't be light and flexible. The blade would be heavy as hell and immobile.

Cold fury throbbed at her temples, and it wasn't only directed at Liam. Self-disgust made it almost impossible for her to breathe. How could she have been so easily fooled? The answer was simple: She'd been angry and in a hurry and she hadn't expected it.

He'd counted on that as he planned and executed the whole setup. She'd been his puppet since the first time he'd laid eyes on her.

Avy focused on breathing, on gaining control of her emotions so that she didn't destroy something in the room. No wonder he'd filched her SIG Sauer. He'd known that when she discovered his deception she'd be mad enough to shoot him.

She peeled off her clothes and got into the shower, methodically scrubbing every inch of skin that Liam had touched, and then doing it all over again. *Think, Avy. What did he do with the real sword?*

She thought about the crate that she'd almost tripped over in the hallway. The doorbell ringing, and Liam seeing it off . . . folding the shipping bill. The bastard had some brass balls.

She'd looked only at the dimensions of the crate, which indicated that it held a painting. But stolen art and antiquities were smuggled all the time using ingenious hiding methods. Solid gold bowls from India encased in cheap pottery. Paintings secreted under the upholstery of chairs. Diamonds hidden in bags of flour or rice.

Liam James had sent the sword off via DHL right under her idiotic nose, and she'd never thought twice about it. How he must have been laughing inside!

Avy emerged from the shower and savagely wrapped her hair in a towel. She supposed she should thank God that she hadn't actually delivered the fake sword to the insurance company. Her reputation would have been utterly ruined.

Kelso's mysterious note made perfect sense now. What didn't make sense was how he'd known of her error before she did—which was mortifying. Bad enough to make the mistake. Worse to have her boss point it out while she was still celebrating victory.

Avy bent over the sink and did her best to brush the stupidity out of her mouth. She tried to rinse the humiliation away. Then she stared bleakly into the mirror and considered how to recover.

All of life's a game, darling. It just depends on how you choose to play it. What's your strategy? What's your attitude? What's your reaction when you lose a point or two? You make a decision to prevail or not in the end.

Avy stood naked in front of the mirror and smoothed some sheer foundation over the razor burn he'd left on her face. She smiled grimly before applying a pretty, flirtatious shade of lip gloss to camouflage the determined set of her mouth. *Yes, you deceitful son of a bitch, I do.*

"The shipment's been made," Liam said to Kay Bunker on the phone. He reclined on the big white modern sofa in his living room, one knee hooked over the backrest.

"The Frog's not stupid enough to sign for it himself, though. He'll make sure it's a housemaid who accepts."

"I hate to agree with anything that comes out of your mouth, James, but I do this time."

Liam laughed softly.

"What's going on with Avy Hunt?"

A lot more than I'm going to tell you. "At this time I have her successfully diverted."

"Good. Keep her that way. I don't need to tell you the importance of keeping her out of this operation."

"No, you don't."

"Nothing can go wrong."

"I understand, I assure you."

"Contact the Frog, will you?"

She referred to the French dealer who was handling arrangements for the black-market sale of the sword.

"All right."

"How do you do business?"

As if he was going to discuss that with her. "We have our ways."

"Well, touch base with him somehow. I want a status report."

"As always, I live to take orders from you, Miss Bunker. Consider it done." He hung up the phone with irritation, regretting the day he'd put himself under her thumb.

He'd dialed precisely four numbers of the Frog's butler's brother's telephone number when his doorbell rang for the second time that day. He opened the door to behold Avy, cool and stunning in a black leather miniskirt, sheer black stockings, and positively lethal spike heels.

"I thought you might have been the deliveryman for my new mattress," he said. "You did extensive damage to the existing one."

"What a pity," she said, clearly not meaning it.

"Nice throw."

She nodded. "Thank you."

Liam studied her carefully but could find no clue that she knew of his deception. He could find no sign of any emotion at all. "Won't you come in?"

"I'd like my SIG Sauer back, please," she said, brushing past him to stand in front of the fire. Liam stared helplessly at her mile-long legs and tried not to remember them wrapped around him last night. They'd felt great in the dark, but visually they were stunning. The skirt hugged her intimately. Was it at all logical to be jealous of a skirt?

She shifted her weight from one foot to the other, and his mouth fell open as he caught just a glimpse of lace and garter strap.

"My weapon, Liam?" She turned.

He forced his gaze away from her legs and noticed that she'd painted her lips the color of ripe strawberries. They glistened invitingly.

Gun, you imbecile. "Right. Your gun." If she didn't know about the sword yet, then she probably wouldn't shoot him. Liam took the chance that it was still wrapped up in the blanket she'd stolen.

He'd stuffed the 9mm under a stack of dish towels in a kitchen drawer. He removed it and brought it to her.

"Thank you. Where's the clip?"

"I'll trade the clip for a kiss."

Her eyes glittered, and for a moment he feared she did know about the sword. Then her mouth curved seductively and her expression turned arch, playful. She took two fist-fuls of his shirt, tugged him to her, and whispered against his mouth, "You know you're the best I've ever had. . . ."

Music to a man's ears.

He nipped her lower lip. It tasted like strawberries, too. Most women's lipstick tasted awful, but not Avy's. "There's more where that came from, love." He settled his mouth possessively over hers, sliding his hands over her hips, enjoying the feel of the butter-soft leather of her skirt. He smoothed his hands over her arse, dwelled there for a few moments, and then made his way down to the hem of the short garment. He lifted it, slipped under it to the naked flesh beneath.

Liam groaned as he touched her there, and any doubts he still had vanished. She wouldn't let him touch her if she knew what he'd done. She'd make him a eunuch before she'd let him touch her.

He grabbed a sweet, sweet handful of bottom and kissed her even more deeply, making love to her mouth with his tongue. And then it occurred to him that this wasn't fair.

My gentlemanly scruples have to choose this inconvenient moment to show up? He consigned them to hell. But they refused to go away. It was one thing to let sex with Avy happen naturally before she'd found the sword. It was quite another to have duped her and then to take advantage of her ignorance.

With a monumental effort he tore his mouth from her mouth and his hands from her delectable arse. "Avy, there's something we should discuss."

"I don't really feel like talking right now," she purred, trailing her fingers down his shirt. "If you know what I mean."

Good God, did he know what she meant. Parts of him he didn't know existed throbbed with wanting to throw her down on the nearest available surface and have his way with her.

"No, really. There's something I must tell you."

She ripped his shirt open, and he looked down in surprise as buttons flew everywhere, bouncing on the hardwood floors. One landed in the fire, where it promptly blackened and melted.

He opened his mouth again to reason with her when she bit his left nipple and tore open his fly. "Christ Jesus!"

She pushed him toward the bedroom even as he stumbled over his falling pants. "What the . . . What's gotten into you?" He laughed weakly.

"Why, a little English, of course."

In seconds flat he found himself on his back in his bed, Avy straddling him as she had the night before. "I want to tie you up," she whispered, and licked the nipple she'd bitten. "I want to do all kinds of dirty things to you, and know that you can't stop me."

Sounded good to him, especially when he could see her breasts straining against her top. Especially when she rubbed herself along his bare cock. Liam groaned.

"Where do you keep your ties?"

"Hanging l-left side—oh, *sweet Jesus*—armoire."

Avy slid down the length of him. He heard the doors open and the metallic clink of the hanger as she helped herself to his handmade Italian ties.

She slipped one around each of his wrists and tied it firmly to a bedpost. Then she trailed her fingers down his naked body, blowing softly on his cock, until she stood at the foot of the bed.

What the hell, he let her tie his ankles, too. His conscience nagged at him, but she was doing this as much for her pleasure as for his—and what kind of man would he be if he denied this beautiful, kinky woman pleasure?

She finished tying the last knot, and he lay there expectantly, grinning in anticipation, his cock almost parallel to the bedposts. The grin faded as she eyed him dispassionately and then walked into the bathroom to wash her hands. Why would she need clean hands to get dirty with him?

She returned in moments to stand over him. "Think you'll seduce me, dupe me, and turn me into a joke—and get away with it?" That dangerous glitter was back in her eyes, and he realized that he was in deep trouble.

"I'm sorely tempted to spray-paint *you* gold and super-glue rhinestones to your *balls*."

He winced.

"Or I could lure that cat of yours out with some treat and then throw her onto your nude body."

"Cruelty doesn't become you, love."

"But I think I'll just take that DHL shipping bill, Liam, instead. You mailed the sword while I was here, didn't you?"

Liam wasn't sure it was at all wise to confirm her suspicions, given the circumstances.

"Didn't you?"

"Er, yes." He lay like a bloody starfish while she prowled his bedroom looking as if she'd cheerfully murder him. *Brilliant, Liam. Sodding brilliant.* "You have to admit it was clever."

"Are you feeling clever at the moment, *love*?" she asked wrathfully.

"Not so much."

"Where is the shipping bill?"

Hell and damnation. "You can't go where the sword is going. It's dangerous."

"Spare me. Where is it? Don't think I won't tear apart your house, because I won't hesitate."

"I'm deadly serious, Avy. These are not nice people and they have no scruples. Do you understand?"

"Where. Is. It."

He kept his mouth shut and just looked at her.

"Fine. You want to play it that way?" She left the room for a moment and then came back with her gun and a clip, which she shoved into it calmly, competently. She aimed it at a part of him that he really didn't wish blown to pieces.

Bollocks.

"Where is it, Liam? I don't have a lot of time to search your house."

"It's in my wallet. Check my trousers."

She left the room again and came back in with them. She removed the wallet and opened it. "Your driver's license photo makes you look like a serial killer."

"Thank you."

She palmed the shipping bill and threw the wallet on the dresser. He supposed he should be glad she wasn't robbing him. "France. Lovely. *Au revoir,* Liam." She headed for the door.

"Avy, darling. Aren't you forgetting something?"

Hand on one leather-encased hip, she said, "No." She checked inside her bag. "Let's see, I've got my compact, my nine-millimeter, my passport, and my self-respect back. Not a thing missing."

Liam gritted his teeth. "You *are* going to untie me?"

"Oh, no," she said sweetly, now powdering her nose. "Whidby can do that, don't you think?"

"Whidby and I don't usually share this much," Liam said, casting a meaningful glance at his personal equipment. "Could you at least provide me with a sheet?"

She pretended to consider it. Then she shook her head. "Paybacks are a bitch, Liam."

chapter 13

Outside Liam's home, Avy called ARTemis immediately. "Sheila, I need you to patch me through to the Nerd Corps," she said urgently. "I have an emergency situation."

"Yeah, yeah, everything's always an emergency. You can't ask how I'm doing? Tell me you miss me? How'd you like the outfits I packed?"

"Sheila, of course I miss you. And the outfits are great. Now, come on. I don't have time to—"

"That Miss Hunt, she's always so polite and Southern. Asks after your granny and your dog and—"

"Sheila!"

"Jeez, all right already."

In the background Avy heard her blowing. "Did you just do your nails?"

"Excuse me, ma'am, but I don't have time to discuss that." There was a click and then the line began to ring again in the department they called the Nerd Corps.

"Miguel."

"Miguel, it's Avy." Miguel looked like a Cuban choirboy, wore nothing but Polo Ralph Lauren, and was the best hacker they had. He defied the standard stereotype of unkempt rebel geek. She suspected that in his off hours he was president of the local Young Republicans club.

"Listen, I'm going to give you a DHL tracking number. I need you to work some magic, okay? I need you to, um, access the relevant files and find the truck this item is on. I need to know where the truck is and what regular stops it has over the next few hours."

Miguel whistled. "*Coño*. You don't ask for much, do you?"

"Can you do it?"

"Of course I can do it, *mi vida*. Might take a few, though."

"I need to pick up this item before it crosses the channel into France. It'll be easier for me to get it off the truck than wait until it's delivered and put under tight security."

"*Sí, sí.* Got it."

Avy frowned as Sheila's comments went through her mind. Maybe she had been abrupt lately. "How's your mother doing, Miguel?"

"She's fine," he said, clicking away at the keys of his computer.

"Your girlfriend?"

"Great."

"So, think it's serious?"

"*Qué pasa*, eh? Is this twenty questions? Southerners usually aren't so nosy."

Avy almost laughed. She couldn't win. "Sorry. Why don't you call me back when you've got something."

"Yup." He continued to tap and click away.

"Miguel? Thank you."

"*De nada.*"

Avy hung up the phone.

Ten minutes later Miguel gave her the truck number, its current location near Covent Garden, and its general route. He was worth his weight in gold.

"Miguel, I think I love you. Thanks."

"Is it serious?" he mocked. "Should I dump Maribel?"

"No, babe, but you are brilliant."

"Yeah, well. So, you turning masked bandit, holding up a DHL truck?"

"Of course not. I'm a little more subtle than that. Thanks again." And after changing clothes at her hotel, Avy was on her way.

For this particular little drama she chose a long flowered skirt, a sweater set, blue contacts, and long blond ringlets. She adjusted her makeup from siren to sweet and added ballet flats and classic pearls to complete the look.

She met her ARTemis driver at the main entrance, and he dropped her into place in Covent Garden. Half an hour later, precisely on schedule, a familiar yellow-and-red DHL truck rounded the corner onto Monmouth Street. Avy, pretending to rummage through a large handbag, walked right out in front of it.

Brakes screeching, tires squealing, driver cursing, the truck narrowly missed her. Avy played it to the hilt and went down in a puddle with a creditable shriek. She kept her eyes closed as footsteps pounded toward her.

"My God, miss! My God! Are you all right?"

Avy opened her eyes with a moan.

The driver, white-faced and shaken, extended a hand to help her up. He was a doughy, middle-aged guy with a sweet expression, blunt features, and a henpecked air. Not too bright—the perfect mark.

Avy felt a twinge of guilt as she cradled the back of her head and blinked up at him. "I-I didn't see you."

"Are you hurt?" His watery brown eyes searched her, panic-stricken.

"I'm not . . . sure." She allowed him to pull her to her feet. "If I could just sit down a moment? Would that be all right? Just there, in the passenger seat."

He almost fell over himself helping her to the truck. "Can I get you anything? Anything at all?"

Avy had planned the location well. There was a bakery and tea shop right around the corner. She looked up at him limpidly. "Perhaps . . . Oh, I do hate to ask, but—"

"Anything," he said, desperate to make amends.

"Perhaps a cup of tea? There's a shop . . ."

"I know it," he said. He cast a nervous glance over the truck. "I'm not really supposed to be out of sight of the vehicle, but under the circumstances . . ."

She looked as forlorn as possible, focusing on brushing the mud off her skirt. She sniffled for good measure.

"Be back in a jiffy," he said. A cautious man, he did take the keys.

He'd barely rounded the corner when she was out of the seat and searching in the back of the truck. The crate was easily identifiable, though heavier than she'd thought it would be. Avy dragged it to the front, heaved it up onto the passenger seat, and inched her way past it to get down.

She whistled to her own driver, who pulled the car up next to the DHL truck. "Backseat," she said succinctly. "It's not going to fit in the boot."

They muscled it into the car. Then Avy climbed into the front passenger side and ducked down so that she wouldn't be visible when they passed the bakery. "Go," she said.

They went.

Liam spent a terrifically uncomfortable five hours before he heard Whidby's key in the lock. He'd had ample time to repent his many and varied sins, but he'd used most of it cursing instead. His hands were purple, and he could have sworn that battalions of ants raced along his arms. His feet were swollen, and he was in danger of losing circulation to them. His impressive erection had long since disappeared.

It was not payback, but Avy Hunt who was the bitch. And yet he couldn't really be angry, sod it all. She had a right to be annoyed. She even had a right to a bit of revenge. He only wished that Whidby didn't have to be a part of it.

Whidby had been with him for twenty years, ever since Liam, busy casing a building, had rear-ended his car while Whidby was on the way to the unemployment office. Liam, feeling guilty, had hired him on the spot and never regretted it. As to whether Whidby had regrets . . . that was another topic entirely.

"Afternoon, Whidby!" Liam called from the bedroom.

"Good afternoon, sir." His stentorian tones echoed in the hallway. "Do you require anything, sir?"

"Yes, Whidby, as a matter of fact I do. I should like a knife and some underpants, in that order."

"Sir?" Whidby's footsteps came closer, and at last his bushy white head popped in. His eyes almost popped out, however. *"Good God!"*

Tall, stooped, dignified, Whidby had a creased face full of character and moved like an old lion. He tried to tame his abundant white mane with gel, but it resisted.

"I am overjoyed to see you, Whidby."

"Wish I could say the same, sir." The butler fell into a coughing fit and quickly covered his mouth with a handkerchief. When he raised his head his eyes were streaming.

"Allergies, Whidby?"

"Terrible, sir." Whidby went another round with the handkerchief.

"For the love of Christ, would you stop laughing at my cock and fetch a knife?"

"To be sure, sir." And Whidby made a beeline for the kitchen. Once in the hallway, he bellowed with amusement.

"I hear that!" Liam yelled.

Whidby returned, poker-faced and funereal, to slice

through not one but three of Liam's favorite Italian ties. The last one Liam didn't care so much about.

Whidby handed him a pair of undershorts. "Drink, sir?" he asked. "Several?"

Liam donned the shorts, shook his head, snatched a pair of jeans from the drawer of the armoire, and shoved his legs into them. He glanced at his watch. Avy was almost certainly in France by now, either by air or Chunnel. *Bollocks.* He had to stop her before she got to the Frog's.

Before Whidby could give him any more grief, the telephone rang on his secure private line, which indicated more trouble.

"Yes?" Liam asked tightly, gesturing Whidby out and closing the door behind him.

"She stole the thing off the goddamned truck!" Kay Bunker shouted in his ear.

"What?"

"She stole the sword off the DHL truck, and you'd better do something about it fast or this operation is history. Want to spend the next ten years in a California prison, James? In a nice orange jumpsuit and rubber flip-flops?"

"I'm not overly excited by the prospect, no."

"Then you'd better track this woman down and recover that sword." She hung up on him.

Liam sat down on his butchered bed, rested his elbows on his knees, and laughed until his stomach hurt and he was gasping for breath.

He laughed out of frustration, he laughed out of admiration, and he laughed out of relief that Avy wasn't, after all, on her way to the home of a very dangerous criminal who'd have no compunction at all about killing her if the need arose.

"Ava Brigitte, you are one hell of a woman."

Whidby tapped on the door. "Sir, I really must insist that

you have a brandy for medicinal purposes. First I find you tied up in the buff, then I overhear you snorting and chortling like some species of primate, and now you are speaking to unseen persons."

Liam accepted the brandy with a nod of thanks. "I only *wish* I'd never seen her."

Whidby eyed him speculatively, one woolly white eyebrow askew. He shot his cuffs.

"No," Liam said. "No, that's not true. Avy Hunt is one of a kind, a masterpiece of a woman. I may have to have her for my own—but I wonder if the price is too high."

Whidby's other eyebrow rose to join its mate. "Are you proposing to steal her, then, sir?"

Liam chuckled and then turned serious. "No. But I may one day be proposing."

"Heavens," said Whidby. "Then I suppose we'd better stock up on Italian ties, sir."

The problem with acting was that the bruises and the mud weren't feigned. Avy ignored the throbbing in her right hip as well as curious stares from the other guests as she walked through the lobby of the Savoy, closely following the bellman who was handling the crate.

Once safely in her room, she pulled her father's Victorinox knife from her suitcase, extracted the Phillips-head-screwdriver tool, and went to work taking the crate apart. Ten minutes and two broken fingernails later, she lifted off the top and stared at the contents. *Son of a bitch.*

The item in the crate was not a sword; it was a Seurat postimpressionist painting in a monstrously ornate gilt frame. Liam, it seemed, had lied to her yet again.

Almost dizzy with rage, Avy glared at the piece.

Her first frustrated impulse was to torch it, but she didn't wish to endanger anyone in the hotel, go to jail for arson, or, as an art lover, destroy great work.

Calming herself breath by deep breath, she thought back to Liam's expression as he told her the shipping bill was in his wallet. The concern in his eyes hadn't been feigned. If he'd simply been sending a painting to a dealer, then what had that been all about?

Avy gazed down at the painting again, her eyes losing focus among the multihued dots of Seurat's style, pointillism. The spots of color didn't make sense up close. It was when the viewer moved back a distance from them that the image on the canvas came into focus.

Avy lifted the painting in its heavy frame out of the crate and propped it against the mirror over the room's dresser. She took several steps back from it, and the blobs and stipples swam into focus as elegant nineteenth-century Parisian ladies in voluminous pastel dresses, conversing in the Bois de Boulogne on a sunny afternoon.

A walk in the park. Very funny, Liam.

She stared at it a bit longer—it truly was lovely. But it wasn't what she was looking for, not by a long shot.

Pointillism. Colored dots. Connect the dots, Avy. . . . For the first time she was beginning to doubt her ability to do her job, and her job meant everything to her. It was her identity, her love, her life.

Avy rapped every inch of the frame with her knuckles, but it seemed solid. She looked for openings or secret compartments; there were none.

Think. She dropped her muddy skirt and sweater set onto the floor and crawled into the middle of the hotel room's bed, where she sat cross-legged in her bra and panties.

All paths led back to Sir Liam James. Liam who had been tailing her. Liam who'd followed her from the U.S. to the U.K. and allowed her to break into his home—for amusement, he'd maintained.

None of it made sense. She should have been chasing after him, not vice versa. Something was going on here that she didn't like and didn't understand.

She thought about Kelso's cryptic message. Was Kelso involved in this? Was this some elaborate test of his to keep her on her toes? All too possible.

At any rate, her current conundrum was that, like it or not, she had to go back to square one again: Liam James. He'd sent her on this wild-goose chase, and he was the only one who knew where the sword was hidden.

She thought about how she'd left him trussed like a turkey to his own bed, and suddenly the image wasn't quite so funny. Because Liam wasn't going to be very happy to see her—of that she was quite sure.

chapter 14

"Why is Avy Hunt still in London?" Kay Bunker demanded. "She's got the damned sword."

Liam lowered the volume on his mobile and continued
to spread a lovely, ripe Camembert onto a piece of toast.
He topped it with paper-thin slices of green apple and took
a bite. "Mmmmmm. Heaven."

"James? Did you hear me?"

"Miss Bunker, do you ever take the time to eat lunch?"

"No. And we're not paying you to eat it, either."

"You're not paying me at all," he pointed out. "But at
any rate, your lunchless state accounts somewhat for your
edge of irascibility."

Her irritation crackled down the line. "Why isn't she
checking out of the Savoy? Why haven't you made a single move on her?"

Oh, but I have. "Because there's no need for an un-
seemly rush."

"Come again?"

Love to. With Avy, not you. "She doesn't know that she
has it," he explained patiently.

"What do you mean? She stole it off the truck!"

"She stole an item. My guess is that she's still a bit
stymied by my packing abilities, however."

"Don't sound so impressed with yourself. Just get the sword back! We need it in play. Which part of that simple concept don't you grasp?"

"All in good time. I'm waiting to see what her next move is. Fascinating woman, I must say."

"You'd better keep your pants zipped on this one, James."

"Buttoned, my dear Bunker."

"Whatever!"

Liam took another bite of his cheese-slathered toast. "You like a good Camembert, Miss Bunker?"

"What's that?"

"A marvelous French cheese. Rather like Brie. Shall I send you one?"

"No. Will you focus, already? There are more important things at stake here than women and cheese."

He sighed. Kay Bunker had no imagination and no sense of humor. He'd noted it from the instant he'd met her in that depressing, dank little room to which they'd ushered him after the Getty debacle.

Navy blue suit, poly-blend blouse, a smell of Listerine and dry-cleaning fluid—that described Kay Bunker. Dark bobbed hair, blunt, forgettable features, a complete immunity to charm.

She'd gone straight for threats, no interesting or amusing cajolery. She'd been earnest and appallingly hardworking; didn't wish to break for tea like a civilized human being. Of course, the American version of tea was revolting—cold, out of a can. . . .

Liam got rid of her as courteously as possible and swapped out the SIM card in his mobile before making a now-necessary international call.

"Monsieur Gautreau, *s'il vous plaît*."

"May I tell him who is calling?"

"His London business partner."

The Frog's harsh Gallic voice greeted his ears within moments. "Where is the merchandise? I expected it yesterday."

"We've encountered a small snag on this end. I'm afraid I can't get it to you for another day or so."

Liam heard a controlled exhale on the other end of the line, a sure sign that the Frog was smoking. "This is not welcome news, *mon ami*. Our buyer may get restless. What is the reason?"

Liam debated whether to tell the truth. In the end, he did. "The merchandise was taken off the truck by a recovery agent with the U.S. firm ARTemis, Inc. But I'll have it back by tomorrow; I guarantee you that."

A small pause ensued. "You'd best make good on your promise, or I will have to get someone else involved to take care of the matter."

"I don't want her hurt."

"Then you keep her out of my way, eh? The people we represent will have little patience for the antics of an American girl. This will be the last time she interferes, *comprendez-vous?*"

"*Oui. Au revoir.*"

Liam swapped out the SIM card again and dropped the other one into his pocket. Then he cut himself a slice of green apple and munched reflectively. Avy must find herself in a pretty pickle at the moment. She was likely furious with him, unaware that the sword was in her hotel room, right under her nose.

She'd also assume that he was furious with her for her little stunt—most men would be incapable of finding the humor in it. He crunched down on a second slice of apple and grinned. It had almost been worth the humiliation just to see the look on old Whidby's face when he'd walked in.

But how did he play the next move in this psychological and sexual chess game with Avy? He rather thought guilt, administered in just the right dose, might be the answer.

The house phone in the kitchen rang, and Whidby answered it, as was customary. "James residence, Mr. Whidby speaking." He raised his eyebrows. "James residence," he repeated. "Hello? Yes, Miss Hunt. One moment."

Whidby started to pass the phone to Liam, but Liam shook his head. Time to play hard to get. "Please inform Miss Hunt that I am not at home," he said, knowing full well that she'd hear the words.

Whidby did as instructed. "Of course, Miss Hunt. I'll give him the message." He placed the receiver back in its cradle. "Miss Hunt regrets the way you two last parted."

"I'll wager that she does," Liam said. "Now that she thinks I'm her only hope of doing her job."

Two hours later he was reading the paper when the doorbell rang. Whidby, dignified as ever, conveyed to him a box from Gucci. Liam opened it to find four very fine silk ties inside, and chuckled gleefully.

"Mark the box, 'Return to sender,' Whidby. Call a courier to deliver it to Miss Hunt at the Savoy."

"Very good, sir." The manservant wore no expression at all, but Liam thought he detected a note of disapproval in his tone.

"Problem, Whidby?"

"It occurs to me, sir, that Miss Hunt probably had very good reason to leave you trussed like a Christmas goose. Is that accurate?"

Liam hunched his shoulders. "Somewhat."

"Like all of us British, sir, I feel sure you have mastered the art of understatement."

"Rather well," Liam admitted.

"Then I also surmise that if, as you say, you may care for this lady . . ." He coughed delicately.

"I'm not at all sure of that, but go on."

"Then how far do you really wish to take the game? At what point will you stop the play, and when you do, will it be too late?"

"You're being dangerously close to avuncular, Whidby. Almost stepping over the line into parental."

"With all due respect, sir, it's only when you're veering toward making a horse's arse out of yourself that I feel tempted."

Liam drummed his fingers on the coffee table in front of him. "You've never even met Miss Hunt."

"No, sir. But I like the sound of her."

Liam sighed. "Here's the thing, Whidby. This isn't the game you think it is. The stakes are high. Very high. And if I don't play Miss Hunt, she'll play me. If that happens people will die—including, quite possibly, her."

Whidby's face took on an actual expression, one that somehow combined weariness with wariness. "I strongly suggested that you get out of this business years ago, but you wouldn't listen."

Liam nodded.

"You'll protect her." It wasn't a question but a statement—almost an order.

"Yes, I will. But she's not going to like it. And she'll probably never forgive me."

Continuing his trend toward expressionism, Whidby looked stern and not particularly sympathetic. He turned to go without waiting to be dismissed. "Well, then. You're right royally screwed, aren't you, sir?"

Liam didn't turn a hair. Instead he said gloomily, "Yes, Whidby, I am."

*   *   *

Avy reluctantly accepted the box of ties back from the Savoy's bellman. Being cute wasn't getting her anywhere with Liam, and she was running out of options.

He wasn't going to let her near him again in the usual way, so it was surveillance time. She needed to know every move of his in order to find out what he was up to. If he hadn't shipped the sword, then he still had it in his possession. Quite possibly he'd deliver it personally to his buyer.

Unless . . . no. She ruled out the possibility that he'd have Whidby do the dirty work. There was affection between the two men, and she didn't think he'd risk Whidby's neck. She might be wrong, but she'd take that gamble.

After rifling through Sheila's various options, she dressed as inconspicuously as possible, as a grungy kid of about twenty or so. There were hundreds of them all over the city of London in clothing similar to what she put on: dirty, baggy jeans, a worn T-shirt with a rip near the hem, and a patched canvas jacket.

She clipped a bunch of keys to a belt loop and shoved her feet (layered in two pairs of socks) into a pair of ugly work boots that Sheila claimed to have bought off a bum. She tucked her hair up into a slouchy hat and completed her look with no makeup and a cigarette dangling disdainfully from her lips.

Avy left her room and did a mental check to get into character. She walked to the elevator in a casual, rolling gait and grunted at the other passengers, well-heeled sorts who gazed at her with suspicious disapproval, probably afraid that she'd pick their pockets. They clearly wondered what a grungy kid was doing in the Savoy.

She gave them her best up-yours glance as she stepped out of the car and headed out the door to the bustle of the street. To remain inconspicuous she took the tube to a station near Liam's and got into position across the street. She'd instructed her car and driver to wait a couple of blocks away, on the off chance that Liam drove anywhere.

She didn't have to wait for long. He emerged freshly shaven and looking like blue-blooded sin in a tailored suit. He checked his watch, a discreet Cartier, and headed for the tube station she'd just exited, stopping along the way to buy a newspaper.

She raised her eyebrows at his choice of reading material, a rag that was known to churn out stories on aliens, UFOs, and D-list celebrities. But Liam was an unusual man, and judging by his hoots, he appeared to take great pleasure from the paper.

They rode the tube to Westminster station, where he got off and strolled straight across Westminster Bridge. Avy kept one eye on Liam at all times, but couldn't resist taking in the iconic sights of Big Ben and the Houses of Parliament. How many Turner paintings she'd studied of the subject she couldn't recall, but there'd been dozens, and she'd gotten lost in the beautiful way the artist captured the light and reflections on the water of the Thames.

Liam had a spring in his step as he waltzed past County Hall. To her relief he did not stop at the Saatchi Gallery or Dali Universe to steal art. Instead he headed along the riverbank to the London Eye, past the Golden Jubilee Bridge and Southbank Centre. The Thames glittered, undulating under the weak English sunlight and reminding her of a long, spangled silver evening scarf.

Avy wondered just what he was up to. Was he meeting someone? Checking a dead drop for stolen goods? Not for the first time she considered that he might have hidden or buried the sword somewhere off his premises and would pick it up when the scandal over the theft died down.

She was vaguely surprised that she didn't spot other surveillance on him—surely the British authorities and Interpol had to have him on their list of suspects for the theft of the sword. But who knew how they handled cases? She found it confusing enough to keep up with the tactics of American law enforcement.

Liam strolled past Waterloo Bridge, Oxo Tower, and Blackfriars Bridge, while she skulked behind him and enjoyed the sights. Once he crossed into the newly fashionable Bankside area, to her alarm he made straight for the Tate Modern. Was he casing the museum for possible new acquisitions? Would he really dare?

Silly question. Liam had balls of solid brass—of course he would dare. She began to sweat as they went inside and he took in the spectacular Turners, those paintings that for some reason had always been dear to her heart. *Leave those alone, you bastard.*

Liam appeared lost in Turner's *Vision of Medea*, standing in front of it for a good five minutes, while a museum guard eyed *her* suspiciously. *If you only knew who that man was, you'd be paying a lot more attention to him.*

Finally Liam yawned and made his way to the coffee bar on the fourth level, where he stood sipping his beverage and enjoying the magnificent view of the Thames.

Avy began to get annoyed. It was all very well to take a stroll through old London, but she wasn't here for a scenic tour. She'd love some coffee too, but it was too risky. Liam would notice her.

Apparently revived he set off again, past the replica of Shakespeare's Globe Theatre and down Southwark Bridge Road to Southwark Street. She followed him into the center of Borough, which had a charming, villagelike feel that was completely unlike any part of London she'd ever visited. When she was in town she usually headed straight for the imposing, postmodern Lloyd's building on Lime Street and took care of business.

She almost lost Liam twice to the gourmet cheeses and baked goods in the wonderful Borough Market, which captivated her instantly. She couldn't cook worth a damn, but she did appreciate fine food when it was right in front of her face. And what was the harm in buying a bit of Stilton and a lush, creamy, ripe Camembert? Her jacket would stink when she returned it to Sheila, but Avy couldn't bring herself to care. She bought a round loaf of black bread, too, to spread the cheese on, and tucked it under her arm.

Liam picnicked alone on the grounds of Southwark Cathedral, blinking like a contented reptile in the afternoon sun while she lurked behind a tree. He winked or smiled at every woman who walked past, melting them in their tracks.

She glowered. Her father did the same damn thing.

Liam finished eating what looked like a small steak-and-kidney pie, as well as some sliced bread with roasted vegetable filling. He brushed the crumbs off his trousers, disposed of his trash, and set off once again, this time heading for London Dungeon, home to thieves like him a couple of centuries ago.

Avy followed him from there to the odd, egg-shaped City Hall, where London's mayor held office, irreverently dubbed "the Testicle." She'd been there once before and stood under the spiral ramp that extended up several stories.

When Liam crossed the Tower Bridge she gamely followed, though she was beginning to get suspicious. Her feet in the work boots were killing her, but she marched after him, all the way past the Tower of London to St. Katharine Docks and—oh, God, when would he stop?—beyond.

Liam obviously had some destination in mind, but she

couldn't guess what. It was only when he headed toward the Monument and cut up Lime Street that she understood. He'd led her on a merry dance all the way to the Lloyd's of London building, knowing damned well that the sword was insured through Lloyd's. She spared only a glance at Richard Rogers's vast, stainless-steel, postmodern building. She was too pissed off to enjoy any more of London's architectural sights.

Liam bent down, ostensibly to retie his shoe, but she was pretty sure he was aiming his backside at her just to mock her. She wanted to run up and kick it. But before she could act on the impulse his hand flew up and something beaned her on the head—a small pebble.

"Damn, I'm accurate—even throwing backward." Liam stood, grinning. "What's that under your arm, love?"

She stalked up to Liam, panting. "You knew I was tailing you the entire time, didn't you?"

He took in her appearance with amusement. "In a word, yes. Did you enjoy our walking tour?"

"No. I have blisters from hell."

"The implication being that I'm Satan." He rocked back on his heels.

She shot him a look that said it all.

"Shall I tell you a little bit about Lloyd's, your contract employer?"

"No," she said through gritted teeth.

"They began in 1688 in Lloyd's Coffee House, believe it or not. They were a small group of maritime insurers."

"I'm really beginning to loathe you; do you know that?"

"I'd guessed," he said cheerfully. "At any rate, I doubt the original founders of Lloyd's ever imagined that they'd one day be insuring film stars' legs or football players' knees. Really quite odd when one thinks about it. Do you suppose that they'd insure a recovery agent's feet? You do seem to pound the pavement quite a lot."

Avy drew in her breath with a hiss.

"It could lead to calluses, corns, hammertoes, bunions. . . ."

"Liam," she said in a warning tone.

". . . even flat feet." He displayed all of his teeth.

"Look, you asshole, I haven't sent those ties back to Gucci yet, and I'm thinking seriously of strangling you with one of them."

"While I'm quite sure that doing so would be of great comfort to you, I don't think you'd ever come across your sword with me dead."

"It's not my sword," Avy said. "It's not yours, either. It belongs to a museum that wants it back. It belongs to the public."

"Does it truly belong to an American museum? Or was it looted from its native land to begin with? Besides, the public doesn't give a damn about it," scoffed Liam. "Are you aware that only a tiny percentage of the population ever steps a toe into a museum?"

Avy poked him in the chest with her index finger. "Well, that tiny percentage should be able to view and appreciate their art objects."

Liam raised an eyebrow. "The Sword of Alexander isn't an art object—it's a weapon."

"A very valuable weapon of historic significance."

"It's also a financial weapon," he said quietly.

"What exactly do you mean by that?"

"Nothing. Never mind." He reached out a hand and tweaked off her hat. "Avy, who dressed you today?"

"Lagerfeld, Hilfiger, Kors, and Karan all met me for breakfast and a fashion consultation."

"Really. Their advice obviously fell on deaf ears." He grinned.

She snatched her hat back from him and jammed it onto her head.

"The makeup artist did a marvelous job, though."

"I'm not wearing any makeup."

"I know. I'm saying that you don't have to—you're stunning without it."

She blinked at him. "How do you manage to be insulting and charming at the same time, James?"

"Why, the same way you manage to be simultaneously annoying and alluring." The corner of his mouth quirked, producing a completely devastating dimple that ought to be against the law.

"At Oxford," he reminisced, "we had a not-so-gentleman's club. The object of the game was to get a woman to box your ears but then stay for a chat afterward. We got bonus points for getting her number."

"You're despicable."

His teeth flashed white. "Yes? What's your point, love?"

"And incorrigible."

"Very true."

"And impossible."

"Quite likely." He looked at his watch. "Well, I must be on my way."

"What's the matter—are you late for an appointment to steal something? Do you have a date to give another woman the special runaround tour of London?"

"Holding a grudge, Avy, darling?"

She wiggled her toes and flexed one of her aching feet. "Yes."

"What was it you said about paybacks before you left the other night?"

She winced and remembered that she had to be nice to

him, since she wanted something. "Yeah, well. So, are we even?"

"Not even close." All trace of the dimple had vanished from his face.

"Oh." She fidgeted with her hat.

Liam shoved his hands in his pockets and gazed at her coolly. "I do hope you enjoyed your tour of Bankside."

"You can't possibly expect me to say thank-you. And after leading me around by the nose for miles, the least you could do is buy me a drink."

"What petulance. Is it my fault that you tailed me? Did I invite you to come along?"

She bit her lip.

"Besides, from what I understand you're expecting a fat commission check from the insurer when you bring back the sword. Why should I buy you anything?" His eyes held a competitive glint.

She shrugged and turned to walk away, trying not to limp, since that would spoil her exit.

"Avy. Come along. I'll take you to the Jamaica Wine House—it's only a couple of blocks away in St. Michael's Alley."

"No."

"Knickers in a twist, love?"

"I'm not dressed for a wine bar. I'm tired and thirsty and I'll go have a pint somewhere in a pub by myself."

"The Jamaica Wine House *is* a pub. An old Victorian fondly known as the Jam Pot. They serve a lot of beer."

"Then why do they call it a wine bar?"

He shrugged. "I have no idea, since it began as a coffee and rum house in the sixteen hundreds. It's one of the oldest pubs in London, though. A landmark."

"All right," Avy said. "If you'll actually be seen with me, then I'll go."

An odd, rueful expression crossed Liam's face. But he held out his hand and she put hers into it, liking the firm warmth and the link between them far too much. "Shall we?" he asked.

chapter 15

The Jamaica Wine House was located in a labyrinth of tall, imposing buildings, marked by a black lantern bearing its name in white letters. It was loud, warm, and cheery, if smoky, with tall stools and wooden tables placed close together. The timbered ceiling overhead was quintessentially British.

The air was redolent with hops, expensive Gauloise cigarettes, men's cologne, and sturdy English food.

The crowd seemed to be mostly investment bankers and business types, but that wasn't surprising, given the pub's location in the Square Mile of London's financial district.

Liam ordered them pints and managed to secure a table in a nook, where they could talk relatively privately and they had a good view of the goings-on. The conversation around them varied from arguments over football matches to workplace gossip and stock analysis.

"So, here we are," Liam said, holding up his glass in a toast.

She met it with her own and they drank. The beer, cold, liquid heaven, slid easily down her throat. She was so thirsty she could easily drink five.

"Here we are." She smiled politely. "Which is where, exactly?"

"At the Jam Pot."

"That's not what I'm asking, and you know it. How do things stand between us?"

Liam rubbed at his nose with his index finger. "Er, are you expecting me to propose, love? We had a splendid romp in the sack and all that, and we've taken a little jaunt today, but I hardly think our relationship has had time to develop." He winked.

"Don't worry," Avy said evenly. "Your very limp ring finger is safe."

Liam choked on his beer.

"I wouldn't marry you if you were the last man on the planet."

Was it her imagination, or did he actually look offended?

"I'm here for a reason, buddy. And it's not to take you home to meet Daddy. Can you imagine how that introduction would go over? 'Liam, this is my dad, the U.S. Marshal. Daddy, this is Liam, the thief. I'm sure you'll have a lot to talk about.'"

He laughed, but uncomfortably. "Yes, I do see how that might be awkward. But Avy, my darling, you wound me. Surely you'd have my children if I were the only man left standing."

"Right. We'd teach one to pick pockets, another to filch jewels, and a third to steal art."

He looked delighted. "I've always wanted three children."

Avy blinked. "Well, you'll have to have them with some other woman, one who appreciates your many peculiarities. Why do you want three?"

He rolled his pint glass back and forth in his elegant fingers. "I'm one of three."

"You have a brother and a sister?"

He nodded.

"For some reason I thought you were an only child."

"No." The tinge of sadness was back in his expression. "May as well be, though."

"Why? You don't speak with them, either?"

"Not often. They'll lose their inheritance if they make contact with me." A bitter smile played around his mouth.

"Must be quite an inheritance to buy them off like that."

He nodded.

She was curious, but liked him better for not going into detail about some massive estate or the family diamond mines. "Can I ask . . . what you did to make your father so angry?"

"You can ask," he said, and drained his pint. He signaled for another after checking her glass. She still had three-quarters of her beer left.

She just looked at him.

"It's not a pretty story," he said at last. "I did something unforgivable. He was very hurt."

"So you're not going to tell me how unjust he was to cut you off and not speak to you for the last . . . how many years?"

"Nineteen. And no." Liam rubbed the back of his skull, as if to comfort himself or stop a pain there.

Again, she was curious. But she didn't pry. People shared with one another in their own good time. And she had to admit that he had absolutely no reason to trust her with any kind of family secret.

She found it odd that they could sit here so companionably, when she wanted something from him so badly and he refused to give it.

Well, and why should he? She tried to put herself into Liam's shoes. If she had pulled off a heist of something this valuable, and had a way to sell it, she wouldn't want to turn it over to anyone either.

The only way she'd negotiate a deal was if she could trade the sword for something of equal or greater value.

And the bottom line was that she didn't have anything worth a fraction of what the historic sword was worth.

She didn't . . . but what if she could borrow an item from someone wealthy? What if she arranged a "trade" that was really a sting operation? If Liam produced the sword in exchange for whatever it was, then the authorities could pick him up—and lock him up. She'd present the sword to Lloyd's, collect her commission, and have done a good deed by getting a low-life burglar off the streets.

She glanced at Liam in his custom suit trousers and handmade shirt. Okay, high-life burglar.

"What's going on in that devious brain of yours, Ava Brigitte?" he asked.

"Nothing. I was just"—she manufactured an embarrassed expression—"thinking how handsome you look."

He cast her a thoroughly cynical glance. "Why, thank you. I'm sure you were also thinking how intelligent and charming I am, not to mention how well endowed."

"Liam!"

"Because you're about to ask me for something, and everyone knows that it helps to butter up your mark."

"I was not buttering you up."

"But you are about to ask me for something."

"No, actually, I wasn't." She took a sip of her beer and then set the glass down. "I do have an idea for you, though. You have something that I want. You obviously stole it for the money."

He shot her an inscrutable glance. "Aren't you clever."

"So if I could provide you with an object of equal or greater value, then perhaps you'd consider a trade."

"Your logic is faultless." Liam's teeth clicked against his glass as he drank.

So far, so good. He was swallowing the bait along with his beer. "You could sell the other object instead, give me the sword, and we'd both be happy."

"Blissful, in fact."

She didn't care for the affectionately dismissive expression on his face.

"So what kind of object could you offer me?" he asked. "The crown jewels, perhaps? Or a nice little Monet from the Met?"

"I'm not kidding—so there's no need to be sarcastic, Liam."

"No, you're not kidding, but you are bluffing. Because you don't steal, Avy—remember? That's the difference between you and me. And to get an object worth eleven-point-three million dollars, my darling, you'd have to either steal it or have a convenient little arrangement to borrow it— with the assurance that the authorities would round me up and give it back."

She kept her face utterly impassive.

"So this little deal of yours doesn't appeal to me at all, you see."

"You're absolutely right. I don't steal."

He snorted.

"But I do know a lot of people with stunning art collections, since I've worked with them. What if I helped you gain access to something you want? You could do the stealing yourself."

"And have the whole scene filmed for the delectation of Interpol? I think not."

"How can you be so sure I'd do that?"

"Because it's your profile, Avy. You're not capable of crossing that moral line."

"How do you know that for sure? I broke into your house, didn't I?"

"Ah, but you felt that justice was on your side. You weren't committing a burglary, but a recovery. You stressed, when I caught you, that there was an important difference between what you do for a living and what I do. Now, two days later, you want me to believe that you've changed your mind?"

Avy took off her hat and settled it over the round loaf of bread she still carried. She pulled the pins out of her hair and ran her fingers through it. "Maybe meeting you has changed my mind."

Liam said nothing, just turned his attention to his beer once again.

"These are very rich people whom I work for. The loss of a van Gogh to them isn't the same thing as the loss to a little old lady of her life savings. I do realize that. I also realize that many of these millionaires buy art not because it means something to them, but because they're hoping it will appreciate and make them even more millions. Or because they like to be able to point to it and tell people that they own an original by a legendary artist. It's disgusting."

Still Liam remained silent.

She pressed on. "That's how you've justified your thefts over the years, isn't it? You've stolen only from the ultra-rich. The oil-happy sheikhs, the moneyed aristocracy, the wealthy, nouveau riche industrialists and technocrats."

"True," he said at last.

"You've never once stolen from someone who couldn't afford the loss. I read your file very carefully. I dug beyond the facts and figures. You, Sir Liam James, have a conscience."

"No!" he exhibited mock horror. "Say it isn't so."

"You might even call it a moral line," Avy said, closing in. "Maybe, as you told me two days ago, we are very similar."

"Avy, my love, I understand exactly what you're doing, and it's not going to work. I will not make a trade of any kind for the Sword of Alexander."

"Why not? How long did it take you to actually steal it—a few seconds?"

He laughed. "There was a lot of research and planning before that, my girl."

"But you enjoy that sort of thing."

He nodded.

"So what's the big deal? You can take something else."

"And you can recover something else. I fear that we're at an impasse, Ava Brigitte. By the way, what is that lump in your jacket? Have you grown a third breast?"

"What?" Then she remembered. "No." Sheepishly she extracted the Stilton and the Camembert and set them on the table next to the bread in her hat.

His eyes lit up when he saw the Camembert. "Aha. You'd have been better off trying to bribe me with this, you know. Wish we could unwrap it, but we'd doubtless be tossed out of the pub."

"What makes you think I'd share?"

"I *am* buying your beer, wench. Speaking of stealing and sharing, there's a nice little Seurat somewhere out there that I should like returned." He raised his eyebrows. "That might go a long way toward a détente between us—and perhaps I'd even be willing to chat further about some sort of arrangement. Especially if it's delivered in person by a gorgeous woman."

chapter 16

Back in her room at the Savoy with nothing to show for the entire day's work but bread and cheese, Avy called her cousin Shari to check on things at home.

"'Lo?" Shari sounded as if she'd been asleep, not working on some killer term paper.

"Hey, Shari, it's Avy. How's it going?"

"Fine. I haven't seen any creepy guy around the building."

"Yeah, that's part of the reason I'm calling. He's gone, so you can relax."

"How do you know he's gone?"

"Friends in low places," Avy said. "Trust me, he's not around, and there's nothing to be afraid of."

"Whatever you say." Shari yawned.

"So how's Kong?"

"He bit me! I really hate that bird."

"Gringa estúpida!" said a disembodied voice in the background. Clearly it was Kong.

Avy bit her lip to keep from laughing. "I'm sorry. I take it he didn't sever an artery?"

"It's not funny, Ave. If he does it again he's going to get a flying lesson off the balcony."

"Look, Shari. I apologize that he bit you, and I really

appreciate your help. He'll probably calm down in another day or so."

"Yeah, well, I want a bonus for this."

"Ladrona!" Kong chirped.

Oh, boy. Avy said in wary tones, "What do you mean, a bonus?"

"Workman's comp. I've been injured on the job."

"You have *got* to be kidding me!"

"Nope."

Avy ground her teeth. *It's not Kong who needs the flying lesson off the balcony.* "We'll talk about it when I get home. I have to go. Don't forget to water the mint, okay?"

"Yeah. Your dad called, by the way."

"When?"

"Couple of hours ago."

"Thanks. Good luck with your paper."

"My what?"

"That term paper?"

"Oh, right. Thanks."

Avy hung up, shaking her head. Shari was a piece of work. Wearily she ran her hands through her hair, ditched her grungy boy clothes and flopped on the bed to think. She thought about returning her dad's call, but that conversation would involve way too much skillful bending of the truth in order to avoid lying outright. She'd call when she got back home.

Avy's thoughts turned back to the painting and she considered returning it. If she gave it back to Liam, would he at least give her a hint toward the whereabouts of the sword?

She doubted it. He'd never been straight with her, not once. He'd played mind games, done the bait and switch, distracted her by seducing her, and led her a merry dance.

There was one other thing that Liam seemed to want: her

body. Would the combination of the painting and another night of pleasure sway him? He was obviously still annoyed about the way she'd left him tied up, but in her experience, sex did a lot to soothe a man's ego.

She heard Gwen's voice, asking her how far she'd go in the name of a recovery, and blocked it out.

She didn't much like what a trade of sword for sex made her, but desperate times called for desperate measures.

Avy paused for a moment to consider why she wanted to retrieve this particular item so badly, and it came down to more than money, more than reputation, more than proving to Kelso that she was equal to whatever he set in front of her.

She was up against the world's most skilled master thief, a certified bad guy, and she didn't want him to win. He was stealing a piece of history and a public treasure, and she couldn't let him get away with it.

She was . . . the antithief, however ridiculous it sounded. The guy—or girl—in the white hat. The one on the side of truth, justice, and the American way. Like her father, no matter what his faults.

Avy's feelings about sex were complicated enough without muddying them further on the job. She cringed. But she'd already slept with Liam once . . . which broke the ice, so to speak. If sex now had to be her weapon against him, then so be it. The end justified the means. All she had to do was stay in control while he lost it.

She dressed provocatively, her hair twisted up but allowed to partially cascade over one shoulder from a sterling silver clip. She applied dark, mysterious eye makeup with slightly smudged liner. She added color to her cheeks, but only Vaseline on her lips for shine.

She wore a simple wrap dress in deep teal, silver sandals, and silver jewelry: tiny bows and arrows dangled from her ears, and a target hung from her throat on a modern, hammered-link chain.

Before she packed the painting back into its shipping crate, Avy ran her hands over every inch of it again, just in case. She carefully felt the backing paper and all around the frame. There was nothing unusual there, no telltale bulge. She pulled every centimeter of padding out and did the same to the crate, with equally disappointing results.

Finally she replaced the padding and carefully repacked the piece. She fitted the top of the crate back on and tightened down the screws with her Swiss army knife.

The bellman returned to help her downstairs with the crate, and if he found her appearance startlingly different, he didn't mention it. He simply handed her into the front seat of her chauffeured car and placed the long crate in the backseat as instructed.

Minutes later Avy was once again back at Liam's house, eyeing the forbidding black door and discreet brass lion's-head knocker with determination.

The door swung open before she could knock on it. An imposing older man with bushy white hair and equally bushy white eyebrows gazed down at her. "May I help you, miss?"

She swallowed. "You must be Mr. Whidby." She took in his dark suit, polished shoes, and snowy collar, his ramrod-straight posture.

She tried not to think about this very proper old gentleman having to cut Liam's naked body free of the bedposts, but she could feel the blood rushing to her cheeks, advertising her shame.

"And you must be Miss Hunt." Was that a tiny twinkle in the man's eye?

She wanted to deny it, but Avy cleared her throat. "Yes. Yes, I am."

"The package next to you looks as if it contains something significantly larger than four Gucci ties."

"Um. Would you believe that it fell off a DHL truck?"

Whidby bent to pick it up. "Oh, yes—if you'll believe that I fell off a turnip truck. And just yesterday, too."

Avy smiled. "Here, let me take one end of that—it's heavy."

"No, no, my dear. You don't need to resort to such measures. I'll ask you to come in anyhow."

"That's not what I—"

"Well, well, if it isn't the luscious Avy Hunt," Liam said, appearing from around the corner. His face was unreadable, his hands were shoved deep into his pockets, and he'd clearly had another drink or two.

On the bright side, he was wearing some pants. "Hello, Liam," she said. "I've brought you a gift."

"A gift!" He clapped his hands. "Whidby, isn't she a sweet, sweet girl?"

The older man coughed, no doubt thinking of how she'd left his boss. "Terribly sweet, sir."

Avy felt her blush intensifying.

"No resemblance at all to the evil creature who left me on my back the other day, like a dead cockroach."

"No, sir."

"Whidby was sorely tempted to leave me that way," Liam said to Avy, "but it would have meant the loss of his pension."

"Indeed," said the older man. "Shall we ask the charming Miss Hunt in for a drink, or shall we rudely force her to stand in the foyer like a salesman?"

Avy tried to evaluate the relationship between the two men, which was clearly more than that of employer to employee. "I'd love a drink, thanks." She still didn't trust Liam not to snatch the painting and throw her out.

"Then may I take your coat, miss?" Whidby extended his arms and she nodded, turning her back to him and allowing him to slide it off her shoulders.

Liam inhaled audibly as she turned again to face him, and she knew she'd scored a hit. He wasn't indifferent to her, even after having her once. His eyes roamed her body as Whidby made away with her coat. "If you have a stitch of clothing on under that dress, I'll eat Whidby's lace-ups."

She smiled.

He groaned. "What are you trying to do to me?"

"Nothing. I came to bring you a gift."

His eyes focused on her cleavage, where the little target hung. He reached out a finger to touch one of her earrings.

"Bloody cheeky to bring me back something that was mine to begin with."

"Oh, but it wasn't." Her smile grew wider.

His lips twitched. "What sort of cocktail would you like?"

"Anything but a Molotov." She moved in close and brushed his thigh with her hip as she walked into the conspicuous luxury of his living room.

Liam headed for the drinks cart. Avy liked the fact that he got the drinks himself, even though Whidby was around presumably to provide such services.

She sat on the English fainting couch and crossed her legs, well aware that the wrap dress bared them to her upper thighs. Under the muted lighting her bare calves glistened with the scented oil she'd rubbed into them.

Liam paused, noticing. Then he smoothly continued to pour Scotch from a decanter into her glass. It looked like liquid gold. He poured a Scotch for himself as well and then brought both tumblers over to where she sat. He handed her one and they clinked glasses. She drank. So did he. His mood seemed odd, different from how he'd been in the pub.

"You had a sudden change of heart," he said, gesturing at the painting.

She nodded. "I told you—I don't steal."

"You did steal it," he pointed out. "Now you're returning it to the thief. Why not recover it? Doesn't your conscience bother you?"

"A little," she admitted.

"I'm sure the owner or his insurance company would agree to pay you a fee."

She shrugged.

"What exactly are you up to, Avy, darling?" Liam continued to stand, dwarfing her as she sat on the low couch. Her eyes were at the level of his crotch.

She dropped her gaze to her tumbler and took another sip. "Where's Whidby?"

"Probably in his suite. Don't you worry about him. He's been with me for a very long time, and he knows when to make himself scarce."

Liam traced her liquor-wet mouth with an index finger and closed his eyes when she captured it between her teeth, then took it deep inside and sucked.

He opened his eyes and stared down at her golden brown head as she released his finger and lifted his sweater to plunge her tongue into his navel. He caressed the curls streaming over her shoulder from the silver clasp.

"What do you want, Avy?" he repeated.

"Isn't that obvious?" She moved her hands to his belt buckle, but he covered them with his own. Forced them down.

"No, Avy. I won't let you do this."

She stared up at him, astonished. No man of her acquaintance had *ever* refused what she was offering. No man except for him. "I *want* to do it."

"I think what you want is entirely different. You're playing me."

Careful how you handle this, Avy. She shot him a thoroughly wicked look from under her lashes. "So let me play you," she whispered. "I'm an excellent musician."

He laughed softly, and she took that as a green light. She eased down his zipper. She wanted him under her control, at her mercy.

But before she could grasp him, he caught her wrists and pulled her up hard. "That's not what I meant, and you know it. You're *playing* me."

She struggled in his grip, but he was unyielding. "Right. And all of life's a game, remember, Liam?"

He looked deep into her eyes, his own implacable. "This shouldn't be."

"Why not?" She tried to free herself again, but he refused to let her go. "Why the hell not?"

"Because for one thing," he said slowly, "there's no trust between us."

She gazed at him in disbelief and began to laugh bitterly. "You want me to *trust* you? You have got to be kidding me. You're one crazy son of a bitch."

He nodded. "Mad Liam," he said, his tone a little sad. "Mad, mad Liam."

"Well, now that we've established your unbalanced state of mind, would you please let go of me?" She wrenched against his grip again, and her silver clip sprang free, falling to the floor. Her hair tumbled over her shoulders.

His irises darkened as he looked at her. "I don't *want* to let go of you, Avy." And he bent his dark head and kissed her.

She resisted for a moment, but the heat of him, the taste of him, went straight to her head. She found herself kissing him back more and more urgently, and didn't even notice his grip on her wrists loosening. When he raised his head their fingers were intertwined.

He leaned his forehead against hers, panting. "I don't want to let go of you, but I will if that's truly what you want." He freed his fingers from hers, and her arms dropped to her sides. She stared up at him. His eyes were as gray as heavy rain this evening; she could detect no hint of wicked green.

She brought her hands up to her waist and untied the wrap dress, letting it drop to the floor. She stood in front of him in nothing but the silver sandals and firelight.

"Sweet Jesus," he said. He reached out and trailed his fingers along the slope of one breast. Then he looked at the silver target again, drew back, and shook his head.

She settled herself onto the fainting couch, crossing one leg over the other and looking at him boldly. She twisted her hair into a knot on top of her head. "If I only had a hibiscus behind my ear," she murmured.

"Manet's *Olympia*," he said instantly. The painting had scandalized all of Paris when it was exhibited in 1865, and Parisians were hard to shock.

"She was a whore."

"Exactly. Sit up, Avy."

"You don't want me to be a whore?"

He shook his head. "No, I don't."

She got up and walked across the room, took a velvet pillow off the L-shaped couch, and tossed it down beside the hearth. She lay down on the floor with her head on it, unknotted her hair, and spread it to either side of her. She took off the sandals and brought one knee up so that her bare foot rested against her other calf, creating a triangle.

"The Tintoretto," he said, his mouth curving.

She nodded. "You'd rather have his model than Manet's.

Tintoretto offers the viewer a gift, while Manet charges a fee."

Liam's teeth gleamed in the firelight. "Exactly." He dropped to one knee beside her and peeled off his sweater, then kicked off his own shoes. She looked up at his solidly muscled chest, bronze in the firelight, and the abdominals you could break rocks on. She too was getting a gift, and she couldn't wait until it was entirely unwrapped.

chapter 17

Avy had had boyfriends, the usual suspects from high school and nearby colleges. And given her taste for excitement, she'd done the dirty deed on a plane (very uncomfortable), on a train, and in automobiles. She'd even done it once in the stacks of a local law library. But none of those guys held a candle to Liam, and nothing beat having sex on a soft rug in front of a hot fire.

She felt as lush as the Tintoretto as Liam's hard body stroked in and out of her and his mouth framed her bliss. She flickered in and out of reality as he took her to another dimension of physicality, one that melded with the subconscious and felt almost spiritual. He made her feel like beauty itself as she rushed toward light and spilled over the edge into white oblivion.

And lying with him afterward, naked in front of the fire, she wished this brief interlude could last forever. She felt ashamed that she'd been willing to cheapen herself and grateful that he hadn't let her. Along with the "something wild" they shared, there was something pure and good between them, and she'd almost let her blind need to win destroy it.

Liam trailed his hand lazily over her shoulder and down

her arm. He nuzzled her neck and bit her earlobe gently. "Penny for your thoughts, love."

"Oh, c'mon, they're worth at least a pound."

He raised an eyebrow and rolled away from her, fishing in his pants pocket for his wallet. He extracted a ten-pound note and gave it to her. "All right, then. Tell me what's going through that mind of yours."

She pressed it back into his palm, smiling ruefully. "I was thinking that I wished this moment would last. But it can't." She sat up and hugged her knees to her chest, staring into the fire.

Liam surprised her by wrapping his arms and legs around her from behind. "It can't?"

She shook her head, and he gathered her hair in his hands, running his fingers through it. He held it up and blew on her neck. She shivered with pleasure.

"Why not?"

"You know why not," she said. "For one thing, we play on opposite sides of the law. For another, it's not my nature to give up, Liam, and I have a job to do. You're standing in the way. That makes you the enemy."

He kissed the back of her neck, licked at the vertebrae there, sank his teeth gently into the flesh of her shoulder. "I'm a tender enemy, though, am I not?"

She didn't enjoy calling him the enemy. She had to face facts. "I like you, Liam. I like you a little too much. But don't think that—" She gasped as he took her breasts into his hands. "Don't think I won't . . . Oh, God . . ."

He rubbed his thumbs over her nipples, and pleasure shot straight to the core of her.

"Won't what, love?"

Her head fell back and he covered her mouth with his, plunging his tongue inside and making love to hers. Any reply she'd planned on making fell to the wayside unnoticed.

He broke the kiss, rolled on a condom, and lifted her easily, though she weighed a solid hundred and thirty-five pounds. He settled her directly onto himself, sliding home until she felt fully, wonderfully impaled.

"Cold steel, here, love. Just what you're looking for." He leaned back so that he lay on the rug with her straddling him. "Something wrong?"

"This feels . . . strange. I'm unable to see your face and yet you can see me intimately. I feel exposed with my back to you."

"Afraid I'll stick a knife in it, are you?" He pulled out a little and then drove upward, making her gasp. "You don't trust me?"

"I don't know you well enough to trust you."

"Sidestepping the question."

"Don't take it personally, Liam—I don't trust any man." Avy rolled off him and turned, on her knees, to face him.

He lazily traced his fingers from her neck to her stomach. "We'll have to fix that, then, won't we?"

"How?"

"Well, I'd say you're quite right not to trust most men, my darling, but me you can trust."

She laughed, as she had earlier. "Don't be ridiculous."

Liam's eyes glinted in warning, and before she knew it she was flat on her belly with him lying heavy on top of her and between her thighs. He raised himself so that he was braced on his forearms, which he slid under hers. Then he took her hands and held them in his. Oddly, this seemed more intimate than the position of their bodies. She tried to free her fingers but he wouldn't let go.

"You trust me enough to come here with no knickers on, correct?"

"Do you see any?"

"I do not." He nipped her shoulder. "And you trust me

enough to realize that even if you teased me to the brink of torment, if you said no at the last moment, I'd respect that—right?"

She hesitated for a moment, and then nodded.

"Good." He nuzzled her neck and whispered into her ear, "Do you trust that I only have eyes for you, Avy? Nobody else?"

Her body went rigid, even as Liam slid partially inside her. She closed her eyes against an unfamiliar stinging sensation in them.

"Avy?"

She said nothing and made no sign. She didn't move.

"Ah. Not there yet, are we?"

She still couldn't say a word; couldn't laugh in his face; couldn't scoff; definitely couldn't cry. She felt paralyzed.

"We'll get there, love," he said, and pushed into her another couple of inches, spreading her thighs farther apart until she felt wide-open and vulnerable beyond her comfort zone.

But he filled the void with solid muscle and heat and gentle stroking. Liam eased into her the rest of the way and pressed her arched back flat under his chest, so that her breasts nested in the soft rug. She could feel him trembling powerfully inside her, at the root of her.

"You trust me to bring you pleasure, don't you?"

"Yes," she whispered, opening her eyes.

But she lost focus as he began to move, slowly and deliberately, while her breath caught in her throat and a hot current began to coil in her belly.

"You trust me to make you come, don't you, darling." He said it as a statement of fact.

She arched her back as much as she could under his weight and pushed against him, the coil tightening, tension growing within her.

Liam never hurried, never broke his rhythm, his hips rolling forward to kiss her buttocks. He scooped her breasts into his hands and squeezed them, toying with the sensitive tips, abrading them.

All coherent thought left her mind, and she melted into the warm honey of sensation. As she did so he kissed something deep within her, coaxing it from hiding.

"You can't see my face now, either, Avy, but you can feel my cock as I move in and out of you. You can feel my thumbs on your nipples and my hands around your breasts and my belly against your back. Can you feel me wrestling for control over myself? You trust me not to give in yet, don't you? You trust me not to be selfish."

An unfamiliar sound came from her own mouth, and she was helpless to stop it as he moved his hips with hers, faster and faster as she clutched and then clawed at the rug under them. "Oh, God, Liam. Please . . . please . . ."

"You trust me," he said again. "You do. You trust me not to stop until you—"

Color burst behind her eyelids, and she cried out as she came in a hurtling rush, feeling as if her spirit were actually leaving her body as she shook. Maybe he really was the devil and he'd just stolen her soul.

He drove into her two, three times more, and then, with a heartfelt curse, he climaxed as well, draping his body over hers and kissing the back of her head. He buried his nose in her hair and just lay there on top of her, panting as if he'd run a marathon.

She liked the human blanket. She didn't think she could move anyway—she was sure she'd be plastered to his floor all night. The French called orgasm the little death, but they had it wrong. It was a large, convulsive, happy death, and especially nice when followed by a good sleep.

They did fall asleep—spooned, because Liam was afraid

he'd crush her. They woke hours later to two rings of a telephone that presumably Whidby answered.

She started to crawl away to find her dress, but Liam caught her and pulled her back into his arms. "Sneaking off to hunt for the sword again?" he asked sleepily. "You won't find it. May as well stay here with me, love."

"How do you know I won't find it? How can you be so sure?"

"I just am."

"Is that because it's not here?"

"It's here."

"Then I'll find it."

He shook his head. "Stay and be a Renoir bather for me instead, and I'll actually show it to you."

"The real sword? Not your—"

"Not my cock." He grinned at her expression.

She narrowed her eyes. "Why would you show me the sword now, after you've been at such pains to keep it from me? And what do you want in return?"

"In return, I want you to promise that you won't repossess it."

She threw up her hands. "Then what is the point of showing it to me? Liam, you're crazy."

"I'll show it to you because you should see it. It's magnificent, and I know that you, of all people, will appreciate its beauty. And I'll show it to you because I'm willing to trust you. Can I?"

"Liam, don't do this."

"Don't do what?"

"Try to prove that we can have a relationship, because we can't. This has been lovely, but soon you'll be rolling on your rug with some other woman, and I'll be off on another recovery. . . ."

"Don't confuse me with your father, Avy. I told you, I'm a one-woman guy. And as far as I'm concerned, you're it."

She stared at him, astonished. "Liam—"

He met her gaze evenly. His hair was mussed, he had crease marks on his face, and his eyes were bleary, but he was utterly serious for once.

"How can you have decided that after knowing me for only days?"

"I've known you longer than that."

"Through binoculars and a file, sure. I don't think that counts."

"Avy, you don't understand. I decided the moment you brought me that cup of coffee on Brickell Avenue in Miami."

Miami, with its beaches and palm trees and nightlife, its South American flavor and flamboyant edge, seemed like another planet compared to this old-world, treasure-filled London home.

Was she really standing here talking about some kind of future with a criminal? She almost had to pinch herself.

Avy shook her head. "You're reading an awful lot into a cup of coffee."

"Am I? The coffee told me that not only were you smart and observant, but confident, bold. That you had a sense of humor. And that particular quality seems to be very rare in beautiful women."

She traced a pattern in the Oriental rug with her finger, not sure what to say.

"You have a natural elegance that can't be learned, you have style—well, except for this morning—and you love art as much as I do."

"You forgot the Camembert," she said. "Which, by the way, is in my coat pocket. I brought it to share with you."

"You see? You're the perfect woman."

Avy snorted. "I'm far, far from perfect, believe me."

"All we need is a little trust in order for this to work. So. I'll show you the sword, but you have to promise me that you won't turn me in or try to repossess it from me."

Avy looked at him, this unexpectedly sweet burglar with the magnificent body and the silver tongue. She couldn't quite believe how badly she wanted to compromise her values and agree to his arrangement. She was beginning to have fantasies of riding into the sunset with the guy—and that scared her spitless.

"So what do you say, Avy? Hmmm?" The green was back in his eyes, and he flashed the sin grin.

She was silent for a long moment. "I don't think I can make a promise like that, so you'd better not show the sword to me."

Avy, are you nuts?! Have him show it and lie! All of this garbage about trust is ludicrous.

His smile vanished. "At least you're honest," he said.

"I wish I could say the same of you."

"Ouch." A shadow crossed his face. Liam stood up and drew her to her feet. "I'll have you know that I'm the most honest thief you'll ever meet."

Later that night they ate the Camembert on chunks of fresh bread in Liam's huge oval whirlpool tub. They drank champagne with it until they were tipsy enough to sing. Liam had a fine baritone, but Avy couldn't carry a tune in a backpack. After a painful sample of her singing, Liam diplomatically popped bread and cheese into her mouth every time she opened it. Finally she promised not to sing.

He lathered her from head to toe and even washed and rinsed her hair. Afterward she lay between his legs, submerged in bubbles. *I could get used to this.*

She felt warm and cherished and oddly safe with Liam.

As if everything in the world would turn out all right as long as he was there with her.

But still she thought about the sword.

He wrapped her in a huge, plush terry bath sheet and hauled her off to his bedroom, where more champagne had appeared as if by magic. Whidby, it seemed, was expert at playing the ghost.

She felt a little uncomfortable at the thought that he was in the house, but he never showed himself.

"You have a new mattress," she said to Liam.

"New sheets, too." He pulled back the covers and revealed burgundy satin. "Just as I thought. Your skin looks beautiful against them."

The idea of him buying sheets with her in mind was exotic to her. "You bought them? Not Whidby?"

"Whidby hates to shop. I, on the other hand, enjoy it. Seeing as I've had plenty of experience shopping the world's museums and private collections."

"You're so brazen about it all."

He shrugged. "As I told you, I'm an honest thief." He smiled disarmingly. "What would you say if I told you I'd made some reparations?"

"That I'm not sure I believe you."

He actually looked hurt. "Suit yourself."

"Okay, fine. I'll bite. How have you made reparations?"

"In some cases I've actually returned the art. In others I've mailed a cashier's check after investing the proceeds from a sale and making a profit off of the money."

Maybe it was the champagne, but that struck her as very entertaining. "Liam, that's just . . . beyond ballsy."

"Isn't it, though?"

She lay back against his pillows and eyed him.

"You want to see it, don't you?"

"No."

"Yes, you do."

"I do, but I don't want to have to make a choice between you and the sword."

"Everyone has to make difficult choices, love."

She shook her head.

"Come on, my darling." His gaze was enigmatic.

"Liam, what is it with you? Everything has been skewed since you entered my life. I was supposed to be chasing you, but you came after me. You're the one who breaks and enters, but I had to play burglar. And now you want to show me what you stole—but I don't want to see it! Maybe we've drunk a little too much this evening, but I have to admit that I'm confused."

He brought her a black cashmere robe, his, and took her by the hand after she'd put it on. He led her to the Seurat, which still leaned against the wall in his vast living room.

"Oh, no," she said. "If you're going to tell me—"

He laid the crate flat on the floor and removed the screws that held it together. He lifted out the Seurat.

"It *is* in the frame," she said suddenly. "It was in the frame the whole goddamned time. How? I checked it!" Anger and frustration warred with resignation in the pit of her stomach.

Liam's gaze flickered to hers and then back to the painting in its heavy, ornate gold frame. He felt along the elaborately carved motifs of the surface until he reached a serpentine shape in the upper left corner. Each corner had one. She assumed that they didn't all turn counterclockwise, though—only this one did.

And the outer veneer of the frame slid right off to expose a slot two inches deep, six inches wide, and forty or so inches long.

Inside was an object wrapped in a simple white cotton cloth, and Liam lifted it out.

She wanted to see it, and yet she didn't. Seeing it would be final proof of what she'd known all along: that Liam was the thief that the authorities were searching for even as they sat here. A single glance at that sword would be final proof that she'd had the bad judgment to sleep with a felon and enjoy it far too much.

It was one thing to know it in the back of her mind, and quite another to be slapped in the face with it. So she stalled.

"But I handled the painting, Liam. It wasn't top-heavy at all. How did you balance the weight?" As soon as the words were out of her mouth she guessed the answer.

Intuitively she turned the serpentine shape in the opposite corner, and the veneer on the bottom of the frame slid open. Inside was another long, thin object, also wrapped.

"Rebar," Liam said in explanation.

Rebar. Why not? It had worked perfectly.

Avy was torn between admiration for the ingeniousness of the hiding place and utter mortification that she hadn't found it. She'd slept in the same room with the damned sword and never realized it. She'd brought it *back* to him, for God's sake! She didn't like feeling stupid.

Then Liam unwrapped the Sword of Alexander, and she forgot all about how she felt.

chapter 18

The sword was forged in highly polished, unyielding steel, and though Avy had seen photographs, none of them did justice to the sheer beauty of it—nor to the aura of blood-thirsty power that surrounded the thing.

The hilt had been fashioned in gold—the kind that did not rub off on the hands—and the inlaid gemstones spoke to the wealth of its former owner. The thing was both lovely and evil, combining greed with violence.

She could almost feel the presence of Alexander himself, surrounded by the bloody ghosts he'd slain on various ancient battlefields.

Avy shivered as she looked at it, imagining the weapon being made by an expert blacksmith for no other purpose than to kill.

She wished more than ever now that Liam hadn't unwrapped the sword. She no longer felt safe, especially given the way Liam was looking at her. "You promised, Avy."

"Actually, I didn't."

"It was implied."

She wrapped her arms tightly around herself and stepped away from it, walking back over to the fire. "You duped me yet again, Liam. What was this little show-and-tell all about, really? Trying to prove to me how clever you are?"

"No. I explained this to you already. It's about trust."

She turned to face him, and though her back was warmed by the fire, she felt cold. "Is it? I can't be sure. Because the other possibility is that it's about embroiling me in your dirty scheme."

Liam rewrapped the sword and got to his feet. He crossed the room and settled his hands over her shoulders. "Do you really think that?"

"I don't know what to think. Liam, if I don't say something to the authorities, I'm an accessory to your crime. And if I don't even try to take it back to the owner, then I'm not doing my job."

He nodded.

"You're asking an awful lot of me. You're asking for my integrity on a platter—and I resent the hell out of that."

He said nothing, just looked into her eyes.

Avy stared back at him furiously for a moment and then pushed his hands off her shoulders. "You're not going to steal my character, Liam. I won't let you—do you hear?"

"Loud and clear," he said.

She picked up her dress, her sandals, and her bag, then walked back into his bedroom with her things to dress—and to buy a little time so that she could decide what to do.

Did she want to see Liam go to jail? The honest answer was no, even though he deserved to be there. She couldn't imagine him living out his life behind bars.

Avy unbelted his cashmere robe and hung it on the back of the door. She slid her arms into the sleeves of her dress, wrapped it around her body, buttoned it, and tied the sash. She slipped on her sandals and fastened the straps. Then she stood and took a good long look at herself in the mirror. She had to face this person every single morning of her life, and right now the woman staring back at her didn't look friendly.

She'd slept with her mark, and worse, she was afraid she was *his* mark. She'd also been on the verge of developing some very silly feelings for him.

She almost snorted at the fact that she'd felt safe in his arms. Safe? First of all, safety and security were anathema to a woman like her. She couldn't afford to feel safe—it was comfortable and it dulled the reflexes. It took the edge off, and in her business she needed the edge. She needed to be razor-sharp and ready for anything—impersonation, manipulation, subterfuge, burglary.

Avy had seen the damage done to women in the name of security. Women like her mother, who turned a blind eye to her husband's serial cheating because the payoff was the "comfort" of staying married. Yet her parents existed in separate houses, for God's sake. Her mother stayed in the main house and her father mostly used the summer cottage, making infrequent stops "home" when he needed something.

Apparently this arrangement worked for them, since her father conveniently couldn't get involved with any of his girlfriends and her mother didn't suffer financially—but what was the emotional cost? And how had their relationship gotten this way? Once, surely, they'd been in love. Now her mother's first love was her church.

Avy tried to imagine living a life with Liam, and couldn't. She quickly brushed her hair and coiled it into a knot on the top of her head, bringing her appearance back to business. She applied a dark red lipstick, one suitable for giving Sir Liam James the big kiss-off.

And then she added a final accessory to her outfit: her gun.

Liam, sprawled on the sofa in his silk pajama bottoms, had almost dozed off when he heard the *click, click, click* of her silver sandals on the hardwood floor and then the whisper of her silk dress as Avy approached.

He opened his eyes with a smile, only to blink as he focused on the cold black barrel of Avy's SIG Sauer.

"Hell and damnation," he said. "I knew I shouldn't have returned that to you."

"We all make mistakes," she said with a small smile. "I shouldn't have gone to bed with you. Now, where is the sword?" She scanned the room quickly, but the Seurat and the contents of its frame were gone.

Her eyes were cool, her voice was calm, and her hands were steady. "I've reached a decision, Liam."

"Excellent," he congratulated her, keeping a wary eye on the 9mm. "I do hope that it doesn't involve two taps to my high brow."

"It's a compromise. I won't report you to the police as long as you hand over the sword to me right now. I think that's fair."

"Oh, quite fair." He nodded. "Unfortunately, I cannot accommodate you."

"Liam," she said wearily, "I don't want to shoot you, so just get it, please."

He spread his hands. "But I don't have it."

"You do."

He shook his head. "No, I'm afraid not. Whidby does."

"Then would you please ask him to bring it to me, and stop playing games?"

"Avy, darling, he's gone." A vein near her temple began to throb, and he knew her temper was rising. He sympathized; really he did.

"Gone where?" she said in a low, dangerous voice.

Liam remarked on the irony: She was at her loveliest, truly, when she wished to end his life.

"Don't be angry, my dear, but I had to take countermeasures

while you were getting dressed. Whidby is none too happy himself, as his arthritis is kicking up, but he's playing courier. You interrupted my scheduled delivery via DHL, so at this late hour the sword had to be sent in person."

Judging from her expression, Avy wanted to drag him off to the Tower of London and go medieval on him with every torture device available. Was he wrong to find that so sexy?

"I know, I know. In your shoes I'd be quite furious." He looked at them. "Actually, in your shoes I'd be a stumbling transvestite, but—"

"Call him."

"Whidby refuses to carry a mobile phone. He believes they provide the government with a way to track one, and that they cause brain tumors."

"I don't mean via cell phone; I mean here, using the lungs the devil gave you."

"But he's not—"

Avy cocked the trigger.

Fine. *"Whidby!"* Liam shouted. "I say, Whidby, if you don't wish to scrape my entrails off the couch and into the dustbin, do show yourself, man!"

Aside from the occasional pop of the fire, the house reverberated with silence.

Avy let out a string of curses that no nice Southern girl would ever be caught dead repeating.

Liam winced. "No, my love, I assure you, I've never in my life sucked a co—"

"Shut up," she said, enraged. She pushed the barrel of the gun against his mouth. "Or you can suck on this."

He had no choice but to remain silent, puckered against the thing, muzzle to muzzle, as it were. He did send her a speaking glance, however.

Avy stood there, trying to control her breathing, which was uneven. The vein in her temple throbbed, and a pulse at the side of her neck went haywire, too. A few droplets of perspiration had gathered at her hairline, and her teeth were tightly clenched.

Hell hath no fury like a woman outwitted . . . yet again. I shouldn't be so entertained, but I can't help myself. Liam said against the gun, "You don't want to shoot me, love."

"Don't tell me what I want or don't want, Liam."

"It's very messy," he argued. "Ever seen a man's brains blown out? I have. Not a pretty sight, I assure you. And with all the forensic techniques available today, you'd have to spend a good deal of time talking with the police. There'd be a great, nasty trial, and you'd have the media looking up your skirt instead of me. . . ."

"You just don't know when to shut up, do you?"

Liam shook his head and gazed up at her soulfully. "May I say that you look absolutely stunning when you're contemplating murder, love?" He pursed his lips and kissed the muzzle of the gun.

She blinked rapidly, and pink stained her cheeks. Then, to his surprise and, it seemed, to her own, she began unwillingly to laugh. Unfortunately she did not remove the gun from his mouth, so he didn't feel safe enough to join her.

"Liam," she gasped at last, "you are such an *asshole*."

"And here I thought you'd never discover my finer qualities," he murmured. Emboldened, he drew back a little from the gun and touched his tongue to it. He circled the tiny hole as she watched, he nuzzled it, and finally he closed his teeth over the barrel and bit down.

"You're also utterly insane." Avy latched the safety on the SIG Sauer and pulled it away from his mouth. "That was beyond stupid."

"Got your attention, though, didn't it, love?" Liam was pleased to see that he hadn't wet himself during the whole episode, but he'd keep that to himself. "Where are you going, Avy, darling? Must you leave so soon?"

"Yes. Liam, I'm sorry, but you've left me no choice: I'm going to your local police precinct station."

Bollocks. He groaned and rubbed a hand over his face. "Please don't do that to me." Kay Bunker would chew him up and spit him out—and he wouldn't be able to fault her.

Avy looked back at him, her hand on the doorknob. "Liam, I'm not doing anything to you. You've done it to yourself. And you've tricked me for the last time."

Gwen was bored out of her mind and had been for the last couple of days. This part of the job was *not* her idea of an adventure. The walls of the hotel room were closing in on her, and a side trip to a museum and a boutique had just made her paranoid that someone would discover the dog— even though she'd left the DO NOT DISTURB sign on the door.

She'd booted up her laptop and started surfing the Net when she stopped cold at the sight of a familiar face.

"The silver's 'ere," Sid Thresher said in a news clip. "A sh—" *bleep!*—"load o' cash is 'ere. Me wife's jewels are 'ere. But me blasted *dog* is gone!"

Sid ranted to a reporter on a video clip. "Did y'ever 'ear of such a thing? It's madness, I say. Madness!"

"It is very odd, Sid. You say this happened in the middle of the night?"

"Yah, about two thirty a.m.! Some"—*bleep!*—"piece o' tail come waltzing in as cool as you please, right into me"—*bleep!*—"bedroom. She coulda murdered us in our very beds!"

"You say the intruder was a female?"

Nodding, Sid continued, "She coulda cut me"—*bleep!*— "—ing"—*bleep!*—"off, she could."

"Er. Well, thank God for all your future wives and children that she didn't, Sid." The reporter winked. "Just kidding around, there, man."

The rock star's eyes bulged. "Oh, you think this is funny, do you?"

"No, no, Sid. It's not funny, not funny at all. We here at ABC extend our heartfelt sympathies to you and your family. . . ."

The reporter shot a startled glance at the camera when the lead guitarist for Subversion began to cry. "It's me meds," he sobbed. "I'm 'eavily medicated, severely depressed. I want me dog back, you see. 'E goes everywhere with me. Please, whoever has 'im, please don't hurt 'im! 'E's me baby."

Gwen closed her eyes in horror. Sid was a basket case, and it was all her fault. She'd had no idea he would react this way. She checked a different network's Web site.

Hand over her mouth, she watched another video clip. In this one it appeared that Sid had been drinking on top of his meds. "You listen to me, you f—"—*bleep!*—"—ing cu—"—*bleep!*—"You 'arm an 'air of me dog's 'ead and I will personally dismember you."—*bleep! Oh, God.*

She checked the last major news network, and this video clip showed Sid bug-eyed and melancholy.

"The intruder gave your daughter a *cookie*?" the reporter asked incredulously.

Sid nodded, his expression outraged. "Poor mite had woken up and gone for some water. She ran smack into the dognapping tramp! I'm lucky the"—*bleep!*—"didn't take her, too."

Gwen didn't even want to know what CNN had to say—she was sure it would be even worse. Her head began to throb as she shut down her laptop and looked at Pigamuffin in despair. "He's calling me a dognapping tramp. And that damned Kelso, *whoever* the hell he is, is laughing his ass off!"

Pigamuffin was lurking underneath the room's settee, since she'd kicked him off the bed. He lolled his tongue out at her and didn't appear to have much sympathy—not that she could blame him.

"I promise I'm taking you back. In a day or two you will be returned to your palace and all your devoted staff. It'll be filet mignon for breakfast and pork chops for lunch. Maybe they'll even cook you beef carpaccio for a celebration supper."

The dog let his tongue loll from his mouth and looked for all the world as if he were deliberately sticking it out at her.

"You know," she said, "if we had a smidge more time together, I bet I could change your attitude and give you a great case of Stockholm syndrome. I'm actually a very nice person. Dogs love me—under more normal circumstances. And I promise you this was not my idea. I was brought up decently. I don't do things like this."

But Pigamuffin maintained his standoffish attitude. He looked at Gwen with disdain and turned to lie down with his wrinkly bottom and ridiculous tail facing her.

She sighed. Like it or not, she was still the bad guy. The Pigster hated her, and his dear old dad wanted to dismember her . . . and now she had to figure out how to get *back* into Sid's palazzo with all the heightened security and media attention. At least her day couldn't get any worse.

chapter 19

The Marylebone police station on Seymour Street was housed in a brick and stone building, and looked the epitome of a house of justice.

Avy sat in a chair with a beige plastic seat and steel legs opposite one Detective Wurlough, a little gray man with a weary expression and an equally weary cheap suit. He had suspicious, beady eyes, and his teeth looked oddly mismatched. She dodged a blast of putrid coffee breath every time he spoke.

"And what basis do you have for filing this report, Miss Hunt?"

"I saw the sword when I visited Sir Liam's home."

"And your relationship with him is . . . ?"

She could feel her face warming. "He's an acquaintance."

"And the purpose of your visit was . . . ?"

Blatant seduction. "To consult with Sir Liam on a case that I'm working on."

"And your profession is . . . ?"

"I'm a recovery agent. Are you familiar with the American term 'repo man'?"

He nodded.

"Well, that's what I do—only not with cars, with stolen property."

Detective Wurlough stopped writing and looked up. "You say that you were consulting with Sir Liam in regard to a case?"

"Yes."

"Was it this case?"

Reluctantly she nodded.

"Why would he have any interest in talking with you if he were, in fact, responsible for this theft?"

"You'd have to ask Sir Liam that."

Wurlough folded his arms and leaned back in his own plastic chair. "We've interviewed the man already. He has an airtight alibi for the date and time in question."

"Then it's manufactured, I can assure you, because I saw with my own eyes the missing Sword of Alexander in his living room."

"Miss Hunt," Wurlough said. "I must say that I find your story somewhat suspect. You say you were invited to the man's home . . ."

Er, not exactly.

". . . and he showed you the stolen sword himself, on a whim."

"Yes."

"Why would he do that?"

"I don't know. Again, you'd have to ask him."

Wurlough smiled, and it wasn't a particularly nice smile. "Perhaps you two were working together, and you've had a falling-out. Perhaps the reason he has an airtight alibi, Miss Hunt, is that you are the one who stole the sword."

"What? That's ridiculous!"

"So you say. Where were you on the date the sword was taken from the transport vehicle?"

"I was in the United States, Detective. In Miami, Florida."

"And what was your business there?"

Dressing like a cheap slut and setting up Dave Pomeroy for a takedown. "I live there. And I happened to be working on another recovery job in town."

"And do you have documentation to prove that?"

"Not with me, no. But I can provide it to you within a couple of days."

Wurlough ran his tongue over his crooked teeth, as if he were searching for a renegade poppy seed or corn kernel.

"Miss Hunt, I would like to talk with you further. It seems to me that you are a person of extraordinary interest in this case."

"I'm a person of interest? You've got to be kidding me! I came here to do the right thing and let you know the identity of the thief."

"How noble of you, Miss Hunt. Then you won't mind if we detain you here for a few hours and cross-check your story."

I do mind, very much. I need to get on the next train or ferry to France before this damned sword vanishes for good into someone's top-secret private collection! But Avy threw up her hands. "Fine. If that's what you feel you need to do, Detective."

It was close to seven in the evening when Wurlough finally saw fit to let her go. Avy walked out the door of the precinct station, intent on finding a cab. *No good deed goes unpunished, does it?*

She'd barely registered that there was a limousine across the street from her when the door opened and Liam's voice called cheerfully, "Can I give you a lift, love?" He unfolded his long, lean body and stood up, resting his arms on the top of the open passenger door.

Avy stared at him, bewildered. "Why would you want to give me a ride when I just reported you to the police?"

"Why, admiration for your ethics, of course." He gestured into the limo. "Shall we?"

She backed away. "No. I don't trust you. What are you going to do, knock me unconscious as soon as I get in there? Dispose of the witness against you?"

"Avy, Avy, Avy," he said sorrowfully. "We must do something to address your cynicism. I'd much rather kiss you than kill you."

"Well, you're not going to do either one." She began to walk away as fast as she could. Then she stopped and turned; she couldn't help herself. "Liam, for God's sake, you're standing opposite the doors of the police station! You're a wanted man. Would you come to your senses and get away from here?"

He put a hand over his heart. "She cares. The lady cares for me."

"I do not care for you," she said. "You idiot."

"She cares," he said to a businessman crossing the street. The man nodded politely and went on his way.

Avy rolled her eyes and checked her watch. She might be able to catch the last Chunnel train for the evening if she could only find a cab. She hurried along the sidewalk, keeping an eye out.

Liam's limousine soon caught up with her. He lowered the window and leaned out. "You care."

"Liam, leave me alone."

"Where are you off to in such a rush, love?"

"That would be *so* none of your business."

Horns began to honk behind him, since the limo was creeping along to keep pace with her, blocking traffic. He turned his head and waved at the other cars. "Avy, you're causing a nuisance, my darling. If you got in Hartswell could speed up and all these people could get home more quickly."

She sent him a scathing glance. "I'm not causing the problem, Liam; you are!"

"A matter of opinion."

Exasperated, she dodged into a gourmet-foods market, heading for the bakery area. A moment later she heard the bells on the door chime again. She ducked down behind a stand of baguettes and crept toward the meats and cheeses. Liam's wing tips and trousers walked by, his step light and confident.

Busy checking behind her, Avy crab-walked right into a baffled woman's path, bashing her shoulder on her shopping basket. "Sorry!" she whispered. She gestured in Liam's general direction. "Ex-boyfriend. Trying to avoid him."

The woman nodded her understanding, and Avy skittered toward the jellies, jams, and chutneys, finally coming full circle to the door. Bent double, she pushed it open and ran. With any luck Liam would take another five minutes in there trying to find her.

But luck seemed to have deserted her entirely ever since she'd met Liam. The next time she checked over her shoulder he was behind her once again. *For God's sake!*

Avy rounded a corner and dodged into a wine shop this time, where she tried to lose herself among the Italian imports. She was studiously examining several different Chiantis when Liam walked in, damn him. She crept around a blockade of Australian imports and then hid on the far side of a glass-doored refrigerator full of champagnes.

"May I help you, madam?" A clerk eyed her curiously.

"No. No, thank you." Avy darted for the door just as

Liam spied her from behind a display of ports and sherries. He grinned like a shark and strode after her.

The look on his face was pure sex, and unfortunately it released a hundred drunken butterflies into her stomach. She began to wonder if it wouldn't be somewhat exciting to be caught. *No! Avy, you have got to get to the damned train station.*

"I do love a lady who jogs in high heels," Liam called after her. "Luscious arse, by the way."

She would give any amount of money not to be so attracted to the obnoxious man.

"Very provocative hips, too."

Ignore him. He's just trying to get a rise out of you. Just ignore him.

"And hot legs."

Pretend he's not there.

" 'She's got legs,' " he began to sing. " 'And she knows how to use them. . . .' "

Avy choked. A snooty Englishman singing ZZ Top—it just didn't work well at all. And people on the street were turning around to stare.

"Legs, legs, legs!" he belted out.

She hunched her shoulders and kept on walking, groaning when she had to stop for a traffic signal. Liam caught up with her, of course.

"If I didn't know better I'd think that you were attempting to ignore me, pretend I didn't exist," he said conversationally.

"Liam." She swung around to face him. "What are the laws on stalking in the U.K.?"

"A harsh term to describe the loyal shadowing of the spurned and lovelorn, my darling."

"You are not lovelorn and I am not your darling," she said evenly. "You *are* a royal pain in the ass, however."

He slipped an arm around her. "I should like very much to be your very own personal royal pain in the arse," Liam crooned into her ear.

"No, see, you're not getting the message. I want you to *go away*."

He laid a finger across her lips and backed her up against the pole that supported the traffic signal. "That's only because you're feeling guilty about turning me in to the police."

"I do not feel guilty!" she said, pushing his finger away. But he simply replaced it with his tender, clever mouth, and she found herself responding unwillingly to his kiss. If only the bastard didn't smell so wonderful. If only his touch weren't so provocative.

"I forgive you," he said magnanimously.

Her eyes flew open and met his amused ones. "I didn't ask for your forgiveness, and I don't want it!"

He kissed her again. "I know, love. But then, I plan to give you a lot of things that you don't ask for." He whispered into her ear what he'd like to give her next, and a flash of heat streaked through her.

"Stop it."

"I could give it to you right inside that limo," he suggested, gesturing toward it. Naturally the car had followed them. "When the privacy screen is up, Hartswell can't see or hear a thing. What do you say, love?"

Avy glanced at her watch again. Half an hour until the last train. "If your driver can drop me somewhere within twenty minutes, then maybe I'll get into the car with you."

Clearly she was crazy, but what else was new?

chapter 20

"Drop you somewhere?" Liam inquired. "That's rather vague, don't you think?"

"Yes, purposefully so. You're going to have—What is his name? Hartswell?—put up the privacy screen before I get in. And I'm going to tell him where we're going while you sit alone in the back."

"Avy, love, forgive me for pointing this out, but that's quite silly. I'll be able to see where we're going."

"That's where you're wrong." Avy removed the fabric sash from around her waist and slapped it into his hand. "You'll have this tied around your head, covering your eyes, or I won't be joining you."

He raised an eyebrow. "We need to discuss your proclivities for bondage, my sweet."

She shot him a saucy grin. "Why, are you disappointed?"

"Not at all."

"Great. Then put that on."

"I'll simply raise it as soon as you get out of the car, so it won't do any good."

"Wrong again. Since you keep telling me what an honest thief you are, you're going to make me a promise."

"I am?" Liam asked dubiously.

"You are. You're going to promise that"—Avy checked

her watch again—"you and Hartswell will leave immediately after I get out of the car and that you'll wait ten full minutes before you take off the blindfold."

"So you'll have a ten-minute head start on me. . . ." He rubbed his chin.

Actually, I'll have a full night's head start on you, but you don't need to know that. "You don't need to follow me. In fact, I'd appreciate it if you didn't."

He flashed her the sin grin, and it did unwelcome things to her insides, making them all warm and gooey. *Damn it.* But he said nothing.

"Take me or leave me, Liam."

"Oh, I'll take you. Don't be in any doubt of that, my darling." The sin grin grew wider, and her stupid, girly insides completed their meltdown.

"If you can," she said coolly.

He laughed softly. Then he opened the door of the limo and stuck his head in. "Hartswell, we're going to go on a ride. I'm not sure where—the lady will tell you after you've put up the privacy screen. Once we drop her off, you'll take me away from the vicinity and drive me in circles for ten minutes."

"Very good, sir." Avy couldn't see him yet, since he remained hidden by the black glass of the driver's-side window, but he sounded utterly impassive, used to the peculiarities of his employer.

Liam tied the scarf around his head, blindfolding himself while curious passersby rubbernecked. She checked it to make sure it was snug.

"All right, get in."

"Your wish is my command, darling."

Avy rolled her eyes and shut the door on him after he'd climbed into the back. Then she rapped lightly on the driver's window. The man lowered the glass.

"Yes, madam?" Hartswell was a small man who seemed to be entirely bald under his billed cap. He had a pleasant, round face with bright, somewhat protuberant blue eyes.

"Will you take us to Waterloo station, please? I need to catch a train."

"Most certainly, madam."

"Thank you." Avy smiled as if she gave instructions to private limo drivers every morning of her life, and Hartswell got out and opened the rear door for her, closing it after she'd gotten in.

Liam had ditched his shoes and was sitting Indian-style on the seat opposite her. "Drink?" he asked. "What can I pour for you?"

Her lips twitched. "How do you intend to pour me anything when you can't see it, you loon?"

"I don't need to see it," Liam said. He leaned to the left, in the direction of the minibar, and unerringly put his hand on the stopper of the decanter to the rear. "Scotch." He moved three inches to the right. "Ice bucket." Four inches forward. "Vodka, Grey Goose." Another three inches to the right. "Vodka, Belvedere." He patted the door of a tiny refrigerator. "White wine and champagne."

Impressed, she said, "And what if I wanted red?"

He pulled out a drawer under the fridge that held three bottles of red, a zinfandel, a pinot noir, and a Shiraz. "You'd have to help me identify which is which," he admitted.

"How do you remember where everything is?"

"I have an excellent visual memory. And I have a lot of experience operating without the lights on."

Oh, lord. The sin grin was back. "I'm sure you do," Avy said.

"So what will it be?" Liam asked.

"Shiraz, please."

"You just want to see if I can extract the cork blind-folded."

She laughed.

He opened the drawer again. "Which bottle?"

"Far right."

Liam pulled it out and unfolded his legs, settling it between his knees. He quickly found a little knife on the bar and broke the seal, then deftly twisted in a corkscrew that had been next to the knife. After a few quick turns he gauged the position of the cork with his thumb, turned once more, and then pushed down the arms of the corkscrew. He pulled and extracted the cork in one smooth motion.

There were four wineglasses hanging by their stems in a small rack in the corner. He slipped one off, righted it, and then poured, stopping when the glass was half-full. He expertly turned the bottle as he lifted the neck away from the rim of the wineglass to stop any tendency for it to drip.

"Here you are," he said, extending the drink to her.

"If I had a hat on, I'd take it off to you," Avy told him.

"I'm quite sure we can find something else for you to take off." Liam got another wineglass for himself and poured. He set the bottle in a holder. "Cheers."

"Cheers." She clinked her glass against his. The Shiraz was full-bodied, warm and velvety on her tongue. "Very nice. Thank you." She barely noticed that they were moving—the only indication was the soft purr of the engine and a negligible vibration under her feet.

"Liam, how old were you when you first stole something?"

"I assume you mean more than a scone from the kitchen."

"Yes."

He took a sip of wine while he thought about it. "I was

seventeen. Came of age early in more ways than one that year."

The sadness was back in his voice, along with an edge of bitterness.

"What was it that you stole?"

He was silent for a long moment, obviously editing his response. "A car," he said. "I got into it and never looked back. Drove the damned thing until it ran out of petrol, and then I left it by the side of the road."

"Whose car was it?"

"A woman's." The set of his jaw was grim, and his lips had flattened into a thin line. His back was rigid.

"Bad breakup?" she asked sympathetically.

He let out a short bark of laughter. "Oh, you could say that. So, Avy, how old were you when you first stole something?"

"You didn't finish your story."

"I'm not going to finish it, love. It's quite sordid and intensely depressing. So how old were you?"

"How do you know I've truly stolen something?"

"Just do," he said simply.

"I was six," she said. "I stole a pack of Bubblicious from the local grocery store. Tucked it into my waistband while my mother was in the checkout line."

"And were you caught?"

She nodded. "I wasn't allowed to have gum, which was why I wanted it. My mother caught me chewing it later and made me tell her where I got it. We returned immediately to the store, and I had to apologize to the manager and give it back to him. I was so ashamed. I never stole anything again."

"Until your first recovery job?"

She nodded.

"You're such an interesting mélange of wholesome

and cosmopolitan. I don't believe I've ever encountered it before."

She narrowed her eyes. "Don't patronize me, Liam."

"I wasn't. I find it quite a charming combination. Most of the elegant people I know are jaded, world-weary. They believe in very little. You, on the other hand, have strong, impossibly black and white beliefs."

"Why 'impossibly'?"

He leaned his head back against the leather seat. "You don't allow for shades of gray, and therefore your world-view is two-dimensional."

"I didn't get into the car with you to be insulted, Liam."

"No, you got into the car for your own efficient reasons. But I honestly don't mean to insult you. Let's talk about this. The Ten Commandments, for example: 'Thou shalt not steal.' You know that one, mmmmm?"

She took a sip of her wine, resolved not to swallow any of his philosophy, however.

Liam asked, "How do you feel about that commandment in cases where the theft is legal?"

"What are you talking about? Be specific."

"We can start with corporations, for example. What Enron did was technically legal, for the most part. Yet would you argue that a theft from its employees and stock-holders did not occur?"

She sighed. "That doesn't make what you do right."

"Governments, Avy. Governments steal from their citizens. . . ."

"Last time I checked that was called paying taxes."

"Ah. Do you enjoy giving away up to forty percent of your income, darling?"

"Of course I don't enjoy it. Who would?"

"Is it fair to say that the income is being taken from you against your will?"

"Liam, you're splitting hairs—"

"Answer the question, yes or no. You wouldn't pay taxes if not for fear of the consequences, correct?"

She hesitated, and then shook her head.

"Then technically speaking that money is being stolen from you."

"I don't agree. It's not the same thing at all."

Liam continued unperturbed. "What about when evidence is collected from a suspect's person or home after a crime has been committed?"

"What about it? The suspect either gives his permission or there's a search warrant."

"Search warrant or no, the evidence is seized. Stolen, essentially."

"For a damned good reason!"

Liam smiled. "Yes, indeed."

She tried to think of a way to refute his maddening logic, but couldn't.

"Another example. The Tintoretto nude over my bed. The owner was allowing it to slowly rot. Because of his penny-pinching ways, the world came close to losing a masterpiece. Was it so wrong of me, under the circumstances, to give it a better home so that many more generations can enjoy it?"

Avy took another sip of wine. "It was technically his property to do with as he wished."

"I own a cat," said Liam. "It's my property, correct?"

She nodded reluctantly.

"Does that give me the right to skin it alive?"

Even the concept horrified her. "No!"

"Would you steal the animal from me if you knew that I was about to skin it alive?"

"Damn it, Liam, you're leading me in circles."

"Answer the question. Would you steal the cat?"

"Yes."

He nodded in satisfaction. "Shades of gray, Avy. You must consider them."

"Shades of gray lead to moral relativity, which leads to lawlessness, chaos, eventually nihilism."

His expression became affectionately tolerant, to her annoyance. "There you go being black-and-white about shades of gray." He laughed. "On the flip side of the equation, love, the rule of law leads often to injustice and to a police state, which leads to totalitarianism."

Avy drummed her fingernails against the bowl of her wineglass and said nothing. What could she say?

"When you look at a pencil or charcoal drawing, my lovely art history major, do you analyze only the contours?"

"Of course not, but—"

"You look at the way light and dark is rendered to show how the object exists in space. And that's done by shading. Two dimensions—the length and breadth of the paper— become three."

Oh, how green his eyes must be at this particular moment, under the blindfold. "Don't look so pleased with yourself, Liam. You still haven't convinced me that stealing is okay."

He leaned forward. "What if you or your children were starving? Would you steal food under those circumstances?"

"If you ever retire from your life of crime, you should become a lawyer," she told him. "And may I point out that you're riding around in a limousine, nowhere close to starving. So you don't have a leg to stand on, Mr. Clever."

"I was afraid you might feel the need to point that out. So it's back to the cat, I'm afraid. She's a very nasty creature—I'd love for you to steal her. What d'you say? I'll even throw in a deluxe carrier with a handle."

"No deal. Kong would dive-bomb her and peck her to death."

Liam threw back his head and laughed.

"I'm not kidding," Avy said. "He'd win. He thinks he's a chicken hawk, not a cockatiel."

"Whatever possessed you to get a bird as a pet?"

"I don't have to walk him. And I can just throw him in a Crock-Pot if he's been bad."

"No, really."

"A little old lady in my building died unexpectedly. Nobody wanted poor Kong, since he's pretty cranky, so I took him."

"And who's taking care of him while you're here in London?"

Avy frowned. "My cousin—for a larcenous fee. She has long hair and could pass for me in a pair of sunglasses, if you're getting my drift. It's because of *you* that I'll owe her almost a thousand dollars by the time I get home."

Liam looked delighted. "You hired a body double to fool me! I'm flattered."

She laughed in spite of herself.

Liam leaned forward again and found her knee with his free hand. "Help me out, here, darling. I can't see you and I should like to kiss you."

He felt around for her glass and took it from her. He set it, along with his own barely touched glass, down on the little bar. "Will you kiss me? Before you go off on your mysterious errand?"

She wished that she felt hesitant. "Stupidly, yes." Avy bent forward, put her hands on either side of his jaw, and touched her lips to his. He smelled so damned good— always so clean in spite of his tainted philosophies, always that tinge of leather. His lips were soft for a brief moment before they turned hard and demanding, insistent that hers should part for him. And too eagerly she let him inside.

He tasted of wine and felony. Why did this feel so right when it was so wrong?

She chalked it up to the psychology of risk. This whole thing with Liam was due to her personality flaw. She was the type of human being who'd jump out of a perfectly good airplane—just as she was the type of woman who'd bypass a happy, boring marriage with a nice, stable man for a fling with a professional thief.

Flaw. Remember that. Liam plays to your flaws. Hadn't her father warned her once that the scariest thing about her was that she had little to no fear? A common characteristic of psychopaths, he'd pointed out in his comforting, fatherly way.

Against her mouth, Liam said, "That's the first time you've ever done that. Kissed me."

"No, it isn't."

He nodded. "I always kiss you."

"What are you talking about? I ripped open your shirt, bit you, tied you to the bedposts."

"But you did *not* kiss me. There's a big difference. It indicates feelings of some kind, depending on what sort of kiss it is."

Feelings? No. Liam fit her usual pattern of men, and she knew it. He was big, handsome, charming, larger than life . . . a born womanizer, same as her dad.

Avy checked her watch just as Hartswell rapped on the privacy screen. The car had come to a stop.

"Feelings?" she repeated, shaking her head. "Maybe of lust. You're a good-looking guy, Liam. And I won't deny that you're great in the sack. You make me laugh. But what else is there to say—it's been real, it's been fun, have a nice life? Look me up if you ever decide to retire? Maybe we'll meet again sometime, while I'm recovering something else that you've stolen."

"*Ouch.*"

"Liam." She sighed. "I don't say that to be snotty or cruel. But I just can't picture taking you home to Mama."

"Why not?"

"Trust me. You would not go over well with her and her church-lady friends."

"Why not?" he asked again. "What's not to like?"

How could she explain this to someone who might as well live on another planet? "My mother is a strict Southern Baptist and tries to live an exemplary life, Liam. I doubt you're very religious?"

"Er . . ." he said.

"And then there's the fact that you drink, fornicate, and steal. She'll love that."

"Meaning no disrespect, but you do the same."

She sighed again. "I never claimed my mama approved of me, either."

Liam rubbed at his jaw. "Ah. Tell me then—why would the woman you describe name her daughter Ava Brigitte, after two voluptuous starlets?"

"You know the answer to that, Liam." She smiled a little sadly. "My father named me."

Hartswell chose that moment to open the door. He handed her out while Liam remained seated in his blindfold, true to his word. The expression on his face was enigmatic, unreadable.

"Have a nice trip," he said.

"Why would you think I'm going on a trip?"

"Back to the States, of course." His tone was bland, and she knew, with a sinking feeling, that he was very much aware that she was off to France.

"Oh, right. Yes."

"I must say that I'm surprised you're giving up so easily, my darling."

"You win some, you lose some," she said lightly.

"And sometimes it's a tie."

"Good-bye, Liam."

"Bon voyage, love."

chapter 21

Liam was true to his word and didn't remove the blindfold. "Hartswell," he remarked, "I have the most wretched feeling that we're driving away from Waterloo station, and that Miss Hunt is even now getting on the last Chunnel train of the evening."

"I couldn't say, sir. Not for another seven minutes, at least."

"Good man. For such ethically challenged people, we have a wonderful sense of what's right and wrong, do we not?"

"That we do, sir. Er, what would you like me to do with the Modigliani painting you stowed in the boot, sir?"

"It's pronounced Mo-dee-ylee-ah-nee, Hartswell."

"Ah. I don't believe my mouth can work that way, sir. So what do I do with that picture of the horse-faced woman with the freakishly long neck? *Hang* her?"

Liam groaned. "That was painfully bad, Hartswell. And no, please send her to Miss Kay Bunker of the FBI—the address is on file—wishing her many happy returns. Ha!"

"And you said *mine* was bad, sir?"

Liam laughed. "I so wish that I could be a fly on the wall when she opens the crate. It'll take her days to figure out that it's a fake."

"Ever the prankster, you are."

"Indeed. Tell me when the bloody blindfold can come off, will you, Hartswell?"

"Four minutes and counting, sir."

Liam's smile quickly disappeared as he thought about the next forty-eight hours. Two short days until the scheduled sale of the sword to a stupendously rich Syrian who'd been vacationing on the Côte d'Azur.

The current plan was that the Syrian's Learjet would stop to complete the transaction at the Frog's country estate before flying home to the Middle East.

Avy was headed for the address on that shipping label she'd extorted from him. Which meant that she was going to walk straight into Gautreau's crosshairs. Which was entirely unacceptable . . . but what the hell was he going to do, kidnap her and lock her in a closet? He hadn't a clue.

"Hartswell, we're heading home so that I can pack a bag, and then we're heading for the airport in a hurry. I'll take the Cessna."

"Very good, sir."

"May I remove this cursed thing now?"

"One minute, sir."

"Bugger." Liam wondered why in the hell he was being so literal about his promise, but he felt strongly about it. He'd made it to Avy, who considered him a man without honor. It riled him. *The truth hurts, doesn't it, old boy?*

He didn't suppose that she'd understand that he had his honor on a layaway plan. That eventually he'd pay down the balance on it and get it back.

"Time, sir!"

Liam slipped the blindfold off his head and blinked in the glare of headlamps and streetlights. "Thank you, Hartswell."

The limousine slid smoothly through the London night,

a luxury living room on wheels. Once he'd greatly appreciated the car, but at the moment he'd rather be low to the ground in something with a whole stable of horsepower under the hood, setting his own pace, driving hell-for-leather instead of riding comfortably like a flea on a dog.

A parasite—that was what he'd become over the years. Some would argue that he'd been born one, into a wealthy aristocratic English family. But that he could shrug off, chalking it up to the lucky-sperm club.

Devoting oneself professionally to parasitic behavior was another thing entirely. He could make all the jokes he liked about bankers sucking interest and salespeople sucking commissions and barristers sucking percentages . . . but at least those people worked legally for their money.

Guilt had finally caught up with him after all these years; God only knew why. He wanted to be free of it, even if he had to put up with the likes of Kay Bunker in order to attain his goal.

Liam grimly packed his bag once Hartswell had delivered him back home. He tossed in a couple of fresh shirts, the necessities, his climbing equipment, and a few useful gadgets.

After weighing the odds of the Cessna being searched by French customs, he threw in his Glock and some duct tape to secure it somewhere on board. He quickly filed a flight plan electronically for Nice, grabbed his logbook, and headed out the door for the limo again. It might make him feel like a flea on a dog, but at least now he was an armed and dangerous flea.

Avy wouldn't arrive in Paris yet for a couple of hours, and then she still had to get a train to Nice. He could beat her there and put the Frog's house under surveillance; with any luck he could take her down before she even got near it.

He still didn't know what the bloody hell to do with her once he had her, though. Tie her up and gag her? Drug her? He sure as shit couldn't tell her the truth. While he could take the chance of trusting her with his own secrets, he couldn't take the chance of trusting her with the secrets of an FBI/Interpol sting. There were too many people and risks involved. It wasn't his decision to make.

Hartswell dropped him at an airfield twenty miles outside of London, and Liam walked straight out to the Cessna 182 that he owned, unlocked the door, and tossed his duffel inside.

He did a thorough preflight check, inspecting for any damage. He moved the rudders left and right and the elevator up and down, testing the fuel level to make sure there was no water in the tank.

Then he got into the pilot's seat and did a yoke inspection, rotating it left to right and looking out the windows to make sure the ailerons moved properly.

He turned on the instruments to make sure they all worked: radios one and two, the GPS, the manifold pressure gauge, and various others.

He tuned radio one to the departure frequency and radio two to local air traffic control. Then he selected radio one and spoke. "Tower, this is November niner three seven zero five bravo. Plan on file. Requesting permission to taxi and departure clearance. Over."

"Roger, seven zero five bravo. You are cleared to taxi for runway two seven zero. Use main taxiway but hold short. Over."

Liam pulled on the throttle and eased the plane forward, stopping before he got to the runway as instructed. Soon he was given the all-clear to take off.

"November seven zero five bravo, tower. Clear for departure on runway two seven zero. Use southerly departure.

Be advised of traffic to the southwest. Have a safe flight, Sir Liam."

Liam spoke into the radio one last time: "Tower, seven zero five bravo. Departing. Thank you for the assistance, John. Over."

He pulled again on the throttle, pressed on the rudder, and eased the plane into takeoff position. Standing on the brakes, he pulled the throttle to full power. He paused for a moment, listened to the engine, and did another quick scan of the gauges. Then he eased off the brakes.

He picked up speed as he hurtled down the runway in his expensive tin with wings. When he reached takeoff speed, he pulled back on the yoke and guided the Cessna into the air, wishing he could do the same with his spirits.

But he saw no way out with Avy until he could explain— and at that point it might be too late. He had to take her down one way or another.

Soon the airfield was little more than a lighted postage stamp beneath him, and Liam was one with the birds, soaring into the sky and defying gravity.

Above the lights of London the night blanketed everything, punctuated only here and there by the twinkles of other aircraft.

Liam reached a cruising altitude and then groped reluctantly for his satellite phone. It was time to make an excruciating call to Agent Bunker—and *before* she received that forged Modigliani.

"Bunker," she answered tersely.

"Miss Bunker, how I have missed the musical cadence of your voice over the past few hours."

"All right, I've had it. You know damned well it's not Miss. It's Special Agent Bunker."

"And *what* a special agent you are."

"Spare me. What's your status report?"

"As usual, my status is exalted. My report, however, is not so cheery, I'm afraid."

"What's going on? Where are you?"

"At the moment I'm several thousand feet above the Atlantic Ocean, traversing the wild blue yonder. I'm on my way to Provence in the south of France."

"I know where Provence is," she snapped. "We already have FBI and French RAID there, ready to move in after the sale is made. Why are *you* going there?"

Liam cleared his throat. "Unfortunately Miss Hunt is also bound for Provence."

"She's *what*? How does she—"

"Miss Hunt somehow discovered the original DHL shipping bill in my trouser pocket."

An ominous pause ensued. "How did her hands get into your pants? Oh, let me guess! Damn it," Bunker shouted, "you are *unbelievable*. I should have known better than to rely on you for anything at all."

"May I remind you that if not for me, you couldn't have set up this whole sting operation? The Frog wouldn't trust anyone else, and you know it. He's been doing this for over thirty years, and he's not stupid."

Bunker growled something he didn't catch, something that ended with the term *screwup*.

"At any rate, Avy Hunt is indeed traveling to Provence as we speak. I think I can handle her, but I need some time—"

"*Think* you can handle her? That's not going to cut it. We'll have to do something about her. I'll have her brought in."

"Under French law, you can't hold her for more than twenty-one hours without charges, and she hasn't done anything wrong."

"She broke into your house, didn't she?"

"I never filed a report, and nothing was taken."

"It's still B and E, and we can file a report now."

"Don't. Look, all I need is a few hours to get into position. I'd be grateful if you could call one of your buddies in French law enforcement and have her detained for just an hour or so at the train station. Suspicion of false passport or something like that."

Bunker was silent for a moment. "All right. We can arrange it. But you keep her away from that villa, Liam James. Take her to the beach, get her dead drunk, knock her over the head with a day-old baguette—I don't care. Just don't mess this up, or she'll end up dead and you'll end up wearing orange. Got it?"

"As always, it's been sheer pleasure conversing with you, Miss Bunker."

An ominous pause ensued. Then she said, "*Agent* Bunker!"

Liam grinned. "I have a proposition for you, darling. I'll start calling you 'agent' when you start calling me 'sir.'"

"Hell," said Bunker, "will freeze over first." And with that she hung up on him.

chapter 22

After an uneventful trip, Avy arrived in Calais at about six thirty p.m. Since she'd left with no luggage, her first move would be to purchase a toothbrush, some toothpaste, and other basics, along with an inexpensive tote bag. Her next move would be to buy some dark clothing in which she could function efficiently. She glanced ruefully down at her skirt and heels. Not the best scouting or B and E gear.

She'd have to take the TGV, or high-speed rail service, south from Calais to Paris—about two hours—and then an overnight train from Paris to Nice, a trip of five and a half hours.

Her thoughts turned to Liam, who'd clearly suspected where she was going, and she wondered if he'd follow this time. After all, he'd fulfilled his part of whatever bargain he'd made with the Frenchman. If Whidby had delivered the Sword of Alexander to the house in Provence, then Liam was finished and could wash his hands of her. After all, it wasn't his problem if the sword disappeared after the Frenchman took possession of it.

Or was it? The man could easily blame Liam for passing along his address. That gave Avy pause. So what? Then he'd be angry with Liam, and she'd have cut off one of his sources. He'd have a harder time unloading his stolen goods. Why should she care?

But she remembered Liam's grave face as he told her not to go near the man, Gautreau. He'd said clearly that he was dangerous. Would she be unleashing violence against Liam by repossessing the sword?

Liam's a big boy. He knows the risks of working with people like Gautreau. He knows that heisting objects worth millions of dollars is bound to provoke ugly behavior.

But the idea of Liam being hurt or even killed got to her. Avy worried as she paid for her TGV ticket and did research on her BlackBerry on places to stay in Nice.

Just as she'd found a first-rate hotel with an ocean view, she came to the realization that Liam would indeed be coming after her. Because unless he was a master thespian as well as a master thief, then he'd be just as worried about her as she was about him.

He was high-handed and absurdly macho in the best of circumstances. He'd be twice as bad if he thought a woman was in any sort of danger—especially a woman with whom he'd indicated he'd like a deeper relationship.

Liam had foreseen her agenda and probably ripped off that blindfold the moment she'd stepped out of the car. For all she knew he'd gotten on the same train. She heard heavy, purposeful footsteps behind her and turned, half convinced it was him.

But the man who approached was not Liam. He was with the French police, in their official light blue work shirt and dark trousers. "Mademoiselle Hunt?"

Her heart dropped. "Yes?" How could he possibly know her name?

"Your passport, *s'il vous plaît*."

Had Liam reported her guilty of some crime? Turned her

in to the French police much as she'd turned him in to the
British police, in a tit for tat?

"What is this about?" She produced her passport—thank
God her own and not Louise Houghton's. He took a cursory
glance at it and didn't hand it back.

"Come with me, please."

"Why?"

"We would like to ask you a few questions, Mademoiselle."

"About what?" Damn it, she didn't have time for this!

"This way, please." The policeman led her to a tiny,
cramped office in the train station and cleared a stack of papers from a wooden chair before inviting her to sit down.
The room stank of stale cigarettes, body odor, and black
coffee.

With a grunt the officer sat down himself and pulled a
notepad toward his belly. He uncapped a pen while review-
ing her passport.

"Full name?"

It was right there in the little blue book. "Ava Brigitte
Hunt."

"Date of birth?"

"July twenty-third, 1979." He was obviously checking to
see if she knew the information in the passport. So Liam
must have told someone that she was traveling with false
papers.

"Full address?"

She told him.

"Social security number?"

She told him that, too.

"The purpose of your visit to France?"

"Sightseeing."

He looked up at her with shrewd, watery brown eyes.

"Sightseeing," he repeated. "And where is your baggage, Mademoiselle Hunt?"

"I left in a hurry."

"I see. You were overcome with the desire to see France and rushed onto a train without so much as a change of clothes."

She smiled brazenly. "My boyfriend called and asked me to meet him on the spur of the moment for a romantic getaway. He found a special three-day package."

"Ah. *Quelle surprise merveilleuse!*"

She nodded and tried to look full of blissful anticipation.

"And where will you meet him?"

"In Nice."

"Yes, but the hotel?"

She gave him the name of the one she'd just booked, the Palais de la Méditerranée.

"And the reservation—it is under his name?"

Oh, hell. She'd said he'd found a package. "Y-yes."

"Which is?"

"Look, what is this about?"

"The name of this boyfriend, Mademoiselle Hunt, is . . . ?"

"James," she said, backed into a corner. "Liam James."

The officer pursed his lips. "This name, it sounds familiar to me. Why?"

Read your police bulletins? Surf the Internet much? Watch any TV? The story of the sword's theft had broken in the media recently. She shrugged. "I don't know. It's a common enough name, James."

"Mademoiselle Hunt, you will forgive me if I make a telephone call to the hotel to verify zis information?"

I will not forgive you. You're going to find out that it's a pack of lies and be even more suspicious because I've been untruthful with you. You're going to detain me for hours that I can't spare, and . . .

Remaining cool, Avy shrugged. "Be my guest."

The policeman aimed a thin smile at her and picked up the phone. He called information and wrote down a number. Then he dialed it in and hit the button for the speakerphone, replacing the receiver. He eyed her smugly.

She produced a bland smile. *Option: Slip off my heels and bolt out of here right now, praying that I can outrun him and any of his cohorts.*

Downside: He still has my passport, and they'd put out the French version of an APB within seconds. I'd be picked up before even getting the two miles to Calais, where I'd be unable to board a train bound for Nice without the passport anyway.

Option: Become an instant sex kitten, thrust my breasts into his face, and playfully take the phone away from him. Seduce him on his desk in return for my passport.

Downside: That whole meeting-my-own-eyes-in-the-mirror thing. And just look at him. Ugh!

Option: Become instant sex kitten, thrust breasts into his face, and playfully take phone away from him. Just as he thinks I'll seduce him on his desk in return for my passport, clock him behind the ear with that hideous ceramic ashtray near his elbow.

Downside: Arrest for assault and battery of a police officer after they put out the French version of the APB.

She was running out of brilliant options, and she could hear the line ringing on the other end of the phone. "Bonjour, Hotel Palais de la Mediterranée," said a professionally enthusiastic female voice.

Her friendly policeman asked to be connected with the room of Monsieur Liam James.

"Un moment," said the female voice.

Avy reconsidered bolting out the door. She thought about claiming that he just hadn't checked in yet, or that there'd been some mixup. Then, to her astonishment, she heard the line ringing a guest room.

"Hello?" No mistaking Liam's clipped British accent.

Avy blinked once, then twice before she recovered, prompted by the policeman's Gallic scrutiny. "Liam, my darling. It's Avy, calling from Sangatte. I miss you and I can't wait to see you!"

Without missing a beat Liam said, "What the devil is taking you so long, my love? The champagne is getting warm, the bed is soft, and I'm, oh, so eagerly naked."

She tried not to think about him naked, and didn't know whether to bless him or curse him. "I'm so sorry I'm late, but I've been unavoidably detained here." *As you know, you jerk.*

" 'Unavoidably detained' doesn't mean that you're enthralled by a shoe sale, now, does it, Lamb Chop?"

No, Pork Loin, it doesn't. "Hardly, my darling. I'm being held up by a most handsome French policeman, who seems to be all too fascinated by my—"

"Ava Brigitte, you trollop!" Liam yelled. "Are you boffing this chap en route to our romantic tryst?"

Trollop? Almost speechless, she croaked, "Excuse me?"

"You're shagging some fellow you met at the train station?"

The French officer choked.

"What? No, I—"

"And you have the unmitigated gall to tell me this on the telephone, while I await you with champagne?"

"No! This is not what you think—"

"Coldhearted bitch!" shouted Liam, obviously having the time of his life.

The French police officer's watery brown eyes had grown to twice their original size.

"Liam, no!" Avy covered her face with her hand and pretended to dissolve into tears. "How can you think that of me?"

"Deceitful whore! I've had it with you and your sexcapades. It's over between us, do you hear?"

"We have to talk about this—"

"There's nothing to talk about. Remember the waiter in Brussels? *Il postino* in Venice? And the bank manager in Zurich? You're insatiable!"

Avy recalled an expression that a friend of her father's had once used: *I din' know whether to shit or go blind. . . .*

It seemed very apropos for her current situation.

"The uniform," she croaked. "You know I can't resist men in uniform, my darling. The badge, the hat, the gun— I lose all control."

"The bank manager wasn't wearing a uniform," Liam growled.

"His tie was Hermès," she pleaded.

"We're done! I've had it with you!"

"No, baby—please don't end it. I love you. . . ." She was horrified as the words came out of her mouth.

"You love me?" Liam repeated in scathing tones. "A fine way you have of showing it—unable to keep your knickers on."

"I-I'll get help," she managed. "I promise I will."

"There isn't any help for trollops like you."

"There is," she insisted. "I'll go to therapy for sex addicts. Please, Liam, just give me another chance. What better place to start over than in Nice, overlooking the Baie des Anges?"

She hung up the phone shortly afterward and, all too

conscious of the bit about the uniforms, carefully avoided the police officer's gaze.

He cleared his throat and held out her passport by the top right corner, as if he were afraid it was infected with several STDs. "*Merci*, mademoiselle. You are free to go."

Oh, no, thank you, *monsieur.*

Avy fled.

chapter 23

Liam smirked about the phone conversation, but he'd obviously just unintentionally helped Avy out of her prefabricated jam with the French authorities. That meant she would arrive here in a matter of hours.

Unintentionally? Yes, well . . . he could have pretended not to know her, after all. But he'd been unable to resist having a bit of fun with the situation, especially after hearing the shock in her voice that anyone by his name had actually been registered at the hotel.

Which meant he'd lost the advantage of surprise. She now knew that he was waiting for her. The question was, what would she do with the knowledge? Would she come to the hotel anyway—or would she immediately find another one somewhere else and do her best to avoid him?

This one had been a fairly easy guess. Avy, like him, enjoyed the finer things in life, which meant she'd want a top-ranked hotel. She'd checked into one of the best in Nice, the spectacular Palais de la Mediterranée. A few easy phone calls had narrowed down his search and provided the information that Miss Hunt had not yet checked in at the Palais. Voilà.

It would not be as easy to find her the next time. Which

meant that he needed to tail her from the train station to wherever she was going.

Liam checked his watch. He still had loads of time before she arrived. He could get creative with some disguise, but she'd be on alert for anything like that. The best course of action was simply to stay out of sight or blend in with all the tourists and people on holiday.

The Mediterranean sun beat down mercilessly, but the view of the ocean from the Promenade des Anglais took his breath away, no matter how many times he'd seen it or how many bodies roasted in the sun on the rocky beach.

The view was even better from the balcony of his ninth-floor room at the Palais, but Liam enjoyed being in the middle of the action and sweating a little. He wished that he and Avy really were here for a romantic interlude, that they could be just another couple on holiday.

But she'd made it quite clear that she had no feelings for him during the limo ride, hadn't she? Liam squinted into the sun through his Serengeti shades as he emerged from the hotel and took off his shoes to walk barefoot on the beach. He smiled back at the women, most of them topless, who cast him admiring glances. But he didn't stop to chat.

No, they were too easy. He wanted the big score of all women, Ava Brigitte Hunt. He just had to convince her that she wanted him, too. And not as a plaything. He knew damn well that to Avy, sleeping with him was the equivalent of passing her hand through a flame just to prove that she could do it without getting burned.

Liam wiggled his toes in a small patch of trucked-in sand and walked down to the water, watching three children laughing, shrieking, playing in the waves. The sight of them triggered old memories . . . his family's trips to the seaside long ago, when he and his brother and sister had fought over who got the biggest towel and had competitions to see who could collect the most seashells. His older brother, Nigel, had dunked Liam repeatedly in the water. . . . They'd buried his sister, India, to the neck in the sand. Then they'd almost peed on themselves laughing as they put a small crab on her head while she screamed and screamed.

They'd been good times, carefree and happy ones. Would he ever watch his own children play in the surf or make sand castles? He wistfully pictured a little girl with Avy's eyes and smile, sap that he was.

The one thing that he couldn't steal was a family.

God, how had he come to this—thinking in homespun clichés? He shoved his hands into his pockets as the water rushed over his toes and rose to cover his ankles.

But it was true. He could take any material object the world had to offer, given enough time and money to plan and execute the heist. What he could not take back was his family. He couldn't filch or finesse his father's forgiveness.

Nor could he change the circumstances that made his falling for Avy a tragic folly. For he had, and he knew it.

After walking for a few more minutes, Liam made his way back to the Promenade des Anglais and put on his shoes. He passed the grand Hôtel Negresco and turned right on the Rue de Rivoli, walking by the Rue de France, Rue de la Buffa, and Rue du Maréchal to the Boulevard Victor Hugo, where he turned right. Two blocks later he turned left onto Avenue Durante and headed for the Gare de Nice-Ville, the station where Avy's train would arrive shortly.

He found a bench in the shade near the front entrance of the building. The round clock set in elaborate stonework at the top of the station told him that it was five until three.

The sale of the sword was scheduled for ten o'clock the next morning, meaning that he somehow had to keep Avy occupied or distracted for twenty-six hours. He knew exactly how he'd like to spend them: in the big bed in his hotel room rolling on the crisp, freshly laundered white sheets. But it was unlikely that she'd share his vision—or admit to sharing it, if she did.

The shrill whistle of a train coming in brought him back to reality and the uncomfortable metal bench creating what felt like grill marks on his tender English backside.

He got up and lurked behind a tree in the parking lot instead, waiting for Avy to come out. Right on schedule she did, wearing big dark glasses, her glossy chestnut hair loose over her shoulders and the strap of her Dior saddlebag. He admired her leggy composure, her utterly unconcerned air.

No, baby—please don't end it. I love you!

He grinned, wondering how much it had cost her to say those words. Then his grin faded. Would she ever say the last three to him and mean it?

She looked left and then right briefly before crossing the parking lot not five feet from him. She didn't bother to catch a cab, just headed straight down the Avenue Durante. To his surprise she stayed on it, never once looking behind her, until it became Rue de Congress. She walked south toward the Promenade des Anglais and the Palais de la Mediterranée, stopping only to purchase a simple black bikini, a sarong, and a pair of flat sandals.

He continued to follow from several yards back, pretending to be a tourist, absorbed in other shop windows and a guidebook. She gave no sign of whether she'd seen him, though he thought it was very likely.

She arrived at the long, white marble, Art Deco facade of the Palais, with its Doric columns and ziggurats adorned with carved female nudes and elegant horses.

He could easily picture her making an entrance in jewels and a couture gown in the elegant heyday of the French Riviera, when the original Palais casino lured rich playboys and international beauties to Nice.

Now all that remained of the 1929 structure was the magnificent facade. In 2001 Frantz Taittinger of the champagne family had gotten behind a restoration project, and Concorde Hotels, with a team of architects, had designed the current showplace.

Avy took a moment to admire it and then went straight up the steps and into the modern cedar-paneled lobby.

Liam followed discreetly, then made his way to the third floor for a drink in the spectacular courtyard. It was over three hundred feet long and its pillars framed peerless views of the sea, while a curved swimming pool flowed from inside the building to the exterior. Terraced guest rooms flanked the other three sides of the place.

Liam and his martini hadn't been there longer than fifteen minutes when Avy strolled out to join him, obligingly enough wearing the black bikini and sarong. He got to his feet and kissed her soundly, snaking one arm around her waist and enjoying the feel of her bare skin.

She made a pretense at merely tolerating this treatment, but as he stroked the tender skin at her nape and coaxed a response from her, she shivered. Her pulse kicked up and he smiled against her ear, inhaling her familiar jasmine-and-freesia scent.

"Avy, I can't help but be filled with joy at the sight of you, my truculent little trollop—despite your quite scandalous treatment of me." He pulled out her chair, and as she sat he whispered into her ear.

"Now that I know about your predilection for uniforms, I've amassed quite a collection upstairs. I can be your fantasy fireman, your serendipitous soldier, or your capable construction worker, my dear."

The expression on her face was priceless.

She ordered only an Evian and then sat back, crossing one long leg over the other. "How did you manage to arrive in Nice before me? And how did you know I'd be staying here?"

"I'm very well; thank you for asking," he said.

"You are not at all well—that was clear from the telephone call, Liam."

He grinned. "I'm waiting for you to give thanks and tell me that I'm your hero, love."

"You're not my hero—you're my worst nightmare."

"But, Avy, you begged me not to end it between us. That implies that you think highly of me. Perhaps you even worship the ground I walk upon."

She ignored that. "Liam, how *did* you get here before me?"

"Wings," he said simply.

"You chartered a plane."

"No, no. I have my pilot's license and a little Cessna 182, darling. I'd gladly have taken a passenger if you'd asked me for a lift. But no, you had to be all sneaky about things. . . ."

"Oh, of course. I should have asked you for a *ride* when I was trying to get away from you." She threw up her hands. "Only in your world does that make any sense, Liam."

He glanced at her, unperturbed. "The more often you visit my world, the more logical it will seem, my darling. You may even wish to take up permanent residence once you get accustomed to it."

She leaned across the table, unaware of how inviting her cleavage was, her mouth determined under the scarlet lipstick she wore. "Don't count on it. I don't care for a world built on a house of cards. One wrong move, Liam, and it all comes tumbling down around your ears: your Cessna, your limo, your real estate and furnishings. Seized by the authorities, along with your freedom. Women won't find you nearly as irresistible then."

Liam pounced. "You find me irresistible? That warms the cockles of my felonious old heart."

"What? I do not."

"Ah." He drained the last of his martini and dug for his wallet, extracting a bill and placing it on the table under the glass. "Well, that's all right—you made it clear in our last phone conversation that you aren't choosy about whom you shag."

He stood up and extended his hand to her as she gaped at him, outraged. "So until you check into that therapy program for sex addicts, you can make do with me."

Several heads turned toward them, and her color heightened. "Keep your voice down," she hissed, ignoring his hand.

"Don't be embarrassed, love. A voracious libido is a sign of excellent health. Just try to keep your paws off the waiters and postmen, hmmmm?" He caught her under the elbow and kissed her temple as he drew her up. "Come along now—we'll have to find you something more than that very fetching bikini to wear to dinner tonight."

For a moment he thought she might very well stomp her heel into his instep or make a scene. But she shot him a sultry smile. "Oh, Liam. You're so thoughtful and sweet to take me on a deluxe shopping spree in the Nice boutiques. Thank you, darling—I *do* need a few things."

She did—specifically some kind of top to cover that provocative body of hers before they got out of the hotel. He could already feel his bank cards melting. By the end of the afternoon, he was sure, the plastic would be grafted to his right arse cheek.

chapter 24

During the course of the hot, sunny, glittering hours she spent shopping and seeing the sights of Nice with Liam, Avy almost forgot that she wasn't there to have fun. That the big, handsome Englishman by her side wasn't really her boyfriend but an irritating, competitive, quick-thinking thief who loved to keep one step ahead of her.

Neither of them ever mentioned once why they were there, as they strolled hand in hand through the streets of Vieux Nice, the older part of the city. They started in the colorful Cours Saleya Flower Market, a feast for the eyes and the nose with its array of canopied stalls full of vegetables, fruit, spices, and other goods.

They wandered among the crooked, narrow streets and in and out of shops, boutiques, and galleries.

To Liam's evident surprise she actually refused to allow him to buy much for her, though he did insist on paying for a strapless white silk cocktail dress and a pair of high-heeled sandals to go with it.

When Avy came out of the dressing room to show him, he took one look at her and handed a bank card to the saleslady without asking the price. "Whatever it is, it's worth it," he said simply.

Heat rose in her face. "Liam, I was kidding about you taking me on a shopping spree—"

"It's a gift. Please allow me."

When he put it that way, how could she refuse?

Avy wouldn't let him come into the lingerie shop, though. "Go have a beer," she said, giving him a small push onto the sidewalk.

"But . . ." He looked longingly inside at the scraps of cotton, silk, and lace, his eyes a bright, horny green.

"It's a surprise."

"I'll see it later?"

She raised an eyebrow. "If you're a good boy."

"I'm never a good boy," he said, his mouth quirking. "You know that. I'm one hundred percent bad, as you've pointed out on more than one occasion."

The hair at his forehead lifted in a breeze from the ocean, and in the bright sunlight she caught glimpses of burnished mahogany and chestnut among the dark brown. "Maybe not a hundred percent." Avy reached out and smoothed it.

He caught her fingers and brought them to his mouth, kissing them as he had that first day they'd met in Miami.

She was mesmerized for a moment before she pulled them back and recovered. "You're more like eighty-five percent bad. The other fifteen percent is quite lovable."

"I'm not at all sure that's a compliment," Liam mused. "I'll just go get that beer"—he pointed at a little sidewalk café—"and drown my sorrows."

She patted his cheek. "You do that. I'll meet you there in a few minutes, once I step inside this little boutique and find something just as naughty as you are."

Avy had the same experience shopping for French lingerie that most women had: It was impossible to choose only one or two items from among the exquisite array in front of her. Lace, ribbons, sheer panels, embroidery—it all called to her. Bras, camisoles, merry widows, high-cut panties, string bikinis, tap pants, and skimpy thongs. Baby-doll nighties, long, slinky gowns, romantic frilly ones, and simple, sexy shifts.

She finally narrowed it down to two bras, two thongs, one lacy camisole, and a Brazilian-style lace tanga. She didn't bother with stockings of any kind, though she was sure Liam would have appreciated some sheer thigh-highs.

Her purchases came to a total that made her blink, but it was nothing, after all, compared to the commission she'd get on the recovery of the sword.

It was the first time she'd thought of it all afternoon, and it gave her pause. *What are you doing, Avy? Buying lingerie to wear for a guy you kissed off just this morning? A guy who's clearly here to stop you from doing what you're sworn to do?*

She pushed the guilt from her mind. She had a right to some fun, and she knew better than to care about Liam James. She could mix business and pleasure—as long as the pleasure stopped around midnight and she made sure he snored peacefully for the rest of the night.

Not an issue—her next stop was a pharmacy. She needed a toothbrush and some basic cosmetics, after all—as well as something to knock him out.

She felt guilty about that, but it couldn't be helped. It was the only way to make sure that Liam didn't interfere with her moonlit plans. A voice inside her head nagged: *And how is that any different from Dave Pomeroy slipping you a roofie?*

Um . . . Any taking advantage of Liam would happen *before* she gave it to him, while he was ready, willing, and able to consent to sex. Avy ruthlessly shoved the guilt aside and hit the pharmacy two doors down from the lingerie shop. She bought the necessary combination of drugs, shoved them into her bag, and walked to the corner, where Liam sat outside, looking impossibly gorgeous as he sipped his beer and flirted idly in fluent French with two women at a nearby table.

The sight unnerved her. The women were chic and one was quite beautiful—and he clearly had them enthralled. She felt sick, and all her defenses came up. "Still okay if I join you?" she asked.

He lifted an eyebrow. "A silly—and loaded—question."

She lifted a shoulder, then let it drop.

"Avy, darling." He sounded a little exasperated. "Sit down. We have a *pissaliadiere* coming as a snack—an onion-and-olive tart. Niçoise pizza. And here's our waitress with a sauvignon blanc for you."

She sat, settling her bags on the ground at her feet.

"Cheers," he said, lifting his glass.

"Cheers." She lifted hers and clinked it against his.

"Now. Why would you be asking me loaded questions, tinged with jealousy, if you think I'm as despicable as you say?"

"Jealousy?" She exhaled dismissively through her nose and took a sip of the light, fragrant wine. "Don't be ridiculous."

"Would you rather that I called it insecurity? Is that more palatable? You say you adore your father, but he's clearly left some scars, *ma cherie.*"

She focused on the Italianate facade of a church on the corner. "Liam, if you want to have a prayer of seeing what's in the bag, you'll gracefully switch the subject. *Tu comprends?*"

"*Oui,*" he said immediately. "So, did you know that Nice was an Italian city until 1860? It was known as Nizza.

Actually, it was founded by the Greeks but then colonized by the Romans."

"Nizza, like pizza?" She smiled.

He nodded, eyeing the lingerie shop's pale blue paper sack with gold lettering. He rubbed at his chin. "So . . . what *is* in the bag?"

"I told you. It's a surprise."

"Give me a hint, at least."

She sipped at her wine. "For a man who seemed so partial to a—how should I phrase this?—knickerless chick, you certainly are interested in what I bought."

"Knickerless chick," he repeated. The sin grin made an appearance. "I like that. But do give me a hint. Is the item black? White? Red?"

"Shades of gray," she said wryly. "You know, so you can see all of my dimensions in space."

He threw back his head and laughed. "Be nice, or I shan't share the *pissaladiere* with you."

"I thought we established on the night I broke into your home that I'm not at all nice. You stripped me of the title Magnolia Blossom."

He poked his tongue into his cheek. "That's not all I stripped."

Avy concentrated on looking cool and collected, though the memories of that particular night raised her temperature a good ten degrees.

His glance was knowing and unsettling. "You wild-riding strumpet," he teased.

"I wouldn't have—"

She was interrupted by their server, who placed the hot, fragrant *pissaladiere* in front of them and asked if they needed anything else.

Liam ordered them another round. Once she'd gone, he

said, "You see? I had to make sure to get a waitress and not a waiter with you around, you insatiable sl—"

"Liam! First of all, let's set the record straight. You did . . . that . . . on purpose that night so that I wouldn't see the damned sword."

"I did what?"

"You know what. *That.*"

"Avy, darling, you're a big girl. You can say it."

She knew her face had to be blazing. "No."

"Come, now." His eyes danced wickedly. "Surely you're not ashamed to verbalize what we did."

"Stop it. You manipulated me in order to stop me from looking up."

"Yes, I certainly did manipulate you, darling. And you enjoyed it. Twice, I believe."

Forget blazing—her face had surely immolated by now, dissolved into nothing but hot ash.

"Is the shame making you hot all over again, sweetheart?" he asked in a low voice.

"Liam, *stop.*"

"Does blaming it on me make it more acceptable that you loved having my face between your thighs? The big, bad wolf took advantage, so you couldn't help yourself?"

Damn him and his perceptions. There she sat, furious and resentful and mortified—and impossibly turned on.

"I truly, *truly* hate your guts right now."

Liam leaned forward. "Mmmm. But I'll bet you're wet."

Her mouth dropped open.

He winked and placed a slice of the *pissaladiere* on her plate while she sat there smoldering, trying to figure out how she felt about this loathsome man. Part of her itched to slap him into next year. The other part wanted to drag him off to her hotel room.

"Go on, love. Have some warm tart. I know for a fact that it's delicious." He grinned and took a big, messy bite.

Warm tart? The bastard. She averted her gaze and drained the rest of her sauvignon blanc in one swallow. She glowered at him.

"Mmmmmmmm," said Liam. "God, this is good. Avy, you have to try it—I was only funning you. You're so easy to rile, darling."

It did smell heavenly. Avy picked up the slice he'd put on her plate and bit into it. *Good* didn't even begin to describe it. She'd died and gone to heaven—just, inexplicably, with the devil incarnate.

"I thought maybe we'd visit the Chagall Museum and the Matisse Museum next," Liam suggested. "Then maybe a nap before a late-ish dinner?" He waggled his brows evilly.

Though she'd love to go look at art, at some point she had to get away from the man and find the villa she was breaking into later. The Nerd Corps had sent her the schematics, but she wanted to see the place in daylight before she tackled the job. She also needed to find out just where in the damned house the Sword of Alexander was.

"You know, I don't recall promising to spend all day with you," she said. "If you want to case museums you can do it on your own. I'm going to the beach."

He looked offended, which didn't bother her in the least after the things he'd said to her. "I wasn't going to case them; I simply thought you'd enjoy seeing the paintings."

"Sweet of you to offer, but no."

"Very well then, we'll go to the beach."

"Liam, I don't know how to say this without being rude, but I need some time alone. It's been a lovely afternoon; it really has. But—"

"Avy." He took her hands and squeezed them. "Look, it's

not as if I don't know why you're here. But please don't go anywhere near Gautreau's estate. Please." His eyes were serious and had changed back to gray. "I'm begging you. It isn't safe."

"I don't know what you're talking about."

"Let's do away with the pretense, shall we? Listen to me, Avy. He has excellent security, and he himself will shoot to kill. You have no idea who this man is or what's at stake."

She'd never heard Liam sound so urgent. There was nothing wry in the set of his lips, no twinkle in his eyes. "Promise me," he said. "Avy, please."

She met his gaze steadily and said absolutely nothing.

His mouth twisted and he withdrew his hands.

"Where would you like to go to dinner, Liam?" she asked, picking up her wineglass. "Or would you rather stay in . . . and order room service?"

chapter 25

By the third day at the Ritz, Gwen and Pigamuffin had become friends. They were playing fetch with a tangerine when Avy returned her call.

"Congratulations, Gwennie—you're no longer a virgin!"

"Thanks."

"I knew you could do it! Didn't I tell you that you could pull it off?"

"Yes. So where are you?"

"I've been shopping half the day. In Nice."

"Shopping? In Nice?"

"For French lingerie."

"Do you have any idea how unfair this is? I'm stuck in my hotel room with a fleabag dog while you stroll through a resort town looking at teddies?"

Avy laughed.

"Wait, why are you in France, and why are you buying lingerie?"

"I had to leave London very suddenly, and my luggage is still there at the Savoy." Avy's tone was a little too glib.

"Wait, something's going on. South of France, lingerie . . . Are you *sleeping* with that thief? Liam James?"

Avy faked static on the line. "You're breaking up, Gwen."

"That's the worst 'static' I've ever heard! I am not breaking up. I thought you said you'd never cross certain lines while making a recovery. You said—"

"Um, yeah. It's complicated."

"What does *that* mean?"

"I'm not sure. I can't explain it."

"Oh, no. Avy, are you falling for this guy?"

"Of course not. I'm not an idiot. So, have you returned the dog?"

"No, but I'll do it tonight, if I can. Security at Sid's palazzo has been a nightmare, but I think they're easing up a little now, since everything's been quiet."

"Damn. I was hoping you could get over here to help me handle some surveillance."

"I could be there by tomorrow."

"Hmmm. That could still be helpful. I want to complete the job tonight, so I might need to give you a certain something and have you disappear with it. But if that's not necessary, we can travel back to Miami together."

"All right," Gwen said. "So tell me," she teased, "does Liam James wear black leather gloves in bed?"

"Good-*bye*, Gwennie. Break a leg tonight." And Avy hung up, leaving Gwen curious and concerned. What was Avy doing? This was completely uncharacteristic of her.

It was late when Gwen coaxed Pigamuffin back into the special carrier and left the Ritz unobtrusively through a side door.

Break a leg, huh? Thanks. Gwen started up the Vespa and, in the light from a streetlamp, looked at her orange-highlighted route again, this time committing it to memory.

She reached back and patted the Pigster. "You're going home now, boy. Nice getting to know you." The dog just hung heavy from her shoulders, like four-legged guilt.

Much as she'd gotten to like him over the past few days, she had to return him. She sped off, her stomach turning flips already.

Once she'd parked and walked around to the back of the property, Gwen saw with dismay that at least thirty armed guards still patrolled Sid's palazzo. She checked her watch. If she'd had more time she could have watched them until she spotted any weaknesses in the patrol—or at least taken advantage when the shift ended and a new group took over.

But she didn't have the time. Kelso had given her exactly seventy-two hours to pull off the entire stunt, and that meant that Pigamuffin had to be back in Sid's possession by two thirty a.m.

Right now her watch said 12:11 a.m. She didn't dare try to return the dog until most of the household was asleep, and Sid, drat him, was consuming the second of two bottles of wine while sprawled in his pajamas in a lawn chair outside.

Gwen settled in to wait.

He complained loudly to various staff in a voice that got more and more slurred, until finally he passed out. A maid tried unsuccessfully to wake him and put him to bed, but he just gave a mighty snore and rolled over. So she threw a blanket over him, turned out the lights, and went up to her room. Gwen wondered where Sid's wife was, and prayed fervently that he wasn't going to sleep there all night. But it appeared that he was.

Pigamuffin wriggled against her back and emitted a series of small grunts and whines. "Shhhh!" said Gwen. Repossessing stolen art would be infinitely easier . . . one, because she didn't have to put it back, for God's sake. And two, because art didn't make noise or try to escape.

The Pigster kept wiggling. She was tempted just to drop him over the high stone wall and be done with it, but she was supposed to put him back exactly where she'd found him. Which meant in Sid's bed, next to Sid's wife. *Ugh.* Why couldn't she have passed out in a lawn chair next to him?

Gwen waited and waited, cramps forming in her shoulders and neck. Then the break she'd been looking for finally came. One of the guards said something to his comrades and then headed to a corner of the grounds. He found a spot with a bit of privacy and lowered his zipper to find relief.

She stole silently around a hedge and a marble statue, drawing her gun. In one clean movement she had it cocked and pressed to the back of his head. "Don't make a sound," she ordered. "Don't move."

The poor man stood there with his hand wrapped around his johnson and did what he was told.

"Take off your pants," she said. "Your shorts, too."

When he hesitated, she increased her pressure on his skull. "Do it." The pants hit the ground. "Shoes and socks, now."

Finally she told him to take off his uniform shirt. When he stood nude she picked up his shorts. "Sorry, big guy, but you'll need to stuff these in your mouth."

His eyes widened.

"Eat 'em!" Gwen was ready with duct tape, and once the shorts were mostly in his mouth, she wrapped it around his head a couple of times to seal them in.

"Now, hands behind your back." She duct-taped those, too, and then his ankles, moving as quickly as she could. And finally she taped him to the marble statue and patted him on the cheek. "It won't be for long, 'kay?"

Then Gwen pulled his uniform over her own clothing, stuffed Pigamuffin inside it, and donned his shoes. He was a smallish man, thank God, so she could still walk in them.

She strolled casually to the house and waved to the guard nearest to her. He waved back.

As soon as his attention was focused elsewhere, she made for a powder room window on the ground floor that she'd spotted when she'd studied the schematics, banking on the probability that Sid couldn't have had his alarm system fixed since her first break-in. If they'd been in Germany, maybe—but it just wasn't going to happen in Italy.

She cut a small hole in the glass, and then reached inside and undid the latch. She raised the window and slipped inside. Whew—that had gone suspiciously smoothly. Almost too smoothly . . .

She listened for a few seconds, on alert for any strange noises, but heard nothing. So she crept out of the bathroom and up the stairs, once again heading for Sid's palatial bedroom.

Gwen pulled Pigamuffin out of the guard's shirt and slowly turned the knob. She was almost home free—a quick check of her watch told her it was 1:58 a.m. She stepped inside the dark room, only to hear a most unwelcome series of sounds.

"Oh, yeah, baby. Harder . . . harder . . ."

Fortunately it was very dark in the room, but Gwen could still see a tall, skinny, naked man, his butt moving rhythmically. On either side of him were the soles of two female feet.

Gwen froze, trying to keep a grip on the now-frantic Pigamuffin, who probably thought that the bobbing butt belonged to Sid, his lord and master. But Sid, as she well knew, was passed out in the lawn chair outside.

"God, yessss!" moaned the owner of the feet, as Gwen stood as rigid as the statue to which she'd tied the guard. What to do?!

Then the door opened behind her and Sid shambled in. It

took him a moment to register what was happening. Then the lights came blazing on.

"Get off my effin' wife!" bellowed Sid, wild-eyed. "I'll bloody kill you!" And he dove onto the bed.

Shrieks and curses and howls bounced off the walls as Gwen made a snap decision and tossed Pigamuffin after Sid. In a voice as gruff as she could make it, and in a terrible Italian accent, she shouted, "We find-a your dog, sir!"

"Pigamuffin!" Sid stopped beating the skinny man to a pulp and embraced his weird, wrinkled dog. "Oh, Pigamuffin, you're back!"

Hyperventilating, Gwen backed out the door and almost threw herself down the stairs, since she was unable to move very fast in the guard's big shoes. She reached the bathroom, locked the door behind her, and scrambled out the window. Then she slid the shoes off and sprinted hell-for-leather back to the hapless Italian guard.

"You're a hero," she gasped, throwing off his uniform and tossing his shoes down. She cut the tape at his ankles and wrists and placed her small knife in his right hand. "As soon as I'm over that wall, buddy, you can untape your face and spit out your shorts. Then I'd advise you to get dressed really freakin' fast and go claim the reward for the return of Sid's dog, which you just tossed onto his bed. Make up any story you want about how you found Pigamuffin. This is my way of apologizing for the discomfort you've been in."

She hauled herself to the top of the stone wall and looked down at him. "But remember: You never saw me. If you set the rest of the guards on me and they haul me in, I will tell everyone the naked story—and I'll also say you're endowed like a jelly bean. *Capisce?*"

He nodded. Gwen jumped down and ran.

chapter 26

Liam wouldn't be able to tail Avy without her instantly making him. She would highly resent being bound, gagged, and locked in a closet. And he couldn't kill her, because he was in love with her.

So he decided to drive her himself to Gautreau's. It was the only way he could keep an eye on her, after all. He'd let her case the joint and make her plans. Then he'd take her to dinner, make mad, passionate love to her . . . and what? Knock her over the head?

He came to the reluctant conclusion that a couple of sleeping tablets popped into her wine were the only way to go. He truly hated to do it, but if the alternative was her probable death, then he had no choice.

"All right," he said to Avy as they waited for the check at the café. "You're not going to promise me anything at all, because you fully intend to ditch me as soon as we're done here and go and do your job. So let me present you with another option."

Avy's hazel eyes glinted as she finished her wine. "I can't wait to hear this one, Liam."

"I know where Gautreau lives. I've been in his home. And I have a rental car, love. You don't."

"No, but I can rent a bicycle."

"It's five or six miles to Cap Ferrat. You won't get there before dusk."

"Liam, this is not a couples outing. Got it?"

He went for the clincher. "Avy, darling, I can get you inside the house. I can give you Gautreau's own hand to shake. He'll even offer you a sherry. Now, will you reconsider?"

Avy took the check before it hit the table, startling their waitress. "When can we leave?"

"Now." Liam snatched the bill right out of her hand. He folded a banknote inside it and slid it under his empty glass. "The only equipment you need," he said, taking her arm, "is a push-up bra and a sweet Dixie giggle."

Avy rolled her eyes. "Oh, wonderful. He's one of those lecherous old men. . . ."

Liam shook his head. "Not at all. Gautreau is in his late thirties and celibate. But he knows that I"—he dropped a kiss on her mouth before she could dodge—"am not."

"Celibate? Who in this day and age is celibate? Is he a monk?"

"He's not a monk. He's just solitary."

"What else can you tell me about him?"

"He's well educated, knowledgeable about art, and deceptively friendly. He's the sort of man, Avy, who would scratch a cat behind the ears before breaking its neck. Are we clear?"

She shivered.

There were other things he could not tell her, such as the fact that Gautreau was of Middle Eastern descent, through his mother. That he hated the West and what he perceived as its hedonism and corruption. And that he had been very specific in his request that Liam steal a particular weapon, the Sword of Alexander. He'd paid well—almost too well.

Liam was still trying to figure out why he would want a

sword that ultimately was the symbol of Western domination over Eastern territory. Alexander, a Greek, had defeated the Persians with this very sword, driven them out of their own land.

"Why would you knowingly work with a man like that?" Avy asked quietly. He didn't care for the way she looked at him, as if he were some revolting species of insect.

Because despite the fun I have with Agent Bunker, I have come to believe in this operation and I want to bring him down. But he couldn't say it. "Avy, his money's as good as anyone's. Just because I take his cash doesn't mean I like him."

"And besides," she added in expressionless tones, "if you didn't take it, he'd just commission another thief to steal priceless objects, right? So where's the harm?"

He sucked in a breath as he saw the blazing contempt in her eyes.

"Shades of gray, right, Liam?"

He was left with nothing to say, an unusual and unwelcome experience for him. He couldn't defend himself and look all right to her without giving away the whole operation. *God damn it.*

They'd reached the hotel, and Liam gave his valet ticket to a parking attendant, who scurried off to fetch the car. He and Avy stood together in stony silence.

"I won't be working with him again," Liam said at last. "This is the final time."

"And I'm sure you'll tell me next that you only recently found out what sort of man Gautreau is."

"I'll say that because it's true. And don't take that pristine, snotty tone with me, darling—as if you're pure as the driven snow. You steal just like I steal, on request and for a commission."

The valet drove up then with the Mercedes sedan he'd

rented, and Liam opened the passenger-side door for her. "Get in."

"I think I'd rather bike there." But she looked at her watch and then got into the car, dropping the lingerie bag and her purse at her feet.

Liam closed the door on her, none too gently, and walked around to the driver's side. He tipped the attendant, slid behind the wheel, and they were off.

Outside of picturesque Nice, with its peach buildings and red tiled roofs, the countryside was beautiful, stretching lazy and idyllic in the sun. They passed small vineyards and fields of lavender bathed in the golden light of Provence.

Cap Ferrat itself was a wooded peninsula full of spectacular luxury homes, such as the Villa Kerylos and the Villa Ephrussi de Rothschild. Somerset Maugham had once lived there.

Liam enjoyed the pleasure on Avy's face as they drove into Beaulieu, where the cape joined the mainland, and promptly forgot his irritation with her. He wished that he had more time to show her the sights, but the sun was close to setting over the harbor.

He changed the SIM card in his phone as they went around a bend, and he rang Gautreau's house. It was terribly informal for him to call and say that they were already there, but Gautreau would just have to get over it. If he was home he'd invite them in. And if not, they'd have a look-see around the property for themselves.

Gautreau was at home, no doubt looking forward to the next morning's sale. "Yes, of course, come in for a drink with your lady friend, *mon ami*," he told Liam.

Avy sat stiffly as they drove to Gautreau's villa, which was situated midway up the cliff overlooking the port. It was built of mellow old stone with the standard Mediterranean red tile roof, and a heavy set of dark wood doors marked the entrance. "I won't be a bimbo; I'll be a brash interior designer. It'll give me an excuse to be fascinated with the house. All right?"

Liam shrugged.

A young manservant opened the doors and politely invited Avy and Liam inside, escorting them over cool tile floors through a formal living room to a covered porch overlooking the water below.

Gautreau was of average height and build, probably in his late thirties, his most remarkable characteristic a very high forehead. He wore dark trousers and an exquisite white cotton shirt.

He didn't look at all like the type of person who would break a cat's neck—he looked like anyone Avy might see in the local grocery store or in the bank. Clean-cut. Normal. Pleasant. Boring.

Liam made the introductions, and she shook hands with Gautreau, who, though he was cordial, did not offer her the use of his first name.

Avy looked around appreciatively. "What a stunning place you have here, Mr. Gautreau! It's like something out of a *magazine*."

He turned dark, enigmatic eyes on her. "Thank you," he said. Was it her imagination or did his lip curl slightly? "May I offer you two something to drink? Sherry, perhaps, mademoiselle? Scotch, Liam?"

"Scotch, rocks would hit the spot, thank you."

"Do you know, wine makes me awfully sleepy," Avy claimed. "I don't suppose you'd have any Diet Coke?"

Gautreau's nostrils flared slightly, the only sign that he despised her request for the American chemical concoction. "I'm afraid not. Perhaps a Perrier? *Un café?*"

"Perrier would be fine, thank you." She smiled. He did not. He gestured at the manservant who'd shown them out to the terrace, who nodded and disappeared.

"Please sit down. What brings you to Cap Ferrat, Liam?"

"Oh, this and that," Liam said easily, making himself at home on a wrought-iron settee. "Checking to make sure a couple of deliveries came through as scheduled. You simply can't always rely on the courier services, can you?" He carefully did not look at Avy, who sat next to him.

Gautreau nodded. "I received your delivery. Everything was in order."

"Are you in the perfume business, too, Mr. Gautreau?" Avy inquired. "Liam says he comes often to Grasse, nearby, because of his work."

Their host exchanged a glance with Liam and said smoothly, "Yes, Grasse has been the capital of the world's perfume industry since the sixteenth century. But no, I'm not in the business. Monsieur James merely sent me a few bottles of scent for family members. It was very kind of him."

Avy fiddled with her Dior bag and then stared vacantly out at the ocean. "Pretty," she murmured. "Look at all the boats." She accepted her Perrier from the manservant, asking, "And what's your name, hon?"

He was clearly taken aback. "Jean-Paul, mademoiselle."

"I'm Ava. Named after Ava Gardner, you know."

"Enchante de faire votre connaissance."

"Uh, me too." She laughed.

He exchanged a glance with his employer and left the room.

Liam and Gautreau had begun to discuss various football matches. That ought to keep them going for a while. "I think it's so funny how y'all call soccer football. Do you have a bathroom I could use, Mr. Gautreau? A WC?"

He got up as if to lead her to it, but she waved a hand at him. "Just tell me, and I'll find the way. I'd sure love to look around at your house while you men talk sports. I'm an interior decorator, you know. Maybe I can get some inspiration."

He gave her a frosty look, clearly unimpressed by Liam's choice of female companionship. "I would be honored to give you a personal tour."

"Oh, no, no. I wouldn't want to trouble you. I'm sure you and Liam have lots of catching up to do, if you're old friends. But you don't mind me taking a peek, now, do you?"

"Be my guest," he said stiffly. "Jean-Paul is available should you have any questions."

"Great, thanks." She ignored Liam's raised eyebrow, which perhaps was an indication that he thought she was taking things too far.

"Apologies, old chap," he murmured to Gautreau as she stepped inside. "She gets a bit enthusiastic over things." Irritated that Liam was apologizing for her, she pretended not to hear, and stepped inside.

The villa's walls were plaster, painted a cool white that made it seem even larger than it was. A journey down one hallway led her to the kitchen, which gleamed with stainless-steel appliances and hanging pots and pans. The windows were open to the ocean breeze, which mixed with the smells of lamb roasting, garlic, and fresh rosemary. Jean-Paul knelt in front of the refrigerator, digging for something in the vegetable crisper.

Avy backed out soundlessly and retreated. The next room she came to was the dining room, which boasted a long mahogany table and twelve chairs. A disturbing tapestry hung on the wall above an antique sideboard. Woven into it were images of army tanks and submachine guns, no less threatening because they were geometric and two-dimensional.

From a crash course at Sotheby's she knew that the rug under the table and chairs was a long, narrow Karadja, a Persian rug from Azerbaijan in rich, saturated scarlets and blues.

Avy found three rather Spartan bedrooms and another with a massive carved walnut bed that had to be the master. Unfortunately Gautreau had not left the Sword of Alexander conveniently dangling over it for her to find. It was very inconsiderate of him.

She quickly searched a media room before she found the breathtaking library, which had floor-to-ceiling shelves full of leather-bound volumes. It smelled pleasantly musty, of old paper and ink and scholarship.

But what caught her eye was a big rolltop desk in the far corner. On it was a white cotton cloth, the same one she'd seen in Liam's living room in London. And resting casually on the cloth was the Sword of Alexander.

She'd been running on a small charge of adrenaline since they'd arrived, but now it flooded her system. She was right here. It was right there. She could take it and run.

But Liam had the keys to the rented Mercedes in his pocket, and Gautreau's own car was nowhere to be seen. As she hesitated, her window of opportunity slammed shut.

"Looking for a good book?" Gautreau asked from behind her.

"Oh, my gawd," Avy said without flinching. "Have you actually read all these? You must be awfully smart." She turned to face him with one of her brightest, most charming Southern smiles. "I have tons of books too—sample books." She laughed but he didn't. "You know, full of fabric and wallpaper swatches."

"I've read most of the volumes here, though not all."

Gautreau no longer looked ordinary, even though his face was expressionless. His eyes seemed to have darkened ten shades, and his bearing had shifted subtly from casual and elegant to menacing and military. If she ever saw this version of the man in the grocery store, she'd run.

He's the sort of man, Avy, who would scratch a cat behind the ears before breaking its neck. . . .

"I don't think I've ever seen so many books outside a public library," she jabbered, hitching the Dior bag up on her shoulder. "And it's so attractive that they all match."

"Did you find the WC, mademoiselle?"

"Yes, I did, thank you. I just couldn't resist having a look around, like I told you. You've got some real interesting things around here, Mr. Gautreau. Tell me about that round shield in the foyer—was that ever used in an actual battle?"

He placed his hand under her elbow and steered her out of the library, closing the door. Though his touch was gentle, she had the uncanny sense that it was costing him dearly to keep it that way. She forced herself not to shudder and kept prattling.

They ran into Liam in the hall. "There you are, love. We didn't know where you'd run off to, and Jean-Paul hadn't an inkling either." He looked at his watch. "If we're going to have time to bathe and dress for dinner, we'd best be going."

"You'd best," agreed Gautreau, his black eyes glittering as he politely saw them to the door.

The hairs at the nape of Avy's neck stood up. He was one man she didn't want to run into in the dark.

chapter 27

"It's in his library, Liam. The Sword of Alexander is right there on the damned desk." Avy spoke urgently as they drove away.

He didn't seem to be paying attention to her. He seemed lost in his own thoughts, grim ones.

"Liam, did you hear me? He's got it in the house."

"Of course he does. Whidby delivered it to him in person. Did you think Gautreau would bend it in half and stick it in a safety-deposit box at his bank?"

"Could we dispense with the sarcasm?"

"You were bloody stupid to be that obvious about searching the house," Liam snapped.

"Oh, it would have been better just to pretend I got lost looking for the bathroom? The villa isn't that big."

"I should never have taken you there. If he comes after you now, it's my fault."

She suddenly understood that he was worried about her, which was sweet. "He thinks I'm dumber than half a brick. He doesn't suspect a thing."

"I wouldn't be so sure about that." Liam took a turn too fast, savagely wrenching the wheel.

Avy stomped on the nonexistent brake on her side and braced herself against the door handle.

"You're right that he's one creepy guy," she admitted. "He hated me on sight, but I got the feeling before we left that he'd have happily pushed me off his cliffside terrace without a backward glance."

"Gautreau doesn't particularly care for women, especially stupid ones with no manners who snoop through his house."

"Oh, you're just mad because my behavior reflected poorly on your taste in women." She smirked.

"I have excellent taste in women," said Liam, "when your head is screwed on straight."

She put a hand on his knee. "Do we have to spend the rest of the evening snapping at each other? Come on. It's so beautiful here. Let's enjoy it. I don't know about you, but I probably won't be back here for a long time."

"That surprises me, since the region is rich in art and museums."

"Exactly." She nodded. "The things get stolen from here, but they're delivered somewhere else. I have to go and get them from wherever they end up."

The coastal road back to Nice had quite a bit of traffic on it, and they crawled along in silence for a while. Avy mentally prepared for her return after midnight.

There was no direct access to the library from a window, so she had two options: She could either get to it from the terrace doors, which was risky in terms of being seen, or she could climb into the villa from a small window at the end of the upstairs hallway. To do that she'd have to lower herself from the roof or climb up using a rope.

She didn't particularly like either option. She could be easily spotted on the roof from any house above Gautreau's on the cliff. Granted, she didn't plan on staying there long, but still . . .

The only other possibility involved the swift seduction

of Jean-Paul, but she had a hunch that he batted for the other team, so that was out.

Liam finally got them back to Nice, and they turned over the car to the parking attendants once again.

"Thank you for taking me to Gautreau's," Avy told him. "I know you're worried, but it will all be fine."

Liam had made reservations for dinner downstairs at Le Padouk, the Palais de la Mediterranée's elegant restaurant, named for the rare African wood that lined its walls.

He was pleased that she wore the white dress he'd bought her, along with the high-heeled sandals and whatever she'd had hidden in that blue bag with the gold lettering. His imagination ran amok, and rather than risk embarrassing himself in front of the crème de la Côte d'Azur, he diverted his attention instead to the way the white silk off-the-shoulder dress dipped, low and inviting, across the tops of her breasts. There was only the barest hint of cleavage, but Avy didn't need to be obvious to be alluring.

The dress fit her perfectly, molding to her curves without revealing anything it shouldn't. She looked, tonight, the very image of an Ava Brigitte. Fitting, since both Ava Gardner and Brigitte Bardot had undoubtedly graced the old Palais casino in their time, and draped their smoldering sensuality over the arms of dazzled men at the roulette tables.

Tonight Avy had done something different with her hair, and it flowed in full, rich waves down her back, pinned up on one side to leave her neck exposed. Liam had never been given to vampire tendencies before now, but her neck looked so long and graceful, even erotic in the dim light as she turned her head to say something to the waiter.

He wanted her, and though he knew instinctively that

he'd have her tonight, he wanted her for keeps. He'd like to see that smile every morning for the rest of his life and feel those lips on his. How in the hell had he gotten himself into this impossible situation?

For when he drugged her later, as he must, he'd have to kiss her good-bye. Avy was stubborn, independent, and straight-shooting. She wouldn't take kindly to his cutting her legs out from under her—and doing it in such an underhanded way.

But what was the alternative? Letting her risk her life, going by herself to repossess the sword from Gautreau? Even if she got out of there alive with it, she'd have overturned the whole sting operation. Hundreds of thousands of dollars of U.S. taxpayer funds would become Monopoly money. Tens of thousands of man-hours would circle the drain. And most important, Gautreau wouldn't be stopped.

Millions of lives depended on his not getting the money from the sale of that sword. Because Gautreau would take that $11.3 million, launder it, and funnel it straight to Al Qaeda. He'd been doing it for years, unnoticed. How much dirty money did it take to buy a dirty bomb?

Liam couldn't say. He just knew that after decades of devoted self-indulgence and caprice, he himself owed a huge debt to society. For the first time in his life he'd put the needs of other people ahead of his own.

He just hoped, when he got his honor out of layaway, that he'd have the chance to gift-wrap it and give it to Avy Hunt. *Not looking good, old boy. Not looking good at all.*

"Penny for your thoughts," Avy said, gazing at him from across the table.

"Now, where have I heard that before? I think they're worth at least a pound." He smiled.

She opened her evening bag and took out a fifty-pound note, which she pushed across the table at him.

He raised his eyebrows. "The stakes have gone up considerably since we last did this on my living room floor."

"Yes, they have."

"My thoughts are of that much value to you?"

She nodded.

"I'm flattered, but you could always steal them."

"That's your area of expertise, Liam. Remember?"

He pushed the banknote back across the table. "How would it be if I simply shared my thoughts with you? Hmmm? Isn't that more romantic?"

A hint of wariness appeared in her expertly made-up eyes. She left the fifty pounds on the table.

"Avy, are there any circumstances under which you'd fall in love with a thief?"

She swallowed and said nothing.

"Say, if the thief in question were to declare himself quite desperately in love with you?"

"Liam . . ." she pleaded. "Don't."

"Don't what, Avy?"

"Don't ruin things. Let's just have a wonderful evening together, okay?"

"So feelings ruin things, love?"

She shifted uncomfortably in her chair, visibly relieved when the waiter brought their glasses of wine. She raised hers to her lips, but he noticed that she didn't actually drink. She hadn't had a drop of alcohol since they'd left the little café to drive to Cap Ferrat.

Neither had he. He'd poured most of his Scotch by degrees into a plant on Gautreau's terrace, and let the ice melt in the rest.

"Developing feelings for a thief must be rather confusing if one has been brought up to believe in truth and justice," Liam continued when the waiter had deposited an olive tapenade and a colorful bruschetta onto their table.

"I wouldn't know," Avy said, her voice flat.

"Of course not. I was speaking hypothetically." He held out the platter of bruschetta to her and, after she took one of the baked bread rounds, helped himself. "Conversely, it must be rather disturbing to the thief to fall for someone whose moral code frowns upon his career. He might even contemplate retiring so that a lady could look at him through different eyes."

She stopped cold in the act of biting into her bruschetta. "He might?"

Liam nodded and scooped some of the tapenade onto a bit of fresh, crusty French bread. The salty blend of capers, olives, and anchovies brought a blissful smile to his face. "Hypothetically speaking."

"Do you think that the thief's fundamental character would change, though?" Avy asked and, seeming to forget she wasn't drinking, took a sip of her wine.

"I think his entire philosophical fundament would change, along with the source of his funds."

Avy groaned.

"I'm not at all sure about his character, however. For example, he's always going to be irreverent and quite possibly annoying. He'll always be proudly English—'God Save the Queen' and all that. He'll never use those flat American A's."

Her lips twitched, and he longed to pull her across the table so that he could kiss them, but he'd doubtless ruin the floral arrangement and the candles might set her dress on fire. So much for that particular romantic gesture.

However, he had another up his sleeve. "Avy, darling. You look impossibly beautiful this evening, but there's something missing." He reached into his jacket for the box he'd tucked into the inside pocket.

Her surreptitious smile froze and then faded into an expression of what he could only describe as horror. *Good God, she thinks I'm going to propose. And that's her reaction?*

Liam set the box on the table and watched her relax visibly as she took in its long, narrow dimensions. Not a ring box. He pushed it toward her. "Open it."

She used her dinner knife to efficiently slit the tape and then placed the utensil next to her plate again before unwrapping the delicate floral paper. Then she lifted the box's lid. "Oh, Liam. It's stunning."

She didn't ask if he'd stolen it—how kind of her.

The necklace was of rose coral and freshwater pearls, and he'd bought the matching earrings as well. She took out her simple gold ones and replaced them with his. Then she held the necklace up to her throat and tried to fasten it. Her hands shook.

Liam noted that with interest as he got out of his chair and went to stand behind her. He moved her hair aside and clasped the piece around her neck, resting his hands there a little longer than necessary.

Then he sat back down and just looked at her in silence for a long moment. The coral brought out the rosy undertones of her skin, and the pearls glowed softly against it. She was a woman who didn't need the hard glitter of diamonds to lend her mystique.

"Thank you," she said.

"You're gorgeous. Like a Renoir portrait, minus thirty pounds or so."

Avy colored. "I like his women. They look much happier at their weight than some of the self-deprived, malnourished swizzle sticks I see walking around on South Beach in Miami."

He laughed. "You're quite slim yourself. Are you one of those, er, swizzle sticks?"

"What? No. I work out because I have to be fit in this job. And I eat a lot more vegetables than I'd like to, but I also have a big, fat chocolate milkshake every weekend, which is probably one of the reasons I'm a size eight instead of a size four. It keeps me from killing anyone."

"You think the South Beach beauties are homicidal?"

She grinned. "More dangerous than sharks. And all for lack of a little ice cream."

They dined on salade niçoise and chicken stuffed with foie gras and mushrooms; fresh-caught sea bass and ratatouille; after-dinner cheeses; and finally lovely little profiteroles and tiny portions of chocolate mousse.

It was one of the best meals of Liam's life, made even more delicious by the scintillating and problematic woman opposite him. He knew that she wanted him, but for how long?

The minutes ticked by on his watch as the time crept toward eleven. He could have dropped the sleeping pill into her espresso when she got up to powder her nose. But selfish or not, he had to have one last night with her before the inevitable explosion tomorrow morning.

She returned to the table from the far side of the room, and he couldn't take his eyes off her: the proud, honest set of her shoulders and the lithe way she walked, the subtle sway of her hips unconsciously provocative.

His thoughts went back to the blue bag, and once again he began to speculate, randy bastard that he was. She couldn't possibly be wearing any kind of brassiere under that dress. It dipped too low, both in front and in back.

There would be no slip—the dress was lined, as he recalled. Which meant that the only thing Avy Hunt had on under it was a tiny whisper of fabric.

Unlike Americans, the French were not known to be speedy about bringing the check after one's meal. Liam usually appreciated the fact that they'd taken both gastronomy and leisure to the level of art forms. Tonight, however, he highly resented it.

As Avy sat down her bare leg brushed against his and he almost came out of his skin.

"What's the matter, Liam?" she asked, her fingers toying with the coral-and-pearl necklace.

Indigo blue balls. "Nothing at all. I'm just thinking about the contents of that bag again. I don't suppose you'd tell me what was in there?"

She shook her head and shot him a smile far more wicked than the Mona Lisa's had ever thought about being. Under the table her sandaled foot slid up to press lightly against his crotch. "Absolutely not. But I'll show you."

God help him. Where was the bloody check?

chapter 28

Once they made it to Liam's room, they stood for a moment in the dark, mesmerized by the view of Nice's glittering coastline at night.

Then he took her by the shoulders and leaned his forehead against hers, inhaling the sweet scent of her hair. "Avy, darling. Don't do it. Don't go back to Gautreau's."

She opened her mouth to lie to him, deny that she would, when he stole the words from her lips. He started there, and then took over her whole body. He stroked his fingers through her hair, sending tingles from her scalp to her spine and then down to her toes.

She felt the tenderness in his touch as he caressed her nape, lifted her hair to kiss every inch of her shoulders, turned her to brush his lips over the skin of her back. He slipped off her clothes and licked his way down her spine, kneeling beside her.

It was the tenderness that got to her. The care that he took to respond to each of her responses. He listened to her body and communicated with it.

His hands were warm and possessive on her breasts, lifting them, coddling them, suckling each of them until she thought she might liquefy or pass out from pleasure.

Liam stroked her like a cat, and she arched her back

under his touch, rubbing her belly against the hard stubble of his jaw, enjoying the scrape and the burn of it. He held her by the waist as she dropped her head back and looked at the lights of Nice upside down.

His hands moved down over her bare bottom, and he braced an arm behind it before lifting her right knee and settling it over his shoulder. Then she felt that same hard stubble abrading her inner thigh and the hot, taunting moisture of his breath enveloping her sex.

She hung there, suspended physically by his arms and held hostage to anticipation.

Liam blew gently, and she thought she might dissolve from wanting his touch there. A sound she didn't wish to recognize escaped her mouth, a whimper, and he answered it with a growl of satisfaction that told her how much he was enjoying his power. On some unconscious level this disturbed her, but her body simply didn't care. He'd stolen her competitive edge.

Then he tasted her, and the lights of Nice blurred as she trembled uncontrollably against him. He enjoyed her as he might a ripe peach, taking mouthfuls of her and savoring every one.

To her disbelief, he stopped just as she was on the brink of orgasm, and she moaned a soft protest as he brought her upright and looked into her eyes. "Not yet."

Liam rolled on a condom. He lifted her, and she wrapped her legs around him as he slipped inside her. He braced her back against the glass of the huge picture window—God, it was cold!—and drove home, his hands cupping her buttocks.

The cool glass, the wet heat between them, the sight and scent of him nude and utterly aroused by her—all of it maneuvered her into an almost unbearable tension. Liam slid out of her for a moment and took one of her breasts into his mouth, sending shocks of pleasure through her system. The tension ratcheted up even further as his lips and tongue abraded her nipple.

He drove back inside her, big and sure and sexy as hell, and she melted and exploded simultaneously. They came together in a crazy rush, suspended nine stories in the air over Nice.

Returning to reality was difficult. They stood in the dark panting, draped over each other, until Liam walked them over to the bed and sat. He rolled into the middle of the mattress, pulling her on top of him, and wrapped his arms around her. "I never want this to end, Avy."

"Neither do I," she whispered. His body was so warm and solid beneath hers, her flesh molding to his, his cock snugly tucked against her bottom.

"Let's just spend the night this way," he coaxed. "Making love in the dark over the Côte d'Azur."

"Mmmmm." She was so very tempted to fall asleep in his arms. After she scored the sword she might never see Liam again. Never feel him moving inside her again, intent on bringing her pleasure. Never hear his voice or smell his scent . . .

The thought upset her more than it should have.

Just one night, a voice inside her urged. *What's the harm? So you delay the recovery for a day. It's not like the sword will sprout legs and walk down the coast.*

But it could. And once a piece like that disappeared into a very rich person's top-secret private collection, it would be almost impossible to find.

She couldn't risk it. And she also couldn't risk developing feelings for the man underneath her, no matter how handsome and funny he was, no matter how skilled a lover. One day, inevitably, he'd make a mistake. And she refused to share her future with someone who'd wind up in a cell.

She lifted her arms and put her hands up to his face, tracing its contours. "Liam, what's the closest you've ever come to being caught?"

"Why?"

"Just curious."

"You shouldn't worry over such things." He caressed her belly and trailed his fingers up toward her breasts, covering them with his palms.

"You *should* be caught. But I don't want to see it happen."

"Why, thank you. I appreciate the sentiment." He sounded amused.

"You've been very lucky."

"Yes. And I've also been very good."

She rolled off of him and turned to face him. "That woman whose car you stole . . . did she never prosecute you?"

He went still.

"Liam?"

"No. No, she didn't. She was a bit tied up when I took off."

"Tied up as in the way I left you?"

He sighed. "No. She was in the middle of a horrible, messy argument. A row to end all rows. So you see, she didn't much care that I took her car. She was otherwise occupied."

"Who was she fighting with?"

"My father."

"You stole your father's girlfriend's car?"

"No. She was his wife." Liam's words were barely audible.

Avy tried to roll off of him so that she could see his face, but he held her where she was. "Liam?"

"I'll tell you the story," he said wearily. "But I don't

want to see the condemnation in your eyes." He sounded as if he were in physical pain.

Avy stayed still, with her back pressed to his chest, and let him talk.

"I was seventeen. I'd just returned home from school for the summer break, and my father had some big, mysterious announcement to make. He wasn't in the house. I went out the back to the greenhouse to see if he was in there, and I saw a stunning brunette looking at his South American orchids. I'd never seen her before in my life."

Liam's body was rigid under hers, and Avy sought his hands. His fingers shook slightly; his arms were tense.

"She looked at me and smiled. I smiled back. And then without a word she took off her sweater and unhooked her bra."

Avy squeezed his fingers, but he didn't squeeze back.

"I was seventeen. A randy little bastard. I didn't question my good luck. Within moments I was—" His voice actually cracked and he paused before he went on. "Within moments I was balling her on the potting bench. She must have thought I was the gardener's kid—I don't know."

Avy dreaded what he'd say next.

"She was my father's new wife," he whispered. "I was fucking my stepmother when he walked through the door."

Liam wouldn't meet her gaze when Avy did roll off of him. When she knelt on the bed and took his face in her hands, he closed his eyes.

"You didn't know," she said gently. "Liam, how could you possibly have known?"

"I *should* have. What other reason could she possibly have had for being there?" His voice was bitter. "Who the hell else would she have been, a real estate broker?"

"An orchid specialist, an interior decorator, a friend, or a salesperson. She could have been anyone, Liam." Avy pressed a kiss to his forehead and tried to bend her mind around the kind of pain he must be in, still, after all these years.

"But she wasn't just anyone! God damn it . . ."

"Liam, look at me."

He refused.

"Open your eyes and look at me. Hear what I'm saying. It wasn't your fault, Liam. *It wasn't your fault.*"

He shook his head, and she didn't know whether he was refuting her words or agreeing with them. And then, shockingly, she saw tears escape from under his lids.

"Oh, sweetheart," Avy said. "Oh, Liam." She kissed his lips, then each eye.

"Don't." He rolled to the side and got out of bed, standing with his back to her. "Please. Don't touch me."

She followed him and slipped her arms around him, pressing her cheek to his muscular back. "I *will* touch you. Because you don't disgust me, and you shouldn't disgust yourself."

She heard his sharp intake of breath. And then his hands moved down to cover hers.

"I've never told anyone that story," he said.

"I know, sweetheart. I know."

A couple of hours later Liam rolled over in bed and fumbled for the light and then the phone. Avy stirred sleepily and opened her eyes. He looked into them and truly saw no condemnation. No disgust.

It humbled him. And any last doubts he'd had about his feelings vanished. He was one hundred percent, helplessly in love with her.

He called room service and ordered a bottle of champagne, which he didn't want and which Avy probably didn't want, either, given her reluctance to drink her wine at dinner.

But he had to make sure she didn't go anywhere tonight, and he couldn't very well dissolve the sleeping tablets in water—she'd taste them right away. So he had to somehow talk her into a drink.

She stirred and sat up, leaning against the pillows. "Liam, that's very sweet of you, but I don't need any more alcohol. . . ." she stopped. "Well, on second thought"—she gave him a kittenish smile—"it does sound nice."

"Doesn't it." He was instantly suspicious; she was many things, but kittenish wasn't one of them. Did great minds think alike? Of course they did.

Liam couldn't help grinning. *Aren't we just two peas in a bloody pod.*

He kissed her and found all sorts of intriguing ways to pass the time until room service arrived. She had such a lovely body, and especially given their earlier conversation, he intended to make sure that it didn't get shot full of holes tonight.

At the inevitable knock on the door, Liam got up and opened it, accepting the champagne in its ice bucket along with two fluted glasses. He sent the attendant away, telling him that they'd open it themselves.

"If you'd like to take a quick shower, I can open that," said Avy.

You deceitful little trollop, I do so adore you. "Are you suggesting that I need to bathe?"

She dimpled at him. "Maybe a bit."

"Well, then. Anything to please you, my love." He went into the bathroom and turned on the shower, returning in time to see her jump guiltily and clamp her hand to her thigh. "But it wouldn't be gentlemanly of me to leave you thirsty, would it?" He showed her all of his teeth as he commandeered the champagne bottle and removed the foil.

"Oh, but Liam, you're wasting water. Really, I can—"

"If you're that concerned about it, then you can just turn it off. You don't mind, do you, love?"

Realization dawned in her eyes. "Of course not." Her shoulders set, she went in and turned off the spray, emerging quickly, but not quickly enough.

He'd managed to tip the powdered pills into a glass, which he now quite calmly filled with champagne. The lighting in the room was low enough that she wouldn't see a cloud at the bottom of the liquid, and it would soon dissolve.

"I'll just go and take that shower now," Liam said with an agreeable smile.

"But you didn't pour any for yourself." Avy's hand, the same one she'd clamped to her thigh, snaked out and caught the other, empty glass. For only a second, but long enough, her palm rested over the top of it. She grasped the bottle with her other hand and splashed some of the bubbly wine into the flute.

She handed it to him and raised her own glass, looking just shy of smug. "Cheers, Liam."

"Cheers, love." He held the crystal to his lips, and she did the same. Funny how the liquid level on both glasses stayed at its original level.

She definitely noticed, and she noticed him noticing. *Oh, the tangled webs we weave. . . .*

Avy's eyes narrowed. Then she brought the rim of her glass up to the hollow between her collarbones and tipped it, so that champagne ran down her naked body. "Oops," she said. "Maybe you should help me clean up."

Damn, she's good. I don't just adore her; I'm flat-out

helplessly in love with her. She's my living female doppelgänger, for Christ's sake.

Liam was tempted to lick her from head to toe. After all, in her glass were simple ground sleeping tablets, three of them. And half the champagne had already soaked into the carpet under her feet. Another good portion of it would end up on the sheets. What did that leave on her body? Maybe three-quarters of a sleeping tablet? Hell, he could just drink another espresso and be fine.

He grabbed her and threw her on the bed as she laughed. He licked the hollow of her throat clean, and then went over each breast lovingly, centimeter by centimeter.

He sucked down the thimbleful of wine in her belly button and went south from there. It was then that she stopped laughing, and he raised his head so that he could see her face.

He registered two things simultaneously. One, that her expression wasn't blissful but evaluative; and two, that he felt suddenly quite dizzy and strange. Her features swam out of focus for a few seconds, and he blinked.

Then he turned his head toward the champagne glasses. He wasn't feeling the effects of part of one sleeping pill. God damn it all, she'd somehow switched the flutes. And whatever she'd put in his champagne would fell a Clydesdale.

Liam's eyes rolled back into his skull and seemed to keep rolling into black infinity. Then he lost all motor skills and fell face-first into Avy's lap.

Oh, God. I haven't killed him, have I? Avy lifted Liam's poor drugged head, rolled him over, and made sure he was breathing. She checked his pulse. It was slow, but steady. His jaw had gone slack, but he still looked vaguely betrayed. And more—appalled by what she'd done.

She began to feel twinges of extreme guilt. *Don't be ridiculous. He was doing the same damned thing to you. He wanted you knocked out. He put something in your drink. Now, move, Avy! Get out of here before he wakes up.*

She helped herself to the terry robe hanging on his closet door, slipping into it and belting it quickly. She opened the closet and found his duffel on the floor, which, oh, so conveniently held not only climbing gear in a backpack but a Glock to replace the SIG Sauer she'd left behind in London. She made sure it was loaded, then grabbed the whole pack, shoved the gun into it, and stuffed her purse on top of that.

Then she snatched up Liam's pants, rifling through the pockets until she found his valet parking ticket.

She quickly left his room and went back to hers. She dressed in black pants and a long-sleeved black cotton top, twisting her hair up and securing it with a clip. She found socks and shoved her feet into black rubber-soled work boots, the only footwear she'd been able to find that was appropriate for this mission.

She checked her watch. With all the people leaving the casino, she hoped she wouldn't be too memorable as she requested Liam's car from the valet guys. But if she was, so what? Liam couldn't fault them for bringing the car to the person who held the ticket. She only hoped he'd be out cold for at least a couple of hours.

When he woke, his temper would not be a pretty thing to experience. Of that she was sure.

Avy went down to the lobby level and requested the car. The young kid who brought it didn't ask any questions, and she didn't volunteer any information. She simply got behind the wheel and drove out of Nice, heading north along the coastal road toward Cap Ferrat.

The evening was warm and breezy, the moon partially obscured by clouds. She let the windows down and drove the curves fast, enjoying the wind whipping in and out, its roar competing with the crashing of the sea below. Salt air filled her nostrils, and adrenaline began beating a course through her bloodstream.

You steal. You and I, we're just alike. The only difference is that you have a permit. . . .

Though she'd left him in a boneless heap on his bed, Liam's voice came to her as though he were sitting in the passenger seat. "I'm *not* like you," she said aloud.

You get a high from it. An adrenaline rush. It makes you feel alive.

So what if she did? A lot of people loved their jobs.

It's like a great, fast fuck, isn't it, Avy?

She pushed down on the gas pedal, and the Mercedes shot along the road, tires protesting as she accelerated through the curves and corrected with the wheel for the next set. *Get out of my head, Liam. You've dogged my every footstep for days, and I'm sick to death of you.*

But even as she thought it, she knew it was a lie. The truth was that she—kind of—missed the rat bastard. He would have come in handy tonight, too. Working alone she had nobody to keep an eye out for trouble, no early warning system.

And the distressing bottom line was that she was worried about him. The drug combination she'd given him should wear off quickly, and she'd rolled him onto his stomach, but what if he managed to flop onto his back . . . got sick . . . choked on his own vomit? Disgusting thought, but a realistic one. How many college kids had lost their lives that way after drinking themselves unconscious?

He tried to drug you, too, Avy. Pull your head out.

But it seemed like a crime to have a cell phone in her pocket and not use it to call the hotel, to send someone up to his room to check on him. She knew instinctively that however ruthless Liam had been about keeping her from the sword, he would call to have someone check on her if their situations were reversed.

She pulled the phone out of her pack and hit the button for calls made. The number of the Palais de la Mediterranée was right there. She hit CALL, and was connected almost immediately.

"Yes, this is a, um, friend of Monsieur James, who is a guest at the hotel. I'm very concerned about him, as he was drinking heavily tonight. Could you possibly send someone to his room to check on him?"

"Oui, madame. Tout de suite."

"Thank you." Avy was tempted to ask them to call her back to let her know if he was okay, but squelched the urge. All she needed was for her cell phone to ring while she was creeping around Gautreau's villa. Even set on vibrate, it could startle her and break her concentration.

"That's all. I appreciate it. *Bonsoir.*"

"Bonsoir, madame."

She arrived at Cap Ferrat, parked the Mercedes a quarter of a mile away from her destination, and ditched her purse and cell phone in the trunk. She kept a pair of needle-nose pliers with her, ones with a sharp inside cutting edge useful for slicing through alarm wires, and a set of tiny screwdrivers. She also kept her lock picks.

If Gautreau had any sort of wireless security system, she'd be screwed, since she had no way to jam the signal. But from her cursory examination earlier, it appeared to be a standard hardwired alarm.

Avy took out the Glock and gave it a quick check. She'd never once had to use a gun in a recovery, but she was always prepared. She tightened the straps on Liam's pack and shrugged into it. Then she slipped into the night.

chapter 29

Liam registered only dimly that someone was knocking on his door, and that was only because the telephone was ringing loudly at the same time next to his ear.

He lay on his stomach, and it was impossible to raise his head because someone had thoughtfully placed a three-hundred-pound barbell across the back of his neck. Or that was what it felt like when he twitched irritably and tried to move. Something had obviously died in his mouth—something furry, judging by his teeth—and a slight shift of his chin against the bedspread revealed something wet and a little foul—his own drool.

So his first conscious emotion was disgust. The second was extreme annoyance as the phone—no, make that phones, since his cell phone was ringing up holy hell, too—did not stop, and the door actually opened to admit a hotel employee who came in to hover over him.

"Monsieur? Sir? Are you all right?" The cretin shook his shoulder, just as Liam tried to remember something extremely important. Something urgent, in fact. What was it?

"Talk to me, monsieur," said the pest. He smacked him lightly on the cheek a couple of times.

"Piss off," Liam told him. Except it came out sounding more like, "p'shoff."

The phones began to ring again, while Liam tried desperately to remember what was so urgent, and the unspeakable arsehole in the uniform rolled him over onto his back. "Can you sit up, sir?"

With his unwanted help Liam struggled to a sitting position, and his gaze landed on a white silk dress left on the hotel room floor. *Fuck. Avy!*

"Lish' 'ere," he said to the Palais employee. "Need 'spresso. Gallon of the shit. *Now.*"

"You want espresso, monsieur?"

Liam nodded. "Urgent." He stumbled to his feet, not caring for the way the room tilted like a funhouse. He made it into the bathroom and slid to his knees in front of the toilet, where he rammed a finger down his throat and purged his body of whatever might be left of the drug.

He rested his forehead against the porcelain afterward, for only a moment. *Avy.* He had to get to Avy. Undoubtedly the person ringing on both phones was Agent Bunker, ready to chew him a new arsehole.

Liam climbed to his feet with the help of the toilet and a towel bar and headed to the sink, where he rinsed his mouth quickly and registered that he was nude. Clothes. He couldn't play white knight in the buff.

He fished in the dresser for dark jeans and a dark shirt and yanked them on, making his way to the closet for shoes and letting out a long string of vile curses as he saw that his entire backpack was gone. Once he made sure Avy was safe, he was going to wring her neck.

The telephone rang again and he groaned. May as well get this over with. "Hello?"

Kay Bunker was so angry that he couldn't even understand the first words out of her mouth. He didn't care and cut her off.

"Look, she bloody well drugged me. I'm going after

her now. Do not try to pick her up. Keep your team out of there until eight a.m. I swear to you that I will fix this. Leaving now."

Liam hung up on her. He fished his wallet out of the trousers he'd worn to dinner and groped for the valet ticket just as a knock signified that his espresso had arrived. Still going through his wallet, he wrenched open the door and waved the man in. No valet ticket. Had he just left it loose in his pocket?

He signed the bill for the espresso, of which there were two pots, and ushered the hotel employee out the door with a gruff thanks. He checked every pocket in the trousers in vain. Liam ground his teeth. Avy had bloody well better not have stolen his rental car.

He tipped back the lid of one of the espresso pots and braced himself. This would not be enjoyable. He poured the hot black stuff straight down his throat, burning the hell out of his tongue and the surrounding tissue. Then he did the same with the other pot.

He paused, thinking he'd quite likely be sick again, but willing the espresso to stay down. He shoved his wallet into his back pocket and ran out the door.

Avy had indeed stolen his car. There were no words bad enough to describe her that he could think of. Liam walked two blocks and promptly commandeered some unlucky bloke's mountain bike. Then he set off for Cap Ferrat, alternately cursing and praying.

Gwen was packing early the next morning when she turned and stared in utter outrage at the television in her Rome hotel room. On the screen the guard who'd "rescued" Pigamuffin preened and couldn't get enough adulation, though he made a weak attempt at false modesty.

"So you tackled the dognapper to the ground?" the helmet-haired news anchor asked.

"*Si,*" he said, punching the air. "I knock him down."

You did nothing of the kind, you liar. Gwen chewed her toast. *You were shaking like a leaf with your shorts in your mouth.*

"He was a big man, you say?"

"*Si, si.* Very muscular."

"Could you see anything of his face?"

"He wear a ski mask, but I see a scar under one eye."

A scar? Gwen scoffed. *Not even from breast augmentation.*

"Which eye? This could be a useful identifier for the police."

The man looked nonplussed for a moment. "The, ah, left one."

"All right, did you hear that, folks? The kidnapper of rock star Sid Thresher's dog is a big, muscular man with a scar under his left eye. He's armed and dangerous. . . ."

Maybe in a shoe store I'm dangerous. Gwen spread butter on her other piece of toast.

"What do you think he was doing back there on Sid's property?"

"I can only think . . . he must have come-a back for the leetle girl."

"What?!" Gwen sputtered.

The camera did a close-up of the reporter's face, looking suitably horrified. "Evil walks among us," he intoned. Then he shifted gears. "Why do you think he brought the dog back to Sid's property, though?"

Mr. Shorts Muncher stared at his host like a brain-damaged sheep. "Ah . . ."

Gwen tipped strong black coffee down her throat with satisfaction. "Yeah, answer me that one, bozo."

"Do you think he planned to use the dog as bait for the child?"

"*Si!*" said the idiot guard. "*Si, si.* That was very clear."

"It's a good thing you were there to save the day, then. We are so grateful to have heroes like you among us, Mr. Galantino."

"I only do my job," he said modestly. "I am hired to keep Signor Thresher and his beautiful family safe. This includes dog, eh?"

"And who knew that being man's best friend could be such a dangerous occupation? If the man is a world-famous rock star, then it's a brave dog who becomes his companion." The reporter bared two rows of suspiciously perfect, blinding teeth. "Isn't that right, Pigamuffin?"

The camera panned to the fat, ugly, wrinkled canine, who blinked. He reclined on somebody's bony lap, dressed in a black leather jacket and a spiked collar.

The lap, not surprisingly, belonged to Sid Thresher, who scratched Pigamuffin fondly behind the ears for all the world to see.

"You look pleased to have him home, Sid," the show's host said. "But I'm sure that I'm stating the obvious."

"I'm overjoyed, I am. Almost slit me wrists, worrying about the poor boy." He patted the dog on the flanks and smiled like a proud parent when the creature grunted.

"He wasn't harmed in any way?"

" 'E seemed hungry—"

That is a lie. Gwen almost growled. *He ate several whole steaks from room service.*

"—and a bit psychically traumatized, but—"

Oh, please.

"—we've 'ad 'im to a top-notch canine behavioral psy-chologist, who's prescribed Prozac, daily massages, and enforced rest. I'll take 'im off to the seashore on 'oliday and 'e'll be right as rain."

"I know that I speak for everyone here at the station when I say that we are so thrilled that he's back home safe and sound."

"Thank you," said Sid, a tear trickling from his left eye.

The host chose this moment of clear vulnerability to pounce. "You know, Sid, I do hate to bring this up under the circumstances, but our viewers are clamoring to know if the rumors of an imminent divorce between you and Danni are true?"

Thresher jumped up, dumping the unsuspecting Pig-amuffin to the floor. The poor dog landed in a heap. "'Ere, you wanker!" he said indignantly. "We 'ad an agreement. No questions about anything but the dog, you weasel. You bloodsucking, vampire, wannabe journalist! F—"—*bleep*—"you!" He turned to one cameraman after another. "And you! And f—"—*bleep*—"you, too!"

Two handlers rushed onto the stage to try to shut him up and contain the public relations damage. In the ensuing melee, Pigamuffin got to his feet and waddled off as fast as his wrinkly little legs could carry him. Nobody seemed to notice—definitely not Sid, who dissolved into a full-blown tantrum.

"Hey!" Gwen sat bolt upright in bed. "Don't forget the apple of your eye, your best buddy, the dog."

But nobody in the station could hear her. They all too busy watching, filming, or attempting to subdue Sid Thresher's skeletal, thrashing, six foot five frame. It was the female PR handler who finally got him under control, simply by yanking on his long, now-sparse, dry-as-corn-husks hair.

Gwen scanned the screen uneasily for Pigamuffin, but he was gone. What if . . . ? She told herself not to be silly.

But while she was en route to the southern coast of France, her cell phone rang.

"You ain't gonna *believe* this one," said Sheila.

chapter 30

Once in Cap Ferrat, Avy stood in the darkness for a moment, inhaling the ocean air. It was wet, heavy, redolent of salt and exclusivity. Waves crashed forward and then whispered in retreat, echoing the state of her nerves tonight. Rustling among the trees, the wind seemed to warn of danger.

She went for the phone lines outside first, to disable a standard alarm. The little pliers made quick work of the wires. Gautreau's house was dark except for a porch light over the front door and some soft outdoor lanterns illuminating the terrace that looked over the cliff to the ocean.

She hesitated. She'd much rather go in that way, since it was easier access on all counts, but she ran a high risk of being seen, and putting out the lights would be a dead giveaway of activity outside the house.

Unfortunately she would have to go around to the darker east side of the house and toss a rope up to the little window in the bedroom directly above the library. There was a tiny balconet on every upper-story window, installed there only as an architectural detail and to provide support for flower boxes. She had to get the rope up over the rail, securing it somehow. A grappling hook would make far too much noise—she didn't dare use one while people were in the house.

Yes, most burglars are smart enough to break in when the residents are away, Avy. Then there's you. . . .

It took her minutes that she didn't have to spare. In only a couple of hours the sun would start to rise and she'd be totally exposed. Again and again she threw the coil of rope up and over the rail of the balconet, but feeding it back through the balustrade proved difficult. It took her thirteen attempts, but she finally did it successfully.

She tested her weight on the rope and began as quietly as possible to scale the wall. She reached the edge of the balustrade and braced her foot on it, peering over the window box. She had a very small space to work in: about thirty inches in width and only twelve inches in depth. She climbed into it, careful not to tip the flower box and send it crashing to the side patio below.

Avy inspected the latch on the window, which opened at the center like a small French door. Constructed that way to let in the cool ocean breeze, it also made for easy access. She fished in a side zipper pocket of the pack for a metal nail file, which she'd thrown in almost as an afterthought.

Sliding the edge of the file into the groove where the two parts of the window met, she jimmied the latch up and heard it fall back with a tiny click.

Avy pushed open the little doors and stuck her head into the room, which was dark and quiet. She'd pegged it as a guest room on first sight: a spare with a twin bed and no personal effects on the walls.

She had a leg over the sill when she heard a creak in the hallway, then the noise of someone relieving himself and the flush of a toilet. *Shit!* She was damned lucky that she hadn't been out there creeping around.

A door closed farther down the hallway, and she forced herself to relax, consciously slowing down her breathing and battling her elevated pulse. She was shaking with adrenaline, and she steepled her fingers, pushing hard against them and holding for a count of twenty to alleviate the tension.

Liam was right, though: She loved the whole game, particularly this nervous sort of foreplay before the score.

Avy climbed through the window and padded soundlessly to the doorjamb in the rubber-soled boots she'd found the day of her arrival. They might win the ugly award, but they were perfect for the job.

Go. She stayed close to the wall in the corridor that led to the stairs, since most creaks occurred when people stepped near the center of floorboards.

She made it to the stairs with no incident, and slid down the banister rather than risk other loud creaks. She swung off of it at the bottom and paused to listen once again. Nothing.

Avy sprinted for the library and turned the knob, only to find that Gautreau had locked it. She dug into the zippered pocket of the backpack again and retrieved her lock picks. The mechanism wasn't complicated, and she got it open within a minute or two. She closed the door behind her and eyed the rolltop desk.

Damn it. Nothing can be easy if I'm involved, can it? Gautreau had closed and locked the desk as well. She only hoped the sword was in it.

Avy went to work with the picks again and finessed the lock. She pushed up the rolltop and almost dropped to her knees to give thanks. The sword was there, in all its menacing glory.

The wicked, forged-metal blade gleamed as it caught the light from the terrace, sending a shiver of foreboding down her spine. How could a thing made for such evil be so lovely? For it was.

But the malevolent cutting edge curved toward the two

inches of skin that showed between her sleeve and her glove, as if it could sense the flesh. As if it were thirsty.

Almost reluctant to touch it, she shook off the silly feeling of foreboding. Her gut told her it was vague and not specific.

She wrapped it in the cotton cloth and shrugged off one strap of her backpack, feeding the blade through the other one so that it rested across her spine. Then she pulled on the other strap, so that the sword was securely tucked behind the pack. It was heavy, but she'd balanced it well.

She gently closed the desk and relocked it. Then she cast a wistful look at the French doors to the terrace. It would be so much easier to exit that way. But instinct told her not to, to go back the way she'd come.

In this business gut feelings were as important as doing her research and surveiling the mark. So she listened to this one and went back through the library's interior door. She relocked that, too, and inched back up the stairs, pausing once again as she got to the top to listen.

Rasping but even breathing came from one door, which she knew from the schematics led into a smaller bedroom, probably Jean-Paul's. Silence came from the master bedroom.

Go. Avy sidestepped down the hallway, belly almost touching the wall, until she got to the spare room that she'd entered by the window.

She stepped back out and closed it, not bothering to try to jimmy the latch back into place. She needed to get out of here, fast. Successful recoveries were part skill, but part dumb luck—and she never trusted luck to hold for long. Still, she had the sword! Avy congratulated herself on a job well-done, and slipped noiselessly back down the rope.

No sooner had her feet touched the ground than a big, gloved hand clamped around her mouth from behind, and an iron arm caged both of hers. Avy's scream was loud in her own head, but no sound emerged from her mouth. She struggled wildly, trying to dig an elbow into her assailant's belly, kicking at his shins, but she simply wasn't a physical match for him.

Panic stabbed through her—and, following that, a sick impotence that froze her. She felt fear for the first time since she could remember. Fear was nothing like adrenaline. Adrenaline galvanized her; fear paralyzed her.

"*Stop.*" Liam's voice was half growl, half whisper, and when she realized that it was him she almost went limp with relief.

"Let me go!" she hissed when he took his hand away. "You scared fifty years off my life, you asshole."

"And you've scared a hundred off mine, you little ninny," Liam said roughly. "I told you not to come here." Before she understood what he was doing, he had the pack unzipped and the Glock in his hands.

To her disbelief he pointed it straight at her, his arm not quite steady.

"What are you doing?" she croaked.

"I'm not doing a damned thing. You, however, are going to get your arse back up that rope, through that window, and into the bloody library. Then you're going to replace that sword exactly in the spot you found it."

Avy stared at him, her mouth hanging open. "Are you out of your mind?"

"Yes, I am, thanks to you. But I'm quite serious." His eyes were hard, the set of his mouth uncompromising, the line of his nose arrogant.

"I've chased this sword for days, through three countries, and in spite of numerous shady tricks—courtesy of *you*, Liam James. If you think that now, when I've successfully recovered it, I'm going to put it back, then *you are smoking crack*, buddy."

He sighed, continuing to point the gun at her. "Don't make me do this, Avy. I love you, but I will not hesitate to take you down on this one."

"You *love* me?" She repeated the words incredulously. "You have a goddamned Glock pointed at my head. You are trying to ruin my career. You've been stalking me for days, and now you are screwing up my recovery. Don't tell me that you love me, you sack of shit. I am not that stupid! Go manipulate some other woman. Now get out of my way."

"I'm not trying to manipulate you. I do love you, Avy." If possible, Liam's face now looked grimmer than it had before. But he had to brace his gun arm with his left hand, and his eyes were glassy. He was obviously still feeling the effects of the secret recipe she'd put in his drink.

"Right," she said scathingly, and turned to walk away.

"Avy, *put it back*."

She shot him the finger.

Liam came after her and touched the gun muzzle to the base of her skull.

She stopped cold.

"Now," he said. "you have three choices. I can shoot you and replace the sword myself. I can shout and wake the whole household, turning you over to Gautreau as a thief. Or you can replace the sword while I keep watch and we can return to the Palais to have a lovely breakfast in the courtyard."

"You're not going to shoot me," she said in derisive tones. "Same as I wasn't going to shoot you in your living room, and you knew it."

He tapped the gun once, twice, three times against her head. "Avy, don't push me on this. There are things going on here that you don't understand."

"Such as?" She whirled and took a step back.

"Such as none of your business." Liam cocked the hammer of the Glock, his aim unwavering. He looked deadly serious.

"You're bluffing." She'd turned and started walking again when he tackled her from behind and knocked her to the ground. Utterly shocked, Avy just lay there for a moment, spitting out dirt.

Liam ripped the pack off her back and rummaged in it for the other length of rope. "Sorry, darling," he said as he tied her hands behind her. She gathered air into her lungs and opened her mouth to shriek, but he anticipated it and stuffed one of his gloves inside. "He'll kill us, Avy. Do you understand? *He will fucking kill us.*"

When she nodded, he removed the glove. "Then why don't we get the hell out of here?" she hissed. "You're the one who's holding things up."

"Because thanks to you I've got to climb up that rope half-drugged and replace this sodding sword! You have no idea what you're messing about with here. And let me tell you, the only reason I'm not tying your ankles too is that you may have to run for your life if I fall and split my skull."

"It would serve you absolutely right," she said. "It's not bad enough that you ripped off the sword to begin with? Now you've gotten into the theft *insurance* business? 'We guarantee our heist'?"

He ignored her. All he said was, "If I fall, if I make noise, get up and run, do you hear me?"

His voice did seem unusually thick and his movements slower, labored. She was surprised at the effects of the drugs on him, but everyone's body chemistry operated differently.

He staggered once as he got to his feet and shrugged into

the pack himself, stowing the sword across his back, just as she had.

God, did she hate the man. "I always knew you were despicable, but this plumbs new depths, even for you."

"More compliments," he said wearily. "Remember what I said. *Run.*"

Avy looked at the rope, saw how he hesitated on the ground, and took several deep breaths. She imagined him falling three stories and breaking his neck. At first the vision brought her great pleasure . . . and then not so much.

Or—he weighed almost twice what she did and was broader, to boot—he might have a time getting inside the window, might smack the sword loudly against something and wake Gautreau. His balance was off, his reflexes were poor, and he'd almost certainly cause the floorboards to creak. He could be shot full of holes.

The concept of Liam perforated and bloody wasn't pleasurable at all, though she wanted it to be, damn it.

And his physical and mental state were *her* fault. Even as she lay there loathing him, she didn't want him to die. It was in that clear, dreadful moment that Avy realized it: *I'm in love with him. I'm in love with the bastard. And I could just shoot myself for it.*

She didn't *want* to be in love with him—or anyone else. But especially not him . . . God damn it. Why did women glow when they were in love? Why did they float around like idiots? *This* was love—lying betrayed in the dirt with your hands tied behind your back.

Liam grasped the rope and tested his weight on it. He braced a foot against the wall and swayed on the other one. He'd never make it. He'd kill himself for sure.

"I'll do it," she said, despising herself and forcing the words past the burning resistance in her throat. *But I'll never forgive you for this.*

He put both feet back on the ground and turned, brows raised.

"I'll put it back. *I hate your guts*, Liam James," she said bitterly, "but you're in no condition to do it."

"See, I told you that you had feelings for me. Hatred is quite encouraging." Despite the flip answer, she saw by the set of his shoulders that he was wavering, thinking about it. He must feel truly awful.

He said quietly, "I'm not sure I can trust you to do it, Avy."

They were back to this trust conversation? "I said I'll do it." Anger infused her tone. "I may be, as you say, a thief with a permit, but I don't lie. You know that about me."

He nodded and knelt beside her, placing a hand on her shoulder. "If I untie your hands, do you swear by all that's holy that you'll put back the sword?"

"Piece of cake," she said, though just thinking about it ignited fury and frustration in her. *God, am I stupid.*

She closed her eyes and literally saw red instead of darkness. Avy pressed her cheek into the cool dirt and fantasized again briefly about shoveling six feet of it over Liam's dead body.

Am I crazy? I should let him climb and fall. As he said, I can still run—and take the sword with me. Avy thought about it quite seriously.

"That's not a promise. Implications aren't good enough this time, Avy. I need your word."

Damn it, damn it, damn it. If she promised she was screwed. If she promised she was giving in to her asinine feelings for this man. *Let him fall and break his neck.*

"Avy?"

"I promise," she said. *Fool.* She struggled up to her knees. "Now untie me. The sooner we get out of here, the better."

He released her from the knots, and she shrugged into the pack again, sword and all. He stood hidden in the shadows while she went to the rope and grasped it in hands shaking with anger.

She braced one foot and then the other, slowly pulling herself up the wall, feeling this time as if she weighed a thousand pounds. Her arms trembled from the strain, her face crumpled in sheer frustration, and tears fell from her eyes. Sobs began to rack her body, but Avy was damned if she'd let them past her teeth and into the night.

"Avy," called Liam softly. "Are you all right?"

She didn't—couldn't—answer. She just kept going.

"For God's sake," he said, "be careful."

chapter 31

As she climbed, she reflected on the peculiar note in Liam's voice, and as she got to the balustrade and the window again she identified it: fear. He was afraid for her. *I love you, Avy. . . .*

Bullshit. Liam might like sex with her, but he didn't love anyone but himself. She swung her leg over the flower box and stepped onto the little balconet, pushing open the window she'd conveniently left unlocked.

The tears kept falling, and her throat ached from the force of her refusal not to give in to real weeping. *Pull yourself together, Avy Hunt. Crying is for little girls. You going to run into Gautreau while sucking your thumb? Maybe ask him for a blankie?*

With one savage swipe at each eye, she stopped the waterworks. Within seconds she was back in the spare bedroom and creeping for the hallway.

The harsh, even breathing still came from one of the smaller bedrooms, while silence continued to emanate from the master. Avy all but pressed her belly to the wall and stepped carefully, quietly, professionally down the corridor. Out on the landing of the stairs she didn't pause, just slid again down the polished wood banister.

She was jumpier this time—when her backside hit the

newel post she panicked for a moment, thinking that it might be a person. *Ridiculous.*

At the bottom of the stairs she hesitated as a clock chimed five times. But nobody stirred.

Avy headed for the library and picked the lock as she had before. The door creaked slightly as she opened it this time, and she didn't close it behind her. She'd be through here in a matter of seconds.

She made her way to the rolltop and unlocked, then lifted it. She shrugged one shoulder out of the pack and, clenching her teeth, pulled the sword out.

I may be a thief with a permit, but I don't lie.

Shades of gray, Avy. Shades of gray . . .

She stood there, stalling. Not wanting to put the sword into the desk and walk away from her recovery job. She could go right to the front door and slip out while Liam farted up that rope.

I don't lie.

Fuck!

She lifted the sword in heavy, unwilling hands and laid it on the desk. Shaking with anger not only at Liam but at her damned stupid moral code, she lowered the rolltop and locked it. She was still grasping her set of picks when light blazed overhead. Gautreau said in deadly tones, "I wouldn't do that if I were you, Mademoiselle Hunt."

She whirled to find him standing there in pressed-silk pajamas accessorized by a matching robe and a semiautomatic Beretta. She'd bet her whole salary that the safety was off, and every bit of moisture evaporated from her mouth as he cocked the hammer.

"Such a pity that you are so pretty, yet so stupid. Did you really think I would fall for your act this afternoon? I'm only surprised that it's you in here instead of the talented Monsieur James. Why is that, Mademoiselle Hunt?"

She decided to tell the truth. "I drugged him."

"So you are here all alone?"

Then again, there were those handy shades of gray. "Yes. I stole his car. I can show you the valet ticket."

"Charming. And how did you know about the sword?"

"Sword?"

"I am not an idiot, Mademoiselle Hunt." He walked slowly toward her, holding the Beretta much steadier than Liam had held the Glock.

"Fine. Liam told me. I have art world contacts from an old job at Sotheby's. We were going to take the sword and move it through other channels—keep the whole black-market sale price, not just his commission from you."

Gautreau's free hand shot out and grabbed her left breast, his fingers digging in as he twisted hard.

She gasped—from surprise and pain, but also at his expression.

He clearly enjoyed hurting her.

"You like that, mademoiselle?"

"No." She tried to pry his fingers loose and back away from him, but he hung on. The fear she'd felt earlier closed around her again, forcing the air from her lungs.

He released her breast only to slap her face, knocking her sideways and onto the floor. "Perhaps you like that better."

She shook her head and tasted salty, metallic blood in her mouth. Her own teeth had cut the inside of her cheek, due to the force of the blow.

"Greedy, treacherous bitch." Gautreau grabbed her by the knot of hair on her head and yanked her upright, holding her face inches from his.

She'd always been able to keep a cool head in emergencies, but she'd never been in a situation quite like this one. Blood pounded in her ears, she was close to wetting herself, and she wanted to throw up. She couldn't control her breathing—she was almost hyperventilating.

Avy sobbed in fear and went limp as Gautreau licked her face from jaw to temple and then bit her cheek hard enough to draw blood.

Her shudder of revulsion was stronger than the pain—so powerful it almost gave her whiplash.

"We're going to have some fun, mademoiselle."

Where was the adrenaline that usually pumped through her, giving her almost superhuman strength and ability? It had deserted her and left behind this pathetic, sniveling creature. *God help me, where is Liam?*

As if she'd conjured him, Liam crashed through the terrace doors of the library, and Gautreau's head whipped around.

In a last-ditch effort to save both her life and her self-esteem, Avy slammed her knee up and into Gautreau's balls. He obligingly fell to the floor, clutching himself and swearing in French, his face mottled. He'd dropped the Beretta.

Liam grabbed her and pushed her behind him. "Go!"

She didn't need a second invitation. Avy scrambled for the exit, her old friend adrenaline back in force.

Out of the corner of her eye she saw Gautreau make a move toward his gun, but Liam growled at him, aiming the Glock right at the Frenchman's head. Of course, Avy knew he couldn't hit the broad side of a barn at the moment, but their unwilling host did not.

That could change at any moment, though. "Liam, come on," she said urgently. "Front door. Too much glass over there."

He took a moment to kick the Beretta across the room before turning and running after her.

Gautreau didn't shout, which made his threat all the

more sinister. "I will hunt you down for this, James. I will find you and feed you your genitals."

The only problem with the front-door exit was about five-foot-ten and hurtling down the stairs. Jean-Paul had awoken due to all the noise, and he looked a lot more lethal when he wasn't serving drinks and petit quiches. He handled a Smith & Wesson .38 Special with more ease than he did a silver tray, and he made good use of it.

Avy spun to the side at the first explosion. The bullet hit the doorjamb as she threw herself out, dragging the bigger, currently slower Liam with her. Why had she drugged him? Why, God damn it? She launched herself at him and knocked him to the ground at Jean-Paul's second shot, but Liam still roared with pain. He'd been nicked in the shoulder.

Glock! "Give me the gun," she shouted, wresting it from his grasp. She rolled and aimed at Jean-Paul, catching him in the forearm. Not his shooting arm, unfortunately, but it was enough to make him falter, and she lugged Liam to his feet and shoved him onward.

Jean-Paul headed back into the house, presumably to check on Gautreau.

Avy and Liam ran for the road. On second thought, it was the first place the two Frenchmen would look. Cap Ferrat boasted a winding, rocky cliff walk, and they made for that instead—precisely because it wasn't logical and might buy them some time.

It was made for strolling and sightseeing during the day, not headlong gallops at night, but Avy had a pattern of doing things backward and upside down. Why should this be any different?

She did make sure to keep Liam on the inside, since scraping his body off the rocks wasn't her idea of fun.

Besides, she wanted to give him a big piece of her mind before knocking him off a cliff.

Even though he'd saved her life in the end, she was as angry as the waves that beat and tortured the rocks below them; as angry as the wind that had picked up unexpectedly and tore at her hair. The briny taste of it was the flavor of her bitterness. The situation back there with Gautreau hadn't needed to happen. She'd been out of there; she'd made a clean recovery; she'd *won* until he'd shown up.

Water under the bridge, her father would say.

But it wasn't. The water was churning below them and churning inside her, too, in a tempest of tears she hadn't let escape. She felt like a female tropical depression, building toward a human hurricane. But she shoved the feelings away and reached for practicality instead.

Once they'd made some headway along the path, she stopped and looked at Liam's drawn face. "Let me see your shoulder."

"It's nothing."

Spoken just like a man.

"Let me see it, you stubborn jerk. However much I may want to, I won't light a cigarette and stub it out in the wound."

Just the idea of it made him blanch. "You are too kind. But I'm perfectly all right, thank you."

"Liam," she said in dangerous tones, "don't test my patience right now. It's nonexistent. Now, take off that shirt and show me the wound before I smack you into next year."

"Admit it: You just want to see my naked chest, darling Avy."

"Liam, shut up and sit down. I'm in no mood for your banter and sexual innuendo." She shoved him backward and then put pressure on his unwounded shoulder. Reluctantly he sank to the ground. He raised his arms to pull off his shirt, but then stopped with a groan of pain.

She saw in the first rays of dawn that the shirt was soaked with blood. So she took it by the crew-neck collar and ripped it down the front.

"Do try to control yourself, love," Liam said with a raised eyebrow. "I know you want me, but I didn't pack a change of clothes when I ran from the hotel to save your neck."

Avy gritted her teeth wrathfully and ripped the shirt down one shoulder seam and then the other, pulling the fabric off his body. "Oh, is *that* what you were doing? Let me remind you that *I had everything under control* until a macho, stupid, interfering Englishman showed up! I'm good, Liam. I was in and then out. I was *gone*—until you mugged me and held the Glock to my head! So don't talk to me about saving my neck, you *unspeakable*, *marauding asshole!*"

Liam got to his feet and stood over her, his face an inch from hers. "You think you're the only one who's angry? I'd like to wring your bloody asinine neck! I told you not to go to Gautreau's. I told you to leave the sword alone. I told you that you don't understand what's going on in this situation. But no, you had to sure as shit waltz in there anyhow, you pigheaded, stubborn wench!" He took her by the shoulders and shook her none too gently.

"Get your hands off of me," she said in deadly tones.

"Funny. That's the first request I've had from you along *those* lines." He smirked as only an arrogant male could smirk.

Beside herself with rage, Avy ripped two long strips from his T-shirt, folded one into a pad, and slapped it down onto his bleeding shoulder wound.

"Ahhh!" Liam hissed in pain. "You *bi*—Gaaaaaah!"

She'd savagely tied the other strip around the wound in a tight tourniquet. Liam launched into a string of utterly disgusting curses.

"Sorry, *love*. You're right," she said with a sweet smile. "I just can't keep my hands off your body."

He squinted at her dangerously.

"Now, come on. We need to keep going."

"Begging your pardon, but you had a cushy ride up here in my Mercedes, you're not drugged, and you haven't had a hole shot through you. Forgive me if I'm not as chipper as you are."

Avy raised her brows. "He cusses *and* he whimpers. I'm falling more in love with every passing moment."

Liam had opened his mouth to offer a pithy response when they were greeted by a now-familiar whine and an accompanying explosion. Clearly Jean-Paul and Gautreau had found them.

Avy dove for the backpack, but Liam got to it first. "It's too heavy for you." He shrugged it onto his uninjured nude shoulder and grabbed her hand. "Come on!"

"Why didn't you shoot that bastard," Avy panted as they ran, "at close range when you had the chance?"

"It's complicated," he shouted.

Seemed pretty simple to her. Fear tried to paralyze her again, but she fought it back. She put a hand up to her wounded cheek and her fingers came away bloody. She'd rather deal with Gautreau's bullets than his other horrifying tactics.

The dawn light tinged the sky with gold and pink, reminding her again of Turner's glorious paintings. Sunrise was both welcome and dangerous. While they could see where they were going, so could the enemy.

"Why the hell are they still after us?" Avy yelled. "They have the damned sword!"

"Er, it's complicated," Liam repeated, ducking as another bullet whizzed by, shattering her nerves.

"*What's* complicated? And don't say that you could tell me, but then you'd have to kill me—or I'll push you over the cliff."

Liam looked down at the water and shook his head. "No, darling. That you won't. I'm not a strong swimmer, and Benchley's *Jaws* left a strong impression on me."

"I'm sorry to hear that." Avy had come to an unfortunate conclusion, just as they came gasping to a hairpin bend in the path. They were both exhausted, and there was no good way to escape from their pursuers. They could be shot, or they could go swimming.

Another bullet hit the trunk of a scrubby tree next to her head, and Liam dropped to a crouch and yelled, "Get down!"

My thoughts exactly.

Sorry about Jaws, *Liam. Sorry about what the salt water's going to do to your wound. And I'll just have to help you tread water.*

Avy planted her boot right against Liam's backside and kicked out hard. Then she jumped after him.

chapter 32

Cold salt water filled Avy's mouth, her nose, and her ears. It slapped her face repeatedly, and the salt burned like a hot poker in her wounded cheek. She struggled to keep her head above water in the tantrum of waves, and spotted Liam about five yards away doing the same.

His eyes were wide with shock and pain as she fought the water to get to him. "I bloody well told you that I don't swim!"

"You can swim," she said urgently. "You can at least tread water. Keep your legs moving, Liam. Keep stroking your hands down, over and over. Do you hear me?" She stayed just out of his reach, in case he panicked.

He didn't. He cursed vilely instead, which she figured was a healthy sign. But he tried to dog-paddle toward shore.

"No! Liam, swim out to sea. The waves will break us like matchsticks on those rocks, and Gautreau is still there with a gun. Come on!"

He spit out water and cursed some more. But he followed her.

Her clothes sucked and dragged at her body, and the boots that had been so effective for burgling a house were now a liability, filled with water and weighing a ton. She reached down, unzipped them, and kicked them off. Then she started swimming again, encouraging Liam as they went.

They were spotted by the captain of a yacht getting an early start out to sea. He was Italian and didn't speak much English, but he comprehended their shouts for help—mostly Liam's—and tossed them a life preserver.

The yacht itself had been dubiously christened the *Sex Machine*, but Avy didn't care what it was called as long as they were taken aboard.

The startled captain tossed them the life ring, which she immediately passed to Liam. She caught hold of the rope attached between it and the vessel and then began to swim, towing him along.

"No," said Liam, breathing hard. "This is utterly demoralizing. I'm being outdone by a woman."

"Oh, stuff your ego, James. As you pointed out, you've been drugged, shot, and don't really swim. Get over yourself."

Between gasps, Liam hung on to the life ring and told her volubly and at great length how displeased he was by her cliffside maneuver, how salt water felt in a fresh gunshot wound, and how, if he were eaten by a giant sea bass, he'd haunt her forever.

A wave came along and smacked him under the surface, and he reappeared, coughed, and resumed shouting at her while he bobbed and dog-paddled with one arm.

She suspected that he was on such a rant because it kept him from thinking about how powerless he felt in the water, and so she just let him rip.

He objected to her logic in jumping, her underhanded tactics, the fact that she wouldn't let him just swim to shore. He pretty much objected to the fact that she'd ever been born.

He'd also dropped the backpack to the bottom of the

harbor, sending with it her cherished set of lock picks, the Glock, and everything else.

"I told you to let me take the pack," she said, hanging on to the rope as the captain of the yacht reeled them in. "But no . . . you had to be a manly man."

"Yes, I felt quite macho sailing through the air with your boot print on my arse," he growled. "How long had you been itching to do that?"

"Forever," she admitted. "But I wouldn't have actually done it if we'd had any other way of staying alive. So don't, as you would say, get your knickers in a twist."

"You know, individuals who are drowning often climb onto their companions or rescuers and drown them in a panic to stay alive." His eyes gleamed.

"Liam"—a wave hit her in the face, so she stopped to spit out water and then gasp for air— "may I point out that you are not drowning, and that if you were, I might not be inclined to rescue you? I'd probably just swim away. Now shut up and just tread water. By the way, it's normal to be cranky as the drugs wear off."

"Cranky?" he sputtered. "I'll give you cranky. . . ."

They finally reached the yacht, and the captain let down a ladder at the stern so they could scramble aboard. Both of them fell to the deck, panting. Avy's sodden trousers had chafed almost every inch of her skin as they'd swum, and now that they were out of the water the chafes began to burn. But she lay there ignoring them, too tired to even snipe at Liam.

Out of the corner of her eye she took in the details of the yacht. It had to be over a hundred feet long, and every inch of it gleamed white and shiny in the sun, as if scrubbed with baking soda. Long expanses of tinted windows stretched along the length of the cabin, providing expensive privacy for the owner. Above the cabin was a luxurious sundeck and the captain's bridge, enclosed in more tinted glass. Over the salt air Avy could smell bleach and freshly minted money.

The captain asked them something in Italian, of which Liam knew the rudiments.

"What did he say?" Avy asked.

"He wants to know how we fell into the water and why we're swimming *away* from shore," Liam replied.

"What did *you* say?" asked Avy.

"I told him that you lost your footing and fell, and that I jumped in to save you. But you panicked, got disoriented, and swam in the wrong direction. You thought the boats were closer than they appeared."

"Unbelievable," she said. "You made me look like an idiot."

"The alternative is that I look like an idiot, and that's simply unacceptable." He grinned. "Because of me being one hundred percent man and all that."

"I truly loathe you."

"Trust me, darling, not as much as I loathe you at the moment."

The captain brought them some towels, which they accepted with thanks. Then he spoke to Liam again, apparently asking where they wanted him to drop them.

It was then that a deeply tanned skeleton with a lot of hair and buglike sunglasses appeared, throwing open the sliding doors from the interior. "What the 'ell is all the bloody noise about, eh? 'Oo are these wet wankers, Franco? And why are they on me yacht at six o'clock in the bloody morning?"

Avy blinked. No . . . surely that wasn't . . . No, it couldn't be.

Liam got up and extended his hand. "This particular wet wanker is Liam James. I've always wanted to make your acquaintance. I'm a big Subversion fan."

"Sid Thresher." The tanned skeleton nodded. Besides the bug sunglasses, he wore nothing but a lime green banana hammock and a Clorox-white terry bathrobe hanging open and flapping in the breeze. "But oy suppose you knew that. And who's me beauty, 'ere?" He gestured at Avy.

She got up and wrung out her hair. "I'm Avy Hunt."

"Avy Hunt, you say? No, really?"

She nodded, puzzled as to how he'd know her name.

"The same Avy Hunt that's with ARTemis, Inc? Recovery specialists?"

"Yes . . . how do you know the firm?"

"Come in an' join me in a Bloody Mary and I'll tell you all about it. Long, strange journey it's been. First me dog is kidnapped. Then me dog is returned. Then I go on the telly, and me dog disappears again. So, at me wit's end, I do some askin' around, and I get the name of this recovery firm. I get your name as the best there is."

"Well, thank you." Avy exchanged a glance with Liam and avoided the sight of Sid's neon bulge.

"Yah, excepting you're not available, if you please. They sent me a Gwen Davies instead."

Avy choked.

"Odd little duck, that one. Sounds strangled every time she speaks a word to me. I told her 'ow she shouldn't be cowed by me fame and me talent—"

Liam fell into a mild coughing fit.

"—but ye know 'ow some women are. I said to her, I said, she could get over 'er bashfulness quick-like if she just blew me a couple o' times. We'd be old friends, like, after that."

Avy just stared at him, speechless.

"Back in the day," Sid said, sounding outraged as he splashed tomato juice into a tanker-size cup, "a girl would ha' been on all me ten inches like a starving sparrow on a worm, eh?"

He stopped, reached for the vodka, and frowned. "Understand me, it's more like a python than a worm, but I exercised me some poetic license. . . ."

"I take it that this Gwen Davies disappointed your expectations?" Liam inquired, somehow keeping a straight face.

"You could say that, man, you could! She gets all poker-faced and informs me it's not in 'er 'job description,' thank ye very much, to suck anyone off. An 'ere I was, just tryin' to calm 'er nerves . . . bloody ingratitude, I tell you." He opened the small refrigerator in the galley and poked around, his bony butt gyrating in the bathrobe. "Franco! I say, Franco, where the 'ell has the celery toddled off to?"

He pulled his head out. "Eh, well. She's good, anyway. She's got me dog—it's why I'm 'ere. Tracked 'im down to some producer's summer house in Cannes. Bloody wanker was still crafting a ransom note." His attention turned back to the refrigerator and his quest.

"Celery," he mumbled. "Where are you?" At last he gave up, frowning, and slammed the refrigerator door. "Can't have Bloodies wi'out celery."

Avy held up a hand. "We've had a tough night. We'll skip the Bloody Marys, thanks."

Sid looked offended. "Ye don't know what ye're missing, lovey."

"Oh, I'll suffer through one," Liam said easily. "I can't turn down a drink with the legendary Sid Thresher."

"Ha! You're all right, you are." Sid splashed more tomato juice into another monster cup and added at least half a pint of vodka. "Franco!" he roared.

The captain popped his head in. *"Si, signore?"*

"Celery, man! Where the fuck's the celery?"

Franco looked troubled. "Signore, you eat it all last night. With jam."

"With *jam*?"

"Signore, you smoke . . . then you are ver' hungry. You remember?"

"Ahhhhh." Sid looked sheepish. "Right. Never mind then, Franco. We'll have to make do with carrots . . . or bread sticks."

Liam's face took on a revolted expression. "Really, old chap, I'll be quite all right without a garnish."

Sid shrugged. "As ye like. Cheers!"

Avy sent a speaking look Liam's way, but he ignored it. Finally she said, "Darling, that won't mix well with your medication."

"Yes, but it will make my shoulder feel loads better."

"What 'appened wi' your shoulder, man?"

"Ah, hell. You know how it is with women. We got into an argument and she shot me. With my own gun, no less."

Sid's mouth fell open, and he peered at Avy over his bug glasses. "You *bitch*, you."

"Thanks. I'll take that as a compliment."

Sid turned back to Liam and jerked a thumb in her direction. "Shall we pitch 'er back overboard, then?"

Liam appeared to ruminate on this. He took a long drink of vodka, then sighed. "No, no. Due to very bad judgment on my part I'm fond of my little homicidal maniac."

Avy stalked out of the galley, through the very posh, polished, wood-lined sitting area, and out onto the deck to join Franco, who shot her a sympathetic look.

"How do you work for him?" she asked.

"Eh?"

She jerked her head toward the cabin and rolled her eyes. Then she held out her hands palm up and lifted her shoulders.

Franco nodded and shrugged. A corner of his mouth turned up. "He, how you say, pay well. And he bring *belle ragazze* on board—many. Some like captain, too."

She stared at him in disgust. *Men.* She wasn't sorry in the least that she'd kicked Liam off the cliff.

chapter 33

By the time Franco docked the yacht in Nice to let them off, their clothes were dry and Liam was back in a sunny and very expansive mood, courtesy of Sid's vodka.

Because Sid's bimbo du jour had not yet joined him, and he'd taken such a shine to Liam, one Bloody Mary had turned into three while six a.m. became nine forty-five.

The beautiful day mocked Avy's mood; light sparkled off the ocean's foam-flecked cobalt waves, the breeze toyed with her salt-encrusted hair, and birds called cheerily to one another as they scavenged for fish.

If she could have zapped the atmosphere and made everything still, gloomy, and gray, she would have.

After they said their fond good-byes to Sid and Franco, Liam rolled happily down the pier while Avy gritted her teeth and resisted the urge to kick him back into the water. "You're a disgrace," she said.

He slung an arm around her shoulders. "And you, my love, are a distress. Come on, now. We have to celebrate."

She shrugged out from under his arm and turned to face him. "Celebrate? Celebrate what, exactly? Me failing for the first time ever on the job?" Kelso would be unimpressed. McDougal and Valeria would be delighted.

"You didn't fail, my darling." He looked woozily at his

watch. "You saved the day. You're quite a hero—well, as long as I'm tolerant and overlook the more pestilent aspects of your personality."

"Pestilent? *Hero?* Yeah, I'm a real hero, all right, for returning the sword to the jerk who commissioned its theft. Now it will disappear into some rich guy's collection and never be seen again."

"It won't disappear."

"Don't be naive, Liam—of course it will disappear!"

Her voice was half drowned out, though, by a small jet of some kind headed in the direction of Cap Ferrat.

He looked up at it, mouth spreading wide in a true shark's grin, his teeth gleaming white in the morning sun. "If that's who I think it is, then it's time for champagne, darling Avy."

"I'm never drinking champagne with you again," she said. "And I'm surprised that you'd want it with *me*, after last night."

Liam chucked her under the chin and planted a salty, vodka-laden smacker right on her lips. "I want it with you anyplace, anytime. And we'll drink many a bottle of champers together over the years."

"You've got some fantasy going there. Have another drink, why don't you? Let's see if it gets any better."

"It couldn't possibly, love. Couldn't possibly."

"Liam, were you smoking funny stuff in the galley with Sid back there?"

He shook his head and ushered her up the front steps of the Palais de la Mediterranée. Liam was shirtless, and they both looked an absolute wreck, so a staff member at reception tried to stop them on the way in. Fortunately Avy had her wallet in a cargo pocket of her black pants. "We're guests of the hotel."

After a check of the computer and an incredulous look at

her passport, the staffer stumbled over an abject apology and escorted them personally to the elevators.

"Could you have a bottle of Cristal sent up, please?" Liam asked, despite looking as if he'd just walked off the set of a Rambo movie.

"Certainly, sir. With our compliments."

Avy said, "I'd rather have a huge breakfast than champagne."

"We can order that, too," Liam said expansively.

To her annoyance, he came along to her room. "You took my car. So I'm going to take over your shower, since I haven't a clue where my wallet has gone—not to mention my room key."

He didn't sound upset about it. He sounded relaxed and happy and buzzed. Like a man on vacation, without a care in the world. She remembered his shark's grin outside on the Promenade des Anglais. *What is going on?*

"Fine. You can use my shower, but then you can tell me just what you're so happy about and why you want to celebrate. Because I'm getting a sick feeling in the pit of my stomach."

He shot her a smug, enigmatic look and made straight for the bathroom. She heard the shower go on. "Want to join me?" he called.

"No. I'm done being naked with you."

"Oh, ouch. Surliness doesn't become you, my darling."

She ignored him and peeled off her dirty, still-damp clothes, exchanging them for the robe she'd taken from Liam's room. He could use the one on the back of the bathroom door.

Then she sank down onto the bed, running scenarios through her mind. This jaunt had Kelso written all over it in red letters. She created a list.

1. Sword is stolen.
2. Kelso assigns the recovery to me.
3. But Liam is already tailing and surveilling me.
4. I fly to London to repo the sword.
5. Liam greets me as I break into his house.
6. Liam plays all kinds of games with me.
7. He screws me—in every way possible.
8. Liam follows me to France.
9. Sticks by me like glue.
10. Wins in the end by making me replace the sword in Gautreau's house.

But number ten didn't make sense. Kelso wouldn't associate with a person like Gautreau, and he also wouldn't have deliberately put her in harm's way.

What in the hell was going on?

The water went off in the bathroom, and soon Liam came strolling out, looking impossibly handsome in the terry robe with wet, slicked-back hair and three days' growth of stubble on his face.

He answered a knock on the door, accepted the Cristal, and waved the attendant away just like the last time. "Perfect timing."

She'd rather have had the chance to shower first, but no way was she leaving him alone with the open bottle. She didn't want any paybacks of the narcotic variety.

"Why don't you fill me in, Liam?"

He nodded. "It's time." He extracted the cork with a soft pop and poured some champagne into each glass. Then he handed her one.

"It's time?" she repeated. "I'd say it's long past time."

"Just promise me that you won't be angry, love."

The sick feeling grew in her stomach. "Like the other occasions, Liam, I can't promise that. Now spill it."

He cast a quizzical glance at the champagne, but started talking. "That plane that we saw overhead, flying in the direction of Cap Ferrat, was carrying a Syrian national who shall remain nameless. This Syrian has been itching to get his hands on the Sword of Alexander, symbol of the infidels, for years. He couldn't find anyone who had the balls to steal it."

Avy gazed at him steadily.

"Gautreau heard of his desire for the sword. He knew the Syrian would pay top dollar for it, and Gautreau has been in the art-theft game for years. However, he doesn't play it for personal gain. He raises money to support Al Qaeda."

"Al Qaeda?"

He nodded, and Avy backed as far away from him as she could. Her skin suddenly felt hot, while inside she went cold.

She remembered the tapestry in Gautreau's dining room, the one with all the tanks and machine guns woven into it. She shivered and touched her hand to the bite mark on her cheek.

"Let me get this straight," she said quietly. "You stole that sword knowing that it was going to be used to raise funds for terrorism. And you don't want me to be *angry*?" Her hand tightened convulsively on the champagne glass.

"No. I stole the sword with the blessing of the U.S., British, and French governments, and passed it on to Gautreau so that he can be stopped."

"What?"

"It was a sting operation. Our biggest concern was you, however. The sword is insured through Lloyd's, and Lloyd's uses ARTemis often. You in particular."

She gripped the glass in both hands now, one on the tulip-shaped bowl, the other on the stem. "You targeted me from the beginning," she said. "That's why you were tailing me in Miami."

He nodded.

She tightened her hold on the glass as she stared at him, fury humming through her bloodstream. A peculiar cracking sound caused her to look down: She'd snapped the bowl of her champagne flute clean off the stem.

"I'm sorry that I couldn't tell you," Liam said. "I really am. It wasn't my secret to share."

She threw the contents of the glass at his face. "Get out."

"The sale was set for ten a.m. this morning. The FBI and French RAID were waiting to close in and take Gautreau and the Syrian down. They just needed the wire transfers as the final nail in the coffin."

"Get out!"

"That's why I forced you to replace the sword. You did a good thing, Avy. You didn't fail in any sense of the word."

Her tears shocked her more than they seemed to shock Liam. "You've played me like a fucking violin!"

"It started that way. It hasn't ended that way."

"All this time you've just been babysitting me, keeping me away from the sword so I wouldn't screw up the op. Do you know how that makes me *feel*?"

"I'm sorry. All I know is that I love you."

"If you say that again I swear I will break that champagne bottle over your low-down, two-faced, lying head."

"But I do. And I've been retired for two years—"

She grabbed the bottle, upended it, and swung at him.

"Bollocks," he said, jumping back. "We really don't have such good luck with champagne, do we?"

She came at him again, and he leaped for the door.

"Christ, woman!" He wrenched it open and got himself out, pulling it closed behind him. Then he spoke through the wood. "I take it that this isn't, perhaps, the most auspicious moment for a marriage proposal?"

Avy threw the bottle at the door so hard that it shattered.

Liam sent a hotel employee to get his rental car. He canceled all his credit cards and had replacements overnighted to the Palais. He thanked God that he'd had the foresight to make a copy of his passport and driver's license.

He asked the concierge to send lilies to Avy and buy him some clothes with a bit of cash he had stashed in his hotel room, which the staff wouldn't give him access to without proper identification. When he finally explained that copies of his papers were in the room, and told them where to find them, an attendant checked and at last let him in.

And the entire time he went through these motions, he felt as if his life were over, when he should feel exultant that he'd done his part to pull off the sting—not to mention ensuring that he'd receive his pardon from the U.S. government.

I finally meet the perfect woman, my soul mate. And I manage to destroy all hope of a happy ending with her. Brilliant. Utterly brilliant, Liam.

He finished wrapping up his business and headed down to the third-floor courtyard in his new silk shirt and Bermuda shorts.

At a table with a marvelous view, Liam gazed out at the Mediterranean and sipped café au lait—not a proper man's beverage, but as he ran his tongue around his blistered mouth, he wasn't sure he'd ever be able to drink espresso again. And he supposed he should sober up.

He rang Kay Bunker in the meantime. "Bonjour, Mademoiselle Bunker! *Comment allez-vous?*"

"*Agent* Bunker. And I'm just peachy. I've got a spitting-mad terrorist to my left, in cuffs. And his ugly Syrian buddy with the tablecloth on his head has matching ones."

"You are a model of political correctness and cultural sensitivity. But may I offer my congratulations?"

"You may. They're both screaming for lawyers, which is entertaining, because no lawyer's going to get them out of this mess. We've got the sword. We've got the wire transfer from the Syrian to Gautreau's account, and then we've also got the automatic rollover from that to a known Al Qaeda operative. These guys are done," she crowed.

Liam waited for at least a cursory thanks, but it didn't come.

"I'm hoping you can solve one last puzzle for me, Miss Bunker. Why would the Syrian have wanted a weapon that is the symbol of Western influence over the Middle East? It doesn't make sense."

"Oh, that. Our sources say that he was set to throw a big party, and they were actually going to melt the thing down in some ceremony, believe it or not."

"*Melt* it?"

"Yes."

"But it's worth a fortune!"

"Yes."

He was glad that Avy didn't know about that little detail. She might be even angrier with him that he'd jeopardized an $11 million piece of history.

"I see. I'm glad they never had the chance." Liam switched the subject. "So, my darling Miss Bunker, when can I expect my get-out-of-jail-free card from the U.S. government?"

She sucked in an angry breath. "Agent. Not *darling*. Not *miss*. Not *anything* but *agent*. And you'll get it within a week or two, along with a letter commending you for your service, which is a big joke, since you've screwed up everything you've touched."

Liam let that slide. "Agent Bunker. May I say that it's been a scintillating experience working with you?"

A strange noise came from her end of the line.

"Are you all right?" Liam asked.

"I'm fine. Just all choked up at your use of the word *agent*, *Sir* Liam."

He laughed softly and broke the connection.

chapter 34

Gwen noted that Cannes wasn't in the least glamorous without the international film festival to enliven it. It was just another small, sleepy little town along the coast of southern France. Still, the sun was warm, the sea was frothy and blue, and Gwen had slept pretty well, considering that she'd once again shared her hotel bed with a dog.

Knocking on the producer's door and taking Sid's pet back had been easier than whipping out her credit card in a boutique. She hoped all her future recoveries were that simple. What she wasn't looking forward to was seeing Sid Thresher again.

Gwen adjusted her Maui Jims and fed Pigamuffin the last bit of her ham-and-cheese croissant as Thresher's ostentatious yacht drew near the dock in Cannes. Pigamuffin didn't bother to chew the morsel; he just swallowed it whole. The dog peered out at the water from under the mass of wrinkles that formed his head, as if he recognized the big boat. Then he yawned.

Sid himself ambled to the bow wearing nothing but an appalling, neon green, minuscule Speedo and a white bathrobe that flapped in the breeze. "Piggy!" he called, waving madly with one hand. The other was wrapped around a monster plastic cup with the tip of something orange—a carrot?—sticking up out of it.

The captain, lurking behind the darkened glass of the bridge, drove the huge white beast carefully to within a couple of yards of the dock, and two men appeared out of thin air to ease it the rest of the way into the slip. Once they'd tied it into place, Gwen approached with Pigamuffin in her arms.

Sid lurched over to meet them and took the dog from her extended arms. "Piggy, Piggy, Piggy!" he crooned. He kissed every wrinkle on his pet's head, and Pigamuffin slurped his haggard, dissipated face. Both of them were so ugly, but Gwen found herself oddly touched.

Finally Sid set the Pigster on the deck and extended his hand to her. "Gwendolyn, me beauty! Welcome aboard the *Sex Machine*." He winked.

"Er, thank you." She stepped on carefully.

"Bloody Mary?"

"Perrier, if you have it."

Sid squinted at her before turning his head and bellowing at nobody in particular, "A Bloody for the lady, if you please!"

Gwen sighed.

"'ave any trouble, did you?" he inquired. "Wi' the producer?"

She shrugged. "Nothing that a derringer and the threat of jail time couldn't overcome. He claimed that he'd just borrowed the dog, of course."

"Did 'e?" Sid exclaimed, clearly outraged. "I've 'ad it wi' people borrowing me Pigamuffin!"

Gwen cleared her throat. "Yes. Yes, I'm sure."

"Something wrong, me beauty?"

"Not a thing." Gwen aimed a perfunctory smile at him. She looked at her watch.

Sid frowned. "We may 'ave gotten off on the wrong foot, me Gwendolyn, when we met. Understand that I was only trying to put ye at ease with me offer of—"

Her face heated instantly. "Right," she said hastily. "Of course."

"'S quite an honor, you know."

"I'm sure. But really, I'm . . . not worthy."

"Oy don't let just anyone gum Sid's big banger."

Eeeeuuuwww. One of the invisible staff suddenly appeared with her unwanted Bloody Mary, and Gwen fell on it like a long-lost relative, narrowly escaping the carrot, which threatened to put her eye out.

Sid looked delighted. "See, what'd I tell you? You didn't want no stinking Perrier. You wanted a nice Bloody!"

"Delicious." Gwen nodded. "Thank you." She took another gulp.

"In me experience—and I've 'ad me a lot—women often don't know what they really want."

Uh-oh.

"And see, Sid 'as a theory, 'e does. Siddie thinks you doth protest too much, lady. You want the big banger, don't you?"

"*No,*" Gwen said emphatically. "I do *not* want the big banger."

"You want 'im." Sid nodded and sent her a sly wink. He cupped himself and ambled toward her.

Gwen skittered away and ditched her drink in case she needed both hands to defend herself.

"Oooh, a little cat 'n' mouse, eh?" He lurched after her. "A bit early in the day, but Sid's adaptable, 'e is."

"Get away from me. I mean it!" Thank God she had the derringer if worse came to worst.

"No, no, don't be mean. Be sweet to El Sid. 'E's been cuckolded. 'E's been robbed of 'is dog. . . . 'E's been abused." Tears sprang to the horrifying man's eyes, and he slumped to the deck, drumming his heels like a child.

Appalled, Gwen said, "Oh, God, don't cry."

"All 'e wants, Siddie, is some 'armless, therapeutic sex. If ye can't do it for me, could you do it for the glory of Subversion?"

Gwen choked. "Look, I'd love to. Really. But . . . I'm saving myself for marriage."

Sid looked up through his tears, clearly perplexed. "Why?"

"What do you mean, why? It's a religious thing," Gwen said desperately.

He swiped at his eyes and gulped some of his Bloody Mary. He sniffed. Pigamuffin came over to his lord and master and sat down, too. Sid cuddled him to his bony chest. "A religious thing," he repeated. "Right. Now that you mention it, I do remember Kelso saying something of the sort. . . ."

Gwen froze. "Come again?" she asked dangerously.

"You bloody tease, you—I 'aven't come the first time!"

Gwen's hands curled into fists. "You know Kelso?" she asked.

"Course I know 'im. 'E was one of the original investors in me first album. 'E's the one who came up with the name Subversion."

"What's his full name? What does he look like? How can I get in touch with him?" *Because I'm going to kill him. I'm going to hunt him down and kill him for this. That is a promise.*

Sid shook his head, his cornhusk hair lifting in the breeze. "There's no getting in touch with Kelso. An' I 'aven't a clue what the bloke looks like. 'E may as well be the Man in the Iron Mask."

Gwen's shoulders slumped. *Here we go again.* "But . . .

if he invested in your first album, the funds must have come from some name and address."

"Came through a bank, me beauty. Holding company."

"You must have spoken with him?"

"No. All communications were cabled."

I'm going to find the man if it's the last thing I do. Gwen reached down and patted Pigamuffin's wrinkly forehead, then extended her hand to Sid. "Well, what can I say. It's been a pleasure."

"An' I keep telling you, lovey, the pleasure could be much greater," he said hopefully.

"*Good-bye*, Sid." Gwen exited the yacht.

chapter 35

Avy huddled under the covers in her hotel room, staring at the ceiling. She felt empty and cold and used, no matter what Liam said.

I never met a man I couldn't handle. . . .

That had been utterly true until he came along to outmaneuver her. But worse, far worse, was the fact that she had begun to trust him, at least on an emotional level, in spite of the knowledge that he was a thief.

And at some point along the way she'd fallen in love with the bastard, defenses and emotional unavailability be damned. He'd filched her heart.

God, she was stupid. This had all been a job to him, nothing more. *She* was a job. He'd pinpointed her vulnerabilities and told her exactly what she needed to hear—all in the name of distracting her. And now he still professed to love her? *Please.*

She felt more betrayed than if she'd caught him with another woman, but how could she even verbalize that: *You cheated on me with the FBI?* It made no sense. She was pathetic.

Avy glared at the lilies Liam had sent, which seemed to wilt as a result of the hostility, though they still extended hopeful stamen in her direction.

I'm truly sorry, he'd written. *It was never my intention to make a fool of you. Please forgive me. I'm in the courtyard if you'd like to talk. With love, Liam.*

In the courtyard, was he? In a surge of rage she snatched up the vase and stalked out the door of her room, barreling for the elevators. Five floors down she emerged at the top tier of the courtyard and honed in on Liam's head like a human radar. She'd lifted the vase, ready to hurl it, when she stopped, afraid that she might injure someone else down there.

Avy ripped the arrangement from the vase and threw the flowers hard with the arm that had helped win the state championship for her high school girls' softball team.

The floral missile shot through the air, spraying water as it went, and smacked Liam with satisfying force on the back of his head. Leafy greenery and orange lily petals scattered over the table, some in his coffee.

Dozens of appalled faces turned and peered up at her. Liam's wasn't one of them. He knew damned well who'd thrown them, after all. He brushed bits of flora off his shirt and gingerly removed the petals from his café au lait. Then he calmly went back to reading his newspaper.

Furious at his utter lack of reaction, she stormed away. So it hadn't been her most mature gesture. Neither had tossing the Cristal in his face. But she quite frankly didn't know how to handle her feelings about him.

It wasn't fair of him to apologize, damn it! How dared he turn the tables and make her look like the bad guy for not accepting his meaningless words? How dared he?

She got back into the elevator, ignoring the disapproving glances of a meticulously groomed elderly couple, and rode it back up to her floor. She stomped to the door of her room—only to realize that she'd run out of there without her key. She leaned her forehead against the cool wood and then banged her skull twice before sliding down in front of it in a boneless heap.

Tears threatened again, and she felt like a madwoman. Liam James, in a final insult, had stolen her sanity.

Twenty minutes later a maid approached her and hesitantly touched her on the shoulder. "Madam? Are you all right?" the woman asked in French.

Avy, still curled into a ball and facing the door, shook her head without moving. Vaguely she registered that someone else was coming down the hallway. She didn't bother to look at the person; it felt like too much effort. She lowered her face back onto her knees.

Then Avy felt strong arms lifting her up—not the maid's. She knew it was Liam just by his touch and his scent. Too bad she couldn't muster the energy even to kick him.

"I'll take care of her," he said to the maid. "If you would just let us into the room."

The woman looked askance at Avy, who raised her head and nodded wearily. "It's fine."

Liam was relentless. If he wanted to talk, then even if it took him a decade of pursuit, they would talk. She might as well get it over with so that she could get on with her life— and get away from him.

After the maid double-checked with security, he walked easily with her into the room, let the door close behind them, and sat on the bed with her still in his arms. "I can't believe it—I've managed to carry you over a threshold."

"Liam, that's not remotely cute." She pushed at his chest, to no avail. "Let me go."

"You've tried to kill me twice, now," he said reflectively. "Once by shoving me literally off a cliff and now by flower arrangement. How do you feel about that?"

"Like a miserable failure."

"The murder-by-flowers approach wasn't terribly gracious, love."

She pushed hard this time, and he reluctantly let go of her. She slid off his knees and went to sit in a chair on the opposite side of the room. She glowered at him. "And I *live* to be gracious."

His hair was still damp and tousled from his close encounter of the floral kind, and he looked good enough to eat.

She wasn't hungry.

"Since I've tried apologizing and you aren't having any, let's discuss something else. I've heard the word *failure* come out of your mouth more than once now. And it's not an accurate description of anything you've done. You recovered the Sword of Alexander fair and square, Avy. I know that and you know that."

"Yeah? Well, too bad nobody else does, namely not my boss or my coworkers or Lloyd's of London. Add to that the sheer frustration of the past few days and the expenses I've incurred, which my company will have to eat. And the cherry on top is that I won't get my commission on the repo—or another contract with Lloyd's—after this." She leaned forward. "So how does all that not end up in the failure category, Liam?"

"I'll have a talk with my FBI contact and tell her what really happened."

"Thanks ever so. What a huge difference that will make."

"Avy, don't forget that you helped thwart a terrorist operation. Doesn't that count for something?"

Burning bile shot up her throat. "No, Liam. I *hurt* the sting more than I helped it. That's part of the reason I'm so angry! Can't you *see* that? How could you have done this to me?"

He sighed. "You're used to being the good guy. And you had me all pegged as the bad guy. Now you're upset."

"Hell, yes, I'm upset! You have screwed me forty-nine different ways, both physically and mentally! You are more bent than a goddamned paper clip! You've stalked me, surveilled me, tricked me, seduced me, tricked me some more, and completely fucked me over. Now you're in my room patting my shoulder and saying, 'There, there, honey, it's all right.'"

Liam looked at the carpet. His silence spoke volumes—he knew he was guilty as charged.

"Well, it's *not* all right! And I don't need your little speeches about how I didn't fail, your award of a gold star on my homework. Don't do me any favors, and *don't* patronize me."

"I didn't mean it that way, Avy."

"But the worst thing of all," she continued, ignoring him, "is that I've . . ."

Liam met her gaze now, his own steady and unflinching. "You've what, Avy?"

She pressed her lips together, threw up her hands, and paced across the room to the window, where the cheery sparkle of the ocean and all the tanned, smiling vacationers seemed to mock her.

"If you had just told me the truth! Why in the hell couldn't you have contacted me at ARTemis and told me to back off in the first place?"

"Because I couldn't, love. In this kind of operation, with all the players involved and informants abounding, it's often difficult to know whom to trust. We had to keep things as quiet as possible. They weren't even sure they could trust me."

Avy's flare of anger had slowly fizzled again. Her head suddenly weighed eighty pounds, and her shoulders wanted to sag under the strain of holding it up. She asked quietly, "How did you get involved?"

"Not willingly, at first," Liam admitted. "Two years ago I had a bizarre attack of conscience and retired from art theft, which is being used more and more to launder funds for narcotics traffickers as well as terrorists. Once it was a sort of gentleman's game—but now it's become a rough game of thugby, for lack of a better way to phrase it. It's smash and grab, with no care for the art. No finesse to it at all."

"You retired because it was no longer an elegant crime?" Avy asked wearily. "It was bad for your image?"

"No. Look, will you stop being so difficult, just for a moment?" Liam looked exasperated. "I retired because the whole racket began to disgust me. And I stayed retired until a friend—" He broke off for a moment. "Well, he's an odd sort of friend, since I've never actually seen him. An acquaintance, I suppose. Anyhow, he asked me to recover a cache of ancient coins that were in the possession of the Getty. He claimed that these coins had been stolen from him, given a false provenance and documents, and then sold to the museum. It does happen with disturbing regularity.

"So I set off to do him this favor. Attempted my first recovery." He sent her an amused glance. "And I failed miserably. I got caught and was soon talking with the FBI. If I wanted to avoid doing time in an American jail, I'd help them with a project. At first I was bloody angry. And then I began to wonder if my friend hadn't set me up for the specific purpose of recruiting me for the U.S. authorities. I'd like to kick his arse, that Kelso."

Avy's mouth dropped open. "*What* did you say?"

"I said I'd like to kick—"

"No, the name."

"Kelso?"

"Is that his first or his last name?"

"He seems to have only one, like your actress Cher."

Beware of what is too easy. Avy cursed. "I'm going to

track him down one of these days," she swore. "I'm going to find out who he is. You have to give me any information on him that you have."

Liam eyed her with frank curiosity. "Why?"

"Because," she said bitterly, "Kelso is my boss. He owns fifty-one percent of ARTemis, Inc."

Liam began to laugh as he thought about it. It really wasn't funny that the mysterious Kelso was backstage pulling all of their strings, but he rather had to admire the irony of it.

The one thing that he wasn't sure he could forgive was that Kelso had put Avy in great danger. Then again, he'd engineered it so that Liam would stop her before she ever got to Gautreau's house. And it wasn't Kelso's fault that Liam had failed.

Kelso had put his trust in Liam to protect his top recovery agent. But there was a reason that Avy was his star performer—she was smart and resourceful. She'd gotten the better of him before he'd finally overtaken her.

"Do you find *everything* amusing?" she asked angrily.

Liam lay back on her bed and gave her a lazy glance. "The alternative to laughing is crying, Avy. I'm not so good at that. You?"

"I've cried once in the past three years. That was last night, and it was because of you."

"The last thing I wanted was to hurt you, Avy. I enjoyed you so, and I kept getting in deeper and deeper. I began to fall in love."

She shot her hand out, palm toward him, in a classic shut-up gesture. "Liam—"

"Hear me out, will you?" He sat up and rubbed his hands over his face. "Afterward you can spurn me, kick me to the curb, as you Americans put it. But just let me have my say. Please."

She stayed silent. He couldn't call it encouragement, exactly, but at least she was letting him speak.

"I told you shortly after we first met that you are a thief with a permit. I said it to rile you, love, but the truth is that you've truly earned your permit—by being honest and straight and very, very brave."

She appeared discomfitted by the compliment.

"I, on the other hand, have been dishonest and rather bent. . . ." He smiled ruefully. "And I'm only just now earning my permit. I'd actually like to work on other stings, though my FBI handler and I might come to blows."

Liam got off the bed and walked toward her. "It's very important that I go legitimate."

"Why?"

His eyes had gone a deep, serious gray. "There's this woman. I fell in love with her in the span of about twenty-four hours. She's tricked me, tied me up, hijacked my property, chased me, drugged me, and tried to kill me twice. I've never met anyone quite like her before, and I absolutely know that I never will again. The kicker is that she won't have anything to do with a thief."

Avy looked as if she couldn't breathe, and her pulse jackhammered at her throat. Liam put his hands on her shoulders before she could skitter away. He looked down at her with infinite tenderness that he hoped would wash away her resistance.

Liam said, "She makes me want to be a better man, you see. So that I can be worthy of her."

Avy was no longer laughing. She looked a little misty around the eyes, in fact. He bent his head to kiss her, but she put a hand on his chest and held him off.

"Avy?"

She hesitated, her other hand playing with the belt of her robe. "But . . . will you still be *you*, after all these changes?"

Good God, this woman had his heart flopping about like a landed fish. "I'll still be me," he said, his voice a little rough.

She looked so beautiful and rumpled, standing there in the terry robe. Even with her face still a bit swollen and the wound on her cheek from that sodding Gautreau. He touched it gently with the back of his index finger. If Kay Bunker would give him just five minutes alone with the guy . . .

But he was digressing.

Liam slid his hands down her arms and took her hands in his. He knelt in front of her. "I have a question for you."

Her mouth trembled, and she tried to free her hands, but he refused to let go.

"Ava Brigitte Hunt, now that I've got my honor out of layaway, will you marry me?"

She made an odd, soft sound and stared down at him. She brought their entwined hands inward to frame his face. Then she closed her eyes.

All he wanted to hear was one three-letter word. Liam hadn't spoken to God since he'd walked out of his school chapel that fateful day at age seventeen and gone home, but he prayed now. *Say yes. Please, God, let her say yes. Avy, make me an honest man.*

His prayers were answered.

When Avy opened her eyes, her mouth no longer trembled. "Liam, there's no doubt that I've fallen for you. I . . . I love you."

His heart leaped.

"But . . ."

Not the three-letter word he wanted to hear.

"But?"

"Your honor isn't out of layaway," she said a little sadly.

"What do you mean?"

"You have to return everything you've stolen, Liam. *Everything*. Then I'll think about it."

He gaped at her, staring hopelessly up at that firm jaw and the tough little chin. "Return," he repeated weakly. "Everything."

She nodded and he got to his feet. "You don't know what you're asking."

"Yes, I do."

"Avy." He exhaled every cubic inch of air in his lungs. "There are *hundreds* and *hundreds* of objects."

"How many hundreds?"

"Five? Six? Seven hundred? I don't know! I was a very hardworking thief, love."

She stared at him implacably.

"I swear that I will never steal another thing."

She shook her head. "Sorry. Not good enough."

Oh, bloody hell and utter damnation. I did just pray for her to make me an honest man, did I not? Liam winced.

Thanks a lot, God. Thanks loads, old man.

"But, Avy, darling." He tried for a smile. "You're the recovery artist. I'm the thief."

"It's the same skill set," she said, unrelenting.

"Be reasonable—it will take me years."

She shrugged. "Those are the terms."

Liam sank onto the bed. "So you'll marry me if I do this."

She nodded. "Probably."

"*Probably?* Listen here, Avy, if I replace several hundred items, then I'll bloody well get you to an altar even if I have to steal *that* and the priest, too!"

She looked mulish for a moment, and then she laughed,

and damn it all, it was like the sun had broken through an endless week of thunderheads.

He put his hands on her shoulders. "Say yes, you annoying woman. Please. Put me out of my misery."

Avy's lips twitched as she touched his cheek. "Yes. I will marry you, Liam, if you put everything back."

He couldn't believe he was even thinking about agreeing to this. But Whidby's words had been prophetic: Liam was indeed "right royally screwed"—because he'd do anything in the world for this woman. Anything at all.

However, that didn't mean he was stupid or inefficient. "Avy, darling. Let's suppose that I agree to this plan. However, without help it will take me a decade to return everything, and I don't want to wait a decade to make you mine."

She'd narrowed her eyes at him as if she knew exactly what he was going to say next.

"So I have a suggestion. Let's work together on this little project, shall we? It will go twice as fast."

She began to laugh again. Her eyes crinkled, her generous mouth fell open, and strands of her chestnut hair fell into her face.

He just watched her. *How beautiful she is.*

Avy stopped laughing, shoved the hair out of her face, and then twisted it into a knot on top of her head. She secured it with a hotel pen. Liam grew uneasy—she did that when she got down to business.

"Five percent," she said.

"I beg your pardon?"

"My commission on each piece, for putting it back."

His mouth fell open. "You're going to *charge* me?"

"Yes, and it should be double that. But I'll cut you a deal."

"What happened to love?"

"What happened to honor? I didn't take these things, Liam; you did. And I can't work for free—I have a mortgage to pay."

"I rather thought you'd move in with me."

"Oh, you did, did you?" She smiled. "Maybe I will. But I'll still have a mortgage to pay and a bird to feed. So it's five percent."

"Extortion!" he exclaimed.

She tickled him under the chin. "Those are the terms of the deal. Take it or leave it."

He growled and then heaved a long-suffering sigh. "My darling Avy, this is grossly unfair. But I've said it before and I'll say it again: I'll take you any way I can."

She took his big, bristly, handsome face between her hands and kissed him thoroughly. "No, Liam. You'll take me *if* you can."

You won't want to miss the next book
in this exciting series from Karen Kendall . . .

Take Me Two Times

Missing: A cursed Venetian mask covered with priceless jewels.
Recovery Agent: Gwen Davies, a new recruit who special-
izes in the art of keeping secrets.
The client: Someone from her past . . . someone she's not
prepared to meet again.

*The door opened and Damon courteously got to his feet.
Then he saw who had waltzed into his office and almost fell
back into the chair.*

*It was her. No doubt about it. Those were the same sweet doe
eyes that belied her intelligence. The nose that was narrow
at the bridge and widened into an upside-down heart at the
tip. The contours of her face, also heart shaped. And the
mouth he'd loved until she'd given him the big kiss-off
twelve years ago.*

*He didn't know whether to laugh or throw something.
"Unless you've changed your name, Gwen, you're not Avy
Hunt."*

She shook her head. The silence stretched on.

*He wanted to hear her voice, wanted to take her by the
shoulders and shake her until she spoke to him, even if only
to swear. But he didn't move from behind his desk.*

*"Your hair is different," he said stupidly, eyeing her short
cut with the soft orange streaks. They were supposed to be*

rebellious, but they were oddly elegant. Reminded him of Grand Marnier in a firelit glass.

She nodded. The expression on her face hadn't changed since she'd entered, but even after twelve years, he still knew her well enough to note the small signs of shock she'd exhibited: the quick, subtle double blink, the surge of color in her cheeks, her small hand tightening on that ridiculously large pocketbook. Her left knee, exposed by the hem of her skirt, quivered.

He wished he didn't know what she looked like naked. . . .

About the Author

Karen Kendall is an award-winning author of contemporary romance who started writing at the age of four. An art history major with a concentration in twentieth-century art, Karen worked in museums and galleries before she was a published author. She lives with her husband in Florida. Please visit her Web site at www.karenkendall.com.

KAREN KENDALL

FIT TO BE TIED

It's The Happiest Day of Her Life, but as Jen moves toward the altar, she feels more like a sacrifice than a bride. What's borrowed is her courage, and what's blue? Oh, that would be her berry-stained teeth.

Jen's divorcing parents are up to their usual antics, a self-help book is making her crazy, and her handsome groom, Tom, is drunk during the service. Then a surprize six-foot blonde shows up to the wedding reception—and worse, she's Tom's secret first wife.

Jen's got to be the only bride to ask for a divorce on her honeymoon, but is it the right choice? And will she lose her mind as well as her husband while trying to figure it out?

Love can be so complicated...

Available wherever books are sold or at penguin.com